CW00659703

ACKNOWLEDGMENTS

I would like to start by thanking my good friends Mitchell Kelby and Hayley Morland, who helped and encouraged me at the very early stages of writing.

Thank you to my husband who stood by my passion and allowed me to vanish randomly to go write.

Lastly, a special thank you to my mother, Nadine, who without her this book wouldn't have been possible. Her guidance and inspiration will stick with me forever.

WITCH'S SORROW

AN ALICE SKYE NOVEL

TAYLOR ASTON WHITE

DARK WOLF PUBLISHING

Edited by Rayne Dowell & Michael Evans

Alice Skye Series

Witch's Sorrow
Druid's Storm
Rogue's Mercy
Elemental's Curse
Knight's War
Veil's Fall

Alice Skye Short Story

Witch's Bounty

This book is written in British English, including spelling and grammar.

Trigger warning: Attempted sexual assault

Your FREE short story is waiting...

Witch's Bounty

When the wrong man's framed, and the Metropolitan Police don't care. Paladin Agent Alice Skye takes it on herself to find the real culprit.

Get your free copy of Witch's Bounty at...
www.taylorastonwhite.com

BOOK ONE

PROLOGUE

What was that? She opened her eyes and stared at the ceiling, the luminescent glow of the many stars and moons barely lighting up the dark room. Another loud bang resonated up through the floorboards, forcing a squeak in panic. She grabbed her teddy, covering herself in a pink fluffy blanket with her eyes squeezed shut.

Wait... She opened her eyes, peeking past the pink fluff.

It was probably Kyle being stupid, trying to scare her again.

She reached over to click on the lamp, a pink glow emitting from the unicorn patterned lampshade.

"Kyle?" she called, her brother's room only next door. Lifting a small fist, she knocked three times against the wall.

"Kyle?" she called again, this time louder.

She shrugged the covers away before swinging her legs off the side of the bed, careful to not let her feet get too close to the darkness beneath. Her door creaked open as she timidly peered into the hallway, noticing Kyle's bedroom door slightly ajar, his 'DO NOT CROSS' yellow tape torn from the wood.

"Kyle," she whispered, "you're going to be in so much trouble." She quickly glanced into his room, noticing his empty bed, the sheets and duvet a messy bundle at the bottom.

Something creaked behind her.

She swivelled to look further down the hallway, squinting her eyes in the dim light.

"Mum?" Her parent's door was wide open, the bed just as empty as Kyle's.

Creak. Creak. Creak.

She ran over to the banister, her heart a rabbit in her chest as she peered down into the darkness below. She wasn't fond of the dark.

"Mum?" she shouted now. "Dad?" No response. Nothing. Her hand shook as she gripped the banister, her feet making no noise as she took a few steps down.

Something shattered, a crash, glass.

"Mum?" she called once more, her voice wobbling as tears threatened. She clutched her bear close to her chest as she walked the last few steps of the staircase, her bare feet cold against the hardwood. Another crash. The lights flicked ahead before turning off, covering her in complete darkness.

"Kyle if that's you, it's not funny."

Still no response, she couldn't even hear the usual hum of the heating, the darkness a void of silence.

She padded down the hallway, pushing the kitchen door gently as soft light flickered beneath the frame.

CHAPTER 1

A lice groaned as she turned slightly, the cheap bed creaking beneath her. A yawn escaped as she absently reached towards the nightstand, her hand touching the familiar coolness of her phone. Light streamed through the cheap curtains, forcing her to squint through tired eyes.

"What the?" she groaned as she brought the mobile phone closer to her face, confused with why it wasn't lighting up. The dark screen caused her stress to spike, especially when shaking the phone violently did nothing. Not that shaking anything violently ever worked.

The phone wasn't on charge, the white wire mocking her beside the bed.

"FUCK!" Alice bounced off the mattress, running half-naked into her living room to squint at the small analogue clock on her TV.

7:56 am

"Fuck. Fuck. Fuck." She grabbed the closest clothes,

pulling them on while she tried to brush through the nest she called hair. Hopping on one foot she pulled on her ankle boots, stretching to grab her jacket and satchel before she ran through the front door a few seconds later.

It had to be today, Alice groaned to herself as she hurriedly made her way down several floors to the street below. *The one day I can't bloody be late.*

The door separating the foyer to the road was already open as she half-jogged out, her attention on the small parking space to the side of the building. Her 'vintage,' as she liked to call it, Volkswagen Beetle sat like it always did in its dedicated parking space. The pale blue colouring more silver than it should be, the rust and scrapes flaking away at the paint. The hubcaps were gone, stolen yet again and some smartarse had scraped a bad luck spell into the back bumper. The joke was on them though, they had done one of the symbols wrong.

She dropped her bag onto the bonnet before she frantically searched for the car keys.

"You have got to be kidding me!" she muttered, searching every pocket. The keys were not in her bag like they were supposed to be. They were probably still sitting beside the kettle where she had left them last. Her eyes rolled over to the clumsy curves of the bad luck spell.

It seemed they didn't get it wrong after all.

I don't have time for this, she thought as she grabbed the satchel and hitched it high on her shoulder.

The bus stop was roughly a ten-minute walk up the road. Her light jog made it in four with only a few minutes' wait. The doors screeched open as the bus driver barely looked up, his long greasy hair hiding most of his face.

"Central Caverns please," she asked politely, her voice

surprisingly strong considering she hadn't had time for her morning caffeine.

With barely a grunt the driver accepted her money before starting the bus. She sat towards the front, scooting over to the window seat so she could watch the buildings blur together as the bus manoeuvred through the residential area towards the central part of the city. The steady vibration centred her as she stared blankly, her brain on override as she tried to figure out why she had to go to a meeting.

One day was not enough warning.

Her role as a Paladin was something she was proud of, something she was good at if she said so herself. She was trained to track and detain Breed, also known as anyone not one hundred percent human, by any means necessary.

Well, within reason of course.

Witches, vampires, shifters, faeries and the occasional selkie was what she was skilled in. Unfortunately, the pay wasn't as you would expect a high-risk job would have, especially considering Paladin Agents had a marginally higher mortality rate compared to other jobs. Which wasn't surprising when the subject she was in charge of bringing to justice was twice her size, had large fangs and the tendency to rip one's throat out.

Most people who hired her through Supernatural Intelligence, the organisation created as a Breed partnership with the local metropolitan police, were genuinely tight-arsed. So she wasn't allowed to use flashy spells or show off because the contracts wouldn't pay for it. Don't even get her started on the internal contracts, ones assigned by the Met themselves when they found themselves in over their heads. They paid even less.

What the hell have I done? She pressed her hand against

the window, allowing the cool glass to comfort her clammy palms. She hadn't done anything wrong.

At least, not recently.

"Central Caverns," a husky voice called from the front, someone that smoked fifty a day.

"Stop it, Alice." She shook her head, clearing her thoughts as she climbed out the bus, barely stepping off before the doors closed and accelerated away. Alice groaned to herself when she noticed the Starbucks wasn't very busy next to S.I. tower, her mouth salivating as she forced her feet to walk past the green canopy and towards the rotating doors.

Conscious of the time she grabbed her security pass from her jacket pocket, barely giving herself time to wave to the security guards before she headed towards an empty lift, her nerves a flutter. She waited patiently for the floor numbers to rise, the obnoxious music not helping with her anxiety. She hated being late.

With a deep, calming breath, she squinted at the reflective surface of the chrome doors, trying to decide if she looked presentable or not. Her hair wasn't awful, the blonde strands up in a half bun that looked almost purposely styled, in a sexy messy way. Last night's makeup was still there, the eyeliner smudged enough that it looked like smoky eye shadow around her emerald eyes. Her lips were cracked, but not obviously so. She looked like she'd had an all-nighter, not ready for a meeting with her boss.

It could be worse.

The lift beeped, the doors opened to reveal the general bustle of the forty-second floor. Alice ignored the stares from her colleagues as she manoeuvred through the cubicles, heading towards the back of the building where the meeting would take place.

"Ah, there you are," a high-pitched voice laughed from the corner. "I thought you weren't going to turn up."

Alice turned to Barbara the receptionist, intending to reply with a snarky comment. Instead, she decided to bite her tongue and be polite. It would do her no good to piss off her boss's favourite receptionist, even if it would be satisfying. Barbara, also known as Barbie due to her likeness to the plastic doll, had worked for Dread for as long as Alice could remember, and considering Dread had brought her into work as a small child that was quite a long time.

"I woke up late," was all she said as she went to stand beside the window, staring down at the many floors below. The view was beautiful. London, a city with thousands of years of history blended seamlessly with the steel and glass of the modern world. Alice sighed as she settled herself into a seat, the clock on the wall showing she had made it in time, with just a few minutes to spare.

The leather cushion squeaked as she relaxed and watched a blue flame dance between her fingertips, the ball of fire common when she was feeling extreme emotion. Or for no reason at all. It was a peculiar little thing.

"If you don't put that fire thingy out you are going to set off the sprinklers," Barb sniggered, her baby blue eyes narrowed.

Alice pursed her lips, concentrating on the pretty blue flame, green sparkles bursting at intervals. With a barely audible pop the ball disappeared, leaving her looking at her hands, her nails short and broken, the black nail polish starting to chip.

What have I fucked up now?

The blue flame burst to life once more, energised by her spike in nerves. She tried to bat it away, but it happily glided along the air. Only she had the luck to be cursed with

7

teenage acne, mood swings *and* spontaneous balls of flame. She pondered the mechanics of the small twinkly flame, trying to remember a time when the little thing didn't pop into existence.

"You shouldn't slouch, it's bad for your posture," Barb snidely commented, her long, perfectly manicured nails tapping loudly against the keyboard on her desk.

Alice automatically sat up as her eyes darted to the bottled blonde witch who didn't have many friends in the office. The woman dressed in the most provocative clothes she could find, her perky implanted breasts on full show. Barb was easily pushing late forties, yet she spent all her money on magic infused jewellery that helped cover her wrinkles.

"Barbie, why am I here?"

Barb's eyes narrowed at the nickname, but didn't comment. "You know Commissioner Grayson loves a good meeting." She pouted her lips, a slight curve at the edge. She knew why she was here, but wouldn't say.

"This is a joke right?" Barb ignored her, her attention back to the computer, but the sinister smile still in place.

Alice still hadn't figured out why she was there. She had only three assignments over the past month, and they all had gone well. The black witch who was caught selling curses and black amulets online was an easy tag. She was stupid enough to have her return address on the parcels.

The second was the wolf shifter that made a scene at the bar, one that was wrecked in the process. What pissed her off was the fact they had banned *her* from the bar, as if it was somehow her fault they had a destructive wolf that trashed two chairs and an ugly looking painting. Her last assignment involved a Vamp, one where his psychological condition wasn't considered when he applied to be turned.

He was only three-years-old in undead terms when he was found bathing in blood, not his own, with his trousers around his ankles. It wasn't a pretty sight.

"Tick tock, it's almost time," Barbie giggled. It would have sounded cute on a small child; on her it was just creepy. She flicked her hair over her shoulder, making sure to pout her bright pink lips even more. It was people like Barbie who gave witches a bad name. She smelt like a sickly mixture of roses and doughnuts, not ozone like other witches, ones who actually practised the art of magic.

Something vibrated next to the computer, followed with a shrill whine that had Barbie reaching over to the old grey-corded phone. The phone was so old compared to the modern computer it was almost prehistoric, which made no sense in a company benefitting from the latest technology and equipment. 'If it isn't broke, don't fix it' was a favoured saying amongst Breed over a hundred.

"Yes sir," Barbie breathed sexily into the receiver, her voice taking on the perfect phone sex rumble, unlike her normal high-pitched soprano.

"Why yes sir, I will send her in immediately." With a click, she put down the phone before she swivelled to face Alice, a smirk plastered across her face. "Commissioner Grayson will see you now."

With a pensive nod, Alice entered through the large oak door, pushing against the heavy metal handle. The room beyond was dark, almost pitch black as she stumbled inside.

"Alice," a deep voice greeted, Dread's whole body hidden in shadow. "Please, take a seat." A hand stretched into the sliver of light created by the open door, his fingers, long and pale, were decorated with a diamond and ruby encrusted ring that encircled his middle finger. She closed the door behind her, the room in complete darkness.

Dread's window, the one that would have just an amazing view of London to the one in reception, was blocked out with a blackout blind, the man preferring to sit in the dark.

Alice stepped forward, feeling for the chair she luckily noticed before she closed the door. She wasn't afraid of the dark, she just wasn't happy with it. She didn't trust the complete absence of sight, especially as the man sitting quietly before her could see perfectly while she couldn't even see her hand in front of her face.

She heard a click, the room illuminated by a chrome lamp that perched on the corner of his oversized wooden desk, clean of everything other than the lamp, a piece of paper and a single gold pen that he had positioned perfectly along the natural grooves of the wood. She tried to hide her jump as his eyes settled on her, ones that were just as dark as the room. Obsidian ovals in a white face, ones so dark you couldn't tell where the irises started and pupils began.

Well, she thought to herself. *This is disconcerting.* She had known him all her life, could read him better than anyone, and he wasn't happy.

Drum. Drum. Drum.

Dread's fingers tapped against the top of his desk in an annoying sequence.

Drum. Drum. Drum.

Dread Grayson has held his position as Commissioner of the Supernatural Intelligence Bureau since it was first built around three hundred years ago. The man sitting before her, who still drummed his fingers across the wood, was one of the most powerful people in the city, not counting The Council. He just stared at her, his face worryingly composed, the grooves, which he received before the turn, seemed etched from stone, not one facial muscle moving. He continued to stare at her unblinking, his dark hair cut close to the scalp, almost bald. Large bushy eyebrows dominated his otherwise hair-free face, the dark hair highlighting his incredibly pale complexion.

"You cut your hair recently. Looks nice," Alice nervously commented as she brushed her own blonde strands from her face. *Why am I here?*

He finally blinked at her as a vein started to pulse in his forehead.

"What are you wearing?" he asked, voice clipped.

Alice looked down, seemingly confused by his comment.

Oh shit.

She bit her lip, heat against her cheeks as she only just noticed what she had thrown on. Her shirt was pure white with two strategically placed avocados on the front. Tucked into her black jeans it looked relatively clean. She was grateful it was one of her politer shirts.

She folded her arms over her chest, trying to hide the design as if nothing was wrong. That gained her a small, familiar smile, just the tip at the corner of his mouth. Dread had always moaned about her choice in clothing, ever since he took over as her legal parental guardian all those years ago. He still moaned regularly, even though she constantly reminded him she was twenty-three.

He thought she was acting up.

She thought the shirts were cool.

The smile vanished, his face immobile once again. His eyes were something he often used to scare people, the creepiness of them enough to force anyone to behave. It was uncomfortable, to say the least.

The door at her back opened, allowed some extra light

to creep into the still too dark room. She fought not to turn, Dread holding her gaze until the door shut once again.

"Now Alice, you will remain quiet until asked a direct question. Do you understand?" Dread betrayed no emotion, he had become the Commissioner of the Supernatural Intelligence Bureau, leader of the Paladins. Not her parental figure.

She just nodded back, deciding it was better not to open her mouth at all. She didn't always have a conscious thought on what came out.

"Okay then, when Mr Wild takes a seat we can start this meeting." His obsidian eyes broke their connection, allowing her to breathe for a second before Mr Wild sat in the seat beside her.

The man was tall, around six feet with long light brown hair that hid the expression on his face in a straight curtain.

She looked back at Dread in confusion. *Why am I here?* she asked silently while his eyes stayed blank. He knew what she had asked, but refused to respond. She huffed to herself as she chanced another glance to her right. Piercing blue eyes met hers for a fleeting second before she forced herself to look away.

Fuck. Fuck. Fuck. She had recognised those eyes, eyes of a shifter, someone that was part man, part animal. One that was *pissed*.

"Let's get on with this then," the man beside her complained, his voice deep but emotionless. Monotone even.

She turned to look at him again as his irises changed, the brightness dimming to a darker blue, ones that showed even less emotion, if that was even possible. It was like staring at a wall.

Alice observed him as he swept his long hair over his

shoulder, revealing an unusually narrow nose compared to his broad chin. His facial hair was messy, as if he was used to being clean shaven but hadn't had the time or just couldn't be bothered. She continued to stare at him even as he looked at Dread expectantly, ignoring her for the moment. He had been the wolf shifter she had tagged a week ago, the one who had helped wreck the bar and had gotten her banned.

"Let's begin then, shall we?" Dread tapped once more on the desk. "Agent Alice Skye, do you know why you have been asked to attend this meeting?"

"No," she murmured, even as she struggled to figure out what was going on.

"Do you remember the gentleman next to you?"

Alice gritted her teeth. "Yes."

"Then can you explain to me why you arrested the Alpha of White Dawn?"

"White Dawn?" Alice opened her mouth in a silent gasp. *Oh shit,* she cursed herself. White Dawn was the largest wolf pack in London, if not Europe. She had royally fucked up. "It was a contract, amber level retrieval." She strained to remember the exact details.

"Who gave you the contract?" Dread asked as he studied her carefully.

"It was emailed across to me. Nothing suspicious about it." She tried to shrug without moving her arms from her chest, which made her look even more unprofessional.

"How did you even find me?" the Alpha next to her growled. His irises flashed the brighter blue, barely a second before returning to the darker shade. From her experience with shifters it was his animal's response, their emotions and instincts rawer than their human counterpart.

13

Alice refused to face him, not wanting to aggravate his beast. "I'm good at my job."

"What happened Alice?" Dread leaned forward, the light from the chrome lamp giving him an ethereal glow.

"I was waiting outside the bar where I had tracked the wolf..." A small snarl to her right. "I mean, Mr Wild," she corrected. "He held a man up by his throat, against a wall."

"You held a man against a wall? In a human bar?" Dread's unnerving eyes turned to the Alpha. His fangs punched below his bottom lip in a show of uncharacteristic annoyance.

"Pack business." Was the Alpha's only response, his tone absolute.

Alice continued. "The man had started to shift, bones were breaking, and his fur started to erupt from his ripped flesh, but it was wrong." She knew it, she had seen enough shifts from human to animal and back again to recognise the difference in the transition.

"Wrong?" Dread questioned her.

"I have seen people shift, and this man was wrong, sick maybe. He changed into a half state, his legs bent at the wrong angle and half his body exposing muscle. He ran from the bar and the..." Alice hesitated, deciding to correct herself. "the Alpha, chased after him. So I followed."

"And because of you, he got away." Mr Wild started to snarl before he caught himself, his face shocked before it relaxed back into its impassivity.

"He wasn't my target." She observed him from the corner of her eye, wary.

"It took me three months to track him. I needed the information he could give me. Because of you..." The Alpha started to stand, his voice deepening as violence threatened.

"ENOUGH!" Dread slammed his hand down onto the

table, rattling his pen onto the floor. The vein in his head pulsed violently, attempting to escape his porcelain skin. "I have heard enough." He stared down Mr Wild until he had returned to his seat. "After discussing the details with both yourself and Agent Skye, I have come to a decision that my Paladin was acting correctly in these circumstances."

The Alpha started to protest until Dread held up his hand.

"However, I will personally investigate how a warrant for your arrest was issued. We both know you're not S.I. jurisdiction."

That caught Alice's attention. The only authority above S.I. was The Council.

"I'm not happy with this," Mr Wild said as he settled himself into a more relaxed position. It looked forced. "It took all my resources to track that wolf and then your Paladin went and fucked it up."

"Be that as it may, she did her job correctly." Dread caught her eye, showing her he was still angry.

But I didn't do anything wrong. Dread's eyes glittered as if he could read exactly what she was thinking, which he could. His own eyes replied *shut up and sit still.* So she bit her lip, deciding to take his advice.

"Now let's turn to another matter at hand, Alice mentioned the wolf being sick? Is there a disease going around that we should be concerned about?"

Alice turned to look at the Alpha once more, watching his jaw clench before he replied. "No."

Body language was something she was trained in, and the wolf just lied. *Now that's interesting.*

"Is there anything else you would like to discuss?" Dread reached down to his pen that had fallen, taking his time to line it back up with the grooves of the wood.

"Not at this present time," Mr Wild rumbled, annoyed but hiding the emotion.

"Great, so that matter can be put to rest." Dread pressed a hidden button beneath his desk. The door opened silently, allowing light to penetrate the tense room.

"Alice, we need to discuss your recent assignments. However, I will wait until we do not have an audience." He stood up before placing his hand over the breast pocket of his jacket, a sign of respect. It looked sarcastic. "Until next we meet Mr Wild. Please contact Supernatural Intelligence if you require anything further."

Mr Wild said nothing. Instead, he stormed out the door as a flustered Barbie spoke to him in hushed tones. Alice stood, but decided to wait, watching Dread carefully.

"Alice, you should probably escort our guest down." He concentrated on the pen.

"Why did you do that?" she asked, confused. "You knew he was lying. Why didn't you say anything?"

"And say what?" He finally looked up, his eyes still angry but more composed. "If you think I'm doing an inadequate job, why don't you tell me what you would have done?"

Alice hesitated, thinking about her response carefully. "I don't know, ask him more questions?"

"He is the Alpha, Alice. Sickness among his wolves has nothing to do with us. Shifters, in general, have nothing to do with us unless they pay for our services. You know as well as I do they are self-governed ever since Xavier took over on The Council."

His forehead furrowed, his expression stolid. Alice didn't know what to say, The Council being a subject she knew little about. The Council of five, or technically six when counting the Fae twins stayed out of the media, reigning over Breed silently. Dread, on the other hand, had met them all, and he wasn't a fan.

"I'll escort Mr Wild out of the building." She turned toward the door.

"Oh, and Alice," he started, forcing her to pause. "Make sure Mr Wild doesn't break anything on his way down."

CHAPTER 2

The lighting in the hallway blinded as Alice walked past Barbie, the receptionist glaring as she adjusted her top to show more of her breasts.

"Mr Wild, if you are finished with the show would you please follow me," Alice said politely, not needing to explain what she meant by the *show*.

She felt his tension behind her a second later, an ominous presence that stormed past her towards the lifts at the back of the floor, easily manoeuvring through the maze of drab grey cubicles spotted around in a confusing labyrinth. The only way to distinguish each cubicle from one another was the bursts of colour pinned to the walls, individuals trying to personalise their little space in a sea of grey.

The Supernatural Intelligence Bureau, also known as The Tower, was on constant speed, everyone having something to do or somewhere to be. The forty-second floor was the main operation for the Paladins, a small desk to prepare for contracts as well as their boss, Commissioner Dread

Grayson's office. The other floors contained I.T. technicians, weapons specialists, mailmen, just to name a few. There were even a whole five floors dedicated to a specialist hospital team who worked alongside the London Hope Hospital, England's largest medical facility specialising in holistic magic as well as general medicine.

Alice stood for a moment, trying to catch her breath.

Well, it wasn't awful, she groaned, covering her face with the palms of her hands. *Fuck. Fuck. Fuck.* The only good thing that came out of that meeting was, A: Dread admitted she actually did a good job. *Sort of anyway.* And B: He didn't mention any warnings or disciplinary meetings. Which was always a bonus.

"Oh Alice," a sing-song voice called to her.

She spun to look at Barbie, a feral smile on her pink painted lips.

"Just to let you know your disciplinary meeting has been scheduled for Tuesday at ten-thirty." Her eyes twinkled as she smiled. "Make sure you're here on time." With a last giggle, she turned back towards her desk.

"Great," Alice whispered to herself. "Just great." A lump in her gut, nerves attacking. "Maybe I could get a job with Sam at the bar?"

"You can't do that, you hate people," a chirpy voice replied.

Alice smiled when she noticed two people hanging around her cubicle. "What are you guys doing here?"

What sort of friends would hang around to see if she was fired or not?

"I thought you guys were both out on a contract?" Rose and Danton (or D as he was known to his friends) looked at her expectantly, waiting for the gossip.

"We were ma petite sorcière. But I missed your belle

smile," D sighed dramatically, his long black hair scraped back off his face.

Rose elbowed him in the chest. "Ignore him, we finished it up early."

"Mon amie you wound me." He feigned hurt, his pale hand draped dramatically over his heart.

"As Roselyn was saying, we finished our expédition early. But enough of that, I would like to know how ma petite sorcière is doing?"

"Yeah Alice, are you okay? Isn't that the Alpha? Oh my god, are you fired?" Rose asked in her usual cheery voice.

At a tall five feet, eleven inches, topping Alice's mundane height by a good seven inches, she looked like a cheerleader, one who could rip your throat out and smile sweetly the whole time. She was a panther shifter, a sleek cat the same dark shade as her hair.

"Oui, how are you?" D asked as his dark eyes turned towards the Alpha on the other side of the room. "Why is that wolf storming around? You piss him off, non?"

"How did you guys even know about that?"

"You know how nobody here can keep secrets." Rose fluffed up her dark hair. "So is it true? Did you arrest the Alpha?"

"Maybe." The Alpha in question paced in front of the lifts, his eyes flicking towards her every few seconds.

"Well then ma petite sorcière, in case you have to leave the tower in a more permanent fashion I would like to say how edible you look. Délicieuse," he said, with a sensual curve of his lips. "I'm sure there are things we could do to cheer you up? Non?"

Alice couldn't help but laugh. "I'm busy." She looked up at D's laughing face, his skin perfect, common amongst the older Vamps. The exception, like Dread, was when they had scars, wrinkles or skin imperfections before their turn.

"One day I will own your heart." He said this to her regularly, enough that she knew he didn't mean it. D didn't do relationships, didn't like being 'tied down'. Unless 'tied down' involved satin bed sheets and velvet rope.

He really liked to talk after a few drinks, or a lot of drinks as it was in his case.

"Well, not any day soon." A ding behind her, the lift doors opening as Mr Wild's patience wore thin. "I have to escort him down. I'll catch up with you guys soon." With a quick wave, she jogged to the lift, barely squeezing in with the Alpha as the doors closed.

The typical lift music couldn't drown out the tension in the small metal box. The picture on the wall showed ten people being able to fit into the small space, yet the air was thick with just the two of them.

Well, this is awkward.

Mr Wild didn't seem to feel the same tension, his arms loosely hooked onto his forearms as he leaned against one of the silver panels, casually staring at her. Alice tried desperately not to stare back, instead counting down the floors.

39. 38. 37. 36.

"How long have you been a Paladin?" he asked, the question sounding genuine. Strange considering his face looked anything but, his brow low over his eyes.

"Around five years."

"Not long then."

"Long enough." Alice frowned, looking up at him then. His eyes flashed a pale blue as she held his gaze, his animal taking a look.

She had never met someone who could morph so quickly and so often. She held his stare, desperate to read

21

him. He didn't look angry anymore, more curious. The annoyance was still there, not that his face gave anything away. She just knew it, could feel the underlying pressure in the air. So she didn't look away, just as curious as his wolf seemed to be. His nostrils flared, as if he was scenting the lift, scenting her. She finally dropped her eyes.

"How long have you been Alpha?" she asked, keeping her tone light.

He ignored her question. "Did you train as a Paladin?"

"How is that any of your business?" she asked before she could think of something polite to say. She opened her mouth to apologise as the lift door pinged open on the twentieth floor, a group of three people looked at the tension in the small space, deciding to wait until the next one.

Mr Wild waited until the door closed fully, and the lift began moving again before replying. "Just curious. Never met a Paladin quite like you."

She didn't know whether that was a compliment or not. Probably not. Alice considered it for a few seconds before replying.

"Yes, I trained at the academy."

"Not at the university?"

"No." Alice fidgeted, feeling uncomfortable, the subject a sore spot. She had been accepted into the University of London studying magic crafts, something she had been excited about. Dread was the one who convinced her to become a Paladin, to go to the academy instead. It meant her magic knowledge was basic and self-taught.

"Don't you have to gain a degree to become a recognised witch by the Magicka?"

"No." *Yes. Dammit.* "I don't see what point you're trying to make." She felt her cheeks begin to burn as she concentrated hard on the lights dancing in the seam of the tarnished brass doors.

10. 9. 8.

The lift finally creaked to a stop, opening to show the marble floor and columns of the lobby, a beautiful mosaic of crushed browns, golds and beiges. The metallic elements glittered as light reflected from the revolving doors, hitting the specs in the stone.

Without pause she exited the lift and quickly walked towards the front desk, having to fish out her pass from her bag and scanning the screen on the turnstile to sign herself out. The front desk was large, almost the same width as the whole atrium apart from a couple of inches each side.

There were four members of security on the desk at all times. Vince Cooker, the head of security was waving enthusiastically. He was a mage, a human touched with magic. While not as powerful as a full-blooded witch he could still do a few tricks, which he enjoyed showing Alice on as many occasions as he could.

"Hey, Vince."

"Hey there, Alice. I didn't get to say hi earlier, you seemed to be in a bit of a rush," the old security guard chuckled, his dark skin wrinkling even further. "Who's the gentleman by the glass?"

Alice chanced a look behind her, expecting the Alpha to have already left. He surprised her by waiting just outside the doors.

"He is..." Well, she couldn't just tell him she arrested the guy. "A friend."

"Well, he isn't a happy friend." His smile turned to a frown, his grey eyebrows pulled together in concern.

"He's just having a bad day," she said as she signed Mr Wild out too.

She waved goodbye as she felt cold air brush across her skin, summer having long ago disappeared into autumn, the temperature dropping uncomfortably low as the trees continued to lose their colour.

"Mr Wild." She nodded to the man standing to the side of the entrance. "I'm sure it's been a pleasure." He just stared at her, his eyes once again unreadable.

"How do you do that?" she asked, deciding that she had nothing to lose.

"Do what?"

"Control your emotions." She studied his eyes carefully, noting the flare of shock before he concealed it once again.

How can he conceal his emotions so easily? What did he have to hide?

He stared back, his eyes lingering for a second longer than they should before he turned and walked away.

CHAPTER 3

The bus screeched as it peeled away from the bus stop a short walk away from her flat, a billow of black smoke chasing it down the street. Alice strode past the *'Welcome to Midnight Glade'* sign, a wide metal rectangle hanging loosely from a lamppost. Fangs and large eyes had been added to several of the letters, the neighbourhood kids playing around. It would take a trained eye and someone with decent magic knowledge to notice the small symbols carved along the bottom, anti-violence hexes and protection spells created by overly concerned residents.

Midnight Glade North was like every other suburb surrounding London, an incredibly large community with modest houses painted in whites, beiges, blues and even a few gaudy pinks. Picket fences, neatly trimmed shrubs and flowerbeds decorate paved driveways with well taken care of lawns. People walked their dogs, children played happily in the community park and cars parked neatly along the roads.

The area looked the same as any other residential zone, the exception being that seventy percent of the community was Breed. While it was no longer a shock to have kids in school with shifter children, or a work colleague who had an unusual liquid diet, most humans felt uncomfortable in a majority Breed area. It was almost like an age-old instinct not to hang around with someone who could see you as lunch.

Humans (commonly referred to as Norms) wouldn't notice the small differences in the neighbourhood compared to their 'ordinary' ones unless they knew what they were looking for. Children drew with chalk on the streets, their patterns specific to enchantments rather than daisies and hearts. Windows painted black, giving protection from the sunlight or that a front door had an oversized 'doggy' door fitted where homeowners who had paws could enter easily.

"Hey, that's mine!" a little girl shouted, running in front of Alice as she chased after her brother who had stolen her doll, the head that which had already been ripped off and thrown into a neighbours garden. "I'm telling mum!" the little girl cried as her small hands sharpened into claws as her body reacted to her frustration.

Alice continued to walk as she flicked her collar up to protect her exposed cheeks, the air bitter cold. Slowly, the houses started to become less maintained, flats boarded up from fire damage. Flower beds, if at all planted, had died, the bushes left untrimmed and a few houses needing a good paint, if not completely abandoned. Some teenagers lurked at the street corners, sitting on the street signs passing cigarettes between them like a shifty drug deal. Potholes didn't get filled and cars became less expensive.

The flat Alice shared with her best friend Sam was in one of the less maintained buildings, one that was built in the seventies and hadn't been updated since. The walls were paper-thin and Alice could already hear an argument from apartment 1C as she made her way up the stairs, quickly followed by banging and shouting. The walls were brown with red squares, although not as garish compared to the putrid green carpet that could have once been a shag pile but had flattened and discoloured over years of use. There was no lift, having been broken years before Alice had moved in.

Her neighbour, Mrs Finch in 3A, explained a few years back that Mr Tucker, the caretaker and resident in 1A refused to fix the *'damn thing'* because a group of shifters decided to use it as a place to party and the jumping up and down broke the mechanics. Mr Tucker, on the other hand, explained Mrs Finch was *'talking out of her arse'* and in fact, one of her many dogs had pissed on the exposed wires and ruined the electrics. So Alice took the stairs to the third floor, her place right at the end of the corridor.

"Oh Alice, it's so nice to have caught you," Mrs Finch called from her open doorway as she held a small black dog that shook in her arms. Alice hid her sigh as she turned around, a fake smile pasted on her face.

"I need you to tell that boy of yours that he shouldn't tease my babies like that." Several barks in agreement from behind her as the dog in her arm stayed silent, his eyes bulging.

"What has Sam done now?" Alice asked, bemused. Sam had a love, hate relationship with Mrs Finch. He loved to wind her up, and she hated him for it.

"I'll have you know that boy prowled outside my door, in his *other form.*" She made it sound like he did it on purpose. Which admittedly, he did. "It makes my babies

27

upset to know there's a cat outside." The small dog in her arm continued to shake.

Alice bit the inside of her cheek, "I'll ask Sam to refrain from standing outside your door when he's a leopard."

With an awkward wave Alice turned hastily towards her door. *I can't be bothered with this crap.*

"Now Alice, I'm not finished," Mrs Finch said, her neck prickling a pale pink in irritation. "I saw another woman sneak away from your apartment the other night. A *different* one from the last time." The revulsion was clear.

"What has that got to do with me?" she asked, her temper getting thin as the day started to take its toll on her mood.

"Well, he shouldn't just bring home every girl he's just met. It's unsanitary." She sniffed in disgust.

"I'll let Sam know you don't appreciate his partners. Now if you would excuse me." Alice lifted her fist to knock, only just remembering she still didn't have her keys. Hoping Sam was in and she didn't have to ask someone to break it down she knocked hard, the door swinging open easily.

"Sam?" She called as she closed the door behind her. "Sam, what's wrong with the door?"

"Oh, hey babe girl," Sam smiled, his white blonde head appearing from the kitchen archway, the area leading off from the living room. "Small technical issue in that someone broke in."

"What? Again?" Alice groaned as she walked past the bathroom on the left to the surprisingly decent sized kitchen in the back. She dropped her bag on the small table before facing him, her arms crossed. "Isn't that the second time this month?"

"Aye," he replied cheerily in a soft Irish lilt, his accent only pronounced on certain words and phrases, having died down from years of living in England. "But I have replaced the lock, and it seems like nothing is missing." He wiggled his eyebrows at her, the same colour as his natural white blonde hair, a long straight curtain that's cut several inches beneath his shoulders.

"That's because there's nothing here to steal."

Sam had been her best friend since they met as kids in a support group. She had sat in the circle amongst the other children who had gone through their own traumas, scared and lonely. He had tugged on her plaited hair one day and asked her how to braid his own long, unmanageable locks. She couldn't help but smile at his impish grin with a small dimple in one cheek.

"No comment," he shouted from the kitchen.

"I don't know why we stay here." Alice sat heavily in one of the two foldable chairs she got for ten pounds at one of the cheap furniture chains.

"I've already suggested we go stay at your house."

"It's not my house." Alice settled her chin on her palm, watching Sam potter around the kitchen. Her house, or parents' house, was a boarded up building on the other side of the city. "And you know I can't."

"I know." He softened his voice. "I'm just tired of this place. Did you know Mrs Finch called me a whore today?" He fluttered his eyelashes in mock horror. "I don't know whether to be offended or flattered."

"Offended," Alice smiled. "She told me in the hallway. She also mentioned you should stay away from her dogs."

"Those wee shits shouldn't be called dogs. What's the small black one called? Sooty? Or is it Sunny?" He turned his back to her, stirring a black pot on the stove. Cooking utensils hung neatly on the wall in front of him, some on hooks and others on a magnetic strip. The kitchen tiles were yellow and broken, the spider web of cracks giving the dull wall a sad type of decoration.

"Sooty is the black Chihuahua, Sunny is the ginger Pomeranian."

"It's sad that you know their names."

"I don't know all of them." Alice got up to investigate the contents of the pot. "Only the ones I see the most. She usually stops me to show me the pictures of them she keeps in her purse." The dark brown liquid bubbled angrily, various unidentifiable meats and vegetables floating around. "She has about seven dogs in there now."

"I don't even see how that's allowed." Reaching up he grabbed two white plates from the cupboard.

"What ya cooking?" Alice asked. "It smells... interesting."

"I'll have you know I am a master chef." He gave her a teasing smile, pouring some brown sludge with various meats onto the plate. He threw the spoon back into the pot, causing the brown liquid to jump out onto the wall.

"Bloody hell Sam, you've gotten it all over me." Alice rubbed the side of her arm, the brown stuff scalding hot.

Sam snorted. "That's what she said."

"So funny," she murmured as she picked up her own plate and followed him to the small two-seater table.

"So..." Sam started, a spoonful of his masterpiece halfway to his lips. "Why the long face?"

Alice scooped a mixture of the rice and sauce onto her fork, her taste buds exploding as she placed it on her tongue. "Hey, this is really good." She ate another mouthful, moaning as she bit into a particularly juicy piece of chicken. Well, she thought it was chicken.

"Stop stalling. What happened?" His amber eyes rolled over to her, the colour the same as the leopard that was his other half. He thought it made him look badass. She actually agreed, but would never admit that to his face. Shifters were born with two parts, both a human, and an animal. It was his animal, the leopard, that gave him his attitude, its instincts rawer compared to the human. It was unusual amongst shifters to have the same eyes as their counterpart, a result of his harsh childhood.

Alice chewed the chicken for longer than needed. "I fucked up."

"You what?" He spluttered some of his food. "What did you do?"

"I may, or may not have arrested the Alpha of White Dawn."

"The Alpha?" Sam burst out laughing, clutching his stomach. "Why did you do that?"

"Well, I didn't personally go after him or anything. It was a contract. There was a warrant and everything."

"Was he hot?"

"SAM!" She threw an unused spoon at his head, he ducked and it clattered to the floor.

"Now that wasn't very nice." He suppressed a laugh, his lips trembling at the effort.

"My career is over and all you can do is laugh." She lifted her arms, exasperated.

"You're being dramatic. What did the dark overlord say?"

Alice smiled at Sam's nickname for Dread. "He didn't really say anything." She looked down at what was left on her plate. "I have a disciplinary meeting with him in a couple of days."

"See," Sam said as he added more food to his plate. "If it was that serious the meeting would have been immediate."

"Maybe." Alice looked out onto the small ledge the

landlord called a balcony. Small terracotta pots stood along the edge, some hanging over the railing with a selection of herbs she used for potions. "What about you? You not at work today?"

"Graveyard shift," he moaned as he leant against the metal sink, his empty plate soaking.

Alice suppressed a laugh when she noticed his t-shirt, the words '*I tried to be normal once. Worst two minutes of my life*' written in bold typography across the black cloth. They both shared a humour for quirky tees.

"Why don't you come with me tonight? Let your hair down, have a few drinks. It could be fun."

"Not tonight." No, she had to practise her sorry face. "But I'm definitely up for it soon."

"You need it." He finished up at the sink. "I need to get changed, feel free to change your mind and meet me later. The new boss is in town and I want you to meet him."

Her eyebrows creased. "Meet him? Why?"

"Because you have no social life outside of work. You won't even go on a date with that Vamp."

"Hey, I have a social life," she pouted. "And Danton isn't serious when he asks me out." She also wasn't interested.

"Baby girl, I don't count as your social life."

Alice stuck her tongue out at him.

"And besides, he's also hot," Sam continued, ignoring her childish reaction.

"You think anybody with a pulse is hot."

"And that's why I have an amazing social life."

"I don't think you banging hundreds of people counts," she pointed out. He just laughed as he exited the kitchen towards his bedroom. Alice followed, flopping onto her stomach on his bed, her head balanced in her hands. "What's your job like?"

Sam twisted as he pulled off his t-shirt, scars criss-crossing his abs and back. Small pale lines barely visible from age, the biggest ones high on his shoulder blades. His golden skin tone an advantage in hiding the worst marks.

"Why are you asking?" He grabbed his work shirt, a black cotton tee with the name 'Blood Bar' written in dark red across the back and left pec. "Looking for a career change?"

"Maybe." She sighed, rolling onto her back to stare at the ceiling. The once white paint had peeled in places, the artex cracked.

"Stop brooding. You love your job." He threw a sock at her. "You could always become one of those phone sex operators?" Sam's eyes lit up with excitement.

"You give the worst advice." She changed into a sitting position as he plaited his long hair. "I need a pay rise."

"Don't we all," he tutted, checking his appearance in the small mirror above his chest of drawers, the top drawer having broken off a few months back leaving a gaping hole. His bedroom, like hers, was small and compact, Sam's bed a large double with baby blue duvet and pillow, the sheets always messy and never made.

He came to sit beside her, his arms coming around in a hug.

"You screamed last night," he said, matter-of-factly. "Scared the living shit out of me."

"Did I?" She could never remember her dreams.

"Do you want to talk about your nightmares, baby girl?"

"No." She concentrated on her hands, twisting them in her lap.

"They're getting worse."

"They always do this close to the anniversary." She hugged him hard, resulting in him purring against her cheek, the vibration comforting. Releasing him with a final squeeze, she got up. "You know how it goes. I get some nightmares, I brood, and then it's all over." Every year.

"We both know that isn't healthy." He leant back on his arms.

"And your obsession with sleeping with every living thing is?"

Sam narrowed his eyes.

"Shit, I'm sorry, I didn't mean it." She was just tired and angry.

"Maybe you should go speak to Dr Lemington again?"

Dr Lemington was their psychiatrist as children. He didn't help either of them then, so how could he help her now?

"I don't need any help. I deal with everything just fine."

"Yeah, sure."

Alice could almost hear the eye roll. "Look, I don't want to fight. You need to get to work, and I need to go soak in the tub with a pot of ice cream."

"Aye, I do." He stood, adjusting his skinny jeans. "You sure you don't want to hang with me tonight?" The look of worry on his face made her turn away. He had his own demons, he didn't need to fight hers too.

"No it's cool, I'll be fine." With a kiss on the cheek Sam walked out, the front door shutting a moment later.

Once she heard the lock click she walked into the living room, heading towards the bathroom when a photograph caught her eye. She stared at the picture, the two adults and two kids smiling towards the camera, the only picture she had of her family, the others having been lost or packed away at the house. The house that Alice still hadn't dealt with, still hadn't visited. She tilted her head as she looked at her mother, her emerald green eyes shining with happiness.

Alice reached up, fingertips' touching the glass, tracing her mother's smiling face before moving onto her father, a tall man who only had eyes for his wife. While her mum was the light with bright hair and eyes, her dad was the dark, black hair and deep mahogany eyes. Kyle, her older brother was a mixture of both, dark brown hair with emerald eyes while Alice, the little girl holding her dad's hand was a perfect copy of her mother.

Alice choked back emotion as she dropped her hand, her family gone. Taking a moment to herself she turned to the bathroom, a hot bubble bath sounded like the perfect distraction.

CHAPTER 4

Alice flicked the dirt from underneath her fingernails, the soil having embedded itself from spending most of her morning tending her few plants and herbs on her balcony. She usually used gardening to calm her temper, but it hadn't worked today. The contract she had been assigned igniting her irritation.

How could they do this to me? she thought to herself. *It's barely above intern level.*

Alice audibly sighed, annoyed that she could hear herself whining in her own head. Frustrated she clicked through her phone, double checking the contract, assuring herself the small guy at the bar was indeed the right target.

Target: 347680
Mr Scoolie Smitt – Fae – Leprechaun. 4ft tall – long brown hair.
Sells dud charm spells to young adults who use them to get high.

Alcoholic
Aggression level – green
Retrieval fee – Basic

She had been training to become a Paladin for as long as she could remember, Dread having prepared her since she was a little girl. It made her great at her job, yet there she was, on a contract with a leprechaun. Not even an interesting leprechaun, one who liked to sell crappy charms.

The screen flashed as she analysed all the information, confirming the details with her research.

The Fang
Red Lion
The Cock Ring

Three pubs the alcoholic leprechaun liked to frequent. As she had already been to The Fang and The Cock Ring, (The Cock Ring having, disappointingly, just a rooster as its logo,) she now sat grumpily in The Red Lion Pub just off Angel.

"Give me n'other one then," Mr Smitt called to the bar staff, his high-pitched voice carrying across the room. A large rucksack sat at his feet, almost the same size as him. It was just luck he was the only leprechaun in tonight, otherwise she was out of options. She tried to examine his clothing, looking for the telltale sign he belonged to one of the two Fae courts. Which honestly were more like cults, or some ridiculous frat/sorority.

The Seelie court, also known as the Light Fae, were relatively nice compared to their darker brethren. In her experience, at least. They usually wore an emerald somewhere on their body to symbolise their connection to Seelie. On the other end was the Unseelie court, also known as the Dark Fae, who were a lot less friendly. Their traditions were more barbaric than their light siblings and were often on S.I.'s wanted list. They liked to use the ruby as their emblem.

As Mr Smitt wasn't wearing any gemstones, he probably wasn't registered with either court, which made paperwork a hell of a lot easier.

From his increasing volume she gathered he was only a few drinks away from toppling over, or leaving. So she decided to wait until she detained him.

With time on her hands she looked down at the newspaper left on her table, she might as well relax and make the most out of the evening. Someone had clearly read through it already, the paper torn in places, the crossword completed and artistic penis symbols were drawn on almost every page.

The main headline on the first page was of a body mysteriously disappearing from the morgue. Most of the story had lovely dicks drawn over the writing, but Alice understood the general idea. As she flipped through the pages a picture of a smiling man caught her eye, one of the few photos without pen marks all over it. The title explained he was the youngest witch to accept a position in the Magicka, the highest members of the magic world.

The Magicka, much like The Council, were a board of witches that specifically govern their own race. They specialised in a tiered system to determine how powerful someone was in each main class, earth, arcane and black.

Earth magic was classified simply as someone who used natural ingredients to create potions, amulets and charms. Arcane was slightly different, using their chi to physically manipulate their power. The witch would use incantation words to throw spells at people and objects and was known to be one of the harder classifications to master. Most witches mixed a little of both classes, however, there was one more class of magic.

Black magic was the worst, and yet the most powerful of the three classes. Those witches use blood and death to create spells and potions, something that had been made illegal for obvious reasons.

Within each class there were several branches, such as herbalist within earth and sorcerer within arcane. Inside each branch a witch could be tiered between one and three, one being the highest and three being the lowest. However, most witches just went by their class heading unless they personally specialised in a particular branch.

Tier four was reserved for mages, humans who were touched by magic. Normally born from a witch and a human they were treated like second-class citizens in the magic community. No mage had ever gotten to tier one even though some were pretty powerful in their own right.

Alice snorted at the picture. "It doesn't take a pretty piece of paper to decide how much of a witch I am."

A loud smash brought her attention up to the stage, a drunken man apologising profusely to the amp he had bumped into. He stood there for a good few minutes, his apology turning into a full-blown conversation. Distracted, Alice lifted her drink to her lips, the bubbles going down the wrong hole until she choked loudly, her hand snapping up to cover her mouth. Throat still raw from the coughing she pushed her glass away, sitting straighter in her chair as her boot squeaked across the threadbare carpet.

What the...? Beneath the table she checked her boot, frowning at the noise. *Oh gross.* Her boot squeaked again, the spongy carpet having soaked in a generous amount of liquid. It's probably safe to say over the years alcohol, vomit and other bodily fluids had helped decorate it.

Alice looked down.

It was probably what all the brown patterns were.

Gag.

The décor unsurprisingly matched the disgusting carpet, brown and blue striped walls with paint peeling straight from the brick. Black and white photographs had been nailed to the surface to try and add some decoration. A portrait showed a group of men smiling, a wide angled shot of the outside of the pub and one of a serene woman, her once pretty face having received similar treatment as the newspaper.

The man over to the left continued to chat animatedly to the amp, one foot planted on the ledge of the poor excuse for a stage, and his other placed on the carpet. He leaned forward to caress the black felt of the speaker, his empty glass placed haphazardly on top. A waitress walked past and picked up the glass, causing him to mutter something at her before he staggered off, collapsing onto a table nearby.

Pints clinked as two bartenders served drinks at the bar, the wood a lot cleaner than the tables and chairs dotted around the room. The old wood scratched beyond redemption, the top's sticky, like a fine layer of glue engraved into the grooves of the wood. There was a deep open fireplace, the fire protected by an ornate iron grate cracking happily to the left, the warmth from the flames a pleasant sensation. Unfortunately, the heat cooked the odd smell in the air, a mixture of mould, damp and old beer.

Something shattered against the bar, dark amber liquid pouring down the front.

"Stoopid fecking bitch," the leprechaun shouted, trying unsuccessfully to stop the drink from soaking into his rucksack, the bag now having been placed on the counter. Alice looked over at the ugly clock ticking loudly above the bar.

It was getting late.

With a sullen look at her glass she returned her attention to the room, deciding if it was quiet enough to just snatch her target and call it a night. It wasn't like it was busy, the bar reasonably empty apart from a few drunken men. A handful sat around drinking quietly, some chatting with their friends and some alone, watching the football game on the painfully old television in the corner.

A laugh came from the pool table, a welcoming sound compared to the dull background noise. A thwack as a billiard ball was hit too hard, the ball smashing to the floor. White fangs flashed as the men laughed again.

Blade tight to her back she stood, making sure it remained hidden beneath her jacket, but within easy reach. Glass in hand she walked over to the bar, sitting on the stool next to her target.

"Hi," she greeted, flashing her most sensual smile. He warily looked her over, taking in her leather knee-high boots, tight jeans and a black t-shirt. His eyes lingered on her breasts for a moment before deciding his Guinness was more interesting.

Eyebrows creased, Alice looked down at her cleavage, deciding she needed to invest in a good push-up bra.

How pathetic.

"Can I get a Guinness please?" she asked the barmaid, a shifter Alice would guess from the amount of hair on the back of her hands.

"A fellow Guinness drinker then miss?" Mr Smitt smiled over at her, his eyes actually rolling over her with appreciation this time.

41

"Maybe," she said, thanking the barmaid before sipping a bit of the liquid, trying not to cough as it went down.

"What ya lookin' for? I may look small but some parts of me are anyfin' but," he chuckled to himself, pushing his rucksack out the way so he could see her better.

"I was actually looking for someone to sell me some..." Alice hesitated, trying to sound unsure. "Charms," she ended in a whisper.

"Aye, well, sellin' charms is what I do second best." He winked at her to make sure she understood the innuendo. "Well, are you lookin' for a good time? I have charms for that, ones that make you irresistible to the opposite sex, or the same sex, depending on what you're into." He looked at her expectantly.

"So you admit you do sell charms?"

"Aye miss. Best there is." He proudly smacked the top of his rucksack.

"Brilliant." She stood up, reaching to the back of her jeans to unhook her handcuffs. "Mr Smitt, I have a warrant for your arrest for selling dud and illegal charms, you do not have to say anything, but what..."

His mouth did a great impression of a fish. "Feck off."

Arsehole. "I have a warrant for your arrest. You will come with me quietly..."

He turned on his stool and pointed his chubby finger towards her, the motion causing him to fall face first onto the carpet. Using his confusion, Alice snapped her cuffs onto both of his wrists, the cuff automatically tightening to his wrist size.

"Hey, what the 'ell do you think you're doin'?" he shouted, dazed.

"I told you, you're under arrest." Alice huffed as she leant down to grab his rucksack, finding the bag full of hundreds of different wooden disks. She pushed the disks out the way, finding several vials of blood and a couple bags of salt.

Idiot. Most of the disks were useless. The salt from his fingers ruining the charms before they could even be invoked. Alice picked up a vial of blood, watching it move as she tilted it to the light.

He started to panic, scrambling as he tried to release his wrists. "Oi!" he called. "They're mine!"

She ignored him, instead zipping up the bag and placing it onto the bar.

"Please," he started to beg, turning to one of the bartenders. "Someone call the cops, this bitch is robbin' me"

"Hey, you need to take this outside." The barmaid pointed her finger at Alice. "We don't want any trouble in 'ere. Leave or I'll call the Met."

Alice stifled a laugh. *What was the Met police going to do?* They had no jurisdiction when a Paladin had a warrant. Besides, they were normally the ones that issued the bloody thing.

From inside her jacket pocked she pulled out her Paladin license, the evidence enough for the barmaid to growl and walk away. The Metropolitan Police dealt with the investigations and boring part of law enforcement, dealing with Breed unless the situation was serious or required a specialist.

She was the specialist.

"There would be no use calling the cops. I have a valid warrant."

Mr Smitt's face fell, the colour draining from his cheeks. "I'll give you anyfin', anyfin' you want. Remember I can find the end of the rainbow!"

"Come on." She went to grab him, but he jumped out of reach.

"I have money." He licked his lips nervously. "Pots of gold. More gold than you could ever want."

She ignored him, grabbing him by the scruff.

"Hey, bloodsuckers..." he shouted behind him. "Get rid of this whore for me an' I'll give ya some cash."

The Vamps stopped their game of pool, turning to look at them in unison, as if they were one person and not three individuals. Their eyes dark in their pale emotionless faces, all hint of fun and humour gone.

Vampires could be really creepy fuckers sometimes.

"Now boys," Alice began. "We're not going to do something stupid are we?"

They smiled, a wide grin showing the edges of their very sharp teeth. A threat.

Oh shit.

She released Mr Smitt's scruff as she faced the Vamps, analysing her options. One: Run away. *Not really an option.* Two: Ignore them and hope they go away. *Unlikely.* Three: Humiliate them with her badass skills but also hope they give up before she does.

The first Vamp calmly walked around the table, his sinister smile still in place as he looked her up and down.

Option three it is then.

Alice pulled out her sword, a sharp blade from her back sheath, ignoring the gun on her hip. Vampires were normally too fast to aim a gun at and get an accurate hit, so it meant close quarters with a blade to take them on.

"Any attack against a Paladin warrants an immediate arrest. I WILL use deadly force." The vampires laughed at her threat. They actually laughed.

Bastards.

A blue flame bobbed around the hilt, not as threatening as she would have liked but at least it was something. The vampires stopped laughing, the one closest to her hissed, his fangs elongating in his jaw as he snarled at her.

Fuck, fuck, fuck.

Vamps were fast, like ridiculously fast. She may have trained, but she could never match the speed and strength of even a baby Vamp. It was why Paladins normally partnered on vampire contracts.

Alice breathed in, steadying her weight on her legs as she waited.

"I SAID TAKE THIS OUTSIDE!" the barmaid shouted.

"Shut up, Mary." A man grabbed and pulled her to the back of the bar, pushing her through a door.

"Yes, shut up Mary," the Vamp at the back of the pool table echoed, his head tilted to the side as he watched her carefully. His hair was dark, dyed Alice thought, his pale roots showing. He smiled, showing off his large fangs.

The three Vamps were serious Goth rejects, all wearing black trench coats with metal studs. One wore black lipstick, making his skin look even sicklier than it should. The mouthpiece of the group seemed to be content to stand and watch, his relaxed posture unthreatening as he leant against the wall towards the side.

He wasn't a threat just yet, so she turned to the other two, tutting at their appearance as they made their way around the pool table. "Don't you boys know that Vamps have joined the modern world? They don't just wear all black now," she teased.

None of them smiled. *Tough crowd.*

"You're no match for us, witch," the one on the left snarled. He even made the word 'witch' sound dirty.

She turned her attention to him, pointing her blade as she smiled sweetly. "I'm sorry Metal face, I couldn't understand you with all that stuff hanging out of your mouth." That got her a small chuckle from one of the other Vamps.

"Shut it Greig," Metal face growled, shooting his friend a dark look.

Alice turned to the one called Greig. "I don't know what you're smiling about, you're wearing more makeup than the whole of the French renaissance combined." That stopped his chuckle. "Hey, I have a joke for you." They all look at her like she had lost it. "What happened to the two mad Vamps?"

The three guys looked at each other warily. Not sure how to take her.

"What's the answer?" Someone from the back of the pub drunkenly shouted, followed by a bunch of murmurs.

"Well, they both went a bit batty." A cacophony of laughs from behind, the Vamps not reacting at all. "What?" she asked them, shrugging. "That was a good joke."

"Enough of this," Metal Face shouted, leaning over to grab her.

"*Adolebitque.*" She threw her hand towards Metal Face, his shoes catching alight with a bang before he even touched her. He let out a shrill cry, hopping from one foot to the next to stifle the flames.

A fist blurred, just catching her cheek as the hit resonated through her teeth. She flicked her tongue against the inside of her mouth, making sure all her teeth were still present and standing.

Fucking, ow.

In no time at all Greig hit out again, his fist only just missing as she bent out the way.

Fuck me, he's fast, she thought, moving so her back was backed against the bar.

She needed him angry.

"Is that all you got?" she sneered.

That did it.

Timing it perfectly she moved out of the way at the last possible moment, Grieg throwing himself headfirst into the solid wood bar, knocking himself out cold.

One down.

Chants came from behind, mostly encouragement for her but some for Metal Face. Much to his annoyance his new nickname seemed to have caught on. Mr Smitt was one of the people not on her side.

Alice knew as soon as the flames died, the air shifting behind her. "I have another joke," she said as she turned to Metal Face.

He just snarled, fangs flashing.

"What's a vampire's favourite sport?" The crowd behind were clapping along, even calling out guesses. "Batminton."

His hand a blur he grabbed a pool cue and threw it at her, barely missing her head before he jumped forward, fangs bared. The cue stuck into the wall, the end trembling. Her free hand grabbed his neck inches before he could bite her throat. His skin pale, with red blemishes, pimples ready to burst spread chaotically around his young face.

Vampires used to be humans who had had a blood exchange with another vampire, the virus attacking the human DNA and mutating the strands creating an almost immortal. The virus was very temperamental, only certain humans survived the transition. The ones that did lived off of special proteins commonly found in fresh blood. His skin was yet to settle down into its perfection, meaning he was very young in undead terms.

A nail scraped down her neck, warm liquid leaving a trail down her throat. His nostrils flared wildly as her arm blocked his attacks, jaws grinding together as his own fangs cut into his lips, pearls of blood dripping down his chin.

Brown eyes swirled, pupils growing before encompassing the whole eye.

Fuck.

A Vamp attacking was one thing, one in the throes of bloodlust was something entirely different.

Alice held him at arm's length, a nail scratching down her outstretched arm, clawing to get to her throat. Her arm strained as he started to thrash, his eyes never leaving her pulse as it beat heavily against her neck, his senses all attuned to that one point.

She lifted her sword, impaling it into his chest in one clean move. His mouth opened in shock, the silver penetrating his heart. The crowd gasped, shocked at the sudden turn of events.

Alice twisted the blade, knowing the pain would distract Metal Face enough to think straight, the blade not enough to give him true death. Fairy tales throughout history had gotten that part correct, the only thing that could kill vampires was wood or fire. One thing Hollywood had embellished was that they didn't turn to dust when stabbed. They rotted and smelt like everyone else, which also meant the older the Vamp the worse the smell. It was a shame their affliction to the sun wasn't true either, just a little extra sensitive skin.

Real life was forever disappointing.

"Holy shite!" Mr Smitt cried.

"Now we both know this blade alone isn't enough to kill

you." She looked him in the eye, the pupils shrinking, showing more of his natural brown. "But as you can see, I can manipulate fire." She waited, allowing it to sink in. "And we both know what will happen if I put fire in the nice hole in your chest." She let that knowledge bleed into her eyes.

"Enough," the last Vamp said, his eyes flickering between them as he walked around the table. "We'll go."

"Yes. You will." She smiled sweetly, making him pale even more than his natural skin tone. With a quick move she removed the blade from Metal Face's chest, holding it loosely at her side. The crowd erupted into applause as all three vampires left, glasses clinking as they cheered and congratulated each other as if they had a great part in it all.

"Shite, shite, shite," her leprechaun jabbered to himself, fighting against the special cuffs. He looked up at her, eyes wide. "Please, please, I've got gold, lots of gold. I've..."

Blade sheathed she grabbed him, interrupting his babbling as he tried desperately to fight her hold. Black rucksack in hand she started to leave as Mary the bartender blocked the exit.

"You missy are barred. Look at this mess." She waved at the dented bar with the cue still sticking out the wall. "Who will pay for this?"

Alice fought a snappy response, instead pushing past with a screaming leprechaun.

She plopped him on the curb, opening the back of her car before throwing him inside. The handcuffs clicked into a special metal plate embedded into the seats, making Mr Smitt unable to escape.

She turned to him as she got in the driving side, making sure he wasn't trying to damage anything. Snot was smeared across his chubby face, his fists, the size of a three-year-old child's, were clenched together, trying to pull out of the magic infused cuffs.

"Please," his muffled voice begged. "Please, I'm sorry, I really am." He choked like he was going to be sick. She glared at him until he stopped. "Ple... as... se?" he hiccupped.

"Shut up." She leaned back in her chair, closing her eyes to drown out the sobbing.

Blood hell. I'm definitely going to be blamed for this.

CHAPTER 5

O ne. Two. Three. Four.
        Alice counted the metal beams running
        along the ceiling of the studio, several halogen
lights hanging from each one. A bird sat and watched from
beam number three, his beady eyes judging her as she lay on
the mat.

How the bloody hell did a bird get in here?

"Alice, get up," Rose moaned, tapping her foot.

"No." Alice rolled her head to look up at her friend's
annoyed expression.

"You're being childish."

"If I get up, you'll beat me up again."

"That's the point." Rose reached down to pull Alice to
her feet. "You need to stop letting anger control your fighting. You're making stupid mistakes."

Alice glared as she adjusted her ponytail, several
strands of hair already escaped.

Without warning Rose kicked out, aiming high.

"Shit." Alice ducked out the way, swinging her own leg around to hit her opponent's flank.

Rose flashed teeth when the kick connected, spinning her before she regained her balance. "Better." With a right hook she hit out, feigning the movement while she kicked out with her leg, easily tricking Alice and tripping her back onto the mat. With a small jump she pinned her, Rose's forearm pressed into the back of her neck. "But not good enough."

"Fuck," Alice growled, double tapping the mat. "You tricked me."

Rose just shrugged. "You weren't paying attention."

Alice continue her glare before sighing, her chest pumping up and down as she settled her pulse. "You're right. I can't believe I didn't see your thigh tense."

"You need to act, not react."

"Yeah, yeah." Alice balanced on her knees, tilting her head back to stare at the damn bird. It just chirped quietly, flapping its wings before settling down. Rose sat beside her, offering her the water bottle.

"What happened? You're normally a much better opponent."

Alice accepted the bottle. "I don't know, maybe I'm distracted?"

"About the meeting?"

"No." She thought about it. "Maybe? I don't know."

"I think you should talk to someone."

Alice stared at her friend, eyes narrowing when Rose wouldn't keep eye contact. "You need to stop talking to Sam."

"He's just worried. He said the nightmares are getting worse."

"They're fine. I'm fine." With an irritated growl she

moved to her feet, her eyes focusing as she noticed a punching bag not being used at the side. Fist clenched she smacked it, her frustration pushing it back to whack against the brick wall.

Rose loudly exhaled. "We love you, you know that?" She went to stand next to the bag, holding it in place.

Alice stopped her assault, her knuckles red and sore. "I know."

"Even after you get fired today and become a stripper that can make slightly above average love charms." Rose ducked at the towel thrown at her head, laughing.

"Very funny." She pressed her cheek against the bag, the sand inside not very comfortable. "We both know I would make brilliant love charms."

Rose tilted her head. "Sure, whatever." With a towel she wiped the sweat from her face. "So, anybody interesting in your life at the moment?"

Alice groaned. "Oh god, please stop talking to Sam. We both know I don't."

"I'm just asking." She lifted her hands up in defence. "I think a good ol' rut is just what you need."

"A good ol' rut?" Alice laughed. "Is that what it's called these days?"

"Well, you wouldn't know." Rose wiggled her eyebrows. "Seriously, I'm sure it will act as a great tension release."

"When you find the other half to that particular equation, let me know." With that she walked towards the locker rooms, moving around the other couples sparring.

The studio was large, several offices converted into the wide, open space. Mats were placed erratically around the floor, each person pulling their own one from the large pile in the corner.

"Oh Alice, I'm glad I bumped into you." A man walked

up to her, his white workout shirt see-through from sweat. "I heard from a little birdie that you've been fired," Michael smirked, his ginger hair tied up in a terrible topknot, giving the impression of a single horn. "I'm hardly surprised, considering."

"I can see you're still an arsehole," Alice muttered beneath her breath before she turned with a grimace. "Nice to see you too, Mickey." She started to walk around him when he blocked her path.

"It's Michael." He sniffed at her, his dark green eyes narrowing. She had no idea why he was an arsehole, but decided years ago that was just his personality.

"Well Mickey, I can see your nipples." She pointed at his shirt. As he looked down she slipped past him, continuing her way to the locker rooms.

Where did he hear that? Alice asked herself, slowly getting worried. If rumours were already going around the office, maybe it was possible and her job wasn't safe.

"Hey, wait up." Rose jogged to catch up, her arm coming round Alice's shoulders as they walked. "Ignore dick weed. You know you can't trust anything that comes out his mouth. Only last week he was telling someone how he tagged a bunch of black witches all on his lonesome with his makeshift wand." Rose patted her on the back before moving away. "We both know he hasn't got the skills to make a wand, never mind the funds."

Wands were ridiculously expensive, the small pointy wood able to concentrate a spell a lot easier for the caster, resulting in fewer accidents.

"He even told everyone how he is going to be given a special recognition for it from the Magicka!" Rose continued with a snort. "Yeah, maybe recognition for the worst witch in town. He has one of the worst track records in Paladin history."

"Yeah, you're right." Alice said, not quite believing it herself.

"Come on blondie." Rose put her arm around her again. "Let's get you to your meeting. Don't want you to piss off Grayson any more than he already is."

"I'm sure I can manage it."

Adjusting her neatly pressed collar, Alice stared at the clock on her grey cubicle wall, it was one of those Chinese novelty cats that every minute or so looked in the other direction.

The realisation that something could go very wrong in the meeting was dawning on her. Not once in the last five years working under Dread had she been called into an official disciplinary meeting. Yes, she had had more than one warning over the years, but nothing as official as an actual meeting.

The cat's eyes moved to the left, its tail swinging beneath it. Swatting the blue ball floating lazily around her head she continued to stare at the cat, the eyes swapping to the right once more.

Stupid bloody thing. She swatted at the blue flame again, giving a better impression of a cat than the actual cat clock. *Why do I get a drunken Tinkerbell every time my emotions go to shit?* Alice sighed. *It's probably a physical manifestation of my insanity.*

The blue flame floated over her face, dancing happily, unaware of her less than kind thoughts.

Eyes closed she breathed in, letting the air out slowly,

concentrating carefully to calm her nerves, stopping herself from surrendering to a full-blown panic attack.

Okay. I can do this.

She stood up, tucking her white shirt into her black pencil skirt, the outfit chosen specifically to look professional. She even added a black leather necklace, the one Dread bought for her for her nineteenth birthday.

"You can just walk in," Barb drawled from her seated position behind her desk, her attention more on manicuring her nails than her actual job. "It's not like this will take long," she smiled nastily.

Alice hesitated in front of the door, her fingers grasping the handle.

"Well go in then," Barb urged. "You look like an idiot just standing there staring."

Biting her tongue Alice plunged the door open, stepping into the surprisingly light room and closing the latch behind her.

"Alice," Dread greeted, his face unreadable as he sat at his desk. "Take a seat." The blind behind him had been raised slightly, allowing a little sunlight into the room.

Alice looked around with curiosity, never before seeing the office in daylight. The room was framed with dark oak bookshelves, each shelf looking like it had been carved straight from the wall, every one full of books. Alice squinted as she tried to recognise some of the titles, most being in an unfamiliar language. Photographs lined the back wall, some of Dread shaking hands with important people such as members of The Council, London's Mayor as well as few select celebrities.

Looking back at him, she took a seat in the only chair available, the chrome back making her sit as straight as possible.

Dread's eyes drifted to her necklace, his face softening for a second before hardening once more. Alice waited patiently for him to speak first, her hands sweaty as she rested them on her lap. A million scenarios raced through her head as she stared at him, possibilities of outcomes she didn't want to happen. Dread's hand disappeared underneath his desk, something thumping onto the wooden surface a second later.

"A Folder?" Alice felt her whole body turn cold. Dread had pulled out a red manila folder with her name scrawled across the front. It was a thick folder.

"So where shall we start?" Dread flipped over the first page, reading a little before looking up at her. "Ah yes, here we go. December 19th 2011, you turned a Norm into a dwarf."

Oh, crap.

"I did," she replied carefully. "He was stealing the presents under the tree in the shopping mall." The Met thought it was hilarious, a fitting punishment.

"He wasn't a contract."

"He was still stealing." It was only an illusion. She hadn't actually turned him into a dwarf. "I gave him over to the cops didn't I?"

"The point is that it wasn't your job to deal with it. You are not a police officer."

"But..."

"What about August 2012? You used a sleep potion to capture a black witch."

"I'm allowed to use charms, amulets and potions."

"You put to sleep the whole first row of people in that cinema."

"It may have had a weird area of effect."

Won't be buying a cheap potion again.

"September 2013 you almost drowned a kelpie." He looked up at her from over the folder. "I didn't even know you could do that."

Alice began to comment, but he had already continued.

"July 2015 you stabbed a shifter to the point they had to be rushed to the hospital because of silver poisoning."

"How was I supposed to know he had an above average allergy to silver?"

"That's not the point I'm making and you know it. November 2015 you captured a vampire by giving him sunburn."

"He wasn't in any real danger. He was new, he didn't realise the sun wouldn't actually kill him." Alice tried and failed not to smile at the memory, the vampire in question sobbing when she opened the curtain, not realising he wouldn't die from a little vitamin D. It wasn't her fault he was uneducated.

"Alice this isn't a joke." The smile dropped from her face. "You recently had a full-blown fight with three vampires, in front of a room full of people."

"Now that seriously wasn't my fault."

"Not according to the owner. She wants compensation for the damage."

"I never started that fight." Alice leant forward, pressing her palms face down onto the desk.

"So you didn't goad them with jokes?" Dread glared at her hands until she removed them, her sweaty fingertips leaving marks.

"Errr."

Bugger.

"You don't take your job seriously."

"Of course I do! I have the highest success rate in the branch than any other Paladin."

"Highest success rate, but also the highest damage rate." He slammed the folder closed with an audible slap. "I'm giving you a formal warning. You should be grateful it's not worse considering there are plenty more examples where these come from."

Alice pressed her lips together, excuses bubbling up her throat.

"No comment? That's a first."

Alice just stared at him, trying not to piss him off any more than she already was.

Leaning back in his chair he stared back, his eyes squinting suspiciously at her. "Now that the unpleasantries are over with there are a few things I would like to discuss." His cufflinks clunk on the table as he straightened his gold pen. Alice noticed the cufflinks were black, matching the rest of his black suit. The only suit he owned, apparently.

"Okay," Alice replied warily.

"I have a contract for you. One that has had the fee paid in full."

"Really?" she asked, startled. "Private or autho?" Private was someone who personally hired directly through the organisation for a substantial fee.

It's where they got their nicknames as bounty hunters. They weren't bounty hunters, at least, that's not what her Paladin license said.

Autho were contracts passed on through the Met. In those situations the government helped fund the work, being as it technically classed as police work. It was the private jobs that kept S.I. running smoothly, as authority contracts were categorised as government work, which meant minimal funding.

"Private. It seems you made an impression with the local Alpha."

"Seriously?" Alice felt excitement bubble, the thrill of a new contract exhilarating. "What for?"

"This is a very unusual situation. He didn't give me much choice in the matter."

"Didn't give you much choice?"

Dread leant over to his phone, clicking a button on the receiver before a deep grumbling voice filled the room.

"*Commissioner Grayson,*" the phone's speaker squeaked. "*While it is in my interest to take matters further regarding the misunderstanding with one of your Paladins, I have an offer that will please both of us. I would like to hire Alice exclusively for a contract regarding pack business. I've emailed across the appropriate details and will meet with Alice personally for the rest. I look forward to hearing from you.*" The receiver clicked off as the message ended.

"Why me?" That wasn't how S.I. worked. You couldn't pick and choose who worked on a case.

"Like I said, it's unusual, but we don't need the attention of The Council right now. His threats might be idle, but we cannot take the risk." Dread reached into a drawer, bringing out another folder, this time yellow. Pushing it across the desk he handed it to her. "Mr Wild has your details and will contact you further with any more information."

Picking up the folder she held it to her chest. "Anything else?"

"Don't do anything reckless."

CHAPTER 6

The car rattled to a stop with a puff of smoke, barely making it into the designated parking space. The Beetle always seemed to sigh once it was turned off, as if it overexerted itself simply by driving around town.

Reaching over she grabbed the folder as a loud bang echoed above her. Without thought, she flung the folder towards the suddenly open car door, holding her palm up in what she hoped was a threatening way. She was just glad she didn't squeal.

"You are late, Miss Skye."

"Huh?" She moved her palm out of the way, having to stretch her neck to see the man standing sullen by her door. He had the folder in one hand, having caught it when she threw it. His other hand was resting on the top of the car, with his body slightly stooped so he could catch her eye.

The Alpha had changed since she last saw him a few days ago, his eyes, as always, shielding any thoughts filtering through his brain. His face was clean-shaven, smooth enough to show his blemish free skin. From what she could see he wore a white buttoned up shirt, with the first couple buttons opened to reveal a tanned chest. His jaw was clenched as if he couldn't control the slight annoyance that she was either late, or that she threw his own folder at him. Probably both.

"How am I late?"

"You left The Tower precisely two hours ago, you don't live that far away."

"You followed me?" she steamed as pushed out with her hand so she could get out the car. He moved enough for her to get out, but not enough that she didn't have to brush against him slightly. She felt even more irritated. "How do you even know where I live?"

"You're intelligent enough to understand how I know where you live, considering you just accused me of following you." He leaned against her car, arms folded as he stared down at her.

She slammed the door shut, internally laughing when the noise and vibrations made him move away.

"As you are in possession of the folder, I assume you have accepted the contract?" He knew he hadn't given her much choice, so she said nothing. "Can we go up to your place so we can discuss it in more detail?"

"Why couldn't we have met at one of the conference rooms?"

"I prefer a more... personal setting." When she hesitated, he handed her back the folder. "Miss Skye, you must understand that this contract is strictly pack business. That means anyone under contract by the pack would come under pack jurisdiction. Do you understand?"

"There's a nice little coffee shop around the corner."

"No. This is private."

Alice weighed her options. "Fine."

She started to make her way towards her home, assuming he would follow. When she opened her door a few minutes later he walked past, his gaze taking in the ruined carpet, cracks in the walls, and mould on the ceiling in one quick sweep. She had the urge to apologise for the state of the place, but didn't.

He was the one who invited himself.

There was a loud techno beat pumping from one of her neighbours, the random thumps and pulses annoying. Alice whacked her hand against the living room wall, something she did regularly. There was no point shouting at them to turn it down, they couldn't hear her anyway.

As Mr Wild went to look at her limited collection of books on her homemade shelf, she heard a knock. It took her a second to realise it wasn't her neighbour whacking the wall back.

"Hello?" A woman's voice called through the front door. "Alice, are you in there?"

Oh god, really?

"Mrs Finch," Alice greeted as she opened the door slightly, blocking the view with her body. "Now is not a good time."

"Oh Alice, turn this awful music down." The old woman pushed the door open further, letting herself in along with one of her dogs. "Oh!" She stopped when she noticed Mr Wild. "I didn't know you had company." She turned her attention back to Alice, the glasses she normally kept secured around her neck sitting on the bridge of her nose, making her chestnut eyes huge in her too-small face. "Alice you should have said you had a young man over. I never see you with anyone, I would have brought over my famous tea."

"He's just a work colleague, Mrs Finch."

"Oh, pity." Her dog cowered by her legs, letting out a tiny growl as it faced the Alpha. "Now stop it Mr Toodle's," she scolded the dog. "I'm sorry, he is never this rude." She grabbed the shaking poodle. "Remember my dear, you would make a great wife." She made sure she looked back at Mr Wild for the last part.

"Goodbye, Mrs Finch." She gently closed the front door behind the old woman. Alice always thought it was strange that she encouraged her to marry any man that would take her, yet Sam wasn't allowed alone with a partner. Admittedly, he did bring home a lot of partners.

"Make sure you turn this music down," she called through the door.

"Nice neighbours," Mr Wild murmured.

"She's okay when she isn't propositioning everyone to be my husband." She thought she heard a slight laugh, but when she turned to face him she decided she must have heard wrong. She threw the folder onto the side table before taking a seat on the sofa. "Now, Mr Wild..."

"It's Rex," he interrupted, distracted. "Do you have cats?" he asked as he perched himself on the chair's arm.

"Cats?" She looked around in case she hadn't realised a cat had somehow gotten in. "Oh, my roommates a leopard."

"Ah." He folded his arms across his chest, nose wrinkled.

Great, she thought to herself. *Not only does the place look awful, it stinks too.*

"So, you don't get many male visitors then?"

No way was she going to touch that.

"Shall we start?" she asked in her most professional voice. She opened the folder, frowning when she noticed only three small Polaroid photographs inside. She tipped the folder upside down just in case there was something stuck, but nothing else came out. She laid out the three photographs neatly, looking at each in turn.

All three were pictures of deaths, two male and one female. They were all different people, yet all three photos were eerily similar. In every one the skin and muscle of the deceased had been peeled from the bone, blood a stark contrast as it congealed along the wounds around their arms and throats.

Alice looked closer, deciding they looked self-inflicted. The female photograph clearly showed skin and blood beneath her fingernails, the size and shape matching the ligature marks around the larger wounds.

"This is all the evidence you need. This is what happens when we don't find my wolf."

"Find?" She looked up at the Alpha then, noticing how he wouldn't look at the photographs, instead watching her. "Is one of your wolves missing?"

"Yes. These are previous wolves that, over the last year, have gone missing. They all end up the same way."

Alice silently gasped, wondering if he was serious. He had said it without an ounce of emotion so it was hard to decide. "Could they not have just decided to leave?" *And had really bad luck*, she wanted to add.

"Pack life is very different Miss Skye, and difficult to understand if you're not a shifter. They are allowed their own lives but they must be part of the pack structure. There are no lone wolves in my territory."

"Have they been autopsied?" She would be interested to confirm how they got some of their wounds.

"No. It wasn't needed."

"Wasn't needed? Something in the report could've helped..."

"It wouldn't have." He wouldn't budge.

She pursed her lips. "How long has your wolf been missing?"

"His name is Roman, and it's been about four weeks."

"Four weeks?" She felt her eyebrows rise. "That's a long time..."

"He isn't dead yet Miss Skye." He quickly looked away. "I would know."

"I didn't mean..." *Fuck.* What could she say to that? "Do you have any other useful information?"

"None that is relevant."

Relevant?

"Do you have any leads for me?"

He scanned her face for a second before answering. His eyes dark enough to tell her it was the man looking at her reactions and not the wolf. "Yes, there is a male wolf in my territory that has become a person of interest. He has been seen on several occasions talking to my men." He glanced down at the photographs before coming back to her. "I hear he will be in Underworld tonight."

"The club?" Alice's ears perked up, she had never been to the upscale Breed nightclub. "It takes months to get on the list..."

"It'll be your job to get in then, wouldn't it?"

She narrowed her eyes. "So you want me to find this mystery man and what?"

"Your job will be to get as much information from him as possible. By any means necessary."

"I can't just torture him." *Also illegal as hell.*

"You will do everything in your power to get the job done. Remember who is paying your wage at the moment Miss Skye."

"It's Agent, Mr Wild. Make sure you remember that."
She had about enough of his attitude.

"My men call me Sire."

Alice just heard white noise. He couldn't possibly be asking her to call him Sire? Could he? "That's nice for you." *No way in hell.*

"Fine *Agent* Skye, you may call me Rex." He started to get up.

"Then you may call me Alice." She also stood, feeling uncomfortable to continue sitting when he towered over her.

She flipped the photographs over, not wanting to look at them anymore.

"This is your target." He handed her another Polaroid, this time from his jeans pocket.

She analysed it as he opened her front door. "Wait, will you be there tonight?"

"No, I have prior engagements." He seemed to hesitate at the threshold. "I have instructed my pack to stay away also, I don't want them to interfere." He patted down his pockets before finding a leather scrap. "Before I forget, this is for you." He reached over and grabbed her arm, his thumb stroking the underside of her wrist as he double knotted the leather. "It's a charm, a warning to any shifters that you are off limits."

She stared at the leather plaited bracelet, noticing a crescent moon pendant attached in the middle. "Will this not warn the lone wolf I'm hunting tonight?"

He looked at her as if it was a stupid question. "I will contact you tomorrow regarding any information you discover. Do not miss my phone call." With that he walked away.

CHAPTER 7

The night air felt electric as Alice waited patiently outside the club, the bright red 'Underworld' sign illuminating the line of people waiting behind the long red rope.

"I knew I would get you on a date ma petite sorcière," Danton smiled devilishly.

"It's not a date," she said, rolling her eyes.

"Ah, that's what you think." D just chuckled, adjusting his white shirt to show as much skin of his chest as possible. The colour made his skin even more ghostly pale, bringing out his dark eyes and hair in contrast.

"I appreciate you getting me into the club, although, I think we're both overdressed," she mused, playing with the hem of her dress as she gazed across the crowd of people waiting. The dress she had chosen was provocative enough to show off her limited assets, her breasts considered on the small side. The black fabric was cut low at the front, hinting at a slow curve of flesh with the hem just above her knee. Twin knives were strapped high on her thighs, small blades unlike the one she normally carried down her spine, her favoured sword not able to hide in the backless garment.

"You, my dear petite sorcière..." D touched her bare back in reassurance, leaning down to whisper in her ear. "Look breathtaking." His breath teased her throat. "These women have nothing on your beautè."

"They also have nothing on," Alice noted, shocked at the women's, and even some men's choice of attire. People were pushing the rule of appropriate clothing allowed in public, some only wearing a G-string and a smile, while others had taken hi-vis on to a whole new level. "What sort of club is this?"

Danton didn't even look at them, his interest only for her. "Come, Alice, our table is booked inside." His hand pressed into her back.

"This is a job, not a date." Alice quickly felt under her dress for her knives, making sure the leather holsters were tight to her thighs. If someone happened to glance over they would think she was flashing the crowd, but who were they to judge? "I'm looking for someone..."

"Oui oui, I know, a man with black spiky hair. Can you give me any more information?"

"Only this." She opened her clutch to grab the Polaroid, allowing D to study the grainy photograph of the man.

"Dark hair, dark eyes with pale skin." D looked up at her, his flirtatiousness gone, replaced with professionalism. He could do that, use his sexuality to tease, get his own way. How could you trust someone who could turn it on and off like a light switch?

This was why she didn't date.

"You sure he isn't a vampire?" A direct question.

She shook her head. "You're here to be my spotter."

"Of course. Let me be your arm candy tonight then."

"Lead the way."

Underworld was situated in the Breed district, an old warehouse turned club with a waiting list as long as her arm. The building was painted charcoal grey straight over the brick, with black painted windows looking more like an abandoned asylum than the nightclub apparently hidden inside. Alice stood underneath the large, red neon sign above the metal door, the clubs name manipulated in the glass as a faint beat vibrated through the pavement.

"Come on." D guided her towards the Bouncer, ignoring the glares from the line.

"Evening Mr Knight," the Bouncer welcomed, a huge man of at least six feet, five inches. "Your usual table is ready." He lifted the red rope blocking the door, biceps bulging.

"Welcome to Underworld, where all your darkest desires come true," the woman behind the desk greeted, a fake smile plastered on her face. Her dark hair was tied up into twin peaks at the top of her head, the strands hairsprayed into fake horns. Her too white teeth flashed beneath blood red lips. "Mr Knight," she nodded towards D, the politeness forced.

"Maggie." He turned on his seductive smile. "How have you been?"

She ignored him, her smile wavering before she recovered. "Ma'am, have you been to our venue before?"

"Oh, no I haven't." Alice tried to ignore the tension.

"Then I will recite the rules. There is no shifting or magic on the premises. Anybody shifting or conducting magic, even something small, will be immediately removed and banned." She pointedly looked at Alice as if she was secretly accusing her of something. "Sharing blood is allowed only as long as it's consented and kept clean. Sex is also allowed as long as it's consented but you can only do that in the booths. Not on the dance floor."

"Sex? That's a joke right?" She looked at D for confirmation. "Bloody hell, really?"

"If someone doesn't leave you alone you are allowed to contact a bodyguard who will assess the situation and decide if one or both of you need removing. Bodyguards can be found hanging around the edges."

"Okay." Alice tried not to worry. She didn't really know what she was getting herself into.

"You may enter through the curtain, enjoy."

"Did you kill her cat or something?" Alice whispered to him as they passed through the thick curtain.

D just laughed, the noise muted compared to the music pumping through the speakers placed strategically across the dance floor. The pulsating beat thumped, the sea of dancers thrusting to the rhythm, sweat a glossy sheen across their bodies.

"Wow." Alice blinked, blinded by the flashing lights. "It's smaller than I imagined."

The room was perfectly square, walls raw, scrapes marking the concrete showing the history of the warehouse. Metal beams lined the ceiling, a string of multicoloured spotlights strung across them. A metal cage hung from the same beams, strategically placed right above the dance floor, holding an almost naked woman dancing provocatively around a pole. To the left was a bar, the entire length of the room with a seating area opposite.

"This way." D grabbed her hand, squeezing his palm against hers as he manoeuvred them through the dancers towards the lounge.

He pushed her into a seat. "What are you doing?" she

scolded as she scooted further into the booth.

"We're on a date." He looked genuinely confused.

"This is work." She batted at his hand as he attempted to caress her face.

"Femme stupide. We're here to attract a man? Non? Then we need to make him see you, make him..." He seemed to struggle with his words. "Jaloux. Oui, jealous. He needs to see you above all the other women. You understand?"

"I think so?" *Nope. Not at all.*

"Oh non. Do you know nothing of shifter men? They want what they can't have. Look around the room Alice, what do you see?"

She humoured him, not really understanding. "I don't get it."

"Look at the men, staring hungrily into the throngs of dancers. Staring at women already taken." His eyes flashed in challenge as he leaned down, laying a soft kiss against her throat, just above her pulse. She froze, unsure how to react.

"A drink Mr Knight?" A waitress interrupted, her hair teased into the same twin peaks as the receptionist. Alice broke the contact, shimmying over in the booth to create a barrier of air between them, giving her time to breathe, to think.

The waitress noticed the move, her lips tilting up into a sensual smile. She flashed her neck, making sure he saw her scars. The blood kiss was an addiction, people doing anything to get their next fix of the euphoria a vampire bite could give. They didn't seem to understand the predator they had at their throats, the ecstasy they felt was a pheromone the fangs secreted into tricking their prey into feeling pleasure, not pain as they drain your lifeblood. Poetic really.

The waitress bent to put the bottle of champagne into the icebox, making sure her short skirt became even shorter.

"Would you like anything else, sir?" she said, arousal heavy in her eyes.

"That would be all," he dismissed, his eyes hard as he looked at Alice. Pouting, the waitress walked away, adding an extra sway to her hips. "Now where were we?"

D reached for the bottle, pouring two glasses before setting it back down.

"The most basic instinct is desire, we need these men in the room to desire you. To notice you. If this man you are after is here, he must pick you above the rest."

"What has you kissing me got to do with anything?"

"Trust me..." Gently grabbing her face he leaned down to press a soft kiss.

When she didn't move, he added a slight pressure, licking gently along the seam of her lips.

"Let me in." His lips were talented as he kissed her again, enticing her into joining in. A subtle movement of her jaw and he groaned, rewarding her with another lick.

She kissed him back, their tongues fighting for dominance. She started to enjoy herself, teasing him with quick movements of her tongue. Feeling brave she wrapped her hands in his hair, angling his face for a better...

Blood on her tongue, her gasp breaking the contact.

"Mon ami, you can ask me to be your spotter anytime," he grinned, showing fangs tipped in red.

Alice stared at his lips, deciding whether to kiss him again. The feeling quickly passed. D wasn't her type. Neither was the Alpha, yet she wished it was him she had been kissing.

Bloody hell. She really needed to get laid.

D's eyes glittered as he looked at her, his gaze drifting as something behind caught his attention. "Ah, the kiss worked."

Subtly, Alice looked over her shoulder, quickly surveying the eyes staring at their little corner in the lounge. "You were right." Picking up her glass she downed the rest of her champagne, not wanting the good stuff to go to waste.

"Of course, like I would trick you into a kiss without having a plan." A dark chuckle. "I'm just waiting for you to confess your undying love."

"You're funny."

"Oui, oui," he dramatically sighed. "My heart bleeds."

"I'm sure one of the waitresses could help with that."

"C'était méchant. Go look tempting elsewhere. I have women to talk to."

She leaned in close, whispering in his ear. "Remember the picture, he has black spiky hair." She made it look as sensual as she could, feeling eyes prickle across her skin. With those words she stood up from the table, feeling him watch her as she made her way across the room towards the bar.

Fighting her way along the dance floor she sat on an empty stool at the end, swinging so she could see along the long length. Hundreds of coloured bottles lined the shelving stacked against the wall, all lit up with a spotlight. A huge floor-to-ceiling mirror stood behind the bottles, dancers replicated onto the surface.

She watched the dancers spin around, dancers who were lost to the music, eyes closed and drinks held high up the air as they swung their hips.

She scanned their faces, trying to find anyone who matched the photograph.

"Now what I find peculiar..." Alice spun her stool, trying to hide her disappointment at the blonde standing behind her. "Is what are you doing with a Vamp?" The man smiled, a sensual curve of his lip as his eyes fell to her cleavage. He flared his chi, a greeting, a test among witches to see who was more powerful. The sensation an electric current across her flesh.

Alice concentrated on not flaring her own chi, something that was almost instinct when greeting another witch. She didn't want to encourage him, or gain any more unwanted attention from the wrong man.

"Not interested," she said, turning away.

A hand came down on her shoulder, spinning her back. "What? Your own Breed not good enough then?" He sat beside her, seemingly unaware of her disinterest. "You want to stay with fang-face?" He nodded towards the lounge. "I'm pretty sure he's busy."

Alice couldn't help but look, spotting D in the same booth she had kissed him in earlier, but this time he was joined by two other women.

"He's an adult." An adult who was supposed to be paying attention.

"You need a real man." He gripped her chin in his free hand, forcing her to look at him. "Someone who can show you a real good time." He flicked his hair, the dark blond razor cut at the sides.

"I said I'm not interested." She added an extra bit of bite to her words, breaking his hold.

"Is this gentleman bothering you?" A large hand came down on the blonde's shoulder, squeezing gently.

"Fuck off man, I saw her first," the witch sneered.

The new stranger leant forward. "She says she isn't interested. So fuck off." The blonde witch paled.

The stranger turned to look at her, his eyes dark, the iris covering most his eye, leaving barely any white.

Holy crap.

"Has he offended you?" His dark eyebrows came low on his face, the same shade on his head, hair spiked up with gel in every direction possible.

She appraised him quickly before smiling, making sure to bite her lip seductively. Well, as seductively as she could manage. "He was just leaving."

"No, I fucking wasn't," the blonde witch scowled. "I wanted to buy you a drink."

"Excuse me." He grabbed the scruff of the blonde and started dragging him towards the emergency exit. "Stay there pretty lady, I'll be back in a moment."

Alice hesitated, her instinct and training telling her to follow them, but her brain telling her to wait. *Shit.*

She couldn't break cover.

Cursing under her breath she turned to the lounge, the booth now completely empty. "Great." She scanned the crowd, looking for Danton. "Dammit." Inside her clutch she grabbed her phone, sending a quick text instead.

A drink was plopped in front of her, a pink sparkly concoction with a long straw and an orange paper umbrella. She jumped as it cracked against the bar, her attention elsewhere.

"See, I said I would be back." The dark haired stranger gently pushed the glass of pink liquid toward her, his knuckles red and scraped.

I hope the other guy is okay, she thought, but not wanting to express her concern and scare him away. "Thank you for helping me," she said instead, making her voice soft and girly.

He started rolling up the sleeves of his black dress shirt,

the hair on his arms black and baby fine. Thick veins pulsated beneath his skin, like snakes stretching beneath the flesh. A band encircled his wrist, what looked like sharp thorns adorning the leather.

"I bought you the drink to apologise for how you were treated." His hand fanned out, his nails a sickly blue as if blood struggled to get to the fingertips.

"I appreciate it," Alice said as he grinned, but she still wasn't going to touch the drink. "I'm Leela."

"The name's Tomlin." His hand reached out, grabbing hers in a quick shake. The thorns on his band sliced into her wrist with little effort.

Alice sucked in a breath, instinctively pulled her hand back, which caused the thorns to cause more damage.

His eyes, like onyx watched her as she checked the cuts, not once offering an apology.

The hairs on the back of her neck stood on edge.

His skin had been ice cold.

Could Rex have gotten his Breed wrong?

His eyes looked similar to a vampire close to bloodlust, yet, Alice knew he wasn't a vampire. She didn't even get a shifter vibe from him.

The music renewed, a dance anthem pulsating through the speakers. The crowd continued to dance, all the bodies thrusting and swaying in tempo with the music.

"So do you come here often?" she shouted at him over the music, wanting to keep his attention.

"Maybe," he smiled, showing a row of sharper than usual teeth.

Alice tried to keep her shudder to herself. It wasn't exactly uncommon for some shifters to file their teeth, but it was creepy.

"What about you? Do you come here often?" He leaned

in close, his breath just as cold as his skin against her cheek.

"My first time." She tried to lean away, using her drink as an excuse as she played with the orange umbrella. "I'm from out of town."

"You here alone?" He watched her throat, his leg vibrating, fidgeting.

"I'm actually here with someone, but he seems to be more interested in other women than me." Alice stuck her bottom lip out, feigning disappointment. "Good thing you're here to keep me company."

He gestured to her cocktail. "Drink up, I want to dance."

Alice took a second to understand his question. "I can't dance." Wait, was her words slurred? "No dance. Two left... toes."

Shit. She blinked, her vision blurring around the edges.

"Feet. I meant feet."

Why was she there again? It wasn't to talk about feet.

Oh yeah. She needed to ask him questions, or get him into a more private area. "Do you want to...?"

He grabbed her hand before she finished the question, pulling her towards the dance floor.

She felt herself drifting, not able to feel her legs.

"You can dance with me."

Alice didn't feel the hem of her dress rise before his cold hands touched her bare skin, fingers kneading into the flesh as he pulled her flush against his chest. Hands tight, he matched their movements to the heavy beat of the music.

"See, you can dance." He twirled her around so her back was now to his chest, his hands coming up to hold her waist.

"I feel sick." She fought the sudden nausea. She had

only taken a few sips, why was she nauseous?

"Don't be silly." He continued to move them, his hands exploring her body through her thin dress. Pulling free she turned around, clutching her head as his face blurred.

"Leela, come here." He grabbed her arm, the pain sharp as his nails dug in.

Who the fuck is Leela?

"Ow." She pushed out, barely moving him.

"ALICE!" A voice called through the crowd. Lights flashed as she tried to look for the source, her head groggy.

Hands grabbed her, yanking her away from the dance floor as she was pushed through the crowd.

"ALICE...MERDE. MOVE OUT THE WAY!" That voice again, yelling.

Alice felt herself fall to her knees, the music pounding in her head as she tried not to be sick. She was suddenly lifted, her stomach pressed against something hard as she felt fresh air against her skin, the stench of rotten food assaulting her nose a moment later.

"Put me down." She tried to wiggle free, the movement painfully slow. "I'm going to be sick." She was roughly settled onto her feet. "Oh my god." She closed her eyes, the cold air amazing against her fevered skin.

"I thought we could speak more privately out here." A cage of arms surrounded her, pushing her against the brick wall.

Concentrating, she looked at her surroundings, trying desperately to figure out where she was through the haze. Huge dustbins lined the brick walls on both sides, each one under a streetlamp. A cat hissed, eyes reflective as it scuttled away.

"Where are we?" Her breathing became laboured as she

felt exhaustion taking over, her heart beating faster than usual.

She had to think fast.

Hand stiff she released a blade, the familiar weight settling into her palm.

Tom leaned forward, not noticing her knife as his lips began assaulting hers, shoving his tongue into her mouth. A hand wrapped around her neck, slamming her head against the brick wall hard enough she saw stars. His eyes were wide, watching her as his pupils narrowed to slits, like a snake.

Disorientated, Alice struggled against him, exciting him further as his lips travelled down the side of her neck.

"Ever heard of the word no?" The words came out slurred, her tongue thick in her mouth. Slowly she brought up the knife, the blade sharp enough to sear into his chest with little effort.

"FUCK!" He leapt back, snarling with his sharp teeth. Lifting a hand he backhanded her, causing her to collapse almost unconscious against the wall. "You'll pay for that," he growled, pulling the blade out of his chest as if it was nothing.

Using the knife, he bent down to cut the straps off her dress, the black material sagging against her skin. Hands gripped in the material, he lifted and pushed her face first against the wall.

"Stop struggling." He settled his weight, her legs pinned with his own.

Something warm against her neck, a tongue lapping across her flesh. His hands ripped more of the fabric, searching beneath under her skirt.

"Fuck me. How many knives do you have?" he growled,

chest vibrating. Her head was wretched to the side, held at an angle as he wrapped her blonde strands around his fist.

"Stop," Alice whispered, legs heavy as a sharp pain sliced into her neck. Heat poured from her throat, dripping down her back.

Tom groaned, his teeth tearing through her flesh much like her knife did his chest.

Abruptly, Alice collapsed, Tom's body no longer there to keep her up. Her knees screamed in shock as they connected with the stone floor, the pain dull and throbbing in time with her pulse. Groggily, Alice leant onto her hands, her head hanging low as she struggled to stay awake, arms shaking violently at the weight.

Something burned against her neck, the pain intense as it ripped through the numbness that threatened to take over her body.

A familiar voice, the words incoherent as the world went dark.

"**M**um?" she called once more, her voice wobbling. Bear clutched tight to her chest, she walked further down the staircase, her bare feet cold against the hard wood.

Another crash. The lights flicker ahead before turning off, covering her in complete darkness.

"Kyle if that's you, it's not funny."

Still no response.

Padding down the hallway she pushed the kitchen door, soft light flickering beneath the frame.

"Mummy?" Her voice wet, close to tears. Door heavy, she pushed it harder. "Daddy?" She stepped forward, the light from the window creating a weird glow across the floor, like it was shiny.

A growl vibrated through the air behind her.

In a panic she ran further into the kitchen, her ankle twisting as she slipped on something wet. "Ahhhh," she cried, using her hand to help her sit up before slipping back into the warm liquid.

Drip. Drip. Drip.

She lifted her hand, the dark substance drizzling down her wrist to her elbow in a hot stream. Holding her breath, she listened, not hearing anything in the room with her.

Thwack. Thwack. Thwack.

Tears left a warm trail down her face. "Mummy?" she whispered.

Something walked down the hallway.

Thwack. Thwack. Thwack.

Scrambling against the tiles she tore open a cupboard,

squeezing her body into the small space, pushing the bottles of bleach and detergent out the way.

Door shut, she placed her hand over her mouth, the warm liquid tasting coppery against her lips. Blood pumped in her ears, making it hard to concentrate on any sounds outside as darkness surrounded her.

CHAPTER 8

Alice jumped awake, a scream caught in her throat, the nightmare fading as her head ached, a rhythmic pounding inside her temple. Closing her eyes, she tried to remember the dream, visualising a shadow standing over her, the face obscured by darkness.

Her nightmares were a shattered memory created by a scared child, too broken to be pieced together.

Something licked her fingers, the tongue rough. Turning her head she stared at the leopard half lying across her legs, Sam's huge eyes staring back at her expectantly.

"Sam?" she asked the leopard, her voice harsh, even to her ears. Sam purred in response, curling further onto her legs so his fur came into focus. His leopard was a glorious gold, his rosettes a deep black that turned into a warm brown. It made him pretty, and he knew it.

THUMP, THUMP, THUMP.

Sam jumped up, his hackles rising as a growl erupted from his throat.

THUMP, THUMP, THUMP.

In one motion she swung her legs off the bed, her knees giving out immediately. "Bloody hell!" Her arms slapped against the side table as she tried to stop her fall.

"FEMALE?" A voice shouted in the distance.

THUMP, THUMP, THUMP.

"SHUT THE FUCK UP!" A different voice, this one further away. Probably one of her neighbours.

Sam paced in front of her bedroom door, shooting through the opening once she turned the handle. He quickly ran to the front door and sniffed along the edge, peering back at her anxiously with amber eyes before disappearing into his bedroom.

"ALICE! ARE YOU IN?"

THUMP, THUMP, THUMP.

She unlocked the front door and opened it, only then realising she was wearing just a sleep shirt, one barely covering her underwear, but it was already too late. Rex stared, a blush burning the back of her neck as his gaze leisurely rolled over her ruffled hair and bare legs. Alice felt herself fidget as he looked at the length of her body, his eyes hardening as he noticed the bruises.

"Can I help you?" she asked politely, pretending everything was normal and she didn't have a hangover from hell.

Silently he walked in, slamming the front door behind him. "Do you ever answer your bloody phone?"

Head pounding, she closed her eyes, trying not to throw up as pain resonated through her skull.

A warm hand gripped the top of her arm.

"You okay?"

"Does she bloody look okay?" Sam leaned against the wall, wearing only a pair of boxers. His long blond hair swept over one shoulder, draped elegantly across his bare chest. Clicking his tongue Sam pointedly looked Rex up and down, his face clearly unimpressed. "You must be the Alpha."

"You must be her cat," Rex replied, ignoring Sam's scowl. He turned back to Alice, dismissing the leopard. "What happened?" He reached out to touch her face, his eyes betraying nothing, yet his hand was feather light on her skin.

"Danton brought her back from the club," Sam stated, bringing their attention back to him. "He said she was attacked, he had to seal her wounds." Sam licked out his tongue in demonstration.

Alice jumped when Rex leaned down to sniff her neck, his clean-shaven cheek rubbing against hers.

"Get off my girl," Sam growled, stepping between them and forcing Rex to move back.

"Your girl, huh?" Rex tilted his head, nostrils flaring.

"Both of you stop it." She put her hand on Sam's arm, quieting him down. "Did D say anything else?"

Sam stared at Rex for a few seconds more, the warning clear. "Not really."

Sam caught Alice's gaze. *How do you feel?* he silently asked, not wanting the Alpha to understand his concern. It was a trick they had learnt from Dread, being able to read someone's eyes.

Could be better, she replied the same way.

"I'll put the kettle on," she said aloud before turning to the kitchen. Her headache thumped, someone clearly dancing the foxtrot across her brain. Painkiller in hand, she swallowed it dry as she turned on the kettle, waiting for it to boil. Her foot tapped as she waited, the motion causing the headache to radiate so she stopped, closing her eyes instead.

"Your boyfriend's getting ready for work," Rex said, a

telltale squeak as he settled himself onto one of her flimsy chairs. "Right after he threatened me, of course."

Alice turned then, hearing slight humour in his voice. She still couldn't decipher him, his face relaxed, his eyelashes low across his eyes, shielding his thoughts. Did he know she was trying to read him? Everyone had tells, facial twitches, rapid blinking, smiles that didn't reach their eyes. All subtle indicators of emotion, even deception. She could read people well.

Yet, she couldn't read him, at least, not when the man was in control. His beast, as she was beginning to learn, was rawer in his emotions. How was she supposed to know what he was thinking if he was constantly in control?

Deciding not to acknowledge his last statement she grabbed a mug, pouring him a drink.

"Here." She handed it over to Rex, suppressing a smile when he lifted it to his lips, revealing the hidden joke.

'TWAT' was written neatly in white along the bottom, only visible when someone tipped the mug at a certain angle.

"Thanks," he grumbled, setting the mug down. "Do you remember anything from last night?"

Alice took a sip of her own tea before answering, the painkiller working miracles as it soothed down her throat. "I was dancing..." She shook her head, trying to remember but stopped when her brain threatened to explode. "I was carried outside," she continued, her eyes closed as she tried to remember.

"Anything else?" A whisper, his voice closer than it was before. Startled she opened her eyes, his face only a centimetre away, his lashes low, eyes watching her mouth. Heart racing, she licked her dry lips, his gaze following the action before he looked up at her, his blue eyes radiating something she couldn't read.

"Erm."

"Baby girl, have you seen my work shirt?" Sam walked in, taking in the situation with a quick sweep of his eyes. Alice jumped back, heat burning across her cheeks. "Well, don't let me interrupt you."

"You didn't interrupt anything," Alice stuttered.

"Sure I didn't," Sam smirked, jumping up onto the kitchen counter, his chest still bare as he swung his denim clad legs. "Nice mug," he commented.

Rex frowned, still not understanding the joke. "Tyler, my second is on his way over, he might know some more information."

"What about how you guys let Alice be attacked?" Sam smiled sweetly, his eyes staring at the floor as he baited Rex.

Alice just audibly sighed. "I need to shower." She stretched her arms up, enjoying the click before she realised both men were staring at her. "I won't be long." She called behind as she hurried to the bathroom.

She tried not to think of them alone, as the possibility of walking out with the kitchen in ruins ran through her head.

They were adults, they could behave themselves.

Deciding to make the shower quick, she stepped in front of the mirror, groaning when she saw the top she was wearing. She thought she had on one of her sleeping shirts.

Apparently not.

The words 'Things to do with a pussy...' was written across her chest. 'Play with it' was on the left breast and 'Lick it' was on the right, both placed either side of the image of a black cat, its paws reaching down to play with the bottom hem.

Yes, the Alpha of one of the largest packs in Britain had

seen her wear nothing but an obscene t-shirt. In her defence, it wasn't hers.

Hopefully he saw the humour in it. Which was doubtful.

Bloody hell.

In one swift movement she pulled off the t-shirt, throwing it into the corner of the small bathroom. She risked a look in the mirror, the harsh bathroom light high-lighting the bruises across her skin.

"Shit." She bared her throat, remembering the sharp pain the night before. The skin had a purplish tone that was starting to turn a sickly yellow. Hesitantly she reached up, the skin smooth and unbroken, as was her wrist.

A vampire's saliva was famous for its healing qualities, a few licks and they could close most superficial wounds, which made sense evolutionarily speaking, considering they have to cut someone to feed. Better to be able to heal them afterwards rather than let their dinner bleed to death.

It's was just lucky her bite wasn't deep enough to cause more damage, and even luckier she had D around to close it.

Turning to the shower she operated the dial. The old shower head wheezed, sputtering before water poured from the many holes. The bathroom, just like the rest of the place, was old and broken. They had painted over the tiles when they first moved in, the colour now an off white unlike the bright green it was before. The shower hung above the old bath, the panels avocado coloured and cracked.

The water was scalding when she stepped into the stream, the water unknotting the tangle of hair as bits of debris and flakes of brick began to fall out. Lathering her lavender soap, she stroked down her arms, across her breasts and lower over her stomach. The water at her feet was a rusty red, the colour becoming paler before disappearing altogether. Startled, she searched over her body for an open wound, not finding anything. She turned to look at herself in the mirror, able to just see if she leaned slightly. Dried blood, mostly washed away was patched across her shoulder blades and back.

Her hand went up to her neck again, reassuring herself that her throat was whole.

A loud crash, followed by a shout.

Wiping the water from her face she listened, thinking she had imagined it.

Another crash, this time the door vibrating as something smashed against it.

"Fuck." She hopped out of the shower, steadying herself as she started to slip on the tiled floor.

Grabbing a towel from the rack she opened the door, almost running into the back of Sam. He stood in the way, his shoulders bunched as he stood guard.

"Sam?" she asked, trying to peer around his shoulders. "What's happening?"

"Dominance issues." He turned so she couldn't see. "I wouldn't come out."

She ducked underneath his arm, her gaze narrowing as she noticed a vase smashed on the floor. One of the small things she actually liked.

"What the hell is going on?"

A loud growl turned her head, the sofa having been pushed across the room. Rex was crouched on the floor, it took her a few seconds to see the man underneath.

"What are you doing?" She took a step forward, stopping when she heard a warning bark. Rex leant forward, his hands on either side of the stranger with his teeth bared. "Enough!" she shouted.

Rex snarled, jumping up to stand in the corner, his eyes gone completely wolf. The wolf watched her, anger, desire, and vengeance flashing across his eyes too fast to read.

"Alice stay back." She felt Sam grab her arm, pulling her away. "Be careful," he whispered in her ear. "Rex's beast is in control." Shifters were one with their beasts, sharing the same body but two personalities, the beast half being the more savage of the temperaments.

"What happened?" she asked, whispering back. The stranger on the floor slowly came to his knees, his head still tilted painfully to the side.

"His second needs to show submission."

"What? Why?"

Sam shrugged against her. "The pack has a hierarchy. Stops them from fighting amongst themselves."

"You're not like that," she commented, continuing to stare at the man on his knees. Confused, she looked up at Rex, his eyes like ice, the wolf having its own internal dilemma. She had no idea what to say to calm the situation, especially to a wolf in human skin. She would describe herself as experienced with shifter culture, having lived with and worked with many. She knew the higher the dominance, the better control over their beast. An Alpha had complete control. Yet, Rex didn't seem to.

"I'm not a wolf." Sam fidgeted next to her, his own beast reacting to the uncomfortable atmosphere.

Rex was pulling an aura, something all Alphas or dominant shifters could do to get weaker shifters to submit. Sam might not be a wolf, but his animal was fighting instinct not to succumb to the power. She could feel it across her chi, the essence of her magic connected to her own aura. It was like a gentle river across her senses, persuasive and calming. It was trying to quiet the room, control the beasts.

She wasn't a beast.

"Are we done here?" she asked the wolf, showing him he wasn't the only Alpha here. At least, if there was such a thing as a witch Alpha.

Rex continued to stare, unblinking focus as he took a step forward. Sam tensed, ready to intervene.

"Go get dressed." Rex's gaze roamed over her exposed flesh, the towel only just covering the important bits. "I'll clean up the mess." His voice was strained, deeper than usual. Looking through her lashes she watched him, his face immobile, jaw still clenched.

He was fighting for control.

Sam pulled her into the bedroom, using his larger body to block the door. Shifters kept their human consciousness when shifted, they were able to see through the eyes of their animal and help decide what actions to take. That's what Sam had told her once. He had also explained that when they shift, the animal can take over. They were a more animalistic personality, more unpredictable. That's what she had felt staring at Rex, his animal reacting to something she couldn't see, the man having no control over his animal's instincts.

"He has little control over his beast," Sam commented as she started to dress, a steady growl vibrating across his bare chest. "How can someone as powerful as that have no control?"

She knew it was rhetorical, but felt herself answering anyway. "I don't know." But she sure as hell was going to figure it out. "Go to work Sam."

"And leave you with the granny killer? I don't think so baby girl."

"Granny killer?" She threw him one of his work shirts

that had been mixed with her own clothes. He quickly pulled it on.

"My, what big teeth you have," he mocked in a high girly voice. "Better to eat you with my dear." He gnashed his teeth together.

Alice let out a snort. Sam, forever dramatic. "He's hired me for a job..."

"He looks at you like you're dinner."

"This is stupid." She wasn't going to admit what she saw in his eyes. Didn't even want to think about it. "You know I have to do this."

Sam pressed his lips together. "Call me if you need me." He opened the bedroom door, storming out. She heard the front door slam a moment later.

Great, now Sam is pissed. Frustrated, she pulled at her hair, tying it up into a relatively neat ponytail before she walked back into her living room.

The stranger was standing in the corner, his arms crossed as his eyes followed her. His hair was dark, darker than the mahogany of his skin and shaved close to his skull, military style. His nose was the only thing ruining his otherwise perfectly symmetrical face, a too large nose that had clearly been broken at least once or twice.

"Hi," Alice greeted, "you must be Tyler." The man just replied with a shallow nod. He openly stared at her, his hazel eyes tracing details across her face. "You don't talk much do you?" That got her a head tilt, otherwise no other reaction.

This was Rex's second?

"You challenging my second, Alice?"

She turned to the man in question, his eyes once again in control. *Challenging him?*

"No."

93

"Then why were you staring?"

"I was watching his eyes, they're almost as unreadable as yours," she confessed. Rex pursed his lips, nodding to Tyler. The other man left quietly a second later. Alice scrutinised the whole scene, not understanding. "I thought we needed him?"

"We do, he will be meeting us at the club."

"So we're going back?"

"Yes." Rex watched her neck, his eyes tracing the bruises.

She moved into the kitchen, noticing how nothing was broken or misplaced. Even the grains of her pentagram she had forgotten to clean up were undisturbed, the salt teased into a five-pointed star within a circle. Pulling her spelling pot from the cupboard, she set it gently onto the pentagram, careful not to smudge the lines. Rex stood silently, leaning against the doorway.

"I can't walk around like this," she gestured to her neck before opening a drawer next to the sink and grabbing a small wooden disk.

Complexion spells were one of the few amulet charms she could create from memory. However, it was expensive to create, so like everybody else with a tight budget she bought ready-made ones. They weren't as good.

Rex just grunted.

"So what's the plan?" she asked while placing the wooden disk into the bowl, pouring the store bought complexion potion over the disk gently. It would create an amulet, specifically designed for skin imperfections, freckles, blemishes, discolouration and even bruises. They would all be covered with the complexion veil, magic that concealed the imperfections under a shroud.

"The plan is to see if we can track that wolf." Rex had

walked quietly behind her, peering inquisitively into the pot.

"How would you track him?"

"Tyler is a tracker. One of the best."

"Like a bloodhound?" She turned her back, gently turning the wooden disk to soak up the potion. *"Ignis."* The disk burst into flame, eating up the remaining liquid.

"An accurate description. However, I wouldn't call him that to his face." The flame died out, turning the wooden disk a few shades darker. With a knife she cut a small line along the tip of her thumb.

"What are you doing?" Rex grabbed her arm, his tongue licking out to catch the drop of blood.

"Seriously, that's the second time in less than twelve hours someone has sucked or licked me." Rex's eyes flashed, his reaction unsettling her. "I need to activate the charm." She tugged against him until he released her arm. Watching him suspiciously from the corner of her eye she squeezed her thumb, letting a single drop of blood hit the disk. Instantly there was a little fizzle, the scent of ozone strong in her nose.

"Why your blood?"

"I have special enzymes, it's used as a reagent that reacts with the ingredients to turn on the magic's effect." Spinning the wood she smiled, feeling the magic thrum into her fingertips. She slipped the disk between the leather bracelet Rex had given her and tightened the cord, anchoring the disk flat to her skin.

"It's gone." A warm hand stroked across her neck, the skin unusually soft for a man. She remained still, not able to see who was in control.

"Yes, that's the point." She stepped back from Rex's palm, unsure of her feelings. Butterflies attacked her stomach, a confusing reaction considering he wasn't usually her type. Yes, she found him fairly attractive, but the reaction she felt was more than just attraction. It was an intense longing, like she couldn't breathe unless he was beside her. She had never felt like that with anyone, was confused by it. Lust, yes, endless desire? No. That's what worried her.

She swallowed, Rex's eyes following the movement. That was the problem with dominant shifters, you never knew if you were prey or not.

Her libido didn't seem to care.

"So are we going?" she asked, distracting him, or maybe it was herself. With a slow nod he turned away, assuming she would follow.

CHAPTER 9

The nightclub looked creepy in the daylight, just a drab grey building with black painted windows, more like a drug den than the upscale Breed club she knew to be hidden inside.

White and blue police tape blocked them from entering the shadowed opening to the side. Alice hesitated at the tape, staring at the array of police officers talking animatedly to one another. One took a photograph behind a dumpster, the flash momentarily washing the alley in white.

"Excuse me," someone asked, stepping around them so they could bend beneath the tape. Alice automatically moved out the way, her eyes fixated on the 'coroner' embroidery on their black jumpsuits.

"Shit." Rex widened his stance, folding his arms over his chest. "What are they doing here?"

"I don't know." Alice tried to peer down the alley, the police officers blocking everything. "Can you see anything?"

"No civilians," a man barked.

Alice spun towards the voice. "Excuse me?"

"I said no civilians." The man tapped his pen to the white notebook clutched in his hands. "You should move along now."

"What happened?" Rex asked, his body language closed off.

"Are you, or are you not a civilian?" The man absently tapped the breast of his shirt, scowling when he realised the shirt had no pockets as if he was used to wearing a coat or jacket.

"I'm Agent Alice Skye from..."

"With S.I.?" he frowned, turning towards the alley. "Hey, who called the freaks in?"

"No one called us," she interrupted, grinding her molars. "We were just passing by."

"Hmmm," he gawked at her, taking in her blonde hair and height. "You don't look like a Paladin." He glared at Rex. "You don't look like one either."

"Well, what do we look like Officer?"

"It's Detective, Detective O'Neil."

"Fine, Detective. Would you rather just tell us what's happened or do I call this in and officially report it?"

"You can't do that. This is my case." He eyes narrowed as he scanned her up and down.

"So from the coroner's van I assume there is a body?" she politely asked, changing tactics.

The Detective grumbled. "Yes, you assume correctly. John Doe found around six this morning."

"Breed?"

"Not sure," he answered as his hand absently stroked his dark goatee, the hair peppered with grey. "Which is why we haven't called you guys yet." He glared between them, his eyes lingering on Rex. "You have any ID?"

She pulled out her phone, showing him the document

and ID proving her Paladin status. He grunted as he checked the details. Charming man.

"Fine. You can come take a look, but only you." Rex tensed, not saying anything. "I don't need civilians walking all over my crime scene."

"Okay."

"This way Alice..."

"It's Agent Skye."

"Skye then."

Detective O'Neil guided her past the array of people, ignoring the distasteful looks from the other Officers.

"Like I said, John Doe was found around six. We can't be sure, but we have been given an estimated death of around eleven the previous evening."

"Who found him?" Alice questioned, her mind already looking for details. From the number of men standing over in the corner, she guessed that was where the body was. There were spots of blood along the floor, small, only specks across the concrete. More blood was spotted across the walls, as if someone was hit with such force blood exploded from an open wound, or an orifice such as the mouth.

"The Bouncer." He got out an e-cigarette from his trouser pocket, slipping it between his lips he sucked it hard. It caused the end light to flare orange, giving the impression of a real cigarette. "He's standing over there giving a statement to Officer Palmer." He nodded in the general direction.

Alice looked behind her, recognising the large man.

"The deceased is over here."

She followed him to the body half hidden behind the dumpster, bin bags and rubbish half covering the male. Kneeling, she looked closer, her breath catching as she recognised the witch from the night before, the blonde who kept pestering her.

"You have a positive ID yet?" she asked, proud her voice didn't show how unnerved she was at the realisation. It was one thing to see a dead body, it was another to see one that she saw alive only hours earlier. She felt her face scrunch up, annoyed and disappointed with herself.

Should have followed my gut. I shouldn't have let this happen.

"Not yet." The Detective watched her face carefully, noting her reaction. She quickly calmed her face, relaxing it to impassivity. He slowly sucked from his fake cigarette, holding it in before looking at the end with disgust. "Nothing in his pockets."

"It's clear he was dumped here, but wasn't killed." She raised her hand to the blood splatters against the brick, her fingertips tracing the formation gently. "He was punched first, possibly in the face."

"What makes you say that?" He watched her face again. It made her uncomfortable.

"The blood specks behind us, quite a distance away from the main pool of blood around the body. Something hit him, hard. There is no spray over here even through it's clear he had his throat cut."

"That's what we thought," he agreed, nodding at her. "Impressive, I didn't realise Paladins did this type of work." He turned the cigarette off, putting it back into his pocket.

"You would have to cross-reference the autopsy but I would give money that it wasn't the initial throat slit that killed him." When he didn't correct her she continued. "The blood surrounding the body is not enough, even added to the initial spray behind us it wouldn't be enough to kill him. The wound around his neck is congealed, dried. Are there any bite marks?" She bent to touch the body, pulling her hand back when she remembered she wasn't wearing gloves.

"Why would you ask about bite marks?" He handed her a pair of plastic gloves from his pocket. She slipped them on before kneeling back beside the body, careful to not touch any of the blood.

"The throat is slit to the bone..." She pulled the head up gently, showing the spinal cord clearly through an open wound. "Carotid artery is cleanly cut, all his lifeblood should have flowed onto the floor. But it hasn't, so my first thought would be he was drained of blood first." She softly felt along the neck of the deceased, eventually finding a row of holes in the hollow between his neck and shoulder. "His throat was slit to try to hide the bite. Have you found the weapon?"

"My boys are looking." He accepted the gloves back when she handed them over. He assessed her, it was nothing sexual, more like a man who was evaluating his prized horse. He nodded to himself as if she passed some invisible line into acceptance.

"Yours or ours?"

"He's a witch, or maybe a mage." She quickly continued when he raised an eyebrow. "I felt some magic residue when I touched him. No human could have made those bite marks." She stared down at the body, most of it covered in tin cans, crisp packets and discarded waste. Hidden. John Doe's eyes are wide open as well as his mouth, a silent scream forever on his face.

"I agree. I'll contact The Tower to get assistance." He patted his invisible pocket again, frowning until he reached up to the left side of his head, grabbing a real cigarette tucked behind his ear. He was obviously trying to quit, but failing.

"You should ask the gentleman I was with over."

"Why?" He slanted his eyes suspiciously.

"He's a wolf, their sense of smell can pick up things we could not."

"A wolf, huh?" He searched over the officers until he saw Rex, who stood in the distance. O'Neil thought hard on the idea before confirming with a passing colleague. "There's also more blood further up the alley."

"More blood? From the deceased?"

"We're not sure yet, have to get forensics to check but my gut says no. There isn't any trail leading between them."

Alice lifted her hand up to her throat, remembering the dull pain. "Someone else's?"

"We're leaving the option open."

"Detective?" A young man walked over, his face sweaty with a green tinge. "Mr Sullivan would like to speak to the woman." He blinked over at Alice, his eyes wide.

"Thank you, Officer Gordon." O'Neil lit the cigarette he had been holding, placing it on the tip of his lips. "Agent Skye why don't you go speak to Mr Sullivan. He hasn't been very forthcoming with any information." He savoured a drag of his cigarette, blowing a billow of smoke out his nostrils like a dragon.

"Yeah, sure."

"Hey lady, over here." Alice followed the officer to the Bouncer she met the night before, the six foot plus man clearly angry at being detained.

"Hello. You wanted to speak to me?" she smiled at the Bouncer, lips wavering when she watched his eyes flick to the officer then back. "Hey," she turned to the Officer, "Detective O'Neil needs help with the body."

"Really?" It was almost a squeak, his face turning even greener. "Okay." He ran off.

"You're Alice right?"

"And you were on the door last night."

"Aye. Danton wanted me to give you a message." He crossed his large arms across his chest, veins straining against his skin.

"D?" She looked around, seeing if anybody was near enough to overhear.

"Not here lass, follow me." He walked through an open doorway, the corridor leading into a small office. Sullivan moved to stand behind the small black desk, a silver laptop sitting on top. "This room is more secure." He gestured to the only chair in the room.

"No, it's fine." She decided to stand, not wanting him to tower over her. "This your office?"

"No, just a generic office." He looked around the room like it was the first time he had been there. "Sometimes the boss sits in here, it's soundproof." He flipped open the little laptop, the light glowing over his face, highlighting his impressive cheekbones. "Danton does us favours from time to time." Little clicks on the trackpad, his fingers moving incredibly slow as if he wasn't used to using the equipment. "So we owe him, he asked the boss to ask around and find out some information."

"Information?" She raised her eyebrows.

"Aye, he left before we could relay the information to him so we were advised to give it to you." He clicked a few more times. "Here." He moved the laptop around, a static image of a man tied to a chair on the screen.

"What is this?" She leant on the table, trying to get a better look. Without a word Sullivan reached around and clicked a button, turning on the video. The screen flashed a few times, the image blurry.

"Are you ready to talk yet?" a voice off camera asked.

The man in the chair just smiled, revealing white teeth. His hands flexed, stretching his fingertips as he tested the strength of the rope on his wrists and ankles.

"Nothing? Pity." The screen went black for a few seconds, screams echoing from the speakers.

Alice continued to watch the screen, the black changing to a pale pink before the image came back. The video revealed the man tied to the chair again, blood dripping from his lips, the smile no longer in place. Reaching over she clicked a button on the keyboard, pausing the video.

"What is this?" she asked again.

"Danton asked for backup when you were forcibly removed from the club. We found you in the alley with the dark man, just before he ran off."

"You find the body then too?"

"No lass, that was later."

Alice hesitated on the play button. "You called him a 'dark man'?"

"Aye, we call them dark men when we can't identify the Breed. They are normally from the Dark Court, dark Fae with expensive glamour."

"So he's an Unseelie caste?" She couldn't remember him wearing anything to give that away. Fae were proud of their courts, would normally want to show it off.

"Relative," was his reply.

"What do you mean?"

He ignored the question. "We promised Danton we would help find you, we did. However, as the situation was more severe than we initially realised Danton now owes us the favour." He turned his eyes to her, they were a deep brown with a fleck of green. "I'm sure you will let him know."

"What would this favour be?"

Sullivan smiled, showing crooked teeth. "We tagged his friend. We have decided it would be relevant information for Danton. You will also pass this on."

"His friend?"

Sullivan reached over and continued the video.

"*I think you should start answering my questions,*" the voice off camera asked again, his voice angry.

"*Fuck you.*" Blood splattered as the man in the chair muttered.

"*That's the wrong answer.*" A hand could be visibly seen as a palm covered the camera lens, the screen going dark. After a few muffled shouts the palm moved back, showing the tied up man slumped down in the chair, his head resting on his chest. "*Shall I ask again?*"

The man in the chair slowly and painfully shook his head.

"*Okay then, let's start.*" Alice heard a crack, knuckles clicking. "*What's your name?*"

"*Louis.*" He rolled his head to the side, his cheek still resting on his shoulder. His eyes were a piercing black, the orbs looking straight at the camera as if he could see right through it.

"*You have a partner. Yes?*"

"*Yes.*" With a grunt, he lifted his head.

"*What have you been doing in my club? Dealing drugs?*"

"*No!*" The man coughed, blood splashing down his once white shirt.

"*Then what? We have had complaints you and your partner have been trying to sell something.*"

Louis laughed. "*We were recruiting.*"

"Recruiting?"

"For the cause."

"Cause?"

"The Becoming."

"The fucking what? A cult?"

"No." He started to pull violently at his bonds. "You are not worthy, you wouldn't understand." He spat towards someone hidden from the camera.

"What I understand is that you have been forcing yourself on people. Your partner has just been caught with his pants down, pockets full of date rape herbs and a dead body."

"WHERE IS HE?" The rope at his ankle snapped.

"He isn't here."

The lights flickered, another rope snapping as the man ferociously shook the wooden chair. His arms bulged, black veins pulsating against his skin. With a screech the remaining ropes burst open, one flicking out to clip the camera, causing it to fall to the floor. The screen cracked, screams erupting through the microphone before the image went dark.

Sullivan silently closed the lid, pushing the laptop to the side of the table.

"What happened?"

No answer.

"When was this filmed?"

Sullivan had stepped back to lean against the wall, using shadow to cover his face. She was grateful, he was huge, like wrestler huge. His hands were as big as her head.

"Last night."

"Where is he now?"

Sullivan remained silent, giving her all the answer she needed.

"Anything else I need to know?"

"Usually no, but I believe you should know that the drug we found on him was agrimony."

Agrimony was a herb used specifically for people with sleep disorders, or in severe cases as a date rape drug. It was supposedly tasteless, and in small quantities could make anybody dangerously drowsy, unable to fight back. Yet she hadn't drunk anything.

"Can agrimony be taken any other way other than digested?"

He raised an eyebrow, but answered anyway. "Aye lass, it depends on the amount but even a little bit in your bloodstream could work."

The fucking thorns on his bracelet.

"My boss isn't happy. Not good biz if you have people dropping that shit into lass's drinks. We have never heard of this 'Becoming.' If it is something that directly influences our business we would appreciate any information."

Alice just nodded, she would need information herself before she could even share any. Back down the corridor she finally found the exit into the alley, the noise of all the police officers loud compared to the soundproofed corridor. She walked quickly past everyone and ducked under the police tape, looking around for Rex.

"Agent." Detective O'Neil came over, a new cigarette hanging from his lips, the end yet to be lit. "Did Mr Sullivan tell you anything interesting?"

"No, he just thought he recognised me. Honest mistake." She looked around again, unable to see Rex. "Have you seen the man I was with?"

"Over there somewhere." He finally lit his cigarette, a look of ecstasy lighting up his face before being replaced with his usual grimace. "Take this..." He handed her a card.

"It's my contact details, ring me if you suddenly remember something interesting Mr Sullivan said."

She crushed the card in her hand.

"Of course."

With one last hard look he dismissed her.

Exhaling, she scanned the crowd again, finally spotting Rex's head. "Why are you over here?" she asked as she walked over, watching him straighten up at her approach.

"I had to get out the way for Tyler to catch the scent."

"Where is Tyler?" She still hadn't seen him in the crowd.

"He's gone. Good call to get someone over to sniff the body. I was waiting for you before we catch up with him. He mentioned the scent is strong, he isn't far." He tilted his head to look at her. "What did the ursine want?"

Ursine? Oh. "Bear?" she asked, confused.

"The Bouncer."

She quickly relayed what the Bouncer told her. Rex's face had been unreadable the whole time, like his face was carved from granite. "The Becoming mean anything..."

"No, never heard of it," Rex said before she even finished the question.

"He didn't really talk much about it, just the fact he was recruiting people..."

"Alice we better be going." He started to move away.

"But it's a good place to start."

"A better place would be to track down that rogue wolf. Are you coming or not?"

Alice gritted her teeth. "Fine."

CHAPTER 10

The walk to Tyler took less time than she thought it would, the general busyness that was London calmer than usual. They found him pacing in front of a large abandoned warehouse, the door and windows covered up half-heartedly with wooden planks, decorated in various multicoloured graffiti.

"What is this place?" she asked, staring up at the huge double storey building.

The front was boarded up, something about a male's large appendage in neon pink graffiti sprawled artistically across it. Alice looked up at the drab building, two sizable windows placed beside the door, both closed off and decorated with similar artistry. Four more windows spotted along the upper storey with two more circular windows at the top. They had no boards, just shadowed over with dust and grime. Several broken shards stuck out, an impenetrable blackness oozing out from the holes. Something moved in her peripheral vision, a shape running across a window.

"It's creepy."

"Must have been an old factory," Rex stated.

No shit Sherlock.

Brushing her hand across the wooden panel she tried to find somewhere weak, something easy enough to pull off. A loud screech as Rex pulled off a board effortlessly, long rusted nails sticking from the wood.

"Move please." Tyler budged past her, grabbing another board and pulling it off. Alice moved back, surprised by his deep bass voice. Tyler ignored her, his attention on the removing of the boards quickly and efficiently.

Bloody hell, he does speak.

Once the hole was large enough Alice nudged past them, turning at an angle so she could fit.

"Alice wait..." Rex said as her sleeve got caught on a nail sticking out. "It might be dangerous, let one of us go first."

She tugged her sleeve free, groaning when she noticed the massive hole in the cotton. "Fuck."

"Are you alright?" Rex came up next to her, his hand roaming across her arm as he looked for any damage.

"I just caught my sleeve." She scowled at her shirt before taking in the building surrounding her. It was huge, even bigger than she initially thought. "This must once have been an old textile factory," she muttered to herself, walking behind them into the dark, dusty room.

Around a dozen tables were lined up neatly in rows of four, all evenly spaced. Piles of fabrics and papers sprawled carelessly over the table tops. Mannequins and tailors dummies lined the walls, all seemingly frozen into place, backs stiff, some with arms and heads, and some without. Eyes seemed to follow her every movement, seeing nothing yet seeing everything.

As she walked further into the room the mannequins became more grotesque, more non-human. Porcelain and fabric creatures once resembling humans warped into face-less monsters, bodies burnt and deformed, eyes having been scratched off their once pretty faces, mutilated. The spray can artists had somehow gotten in there too, offensive words and images painted onto the pale flesh.

Alice felt disturbed, almost repulsed at the sight, not quite wanting to turn her back to the army of dolls. A bird squawked, making her glance up as a black shadow flew out through one of the cracks in the windows, the large room having no second floor.

"Tyler can you smell that?" Rex kept his voice low.

Tyler lifted his nose to the air, but didn't confirm or deny. He started to pace the room, his face scrunched up in concentration before storming over to the back end of the abandoned building.

Alice followed quickly behind, almost slamming into the back of Tyler when she followed his eyesight, her eyes unable to make out what he was watching until sunlight finally shone through a broken window.

Hung from a beam was the wolf they were tracking, Tom. His once black eyes misted over in death. Rope was knotted around each of his arms, anchored to the wooden beams running parallel along the ceiling.

Alice felt bile rise up her throat, the creak of the rope against the wood too much. The room was full of old dusty fabrics, rolls of cotton, linen and organza piled high against the walls, dark blue paint peeling off the brick. Dust hovered in the air, creating bursts of sparkle as they reflected off the rays of light from the cracked windows high above. A couple of industrial sewing machines had been pushed to the far corners of the derelict room. The once working machines had rusted with age, their needles dulled.

Blood dripped to the floor, leaving a red splash across

the concrete. Looking back at the body Alice hesitantly walked forward, feeling the urge to check for a pulse, to check for any sense of life. A stupid notion considering his intestines were on show, hanging precariously by his feet, the blood dripping off in an irritating patter.

"Alice," warned Rex, as she felt a warm hand on her shoulder.

"Let me do my job." She shrugged him off.

Tom's head was slumped down, chin to chest, his hair covering his barely recognisable face. Pale skin decorated in bursts of blue, purple and yellow.

"He has broken ribs," she mumbled to herself, hovering her hand over the patterns decorating his chest, next to the large lacerations so deep she could see muscle. Black moved underneath his skin, veins and arteries continuing to leak through his various wounds. The ropes creaked again, the body swaying slightly in the non-existent breeze.

The guys hadn't spoken a word, their attention on the swaying corpse. Concerned, she looked at them, their faces pale as they continued to stare at the body.

"Hey, are you both okay?" They didn't even look at her, their eyes trained on Tom's chest. Taking a step back her breath caught at the back of her throat, blood turning to ice in her veins.

The phrase 'Time's up' was carved neatly into his flesh.

"Rex?" she asked. "What does that mean?"

He didn't say anything for a few minutes, his eyes never leaving the body before he turned to her, his eyes bright, the wolf prowling behind his irises. "A warning. A threat."

"From who? What aren't you telling me?"

"I don't know." He moved towards Tyler, starting a low conversation between them. She couldn't even tell Tyler was speaking but for the gentle vibrations of his throat, his mouth barely moving. He seemed angry, his movements agitated. His eyes connected with hers when he noticed her staring, they flared wolf, a bright yellow before he turned his back to her.

"I'll call the forensics in."

"We don't need them." Rex stormed across the floor towards her, his stride powerful and irritated. Even his face was surprisingly angry. "I'll call in my wolves."

"No, that's not how this works." She stood her ground as he glowered over her. "We need to run blood work and look into what carved that warning in his chest. Your wolves are not trained..."

"I said no," he growled.

"It's part of the package. When you hired me..."

"I hired you to listen to me."

"You hired me for my experience and advice." She felt her own irritation ignite, could feel an intense heat low in her stomach. Her fingers twitched, fire prickling her skin.

"Let her contact them." Tyler intervened. "We could find something out that benefits us." Rex turned to Tyler, full wolf in his eyes. Tyler dropped the eye contact instantly, his throat tilted to the side in submission.

"Rex, it makes sense." He didn't want to listen, his ice eyes bright in the dark room. She could feel the power behind them, could feel the authority that was bred into all Alphas.

She lifted a hand to his chest as he stepped into her, his skin hot beneath his shirt. "Stop it." He pushed against her hand, the wolf in his eyes excited. She released her pent-up energy, allowing a thin wall of flame to line her either side. She didn't want to hurt him, but she wasn't one of his sheep to manipulate and control.

His nose flared, his head tilting as his wolf studied her.

She was running out of ideas fast, she had never seen him react this way. His wolf was still excited, almost playing with her as he showed her his teeth.

"Sire." Tyler whispered beside her. She hadn't even heard him move.

Rex let out a deep growl, one that started at the bottom of his chest and erupted out of his mouth. "Contact them." He pushed away from her, storming out of the warehouse.

Extinguishing the flames she grabbed her phone, texting the appropriate team. The reply was almost instant.

Sending out to your coordinates now. Please standby.

"You shouldn't challenge him," Tyler stated.

"I didn't," Alice said, confused. Not intentionally anyway. "What was that even about?" She waited for the reply, not expecting an answer. She knew shifter etiquette, knew that another animal shouldn't look into a dominants eyes. But surely he knew she wasn't an animal?

"No one has ever challenged him."

114

CHAPTER 11

Alice had never seen anything like it before, and was happy to never see anything like it again.

"As you can see, the organs have been moved towards the back, pressed against the spine," Dr Miko Le'Sanza, Head Pathologist for London Hope Hospital stated as he opened the chest cavity of Tomlin, the wolf they had found hanging crucifix style only a few days earlier. She had pulled as many favours as she could to get the autopsy pushed through, knowing Rex was on a time limit.

"What does that mean?" Alice asked as she followed Miko around the lab. She was told to meet Tyler at the reception desk, but instead turned up early to have a catch up with her old friend. Although, he was more interested in showing her as many gory details as possible.

"You will see." His slightly upturned eyes shone in excitement, a gift from his Asian mother. His father, on the other hand, gave him his dark curly hair and naturally tanned skin. The combination made him beautiful, in a delicate feminine way.

He moved around the body with a metal cart, full of instruments that would be better suited to a torture chamber than a hospital morgue.

"If you look here..." Using a sharp knife he sliced a few layers of skin beside several vertebrae, peeling back the skin.

"What am I looking at?" She walked towards the table.

"There are unusual patterns along the underside of the ribcage, almost like a spider web." Grabbing an instrument, Miko pointed to one of the black vein-like tubes that crisscrossed underneath the skin.

"What are they?" she asked, having no clue what she was looking at. Not that she had the first idea about forensic science.

"I have no idea. But once your friend turns up, you will learn that this particular cadaver is anything but normal." He poked one of the black tubes, the spider web seeming to pulsate before settling.

"That's disgusting."

"Is this a bad time?" a voice asked from behind. She knew who it was immediately, but turned anyway.

"Oh, hey." She blinked up at Rex, surprised to see him dressed so casually. He wore a plain white t-shirt with khakis, compared to his usual dress shirts and expensive jeans. He even wore trainers. "Where's Tyler?"

"He's preoccupied." He looked towards the Doctor, his face cold. "Alice seems to believe you might give something of relevance."

"Relevance?" Miko chuckled, grabbing a clipboard from the corner of one of the desks and handing it to Alice. "I'll have you know I'm always relevant."

Alice glanced at the paper before she heard a weird,

forced laugh. Surprised, she faced Rex who gave her a quick smile, one that didn't reach his eyes.

"What's that?" Rex asked, pointedly looking at the paper on her clipboard, the fake smile fading from his lips.

"Oh." She checked the paperwork again, reading the report a few times over before she understood all the letters and numbers. "This can't be right." A frown creased her brow.

"I've run the tests several times just to check, the DNA matches up. I've never seen anything like it." Miko grabbed the report from Alice before handing it to Rex.

"This is unbelievable."

"What are you guys on about?" He read through the paperwork, not understanding the report.

Miko walked over with a handful of vials and syringes, each already filled with various substances. "What it means is that the blood we extracted is unique and believed to be impossible."

"You're still not making any sense."

"What the report says is that the DNA matches with a shifter, but a couple of unusual strands have appeared in the blood-works." Miko clapped his hands together excitedly before going over to a cabinet and opening a metal cupboard, cool air floating out before he closed the door again. "So when we opened him up it was very unusual."

"Unusual how?" Rex asked. His face stone as he leant carefully on the wall next to the door, his nose turned away from the selection of chemicals and formaldehyde.

"This." Miko shook the large jar in his hands, something pink inside hitting the glass wall before settling in the middle.

"What the fuck is that?" Alice stepped closer, trying to look into the jar with condensation rolling down the glass.

"This, my dear friends is a heart."

"That is not a heart." Alice eyed the bulbous flesh in the water, the shape similar to a heart but at least twice the size.

"This is actually the heart of the wolf you brought in. As you can see it is clearly oversized."

"Clearly," Rex said dryly.

Miko shook the glass again, the water becoming murky before clearing as the heart thudded against the glass. With a few pops, the heart contorted, constricting before releasing, causing bubbles to pop out of several holes and floating to the top.

"Holy shit did that thing move?" Alice went to touch the jar, snapping her hand back as the heart pumped again.

"Yes, believe it or not, it is still pumping." Miko put the jar down. "And it's not even a delayed muscle spasm, like a chicken who would continue to run around even after losing his head. I've been watching it for the last couple days since you brought the body in. It is somehow still living."

"Why is it so large?"

Miko shrugged. "No idea, I can tell it's deformed, most Breeds, at least humanoid have a heart with four valves. A mitral valve and tricuspid valve, they control the blood flow from the atria to the ventricles. We also have an aortic valve and a pulmonary valve that controls the flow out of the ventricles. Now this heart has eight valves."

"Eight? Why would you need eight?"

"That is the big question isn't it?" Miko tapped his nail against the glass, the heart continuing to pump every thirty seconds or so.

"So what does this all mean?" asked Rex, his attention on the pink flesh.

"I have been researching along with a couple of specialists," Miko started to move around the lab, grabbing bits of paper from various work surfaces. "Like I said before, it's almost impossible."

"Doc, what does it mean?"

"Well, between myself and several of my colleagues we have come to the decision that it could quite possibly be a Daemon transition."

"A Daemon?" Alice frowned, trying to remember the last time she had even heard of a Daemon sighting. Something clicked in her head, her nightmares starting to make sense.

Shit. Shit. Shit. Alice stepped back, facing the wall as her stomach rolled.

"Technically, there are no records that Daemons exist, they're not a registered Breed. However, there are medical archives going back hundreds of years depicting such transitions... Alice, are you okay?"

She sucked in a breath. "I'm fine." She was closer to knowing, to finding out what happened.

"Like I was saying, there have been autopsies of creatures that medical professionals at the time have named as Daemons due to their likeliness to the biblical stories, although they are nothing to do with religion."

He scanned through sheets of paper, seeming to forget he had company before looking up, surprised.

"Oh, yeah. There are also newspaper articles and police reports with matching descriptions, but as I said, because Daemons have never been actually classified as an official Breed, no one ever investigated further."

"So, in your professional opinion?" Alice asked, needing to confirm. "You believe that to be a Daemon?"

"I believe that is exactly what he was, or at least would be if the transition was complete." He pursed his lips.

"What can we do with this information?" Rex asked, putting the clipboard down on one of the shiny surfaces.

"Unfortunately not a lot. I'm currently getting my apprentices to look into unusual blood works in autopsy reports over the past year. I'm hoping once I have something to compare my results with I could work out how far the transition is and what actually killed him."

"You don't even know what killed him?" Rex said in his usual arctic tone. "His organs were on the floor."

"It isn't that simple," Miko snapped as he ruffled his hair. "I'm not exactly working on the usual body, now am I?"

"Do you mind if I come back tomorrow?" Alice asked, "I would like to look through some of the reports."

"Sure, ring me later to organise a pass." He absently waved his hand.

"So you haven't found anything useful." Rex crossed his arms. "This has been a waste of time."

Alice glared at him. "Did you find anything else unusual?" she asked the doctor.

Miko ignored Rex's comment. "Yes and no. His internals are messed up, like his lungs and stomach didn't know where to go when his heart grew." Miko pointedly gave her a look. She remembered him showing her the damaged tissue surrounding the spine.

Wonder what that could mean.

"He had blood in his stomach, but I can't really tell if that's unusual or not. I know some shifters drink blood through ceremonies and when hunting."

Alice glanced at Rex, looking for confirmation. "Rex?" she called.

No response, he seemed to be staring at the body.

"Rex?" she said again, slightly louder this time.

He looked up then, his face pale. "What?" His eyes flashed, his wolf reacting.

"Dr Le'Sanza was saying some shifters consume blood for ceremonies and stuff? That true?"

He seemed to shake himself, a full body vibration. "I need to go."

"Rex?"

He faced her, eyes glistening. "Contact me if you find anything else." With that he left the room.

What's up with him?

Alice leant against a stainless steel cabinet, waiting for Miko to be finished with whatever he was doing. She felt herself stare towards the body, his feet bare, with a white tag tied around his big toe.

What can I remember about Daemons? Alice bit the inside of her cheek, trying to think. Dread told her stories as a child, warnings. She didn't believe him. Why would she?

"Alice?"

What else did he say?

"Alice?"

She needed to learn more.

"ALICE!" Miko clicked his fingers.

"Huh?" She blinked at him.

"I've been calling your name." He raised an eyebrow. "What were you thinking about?"

"Nothing important." She cleared her throat.

"So, we going to talk about your wolf?"

"What? Rex isn't my wolf." She felt heat against her cheeks. "We're just working together."

"I meant him..." He pointed to the corpse. "But it's interesting you mentioned Rex now, isn't it." His brows knitted. "Have you seen the way he looks at you?"

"Looks at me?"

"He looks at you as if you're his."

"Excuse me?" *He doesn't really look at me like that, does he?* That confused things. "Anyway, what do we know about Daemons?" She didn't want to think about anything else right now.

"Other than the fact they are beyond rare? Not a lot." He gawked at the corpse. "They were more common in the nineteenth century, but have been hunted to near extinction."

"Hunted? Who has hunted them?"

"Well that's the interesting thing, I don't know." He threw his papers onto a counter. "I have asked anybody who should know and I got nowhere." He tugged at his hair. "Don't suppose you know anything?"

"No." She thought about it. "You said the body was transitioning? Is it magic? Or like a shifter?"

"Magic? That's interesting. Shifters in general, while not widely known, do actually have magic. It's how they are able to shift between their forms."

"So Daemon's could be a type of Shifter?"

"That's relative, they seem to shift from one form to another but there isn't any evidence to suggest that. There is also no evidence to suggest anything else either." With a pen he started to write notes on a piece of paper. "It's an interesting theory though, something I will definitely explore." He peeked at her over the paper. "I'm going to run the bloods again, see if I can break them down further." He turned back towards his work.

"I guess that's me dismissed."

Miko didn't respond, his attention on his new project.

"Bye then." Her voice was lost as she walked towards the lifts, just about to press the button when the door opened unexpectedly. A man stood in the centre as the doors opened, his face puzzled before recognition flowed across his features.

"Agent Skye," he greeted as he stepped out, letting the door close behind him before she could step in.

"Detective." She eyed the button to the left, analysing if she could reach around and not seem rude.

"What are you doing here?"

"Visiting a friend."

He played with the unlit cigarette on his left ear. "Interesting I found you, I was on my way to talk to someone about the body found behind the club. It seems that someone did bleed John Doe virtually dry before using a tin can lid to slice through his jugular."

"A tin can?" That was surprising, the cut looked too clean. She would have put money on a knife.

"That's what the professionals say. What was interesting was he was severely dehydrated. When the guys finally moved the body, a few of his bones disintegrated."

"What could have caused that?" She had never heard of anything like it.

"They're still looking into it." He checked his watch.

"Do you have any leads?"

"Only the extra blood found at the scene, it was magic infused. Identified as belonging to a witch."

"You sure it wasn't a mage?"

"No, the blood was too strong." He frowned, his eyes moving behind her.

"Alice," someone hissed to her back.

Alice spun, heart in her throat. "Dread, you almost gave me a heart attack." She hated that vampires were virtually silent in their movements.

"We have matters to discuss." His eyes flicked to the Detective. "O'Neil, haven't spoken to you in a while."

"Commissioner. Have you looked into the proposal I sent over?"

"About the liaison team? I'm currently working with my Paladins to decide who would be better suited."

"Good. The big bosses are pushing for a more blended variety in the workforce. Liaising with a Paladin would be a start."

"I agree, I believe it would benefit both sides. I will get back to you as soon as I have come to my decision. Now if you would excuse me." Dread grabbed her arm, escorting her further down the hallway.

"Dread what is this?" She dragged her feet until he stopped, making him face her. "Why are you even here?"

"I have just got the report about the wolf. I'm here to personally remove you from your recent contract. Starting now you will no longer be working for Mr Wild. I have organised Danton to replace you."

"Replace me? Wait... back up. Why am I being removed?"

He waited as someone walked past, not wanting anyone to overhear.

"We cannot discuss this in the open."

Mouth tight, she opened a door to their right, walking into the small cupboard before Dread could complain. "You wanted privacy?" She flicked the switch for the light, the bulb choking to life with a high-pitched whine.

Dread closed the door behind him, looking around the small room in disgust. It was literally a cleaning closet, several wooden brooms were stacked against each other on the left while the right wall was full of shelves holding cleaning supplies.

"This isn't what I had in mind, Alice."

"Start from the beginning. Why am I being removed

from the case? I feel like I'm really starting to make a break-through..."

"The risk is too high."

"Dread, I'm a fucking Paladin..."

"Language!" he hissed, his obsidian eyes narrowing. "You're a Paladin who isn't trained to deal with Daemons, especially abominations like that."

"Then who deals with them?"

"There is an organisation that specialises in such things."

"An organisation? Who?" She needed to speak to them.

"I do not have to explain myself to you Alice. There's a reason behind every story I have ever told you. You should try to remember that." He exhaled, calming himself. "I can't risk any of them finding you, if they found out..." He caught himself before he revealed anymore.

"If who found out?" Panic built in her blood. "What haven't you told me?"

"You were never supposed to know," he murmured quietly, almost to himself.

"Dread..." She wanted to tell him about her nightmares, but couldn't seem to get the words out of her mouth.

"Alice..." he sighed. "You must understand, I see you like a daughter, one I want to protect." He hesitated, trying to find the right words. "No, this isn't the right time."

Alice let out a little scream, frustration creasing her features. "I don't understand, you demand I leave something alone but you don't explain why." Her eyes blurred.

Alice dropped her lashes, shocked as moisture filled her eyes.

"You *will* drop the case." He paused as the closet door rattled, as if someone knocked it as they walked past. "This is over Alice. My decision is final." Dread paused, almost as if he was going to say something else.

She turned her head and held his gaze, seeing if she could read through his evasion.

"I'm pulling you off this case. Mr Wild will just have to deal with it." He moved to put his hand on the handle, his back to her. "I know this is hard but my priority is your safety. It's what I promised..." He cleared his throat. "The risk is too high. Not when it's your life."

The door creaked open before he disappeared.

Alice let her head rest against the wall, her eyes closed, refusing to let her tears fall. She wasn't stupid, she knew her broken nightmares that haunted her were memories.

It didn't matter how many years went by, Alice still felt the empty ache in her chest when she thought about her family, her mother, father and brother who were all brutally murdered late one night in their family home. The only exception was her, a small child who had been woken up by a strange noise. A child who had ran and hid when she saw a monster, a shadow.

CHAPTER 12

"He can't take me off the case," Alice grumbled into her polystyrene cup early the next morning. She had checked her Paladin status on the S.I. database at dawn, delighted to see the paperwork hadn't gone through. That gave her at least two days. Until then, she wouldn't be contactable by The Tower.

Blowing along the top of her coffee she stared at the large converted townhouse that housed the local hospital. The front of the building was made up of five-story townhouses that have been connected to the sleek glass and steel structure built behind. Alice quickly moved past row of ambulances, walking into the general reception area. The smell assaulted her nose almost instantly, the strong mixture of copper and disinfectant polluting the air strong enough to choke on. The accident and emergency centre was situated directly behind the reception, rows of benches lined the white lino flooring, almost every available space taken up by someone moaning, bleeding or clutching some part of their anatomy.

"Morning, I'm here to see Dr Le'sanza," she politely asked the tired looking receptionist behind the desk. "He should be expecting me."

"Name?" the woman, Betty according to her name tag, asked.

"Alice Skye."

Betty nodded before scanning through a book in front of her, a frown creasing her brow.

"Is there a problem?" *Was I too early?* She looked up at the clock on the wall, noting how it was only just past eight. She had been too wound up to sleep.

"If you could please excuse me Ma'am, I need to make a phone call." Without waiting for a response Betty grabbed the handset by her computer, clicking a few buttons before murmuring into the phone. Alice could feel the eyes on her back, an accusation of impatient people having to wait too long.

As if it was her fault they had to wait.

"Miss Skye, was it?"

"Yes, that would be me. I spoke to Le'Sanza yesterday..."

"Yes Miss Skye, he has confirmed your meeting. He just didn't follow the proper protocol to register a visitor, doctors do that sometimes." Leaning down into one of her drawers she pulled out a long lanyard with '*VISITOR*' written across it. "Please wear this at all times," she said, passing it over. "It will gain you access to the lower levels of the hospital, please do not go into any patient's rooms unless supervised. If you walk to the large lift and press 'B1', you will find Dr Miko Le'Sanza's office. Take a left, down the corridor and it's right at the end, you can't miss it. Any questions?"

"I've been there before, thank you."

"Have a great day." With that practised smile, she turned to the next person in line.

Clearly dismissed, Alice walked to the lift, waiting patiently in line with the other people. With a bing the lift doors opened, allowing everyone to squish themselves into the small space.

"Press floor one please," a woman asked politely as she read from her clipboard. Pushing the hair away from her face Alice obeyed, pressing the two floors and stood quietly beside the woman. The lift music started almost instantly, an annoying raucous of instruments as if the orchestra all stood up and took a step to the right, playing an instrument they were not familiar with.

A few stops and people started to filter out, leaving more space to move around.

Stepping back she allowed someone to pass, placing her at the back of the lift with the metal banister digging into her back. An annoying ringing broke through the music, adding an obnoxious tone to the already terrible song. A man who wore all black answered his phone, flipping the front open and putting it to his ear. Alice couldn't help but stare, surprised to see a flip phone in this day and age.

"Yes?" the man barked into the receiver. "Yes, we have already found the appropriate information. No, but we haven't got access yet." The man stopped his conversation, turning to glare at Alice. "Excuse me." He held his hand over the microphone, his palm bigger than the black handset.

Alice blinked up at him stupidly. "Oh, sorry."

He just tutted and faced the doors.

"Sorry about that. Yes, of course. I will keep you updated." He tucked his phone into his front pocket, grabbing his sunglasses and planting them on his nose.

The lift dinged once more, signalling that she had reached her desired floor. The door moaned, revealing a very similar white corridor layout. It must be a rule somewhere that all hospitals must be painted a sickly white colour. Shoulders stiff, she walked out, barely stopping herself from looking back at the man, her gut telling her something was wrong.

Dr Miko Le'Sanza's office was right at the end of the corridor, his name embossed on a gold plated sign hanging on the solid wood, unsurprisingly painted white. She knocked gently before walking in.

"Miko?"

"Hello?" Miko swivelled his head towards the door, a surprised look on his face. "Hi Alice, didn't expect you today."

"What are you on about? I said yesterday I was coming?"

"Well yes, but Commissioner Grayson said..."

"Dread came in?" She felt the blood rush from her face. *Shit. Shit. Shit.*

"Well, yes."

Miko shuffled the papers in his hands as he stood up, a tower of envelopes and coloured folders engulfing what she knew to be his desk, various pens and pencils thrown precariously across the pile. "He wanted to organise a team to take over examining the body," he smirked. "I politely told him to shove it. No way was I letting anybody take this over."

"You said what?" She really wished she could have seen Dread's face. "How did he even know about it?"

"No idea. I told him I'm not letting some buffoons come over and mess up my research. So he had no choice but to hire me directly under The Tower until further notice." He sniffed as if displeased, but grinned at the same time. "Which means I also know you're no longer the Paladin on this case."

"So you're not letting me see the reports?" She felt the energy leave her. What would she do now? That was her main lead.

"Of course I am. What he doesn't know won't hurt him."

She beamed, looking around the small office. His desk has been pushed to the far wall, under a light box showing someone's broken bone. The computer sat on the left corner, the screen showing a black screensaver with a pink square bouncing from one corner to the other.

"When's the last time you cleaned?" She sat on the pile of folders on the one chair available in the room.

"I call it an organised mess." He pulled out a few boxes from under his desk, planting them on her lap. "These are the files you were after."

"Really?" She pushed the top box off, letting it land on the floor at her feet. "Oh man, I think I owe you dinner." She smiled at the number of folders, hoping some of them contained something helpful.

"Actually, you owe about six people dinner. We have all agreed on steak." His eyes sparkled. "These particular reports are based on unusual deaths with no known family," he shrugged. "Normally in these situations they are never re-opened, just closed once all the leads go dead. So any unusual abnormalities aren't investigated further."

"Have you read these?" She nodded to the pile on her lap.

"I skimmed them last night. There's one I think you should see." He went to the mess on his desk, shuffling through layers of paperwork before he found what he was looking for. Accepting the report she opened the first page.

Office of the medical examiner
London

Report of examination

Decedent: *Maxi L. Swanson*
Case Number: *RF 12466-892029*
Cause of death: *Unknown*
Identified by: *Teeth were used to check medical records. Concluded with the nuclear DNA comparison done by medical staff laboratory. (Skeletal specimen for identification: Right Tibia) **
*Disclosure – Unusual strands in DNA
Age: *Bones are consistent with an age of around 32 years*
Sex: *Male*   **Race:** *Caucasian*
Date of death: *(Found) 10/11/2010 (Estimate) 8/11/2010*

....

Date of Examination: *12th November 2010 through to 20th November 2010*
Examination and summary analysis performed by: *UNDISCLOSED*
Cause of death: *Exsanguination (Loss of blood to a degree sufficient to cause death)*

....

Findings

¥ *Blood found in the body was less than 40%*
¥ *Unusual substance found in the blood inside the body*
¥ *Bite marks around throat and wrists*

¥ *Found in same clothes reported last wearing.*
¥ *Wounds consistent with self-harm*
¥ *Blood under fingernails – own DNA*
¥ *Reported missing on the 20th of October 2010*
¥ *No proof of struggle*
¥ *Toxicology detects no drugs but cannot determine substance found in blood.*
¥ *Shifter DNA – Species unknown*
¥ *Unknown substance also found in the back of the throat*
¥ *Internal organs larger than usual.*
....

Conclusion:

The subject's self-inflicted wounds have tiny incisions consistent with fang marks.

The unknown substance found in his blood was also found in the back of the throat, ingested.

Died from blood loss and sepsis caused by the open wounds across the body. Little medical history can be found. The front teeth were deformed but the molars towards the back of the throat were used in conjunction with the DNA check. Due to the limited proof and evidence of third party, the cause of death cannot be completely determined with certainty. The manner of death is unknown.

"Unusual strands in DNA?" She flicked through the pages.

"His blood is similar to the wolf you brought in, the abnormalities matching."

"What does that mean?"

"Not really sure yet. But if more of these files match it would be a breakthrough."

BEEP. BEEP. BEEP.

The lights above flashed several times.

BEEP. BEEP. BEEP.

"Shit!" Miko ran to his door, peering out into the corridor.

BEEP. BEEP. BEEP.

"Miko, what is it?" Alice chased behind him, the one file clutched to her chest. The lights overhead turned off for a few seconds before fluttering back to life, the backup generator kicking in.

"Someone has set off the alarm," he replied in between the obnoxious beeps. He started to move towards the stairs, following the crowd of mildly panicked people as they passed beneath a violently flashing red light.

"As in a fire test?" she questioned, following quickly behind.

"Not that I know of."

"Dr Le'Sanza!" someone called. "Doctor..." Miko turned to the sound of his name. "Doctor I'm glad I caught you, someone set the fire alarm off from the morgue."

"The morgue? Wasn't Dr Washington down there?"

"No, sir. Dr Washington got called to a meeting. Security is trying to reset the alarm but it could take a few minutes."

"So there is no fire?"

"No, CCTV has just confirmed."

"Thank you James, could you please go up to reception to help settle the patients?"

"But Dr, I should go help clear up the morgue..."

"It's fine, I have someone to help." James's eyes flashed to Alice. "Oh, of course." He started to run off, his white lab coat flying behind him.

Alice waited a few seconds while the beeping cleared, the sound resonating inside her skull. "What did he mean clean up the morgue?"

Miko turned to her, his face pale. "Shit."

The mortuary was empty by the time they both descended the stairs, having to calm several people on the way down, reassuring them everything was fine.

The corridor leading to the main autopsy room was eerily quiet, nothing like how it normally was. Metal trolleys abandoned, paperwork scattered across the floor.

"Miko, who did you tell about the heart?" Alice heard herself whisper, her eyes scanning the rooms breaking off from the corridor. The emergency lighting was still activated, making everywhere darker than it should be, allowing shadows to swallow up the corners of the rooms.

Ignoring her, he walked past the main autopsy room and through a side door where floor to ceiling metal squares patterned the walls. One of the squares was open, the metal door open with a silver gurney half hanging out. A white cloth draped from the metal, the fabric caught on the edge of the door. A large fridge was at the back, next to a few racks with vials of different coloured liquids.

"It's not here." Miko panicky moved over everything on the shelves, even bending to check behind the rack. "It's not here." He opened the fridge next, closing the heavy door only moments later. "Shit. Alice, it isn't here."

"What about the body?" she asked.

He turned to the only open mortuary refrigerator, pushing the gurney violently with a high screech. "Someone has taken it," he said hopelessly.

"Miko..." She went to stand in front of him, his attention on the black hole in the wall. "Who did you tell about the heart?" He didn't seem to hear her, his attention still on the hole where the body should have been. "MIKO." She clicked her fingers, causing him to blink and shake his head. "Who did you tell?"

"No one I couldn't trust," he said, voice croaking. "Alice why would someone break into a hospital for it?"

"I don't know." The room suddenly brightened, the main power kicking back in. "How can someone just stroll in here and leave with a body and no one notice?"

Miko finally met her eyes, the pupils narrowed. "I don't know." He turned to punch a cabinet. "FUCK!" The sound resonated as Miko grabbed his fist, swearing.

Alice ignored him, instead picking up some debris off the floor and placing them on the side. She had noticed all the rooms, ones that normally locked with a key card, were unlocked. Going over to the double doors she peered at the black box on the wall, one that looked completely undamaged. Frowning she went to touch it, pulling her hand back at the last second when a spark flashed.

What the fuck?

"Miko? What would set off the fire alarm if there was no fire?"

He walked to stand beside her, frowning at the wall. "Someone could have pulled the fire alarm?"

"What about if something tripped the electric?" The black box sparked again, making them step back.

"Not normally, but a slight smoke from the spark could affect the sensitive detectors."

"How long does it take for the alarm to be reset?"

Miko thought about it for a few seconds. "Up to ten minutes."

"So they had ten minutes from when the alarm went off to grab what they came for and escape through the confusion." That was obviously plenty of time.

"The alarm could have been planned."

"Possible." She checked another door, noticing it also had the same treatment.

"Do you..."

Alice held up her hand to silence him, concentrating on a sound from the corner of the room. She heard it again, a soft moan.

"Hello?"

The sound again, slightly louder.

"Shit." Miko walked to an overturned gurney. "Over here." Together they gently moved the obstacle, spotting someone lying along the floor, their back towards a metal cabinet. "Hey, can you hear me?" He gently ran his hands over the unconscious woman, checking her body for any damage.

"She was thrown into the cabinet," Alice commented as she pulled some broken glass away. The woman's face was swollen, the skin around her eye swelling to the point her eye was forced closed. "She must have gotten in the way."

"Barbarians, this is a bloody hospital for goodness sake." Miko gently helped her up as the woman slowly regained consciousness. "Hello, it's Dr Le'Sanza, can you tell me your name?" The woman just stared blankly through her one clear eye. "She's probably concussed. We need to get her upstairs."

"I'll call for help."

The air was chilly when Alice left the hospital, happy to leave the woman with a series of doctors. She had to leave the reports with Miko, who promised to contact her if he found anything. She wanted to stay but couldn't risk running into anybody from the office. They wouldn't have the body to study anymore but someone would definitely be investigating its disappearance, as well as the heart.

The floor squelched under her shoes as she paused outside the doors, water from the heavy rain leaving the floor and roads dangerously wet, the cold weather discouraging the water to evaporate. Eyes dry and gritty she wiped her face with her hands, her breath coming out in a long sigh. It was like they were a step ahead of them, first with killing the wolf and now with his body. Was that their plan all along? To leave the dead with a warning and then recover it?

Rex wasn't telling her something.

A vibration in her pocket. Alice quickly peeked at the phone screen, ignoring the text from Dread. Her finger hovered over Rex.

This wasn't just about his wolf anymore.

A sudden screech made her jump, her phone leaping from her hand to land in a heap on the ground. Heat scorched across her face, her body weightless as she was thrown back, her arms catching her fall as she was hurled to the wet concrete.

Screams rattled, surrounding her from all angles followed by heavy footsteps.

BANG!

Disorientated, she pushed herself up onto her arms and lifted her head, trying to make out the chaos that surrounded her.

"HELP, SOMEONE PLEASE!"

She shakily climbed to her feet, looking around at the carnage, blood a harsh red against the dark ground. A car had crashed into an ambulance, the white metal destroyed, crushing both vehicles completely. The impact had pushed the ambulance into the road, causing a few cars to swerve dangerously to avoid a collision, one being unlucky and crashing head on.

"MUMMY!"

"CALL THE DOCTORS!"

"THIS IS A HOSPITAL FOR FUCK SAKE!"

Voices shouted in the chaos, getting louder as cars continued to avoid adding further carnage. She felt the heat on her face intensify as something caught fire, igniting the first car instantly.

"PLEASE. SOMEONE. SHE'S TRAPPED!"

Alice moved through the crowd, running towards the people desperately trying to free the woman trapped in the car. The door had been caved in, people unable to pull the lock open as they scrambled to gain purchase. The woman groaned and rolled her head to one side of the airbag, blood dripping down her face.

"It won't open." Alice desperately searched for something she could use to help open the door. "Try the other door," she cried to anyone who would listen.

She could feel the heat lick her skin, the scent of oil and petrol strong in her nose as it leaked across the asphalt.

"Hey, we're just getting you out," she spoke calmly to the woman in the car, her eyes glazed over in pain. "Can you undo your seatbelt for me?" The woman stared before sluggishly reaching over, trying desperately to release the belt.

"It won't open." The woman started to cry, violently tugging at the belt. "Why won't it open?"

"It's okay, we can cut it open. It's not a problem." The heat at her back was getting worse, smoke a thick plume surrounding them.

"Ma'am please step away from the car." A fireman rushed over, his suit protecting him from the intense heat. "Ma'am I need you to get back from the car, it's dangerous." He pushed her out the way, and began to frantically work on the metal door with one of his instruments.

Alice stumbled back as coughs constricted her lungs, the smoke thick enough to obscure her vision. She thought she could see the red fire engine in the distance, but couldn't make out the details.

"EVERYONE GET DOWN."

A pop as petrol ignited, causing a fireball only meters away. Metal creaked against the heat, a car becoming engulfed as the flames raced to devour everything in its path. Another firefighter became immersed in smoke beside her, his friends struggling for control, ignoring her as she stood motionless. Burning flesh assaulted her nose, choking as it became hard to breath.

Without thought she approached the flame, the orange and yellow element dancing, fighting against the breeze and the water being poured from the hose.

"It's not working," she whispered to herself, watching the fire grow rather than die. She couldn't understand why, but she felt the biggest urge to touch the fire. She thrust her hand into the blaze, coating her skin with her own blue power.

A cyclone of sound surrounded her, voices and screams she couldn't distinguish as she concentrated on the flame. The fire reacted, surrounding her completely rather than following its desired destination along the oil. Alice peeked over her shoulder, making sure the fireman was still working on the car door, prioritising the injured.

"DON'T MOVE!" Another fireman mouthed at her, unable to hear him above the roar of the flames.

Alice threw her head back, a scream breaking free from her throat, her chi electric as she tried to fight the fire, absorbing its energy. Her hair whipped around her head as her fingertips started to burn, blue fire meeting the red. Slowly the blue conquered, swallowing the danger as her own power burned past her elbows. With one last pop the last of the flame went out, taking with it her breath.

Lungs tight, she held her hands to her chest, her arms still holding her blue flame, the edges licked with green. With a last thought, Alice extinguished the flame, turning off her power like a faucet.

The abrupt emptiness staggered her, causing her to fall to her knees below the smoke. Blood pumped in her ears, breath struggling as her lungs struggled to move in and out. Her hand shook as she reached to her face, her fingertips coming back red as she felt something warm drip down her face.

She surrendered to the sudden exhaustion.

CHAPTER 13

B eep. Beep. Beep.

What the bloody hell is that?

Alice reached over blindly, trying to turn off the annoying sound.

Beep. Beep. Beep.

Unable to find the source of the sound she stretched, feeling something in her hand tug.

"Keep still please."

"OW!" Alice jumped into a sitting position, staring at the red hole that was now in her hand. "What was that?"

"Just removing your drip," a woman in white and blue answered, her attention completely on the task of cleaning the small cut quickly and efficiently. "You might feel slightly disorientated, we had to sedate you because you kept burning my colleagues."

Beep. Beep. Beep.

Alice groggily blinked the remnant of sleep from her eyes, trying to pay attention to the surrounding details. Panic slowly settled in as she recognised the room, an adjustable bed with itchy wool blankets, a single wooden chair at the foot and ugly blue curtains. A TV was on in the top corner, an old small box with a huge heavy back.

Beep. Beep. Beep.

"Oh, let me get that." The nurse clicked a few buttons, stopping the repetitive noise.

"Why...why..." she stuttered, her throat dry. She heard a loud commotion towards the gap in her door, could just make out Dread arguing.

"You did an amazing thing you know."

"I'm... I'm sorry, what?" Confused by the statement she twisted to face the nurse.

"Because of you, that woman and possibly more survived that inferno." With that statement she left, allowing Dread to enter.

"Wow, private room. Snazzy." She coughed, clearing her throat.

Dread just stared, his face creased in worry before he began pacing back and forth.

"Dread, seriously, I'm fine." He just continued to pace, the action making her nervous. He was the calmest and most collected person she knew. He did not pace. "What was I supposed to do? Let her die? The water wasn't working..." she started to babble.

"What you did was brave and stupid." He stopped pacing, his black eyes scary as he reassured himself she was okay. "Mostly stupid."

"But..."

"You were caught on camera."

"Camera?" she asked, confused.

"On a phone, someone caught footage of you absorbing all that fire."

"So?" She swung her legs off the hospital bed.

Dread was suddenly in front of her, his body blocking her from getting off. "Do not move."

"Is that why you're pissed at me? I don't understand."

"I'm not angry, I'm just..." Dread looked around the room, searching for an explanation. "Alice you can't get caught doing things like that on camera."

"What? Why?" She lifted her chin defiantly.

"Since I found out Daemons have been sniffing around," he snapped at her, his burst of irritation and worry evident from the vibration of his pulse. "We both know your affiliation with fire is unusual, that alone would gain you unwanted attention. Add that to the fact..."

"The fact what?" She wiggled her toes, satisfied that she felt every movement.

"I have already said too much." Dread cleared his throat.

"Were you going to say that Daemons killed my family?" She watched the surprise flash across his face before he looked away. That was all the confirmation she needed. She knew she would never get him to admit it out loud, yet that one look gained her a little more of the missing puzzle.

Instead of replying he took a moment to compose himself, the move bringing the small TV in the corner into view, 'BREAKING NEWS' flashing across the screen.

Alice leant forward to watch the poor quality video, clearly recorded on a mobile phone. The image shook but showed a blonde woman in a circle of fire, blue power a river flowing from her hands, eating up the flame. The video cut off just before she collapsed.

"Turn the volume up," she asked, watching the screen.

Dread turned it off instead. "Alice, you must never tell anyone about this. It could put you in danger."

"Why did you never tell me?" she quietly asked. He

knew she wanted to know everything about that night, wanted to understand why.

"And what would you have done with the knowledge?"

Her mouth opened to reply, but nothing came out. She didn't know what she would have done.

"I have brought you up the only way I knew how..."

"Knock, knock." A man wearing a white coat walked in, interrupting their conversation.

"Alice, I would like you to meet Dr Richards. He will be your physician." Dread lifted his palm, shaking hands with the doctor.

"Please. Call me Dave," the doctor replied smoothly, a friendly smile on his face.

"It's nice to meet you Dr Dave, but why do I need a doctor?" She looked between the two men.

"It's just a precaution," the doctor smiled, making Alice stare at the several rings pierced into his lip.

"Do you not set off every metal detector you go through?" she asked as she assessed the rest of his piercings. Along with the lip rings, he had a ring through his nose, like a bull. He also had a bar through his left eyebrow while his right eyebrow had a tattoo of an eagle soaring above it. The small artwork impressively detailed.

"Sometimes." A close-lipped smile. "I have even more piercings below the coat."

Alice blushed as she fought not to look down, interested to see if she could see anything through the fabric of his clothing. "That's nice," she said, concentrating very hard on his face. "So why do I need a doctor again?"

"Like Dr Richards said it's just a precaution," Dread answered. "You shouldn't have been able to absorb that fire, but you did. You also collapsed afterwards."

"I'll be based at The Tower, I just want you to visit me

once a week to check your vitals." He grabbed her chart, reading the paper clipped to the front. "How are you feeling?"

"I feel fine."

"Any aches or pains? Headache?"

"No." *Surprisingly.*

"How often have you been having power flares?" He caught her eye, watching her reactions.

She bit her lip, thinking about her answer. "Not often. I just lose some control, it takes more effort than normal to calm down."

"Is it when you get angry?"

Alice hesitated. "Sometimes."

"Ok," he said carefully as he flared his chi.

Feeling the electric across her aura she flared her own back, shocked at how desensitised it had become.

"My chi..." she cried.

"Will return to normal in a few hours, I think you just over stimulated yourself. Magic is like a muscle, it needs to be trained otherwise it will become exhausted, especially with how much you made it stretch today. I wouldn't panic, it feels normal, but I wouldn't go around absorbing any amount of fire for a while," he chuckled to himself.

She couldn't argue. "Sound advice."

"I'm just going to assess your development over the next few months. We need to find out why you fainted." He took out what she thought was a pen from his coat pocket, clicking it to reveal a small light. He shone it into her eyes a few times, checking her pupils intently. "You also started bleeding from your ears and nose. You don't need a doctor to tell you that's bad." He clicked off the light. "Physically you're healthy, the only damage you seem to have sustained were a couple grazes when you collapsed."

"Hey, did anybody call for a ride?" a familiar voice called.

"SAM!" Alice ran into his arms, thankful to see him. Sam didn't do hospitals.

"Oh, hey baby girl, you giving the docs a run for their money?" he chuckled, hugging her close. "You okay?" he whispered against her hair.

"She's fine." Dr Dave replied, overhearing. "She just needs to rest for a few days."

"Of course she's fine." He stepped back, checking her from head to toe.

"Alice you have already been discharged," Dr Dave said. "But please come see me next week."

"Of course she will doctor," Sam tugged her towards the door. "I'll make sure she goes to every appointment."

CHAPTER 14

Alice cradled her third glass, Sam topping up her vodka and cranberry mix whenever she was getting low. He had convinced her she needed to come and relax, enjoy a night out at the bar he worked at. So far it was working.

"Don't you think you've had enough?" he asked, pouring her yet another new glass. Sam looked great in his tight black work t-shirt, his long beautiful hair flowing free around his shoulders. His eyes were serious, mouth tense with concern.

"Nope." She sipped the liquid again, sighing at the burning sensation.

"When I invited you to hang out I didn't realise you would drink like a fish." He eyed her almost empty glass once more.

"You said I should drink and have fun."

"Yes, *have* fun. Baby girl, your face says anything but." He twirled a finger around a curl of her hair. "You look stunning yet you haven't even stepped on the dance floor."

"I'm taking my time," she pouted.

She had enjoyed getting dressed in the dark red satin midi dress she bought years ago but had never worn, matched with the same shade lipstick. She just wasn't yet ready to immerse herself with the other dancers, pretty dress or not.

"You're sulking." He pulled away her glass, folding his arms across his chest.

"Am not." She knew she sounded like a child, but her deliciously fuzzy brain didn't care. "Why aren't you doing bartender-y things?"

"'Bartender-y' things? Bloody hell, I think you need to stop drinking."

"Just one more?" She smiled cheekily. She wasn't sulking, she was thinking, two entirely different things.

He just stared at her.

"There's plenty more bartenders."

"We shall see," he sighed, handing her drink back. "What are you going to do about the contract?"

"I can't just drop it. I've learnt more in the last few days than I have my entire life."

"Did you really want to know though?"

"What do you mean?"

"Like, does it make it any easier? Knowing?" He waved as someone shouted for his attention.

Alice hesitated. "I don't know." She downed the last of her drink. "Sam I don't know what to do."

"You should stay away from anything that involves the D word."

That made her chuckle. "We both know I don't get any."

"Aye, very funny. You know what I mean." He leant

forward on his elbow, half climbing onto the shiny black worktop as he whispered above the music. "Daemons."

"Yes." Things really did go bump in the night, she would know. "It's busy in here." She changed the subject.

"Yeah, since the new management it's been hectic." He squinted down the bar, someone as called for him once again. "Babe, I have to go serve, you just going to hang here?"

"For a while longer." His look of concern didn't change. "Then I'm going to go dance."

"Good, go enjoy yourself." He kissed her cheek. "Last one." He stole her cup and replaced it with a tall glass that was orange juice mixed with cranberry. "Sex on the beach." With a wink he walked towards the throngs of people at the other side of the bar, his sway in full swing.

Sam had worked in the Blood Bar for a few years, always enjoying the social life that came with being a bartender. He was right with the new management making the place busier, changing the old generic bar into something more stylish and modern. Gone were the cheap seating and sticky floors, replaced with high-end leather stools with chrome detailing and shiny wooden flooring. A stage was newly built from the same dark wood, designed as if it just erupted from the floor.

Blood Bar was notorious for its blood infused cocktails that brought in mainly Vamp clientele, but never really catered to anyone else. The new menu kept to its original taste from where the bar got its name, plus it included a wider range of beverages tailored to almost every Breed.

It was definitely a pleasant place to sit and contemplate her interesting life. Well, at least decide what her next step would be. She needed to know more, as if the more she knew the more she could unlock her memories, unlock her nightmares.

Flaring her chi she gave a satisfied sigh, feeling the usual electric undercurrent from the room. Over the last few hours she had felt her magic restore back to its natural level, like a bottle slowly refilling. Content, she continued to drink her cocktail as she enjoyed the music coming from the beautiful tenor of the singer on the small stage. The band behind filling the room with a steady beat that had most of the bar on their feet dancing.

Something brushed across her chi.

"Maybe you should stop drinking," a husky voice said next to her.

Ready to turn around and tell the person where to shove it, she hesitated, blinking stupidly at the tall man leaning against the bar. His chi continued to stroke hers as his steel grey eyes appraised her face. She had never felt anything like it, sparkles teasing across her aura. She couldn't decide if she liked it or not.

"Excuse me?" she asked, staring at him as she quickly adjusted her own chi. "I didn't realise you were my keeper."

The man smiled, a slight curve of his lips at her comment. He folded his heavily tattooed arms over his chest, a black shirt showing the bars logo across his left pec.

He must work here.

"Maybe you should mind your own business?" She searched desperately along the bar for Sam.

The man chuckled darkly, unfolding his arms from his chest. "Come on sweetheart, you need to go home."

"I'm good here thanks." She knocked the bar for emphasis. That got her another chuckle. "Go play with those lovely ladies over there..." She pointed in a vague direction behind her. "They seem to want your attention."

He followed her finger, frowning when he noticed the group of women staring at him, his eyes narrowing before he looked back at her, his face serious, the flirtatious arrogance gone.

She slipped off the stool, stumbling on her heels before his arm snapped out, steadying her.

"Oh, thanks." His hand didn't move off hers, his skin radiating heat. She tapped his hand, failing to not stare at his tattoos. "I'm not drunk." She could even dictate the alphabet backwards. Probably.

"That's not what a drunk person would say at all." He released her arm.

"Crap." He had her there. "Well, I'm going to dance." She turned and stumbled again, barely catching herself on the bar. So she may have had a few more drinks than she initially thought.

Fighting a blush, she pretended nothing happened and straightened, yanking her skirt back down to an appropriate height. With a nod she walked unsteadily towards the dancing crowd, the musician now singing a heavy ballad.

Letting the music take over she felt herself start to sway, her arms rising in the air with her eyes closed. The beat changed and she altered her moved to match, her hips curling in tempo with the rhythm. She allowed the music to calm her inner turmoil.

Arms wrap around her from behind, a body pasting itself against her back as she danced. His hips moved in rhythm with hers before a hand came round to her stomach, controlling.

His breath against her ear. "What the bloody hell do you think you're doing?" Rex asked.

She knew who it was almost the instant she felt his presence. Twisting her hips she danced against him, feeling his breath hitch, his palm tightening against her stomach.

"I'm having fun." She tried to turn in his grip but he kept her back pressed against his front, his own hips continuing their dance. "Rex, let me turn."

He bent her head slightly instead, his nose pressed against the side of her throat before she finally twisted in his arms, enough to see his white shirt, blood dried into the collar.

"You're drunk." His hands travelled down to hold the bottom of her back, pressing gently.

"I'm an adult." She continued to dance, allowing the music to move her muscles against him. She thought he would tense up, retreat into his intensity as he had done every time before, but he surprised her, instead matching her rhythm with his own.

"You don't think I know that?" he growled. That statement stopped her short, making her gaze up into his eyes. They were electric, clear as anything yet, just as unreadable, as if he didn't understand himself either.

"Why are you here?" she asked, not trusting her own eyes. "How did you find me?"

He pulled her toward him, placing her hands on his shoulders so he could bend down to her ear. "I'm here to ask why *my* Paladin is here getting drunk."

"I *am not* drunk!" She laughed loud enough to disturb the other dancers. "Am I seriously not allowed to enjoy myself without being judged by people?" She clenched her fists. "Haven't you heard? I'm off the case."

"I know." His fingers dug into her back, his voice intimate against her skin. "You think I take orders from anyone?"

She stopped dancing. "What are you saying?"

"I already said you're my Paladin." His eyes traced her lips, their natural blue flashing pale.

She gasped, finally able to read his emotions.

Hunger.

Lust.

The raw openness should shock her, but didn't.

"Why don't you ever smile?" She licked the edge of her suddenly dry lips, his eyes following the action carefully.

"I smile."

"Not at me."

"You just don't see it." She felt his heat against her as he pushed into her personal space. "I have never quite met a female like you." His mouth came down to slant across her own, tongue pushing unapologetically between her lips. She felt the roughness of his kiss, the raw emotions leaking as he gave into his wilder nature, breaking free from his constant control. She pulled his head against her, moaning as she lets him devour her lips.

Her front door was barely closed before Rex was on her, his hands under her dress to lift her up against the hard wall. His freshly shaven skin brushed across her cheek, his tongue licking, teasing along her tongue. She knew in the back of her head it was wrong, but apparently her body didn't care.

She clawed at his shirt, buttons popping in every direction as she pulled it apart to stroke her nails across his chest. He growled into her mouth, his hand boldly pressing against her breast before he pinched a nipple through the thin material of her dress. Her brain short-circuited, arousal heating her up from the inside out as liquid heat grew between her legs.

"Bed?" Rex growled, kissing her again.

Alice just nodded against his mouth, her lungs fighting for air. Lifting her up he carried her into her bedroom, throwing her on the bed as soon as he entered. She bounced in the middle, her hands scrambling against the duvet for support. Rex looked intently down at her, his face hard to read.

Nerves burst through her arousal, confusion. "Wait..." She couldn't finish, her eyes widening when he reached beneath his shirt, pulling it over his head in one sweep. Mouth dry Alice stared at his gorgeous wide chest, over his chiselled abs down the line of thin hair leading into his dress trousers.

He was on her in the next instant, his mouth on hers as his hands roamed under her dress, his touch an amazing contrast to her sensitive flesh. Lifting her dress he pulled it over her head, wrapping the fabric around her wrists, pinning them above her head.

"Rex?" she breathed, feeling vulnerable. It was going too fast...

He kissed down her neck, her wrists still pinned above her head, pushing her breasts together seductively. His tongue licked around her nipple, blowing against the wetness. Alice let out a small noise, almost a sob as he bit down on the sensitive nub, tugging it between his teeth. She pushed at his wrist, writhing underneath him.

Fuck!

The dress burst into flames, the threads burning into smithereens within seconds.

"Shit." He released her.

She hooked her leg around, pushing against his shoulder as he stared confused at the remains of the fabric. The sudden distraction gave her a sudden advantage, flipping them so she was straddling him, his erection continuing to strain. He just sat back up, biting down on the neglected nipple.

"Oh," she sighed, her voice low, husky with arousal.

With a snarl he twisted them, gaining dominance once again. Undulating on the bed she rubbed her thighs together in anticipation, excitement running over her. She had never felt like this, never wanted something so much.

A quick flick of a claw and he cut the edges of her underwear, tearing it clean from her hips in one clean motion.

"That was my favourite pair," Alice moaned up to him, his face expressionless, his eyes too intense as he gripped her, pulling her down the bed.

"No talking." He released her for a second, removing his trousers in a quick movement before his hot body was once again over her. Reaching down, he slipped one finger inside her, teasing the moisture, checking her readiness. He brushed the pad of his thumb against the small bundle of nerves that begged for his attention.

"Yes," she almost begged. Lifting her knee he placed it over his shoulder, opening her to him. She felt the head nudge at her opening, just teasing the entrance. "REX!" she shouted, his cock impaling her seconds later.

Growling low in his throat he started to thrust, powerful movements that pushed her up the sheets. Gripping his arms she held herself in place, her nerve endings screaming at the onslaught. Suddenly pulling out he pushed her hip, tossing her onto her stomach. Lifting her back up on to her knees he thrust into her once more.

He gave her no time to get used to him before he started moving again. Pumping his cock in and out in powerful thrusts. Alice braced herself, taking every inch of him. He grunted as he pumped, reaching below to rub her bundle of nerves, flicking his finger over it in time with his thrusts. Feeling the tell-tale signs of her tightening around him he pumped impossibly faster, spilling himself into her as she moaned his name.

Sneaking a peak she opened the cupboard slowly, seeing nothing through the small gap. The door swung open violently, a shadow standing over the opening. "Come here, little girl," the shadow snarled.

She screamed as a hand grabbed her ankle, pulling her from her safe place. Her head hit the floor with a crack, creating bursts of light behind her eyes.

"You trying to hide from me, little girl?"

With a squeal, she pulled from the stranger's grasp, the warm liquid lubricant against the strong hand. In a rush she threw herself against the back door, the wood groaning from the impact. In her panic she stumbled with the doorknob, turning it at the right angle. The door opened a sliver, catching on the security chain.

She squeezed through the small gap as suddenly a hand snaked out, grabbing her nightgown.

"Got you," the voice growled, the shadow's eyes glowing red in the darkness.

CHAPTER 15

After what felt like forever, Alice finally pulled into a parking space in the busy high street, her car choking as it settled.

She had woken up with a silent scream, her pulse racing as the remnants of her nightmare faded. The dread had felt so real, so vivid compared to usual. Realisation of what the creature was, the shadow making her subconscious go wild.

Yet, the nightmares were still in faded puzzle pieces, repeats of the same story, over and over with no context.

She hit her hand on the steering wheel in frustration.

What was worse was she had woken up alone.

From the absence of heat on the other side of the bed, she had been alone for a while.

Stupid. Stupid. Stupid. She hit the steering wheel again, calming herself.

She had never expected she would end up in bed with Rex, he just happened to be at the right time and place. Yet she felt hurt, embarrassed that she woke up alone in bed after everything that happened.

A dirty secret.

Her body ached, muscles that were rarely used protesting as she shifted in her seat. He had been rough, she had wanted it that way, but could she forgive him for using her and then leaving? No note. Just an empty, cold place beside her in bed?

"I used him too," she admitted to herself. Which was true, she wanted to be able to feel something, wanted someone to make her feel alive. Wanted something constant as her life seemed to be derailing around her.

With a sigh she flipped down the mirror, tilting her neck up into the light.

He had to bite me, didn't he? she cursed him.

She had used the last of her potion to create that amulet, so the red sore on the side of her neck, just above her shoulder blade wouldn't stand out in stark contrast to her pale skin.

Annoyed at Rex she jumped out of the car, the door swinging shut leaving her standing in the busy high street. Someone nudged her, causing her to step straight into a puddle.

"Hey lady, move out the fucking way," a young man shouted as he continued his fast pace further up the high street, shopping bags swinging violently by his side.

She replied automatically with a hand gesture as she moved towards the magic shop, deciding that from now on she would be nothing less than professional.

But first, she needed to hide the bite.

The black washed out 'Mystic Medlock's Magic Shop' sign hung from the old wall, squeaking as it flapped gently in the breeze. The outside of the shop had two large glass pane windows, one side advertising novelty magic tricks for the Norms, and the other showing around three different sized chests with drawers Alice knew to be filled with different amulets and herbs. She walked past the large stone gargoyle that guarded the entrance and into the deserted shop.

The shop was empty other than a bored looking man in a blue apron, who leant against the wall. His algae green eyes lit up as he noticed her enter, his back straightening and his hands patting down his front.

"Welcome," he greeted, smiling with his teeth. He gave a slight flare of his chi before retreating back behind the counter.

"Hello," she smiled back.

The shop was decorated with novelty witch hats and pumpkins that grinned with sharp teeth. A fat black cat sat in the corner, licking its paw lazily, not even looking up to see who entered. A display unit had been moved recently from the scratches on the floor, to be replaced with a cardboard box holding different Hallows Eve cards.

"Isn't it a bit early to be selling Samhain decorations?" The week long festivities were over a month away, the twenty-fifth to the thirty-first of October a huge Breed event where most of the world partied for a week straight in celebration of Breed becoming recognised citizens over three hundred years ago.

"You can blame the card companies. They try to squeeze as much money as they can out of the holidays," the clerk chuckled.

He was just shy of six feet tall with short lank brown hair, his face was pale and Alice noticed faint freckles spotted across his high cheekbones. His mouth was full, turned up at the corners as his green eyes glittered underneath the artificial light. He obviously thought he was hilarious.

"Anything I can help you with?" he asked politely.

"I need a concealer charm, I seem to have run out." She watched as he moved around the shop, opening drawers and looking in cabinets. "Er, are you new here?" she squinted at him.

"Not exactly." His eyes flashed slightly. "My father owns the shop and he needed someone to help out, so I came back home." He shrugged as if it was no big deal.

"Oh, Mr Medlock?"

"Yes, you know him?"

"I do." Alice smiled, having known the old man for years. He was always complaining the bigger chains were going to put him out of business, yet Alice couldn't shop anywhere else. "How is he?"

"He's fine, thinking about retiring." The man continued to search absently for the charms. It was clear he had no idea where he was looking. With a chuckle she walked towards the south wall, opening a drawer clearly marked 'cosmetic charms' and grabbing one of the small cylindrical disks.

The cat in the corner hissed at something before jumping to the floor, slowly hobbling to Alice's feet to look up at her with large yellow eyes. Letting out a yowl the cat waddled past, passing through the beaded curtain into the back.

"He can't retire, he knows everything." She smiled when the man finally turned, holding the disk gently between her fingertips so he could see.

The man grinned back. "Trust me, he doesn't know everything." He coughed, clearing his throat. "The name's Alistair, but my friends call me Al." He held out his hand.

"Alice." She brushed her own hand across his before handing over the disk.

"So where have you been hiding? I wasn't even aware Mr Medlock had a son."

"I've been studying abroad, just finished my degree when my father called asking for me to help out in the shop." He started to ring up her purchase on an old vintage looking cash register. Each button released a loud ping noise, the vibrations gently echoing against the various glass displays set behind.

"What did you study?" She found herself asking, suddenly interested.

"Engineering."

"Engineering?" She noticed the scraps of metal and screws on the desk.

"Yes, The mechanics of magic in machinery. It sounded cool at the time," he smiled gently, almost shy. "Working here has given me some time to play around with some ideas. The shop isn't as busy as I remember it."

"Yeah, the new chain came in down the street..."

"Ah yes, my father is always standing outside shaking his fist at them. Like it would help." Wrapping up the charm he handed it back over, the price flashing up.

Swallowing, she handed over the correct money, wondering if she gave the receipt to the expenses team she could claim it back. She was sure she could make up a decent excuse for why she needed the particular charm.

"Thank you."

"You're welcome. It's one my father made personally so I know it will definitely cover up that nasty bite on your neck. You need to find a boyfriend who doesn't treat you like food."

Alice's hand automatically covered the mark, her cheeks heating in embarrassment. "He's not my boyfriend," she replied before quickly shutting her mouth. Like that didn't make her sound worse.

"Then things just got a lot more interesting." Al leant across the desk, accidentally brushing some metal and screws onto the floor. "Shit!"

A loud buzz filled the shop before a whirling sound dashed across the floor. Alice stepped out of the way as a small circular black contraption began greedily sucking up the debris through a nose at the front. It was the size of a small plate and resembled a strange elephant. The back looked broken, or maybe even unfinished as she could see all the mechanics working inside its open shell, like a clock. The metal and screws it was trying to clean up kept shooting out its back onto the floor behind it, making it turn to collect them again and again.

"What is that?" She watched in awe, never having seen anything like it.

"Shit, shit, shit." Al scrambled to catch it as it whirled around his feet, happily chatting away to itself. "SIM STOP!" he shouted at the metal thing. The mechanical elephant halted, twirling to face Al almost expectantly. "SIM, off," Al declared in clear words before leaning down and picking it up.

"Well, that's curious."

"This is SIM, Suck. It. Mechanics. It's a working name." He hugged SIM to his chest, scowling down at it.

"Well, your degree just got a whole lot more interesting." She clutched her purchase. "I have to go to work, good luck with SIM."

She smiled to herself as she left the store, listening to the fading sound of Al scolding the mechanical elephant hoover.

Having already applied the charm, the small wooden disk hidden beneath her bracelet, Alice felt herself finally begin to relax as she sat down in her small workspace. Each cubicle was made up of three grey felt walls with a desk, every single one identical in their uniformity. It was up to the owners of the desks to personalise their small little space, and that is exactly what Alice had done.

Her desk, just like the others, was a pale wood with two drawers on each side. Mostly filled with pens and notepads, normal stationery things you would expect from a desk. A computer sat on the right corner, still turned on from the last time she had sat there with nothing to do, her game of solitaire patiently waiting for her to finish.

The grey walls had various pictures pinned to the felt, photographs of Sam, old contracts as well as her Chinese knock-off cat clock. Sam liked to buy her things that had a cat theme, her newest addition was a poster with a sleeping cat curled on the front, and the words *'Don't talk to me'* printed underneath.

She closed the solitaire game that always popped up when she turned on the computer and clicked open her emails. "Why am I getting emails about Viagra?" she muttered to herself, clicking through the various correspondences about penis extensions, amazing weight loss pills and badly written pleas from princes asking for help to move their millions. "Aha." She finally opened the email she was looking for.

Alice,

Considering you discharged yourself at the hospital before I

could come visit I'm going to assume you are okay. Which is
good but don't do something like that again.
I have attached my notes regarding the reports in the last
year, most are a waste of time but a few should be of
interest.

I have managed to stay on the case and will be liaising with
the Paladin in charge, Danton, so you will see me more in
The Tower. I will try to give you any more information I
come across.
Don't get caught.

Kind regards,
Miko
P.S. Feel free to give me Dr Richards number.

Alice smiled at the email. Only Miko would turn something this important into something he could get a date from.

Actually, she corrected, Sam would probably do the same. Her mood lifted as she opened the attachment and clicked print, hearing the printer roar to life a few cubicles over.

Notes-
John Doe – Unknown
• Elongated canines, blood found in the stomach. Scratch
marks across the torso. Skull deformed, bone protruding
through skin on top of the head.
John Doe – Unknown shifter
• Elongated canines, blood found in the stomach. Shifter
DNA doesn't match blood in the stomach
Maxi L. Swanson - Unknown

• *Elongated canines, blood found in the back of throat. Self-inflicted wounds.*

John Doe - Unknown shifter

• *Elongated canines, blood found in the stomach. Scratch marks across the torso. Shifter DNA*

Sahari Mooner – Unknown

• *All teeth have been forcibly removed. Blood found in the stomach and back of the throat*

Jane Doe – Human

• *Bruises on the wrists and ankles. Sticky residue around the mouth (Awaiting analysis). Broken teeth. Blood found in the back of the throat*

Mischa Palmer - Unknown shifter

• *Elongated canines, blood found in the stomach. Skull cracked*

Rachel Langly - Fae

• *Teeth completely deformed, blood found in the stomach. Nails torn from the fingertips.*

Francis Carter – Lion shifter

• *Teeth deformed, DNA came back with unusual strains.*

Alesha Morgan – Human

• *Paper ripped – No formal information*

Bobby Dust – Hyena shifter

• *Head had been cut clean off*

Tomlin (Surname unknown) – Wolf shifter

• *Purposely killed?*

Reading the notes she typed the names into the S.I. database, the screen flashing between pages, the police directory searching through hundreds of thousands of records. If any of these people had had any trouble with the police, even just a parking ticket a record should flash up.

Sitting back she closed her eyes, the screen flashing

through the pages too fast for her to read. Relaxing into the chair she thought back to the hospital, running all the conversations through her head over and over again. She hadn't exactly lied to the doctor, she just hadn't told the whole truth. It was only once that she had ever lost control to the point her own power had almost consumed her, but it wasn't uncommon for her to lose a little bit of control. Her annoying dancing ball of flame was proof of that.

An audible beep made her jump, knocking her cup of tea onto the floor with a crash. "Shit." She quickly picked up the cracked cup and placed it back on her worktop, using a tissue to dab at the spill. The computer beeped again, waiting for attention. Using the mouse she navigated through all the information.

Rachel Langly – Water Fae (Siren) – Reported missing 1974 – Arrested on 15th May 2016. Fraud.

Francis Carter – Shifter (Lion) – Sun Kiss Pride – Arrested on 27th July 2016. Possession of Class A drugs and charms.

Bobby Dust – NO RECORD.

Maxi L. Swanson – Reported missing 1999 – DUI 1987.

Sahari Mooner – Reported missing 2010.

Mischa Palmer – NO RECORD.

Alesha Morgan – Human – Arrested on January 10th 2015. Theft.

Rachel Langly was a beautiful woman, at six foot one

she was all long legs, her red hair emphasizing her luscious lips and sharp cheekbones. She definitely looked like an epiphany of a male wet dream, a siren in every sense of the word.

Her supermodel looks showed just how easy it would be to sing men to their deaths at sea, just looking at her most men would bow at her feet. Even in the police mug shot she had a sensuality about her, her luscious lips tilting up at the corner, her eyes rimmed in black.

'No known family'

"Great." She clicked through the pictures, cringing. It was nice to know that when sirens died, the charms they used to survive on land disintegrated. Her long beautiful legs melted together like wax, pearlescent scales growing from her webbed feet up to her navel. Her neck developed gills, and her eyes became inhumanly large.

Alice closed the tab and returned her attention to the list. Using a pencil she crossed out Miss Langly's name, the pencil cutting through the paper from frustration.

"Fuck, Fuck, Fuck," she chanted to herself, rubbing her palms across her face.

She looked up from between her fingers, a photograph of a blonde male staring back. Alice clicked on Mr Francis Carter's photograph, enlarging the details. The dark chocolate eyes were void of any emotion, his emaciated cheeks stark against his natural tan.

"Francis Carter. Sun Kiss Pride, Lion Shifter... where is Sun Kiss?" Alice minimised the page, intending to search for local prides.

"What the fuck?" The computer cut out, the screen flashing before showing the login screen.

Error. Log in details incorrect. You have been blocked. See helpdesk for more information.

"Seriously?" Alice huffed.

This can't be happening.

She scribbled down Francis Carter's name and she tucked the paper into her jeans pocket. The I.T. guys were only a few floors down so she decided to take the stairs.

"Hello?" She knocked on the door leading to where the I.T. technicians work. Alice tried to fight a smile at the poster on the door, a giant A2 print of *'I.T. GUYS. HAVE YOU TURNED IT ON AND OFF AGAIN?'* written in bold typography.

"Hello?" She knocked louder, knowing someone would have to be in.

"It's open."

"Oh." Alice pushed the door, stepping over the threshold into what looked like a spaceship. Computer monitors were arranged around the large room, each screen showing something different. A half built computer tower sat in the middle of the room, bright wires attempting to escape.

"Hey, Alice." Lewis, one of the I.T. guys swung his chair around to give her a little wave. Crisps layered in his incredibly long beard, long enough that it covered most of his bright green t-shirt.

"You on the late shift, Lewis?" Alice asked, closing the door behind her gently.

"Yeah, me and Billy. He's gone to go get us some more crisps." He lifted up the empty crisp packet, even tipping it upside down just to emphasise how empty the packet was. "What can I do to help you doll? I don't normally see you down here."

"It's not letting me log in. Just keeps giving me an error message."

"Ah okay, let's take a look shall we." He spun his chair

to face one of the monitors, his chubby fingers racing across the keys as he typed something into the computer. "It looks like you have been locked out."

"Locked out?" She leant over to look at the screen. "How can I be locked out?"

"Looks like..." He clicked some more buttons. "Commissioner Grayson has put you on medical leave. Look." He pointed to her picture on the screen, the one every member of the building had for security. Her picture was easy to spot, her blonde messy hair bright compared to the darker tones of her colleagues. It hadn't helped she wasn't aware it was picture day, so she had the previous night's makeup smudged across her face. They wouldn't let her retake it.

The words *'Medical leave until further notice'* flashed across the bottom of the picture.

"Shit. Is that why I can't access any systems?"

"Pretty much.," He read the small print. "Top restrictions too." He shrugged his shoulders, the motion causing some crisps to escape from his beard and land on his stomach.

"Okay." *Crap.* "Can you reverse it?"

"Not without risking my job."

"Fair enough." She lifted her hand to her face, wiping across her eyes. *Shit.*

"I might not be able to reinstate your restrictions, but..." he beamed at her. "I don't have such restriction."

"You sure you won't get into trouble?" she said hesitantly.

"I owe you. You helped me catch my cheating wife, if it wasn't for you, I would still be with the bitch. What do you need?"

"Thanks Lewis, you're a star," she grinned, grabbing the notes from her pocket.

CHAPTER 16

T*his was a stupid idea*, Alice thought to herself as she sat in her car outside a large derelict house, scowling at the crumpled map in her lap. Squinting her eyes, she double checked the roads that were supposed to lead to Sun Kiss Pride.

"This can't be right?"

The large Georgian house was set back in a few acres of land, the pale bricks crumbling. Green and brown ivy hugged the walls, hiding most of the damage. The surrounding trees and bushes were a spectrum of the same dire shades, a mixture of browns, reds and yellows, summer pushing into autumn. There were two large windows at the front of the house, all covered by heavy dark brocade curtains, an uncomfortable contrast to the dirty white of the window frames.

Black smoke darkened the sky above signalling someone was home, yet the drive was empty of all other vehicles but her own, which was parked slightly behind a large over-grown bush.

A shrill ring made her jump in her seat. Scrambling for her phone she checked the number before answering.

"Hello, you have reached the mobile of Alice, please leave a message after the..."

"Alice, you're not funny."

"Hi, Sam." She heard his small laugh at the end of the line.

"Why are you in Little Birmingham?" His voice took on a serious tone.

"Well, to be honest I'm currently staring at a house." She had actually been staring at the house for a while, waiting to see if anyone moved behind one of the windows. So far nothing. "Wait, how did you know where I was?" She sat up from her slouch, frowning at the phone.

"Rex turned up and..."

"Rex? What's he doing there?"

"He... Rex... turn..." he began, voice breaking up.

"Hello? Sam? I think I'm losing you."

"Sorry about that," he said, voice strained.

"Just tell him I'm checking out this house, it's supposed to be the pride's den. But, I'm pretty sure Google lied."

Something moved in her peripheral vision, a twitch in the curtain. She watched carefully, waiting for it to move again. When it didn't she released a breath she didn't know she was holding.

"Pride?" a slightly deeper voice said, ending with a snarl, *"what the fuck do you think you're doing?"*

Alice could hear Sam arguing in the background, the microphone unable to pick up his exact words. "Why are you with Sam?" She felt her face scowl. "Put Sam back on."

He ignored her request. *"You were supposed to ring."*

For a man that was emotionless, he sounded pissed.

"Well if you were there when I woke up I could have

173

told you then couldn't I?" Okay, she was only a little bit sour.

"*Sun Kiss Pride?*" A growl. "*Don't do anything stupid and wait for me. You shouldn't have gone there alone.*"

"I'm not stupid Rex, I have thought this through." She hadn't, but she wasn't going to admit that. "I was only going to ask a few questions."

"*Wait for me. I'm leaving now, I'll be there in three hours.*" He would have to make up some serious speed to get to Little Birmingham in three hours. "How did you even know where I was?"

"*Just wait.*"

"Rex I don't need your help."

Another snarl. "*Wait.*" He wasn't giving her much choice. "*Meet you at Manor Green Park.*" He gave her the directions and once she confirmed she understood he hung up without a goodbye.

"Arsehole," she scolded the phone before throwing it onto the seat beside her. Laying the map back over her lap she checked where the park was, happy to see it was only a short drive away. Car in gear, she took one last look at the house. It probably wasn't the right place anyway.

Alice watched an old man walk painfully slow across the path towards the ducks, stale bread clutched under his free arm, the strong breeze doing nothing to stop his journey. Cold, Alice pulled her jacket around her tighter as she looked around the park, enjoying the sun's warmth between the gusts of wind. A group of shifter and human children were running around the grassy area, kicking a black and white football around. A shout as the ball went wide, heading towards the flock of ducks sitting by the pond. With a loud squawk the birds fluttered away, landing further up the pond and away from the children's ball.

The old man stopped his walk, puffing. With determination, he set off again towards the other side, back towards the ducks.

Alice smiled despite herself.

She'd been sitting for long enough for her arse to go numb. She had already walked around the park several times, resigning herself to just sitting and watching. It didn't help that anger still bubbled, not being able to let the conversation with Rex go. She was getting grumpy.

Flicking her phone on she scrolled to Sam's number, hitting the video call.

"Alice, I can't talk now." Sam lifted his phone to reveal half his face. *"I'm still at work."* She could just see the collar of his work t-shirt, his hair in his usual plaits.

"I want to know what happened with Rex? How did he know where I was?"

"He just turned up here," Sam propped the phone up on something, the angle revealing the top half of his torso. *"Had to get him kicked out by the bouncers..."*

"Sam, what is that on your face?" Alice tried to zoom in on the image. "Is that a bruise?"

Sam touched his cheekbone, brushing across the purple mark that was already healing, would be completely gone by tomorrow.

"It's nothing." He buffed a glass before placing it onto a shelf. *"What do you even see in Rex?"* He tossed the rag onto his shoulder. *"He's getting a bit territorial."*

"No, he's not." Alice quieted her voice as someone sat beside her. "It's nothing."

"*He's an Alpha...*"

"We're just working together."

"*Sure, baby girl.*" A sphinx smile. "*Don't ya think it's strange? The way you were hired for the job?*"

She hadn't given it much thought. He had lost three wolves, and had been hunting alone before he hired her. So what made him change his mind?

"*Look, I'm getting off in an hour, we'll talk then.*" A yawn, eyes sleepy as he bent to his phone. "*Love ya baby girl.*"

"Wait, Sam..." The phone went dark. "Dammit." Unable to sit any longer she started to walk the length of the park once more, heading towards the iron wrought bridge.

"Salve dominam," a voice gurgled as soon as she stepped onto the first step.

Startled, Alice searched around for the owner of the voice, seeing no one close enough to have spoken.

"Lonii pro troll?" the voice gargled once again.

"Toll for the troll?" she repeated in English, her Latin rusty. She still knew some basic words, Latin a language taught to all children, especially as it was used in spell-work as well as being favoured amongst the older Fae.

"Oh yes mistress, toll for the troll." Long black finger-nails burst through the green sludge on the wall on the underside of the bridge. It grasped the sides, pulling the rest of its body through the small hole with a wet noise. Rust from the metal moulded itself into the sludge, hardening to become scaly skin as small black ovals popped out of the top, eyes staring. Trolls were the only Fae that iron didn't affect, indeed an annoyance to the High Lords of each caste considering they were classed as the lowest of the Fae possible.

Alice stepped off the bridge, making sure she stood in direct sunlight. "Why should I pay the toll when I haven't crossed your bridge?"

"Silly malefica, you always pay Muck."

"Muck?"

"Muck myself." He leant over an arm, bowing towards her. Well, as much as a bow as a creature with no bones could do.

"Hello, Muck, nice bridge you have." The troll slurped in response. "I don't plan to cross your bridge, but I'll pay the toll if you answer some questions for me?"

"Questions?" His black eyes squinted in confusion.

Great. An intellectually challenged troll. "Questions as in...erm, interrogo?"

The troll smiled, showing a row of pointy nails along his jaw. His green skin swirled, melding into a calmer blue before hardening again. "Ask away mistress."

"Erm, okay." She tugged her jacket in thought. "Who are the local shifters?"

"Bestia leo."

"Lions?"

"Yes." Muck grinned even further, enjoying the game.

"Any other local bestias?"

"No local." He paused for a moment, thinking. "Visitors." He shook his head, sludge slopping across the floor. One bit reached her boot, the sludge sizzling before hardening in the sunlight. As subtle as possible she tried to dislodge it, but it was impossible.

"What sort of visitors?"

Muck smiled, showing even more teeth. "Toll." He held out his hand, stretching as far as possible without coming into direct sunlight. Alice removed one of her gold stud earrings, trying not to touch his skin as she dropped the gold into his hand. "Gratias mistress."

"You shouldn't be talking to the bridge dweller," a new voice said from behind.

Alice turned, watching the painfully thin man approach.

"They will tell you anything for some gold." The stranger stood a few feet away, his dirty blonde hair scruffy, his long stubble a shade darker.

"HSSSSSSSS LEO." Muck spat towards the man, the sludge barely reaching him as he gave a garbled growl. "Nec leo." Muck braced his arms on the iron, sludge splitting into two legs as he absorbed the surrounding water, gaining mass.

"Shit." Alice stepped back, not wanting to be anywhere near Muck when he reached his full size. "Muck, look at me." She waved her arms, trying to get his attention.

"Aut tu præterieris."

He wasn't listening.

"Muck, what visitors?" She tried again, but his attention was completely on the man walking towards them.

"I think you should step away from the..."

Alice grabbed the stranger's outstretched arm, twisting it behind his back.

"Owwww."

Alice knew the hold was painful, but it was hard to keep pressure with the height difference.

She slowly stood on her tiptoes, whispering into his ear. "I don't know who you are, but you shouldn't touch me." She put more weight on his bent elbow, getting her a hiss in return. With a last twist she released him, her eyes trained on his muscles, waiting to see if they tensed for an attack.

Muck made a thunderous noise, his skin becoming a sickly green, head and shoulders taking up almost the entire space underneath the small bridge. Without taking her eyes off the lion she reached to her other ear and removed her remaining earring, tossing it at him. It bounced off his hardened skin, landing in the sun. He would have to wait until dark to claim it.

"I don't think he likes you," she said to the tall man who held his arm protectively to his chest.

"No." A worried glance. "I'm Preston, from Sun Kiss. Coleman sent me."

"He did?" She felt her eyebrows rise, remembering from her research that Coleman Grant was the Pride Leader. *How did he even know I was here?*

A nod. "He's expecting you for dinner, if you would follow me I can take you..."

"How did you know who I was?" she interrupted.

"Mr Wild is at the manor..."

He couldn't possibly be calling the derelict house a manor? Surely she had the wrong place before.

"He told us you would be here." Preston looked at his watch. "We have to hurry, dinner will be ready soon and we can't be late." He shifted his eyes to look around the park, as if he was worried someone might overhear.

"That didn't answer my question," she pushed him. "How did you know who I was?"

"Mr Wild has a photograph of you in his wallet."

He does? Alice saved that information for later. "I'll follow you in my car."

"NO!" A panicked look. "Cole was specific, I have to drive."

"No thanks, I can drive myself." She folded her arms across her chest.

"Please let me drive you." The panic started to grow, his

eyes darting around as he licked his dry lips.

Guilt settled in her stomach. "What about a compromise? I'll drive, but you can come in the passenger seat?"

"I suppose... yes. That should be okay." Open relief on his face.

"Okay."

She guided him towards the car park, making sure he walked slightly in front.

Lions were predators. Everything about this man, from the scruffiness of his clothes to the gauntness of his face suggested he was more prey.

CHAPTER 17

"**N**ice house," Alice commented as she pulled into the same large driveway she was in earlier, the only difference was there were around six other cars along its edge. Car parked at the end she stepped out onto the stones, glancing up at the neglected house. It was just as bad as it was earlier, the darker sky not hiding any of the damages.

Preston said nothing as he walked slowly towards the front of the house, or manor as he laughingly described it. The loose stones crunched beneath her shoes as she paused next to him, trying not to stare at the huge claw marks and cracks patterned along the inside of the columns. The large door opened at their approach, revealing a hollow cheeked young man dressed in a white shirt and slacks.

"Preston," the man greeted. His eyes roamed across her, taking in the black Chelsea boots, blue jeans and black t-shirt with 'Sorry I'm late, but I didn't want to be here' written across it. Fitting really.

Alice tried not to crack a smile, knowing she looked severely underdressed for a formal dinner.

He sniffed as if unimpressed. "We've been expecting you." He walked down the hallway, leaving the door open.

The walls, which she tried not to gawk at as she followed the man, weren't as bad as she would have guessed from the outside. The striped wallpaper looked freshly applied, albeit a bit badly and the paint was newly coated if she went by the strong smell.

"If you would wait in here," the nameless lion pointed into a room at the end of the hall. "My Pride Leader will join you shortly."

That wasn't weird at all, she thought as he left her alone.

"Miss Skye."

She froze in the doorway, fisting her hands.

Rex sat at the large table, watching her with pure focus. She held his gaze, letting him know from the tension of her shoulders that she was beyond angry. He had recently shaved, his skin smooth enough to caress. His light brown hair had been pulled into a bun, a few strands framing his face. She wasn't a fan of men with buns, yet she felt the strongest urge to stroke it, to paste her body against his like a dog in heat. She had never quite felt such a strange compulsion.

"Nice of you to join us." He stood, stalking towards her.

Alice allowed her nails to cut into her hand, the pain stopping her from pulling him against her. "Nice scratches." She stared at the trio of claw marks across his face, the wound already fading to a pale pink. "I wonder how you got them."

"You should have called me." He barked out the words like bullets, his hand coming up to her jaw.

She smacked the hand, breaking the connection. "Those scratches look like a cats."

"I'm impressed with your knowledge of cat scratches. Is that some sort of kink you're into?" a chuckle from the doorway.

"Careful Cole." A warning, Rex's jaw clenched as he fought for control. "She's mine."

"Well, isn't that interesting," Coleman murmured. He was an average looking guy, his blonde hair scraped back from his scalp, a rubber band holding the pale strands in a lank ponytail. His eyes were mean and narrow, constant frown lines indented into his forehead. His mouth a harsh line, hidden faintly behind his ginger beard. "You must be *his* Alice."

"Hmm, must be." She looked between the men, the tension palpable in the small room. They knew each other, and it wasn't friendly.

"You look fine to me." Cole leisurely checked her up and down, eyes glistening as he smiled at her shirt. "Not a mark on you. Those news stations are always exaggerating." He clicked his tongue.

"What does he mean?" Rex gripped her jaw once more, staring into her eyes.

She kept her face passive. "Nothing." Rex's eyes narrowed, he knew she was lying.

"Now, now children. No fighting, we are among friends." Cole clapped his hands and a group of men walked in as if called. They positioned themselves behind certain chairs, forcing Alice and Rex to split.

"Alice, take a seat." Cole motioned with his hand. "I saved this space for you, opposite me," he said with a toothy grin. She passed Rex as she sat in the seat Cole pulled out, tensing as he brushed his fingertips through her hair. "Such a pretty blonde. Like your mother's..." he whispered along her neck.

"Excuse me?" She whipped around to face him, his attention on the decanters on the bar.

"Boys," he proclaimed as he started to pour, the men sitting down in one fluid motion, practised in their precision.

She watched them carefully, knowing something was wrong, but unable to put her finger on it. They all sat there, all six of them, all different ages with no expression on their faces. No emotion in their eyes. It was like a blank canvas, a puppeteer pulling the strings. Their suits were all the same, almost uniform in their blandness, many of them too large for their small forms, cheekbones sharp against their skin.

Cole continued to meticulously pour a red liquid into a glass, repeating it several times as an uncomfortable silence filled the room. The lions were yet to react, all barely breathing as they stared blankly across the table. Moving slowly Cole handed one glass to Alice, his fingers lingering on her own before he went to Rex.

As if a spell was broken the young lions started to fidget, pulling at their lapels in panic. The three to her right started to squirm uncontrollably, their eyes mostly white as they frantically took in their surroundings.

"Hitting the alcohol already honey?" A woman strode in, her dramatic neckline leaving nothing to the imagination. She pouted, making her bright red lips, the same startling shade as her hair, look bigger, more sensual.

The atmosphere became thick, fear heavy as all the lions froze, becoming once again unmoving mannequins. The woman smiled seductively along the table, lingering slightly longer than she needed to on Rex before kissing Cole on the lips, leaving a red smear.

"This is my wife, Poliana." Cole smiled lovingly before helping her take a seat.

"Wife?" Rex raised his eyebrows. "Congratulations, I never knew. How long?"

"About a year," Poliana replied, her eyes slanted as she stroked the skin of the young man next to her, his face pale as he stayed completely still, his chest barely moving.

"Welcome pride members, new friends and old." Cole lifted one of the glasses up to the air, saluting the room. "I hope you enjoy your stay." He stared intently at Alice as he took a sip.

Picking up her own she brought it to her nose, a sour copper smell coming from the deep red liquid. She tensed, looking over at Rex as he sipped his own. He shook his head gently, almost imperceptibly as he placed his drink back down. Following suit she placed her hands beneath the table, careful not to get too close to the lion next to her.

Cole finally sat at the head of the table.

"So, please tell me. Why is the Alpha of White Dawn gracing my presence after all this time?" A slow smile. "Or better yet, why has he brought a Paladin into my home?"

She glanced away from the lion beside her, catching Cole's eye. His smile widened.

"She's a bit small for you isn't she?" He continued to openly glare at her, his eyes roaming across her face. "I get she has some curves, but she must break easily? Nothing like the women you used to have." With a tut he took another drink, sipping loudly on the rim.

Alice felt her face burn. "We're working together."

"Are you now, pretty lady?" A predator's smile, one showing his sharp teeth.

A bark of a sound. The man Poliana was caressing

doubled over in pain, his forehead touching the table, a choking noise escaping from this throat.

Cole looked over angry. "Lukas, calm down."

"Sorry, sire." The man known as Lukas continued to cough, shaking as he gained control.

"Where was I? Oh yes, Miss Alice Skye. I knew of a family in London with that name once. Shame what happened, don't suppose you know anything of it?" A smirk.

She remained silent.

"What? You're not even going to deny it?"

"You seem to be talking enough for the both of us," she bit back.

Cole's eyes narrowed, his hand crushing the glass enough to leave a crack. "Hmm. I can see why he has taken you to his bed."

"You sound so sure."

"Concealer charms might cover up the bite, but I am the lion equivalent of Rex. Our sense of smell is beyond your comprehension, even my lions can smell him on you."

"Cole," Rex growled a warning.

"Interesting," Cole chuckled. "I suppose that would be a conversation for you to have in private." He sipped from the broken glass, red liquid leaking through the small crack.

Alice tried for patience, her fingers digging into her knees as she failed. "This isn't about me..."

"Is it not?" His face was impassive, eyes bright. "You are nothing. I'm just reminding you that you're just a pawn in something bigger than all of us."

"Cole that is enough," Rex stated, his fist coming down hard on the table, making the cutlery rattle. "You know I wouldn't have come here if I didn't need to." His eyes were serious as he glared.

Cole stared back, no smile on his face. "Interesting how you have come back. After all this time." The intensity between the two shifters, the two leaders was electric.

The lions started to murmur, their attention not on the Pride Leader but on Poliana, the only other woman at the table.

Where are the other females? Alice eyed the lion next to her, his face twitching as she watched him, frowning. He was pretty, apart from the clear malnourishment. His face was perfectly symmetrical with the straightest nose she had ever seen. The other lions too, Alice had noticed, were all handsome men.

"Where are the women?" she asked him, studying his reaction intently.

He flinched, his eyes darting wildly. "I'm not supposed to talk to you," he whispered back, his voice surprisingly deep.

"Why not?" she asked in the same volume. He just swallowed and shook his head, his attention on the Pride Leaders wife. She tried to speak to the lion on her other side, but his eyes widened in alarm before he faced the wall, away from her.

A cough brought her attention back to Lukas, his chest rattling as he wheezed in and out. He looked scared, the whites of his eyes huge as he stared straight ahead. Poliana had moved closer to him, her hand stroking his thigh, her tongue licking lazily along the side of his ear. The wheezing noise continued, an uncomfortable screeching sound that hitched in intervals, his breathing shallow.

Alice glanced around the table, not one lion would look her in the eye, all either concentrating on their plates or on Lukas, their eyes full of pain.

There's something wrong. Alice couldn't figure it out,

but she just felt something in the air interfering with the lions, something she had never felt before.

Alice concentrated as her vision blurred, her third eye opening, allowing her to see perceptions beyond ordinary sight. Auras appeared in a burst of colour, a distinctive atmospheric film that surrounded any living being like a personal shield. What separated the humans from magic users was the ability to harness their aura, creating a chi.

The sounds in the room became a low hum, background noise as she focused on Rex and Cole who continued a conversation she could no longer hear.

Searching straight for Poliana she gasped, watching her aura swirl with a spectrum of colour Alice had never seen before. Most people have a dominant colour that is unique to them, with other colours spotted throughout to show sharp emotions. Poliana's was different. Hers was a burst of reds, oranges, yellows and greens that merged together in a beautiful concoction of colour.

Concentrating, Alice watched the hand Poliana stroked Lukas with, his aura an incredibly pale blue, almost transparent. Holes appeared wherever her hand touched, Lukas's aura becoming weaker, disappearing before her eyes. The blue colour whirled, crawling up Poliana's fingertips.

Alice sucked in a breath. She knew exactly what she was. A type of Fae whose sole purpose was to seduce men so they could feed. A Succubus.

Bloody Hell.

She was literally eating his aura, gaining sustenance by absorbing his life force. It must be why many of the lions were so malnourished and weak, she was slowly killing them.

Alice looked over the remaining lions, their auras just as damaged as Lukas's, holes floating across her vision, everyone except Cole. His aura was a dull grey, spotted with black but completely whole.

Letting her third eye slip she blinked the remnants of the sight away. Intense anger bubbled in her blood, her eyes flicking across the lions, now noticing the bruises, new and old marked across their flesh like sirens of abuse. Cole had destroyed his pride, turning the strong, proud predators into prey, food for his wife.

"They're dying," she said quietly. The lion next to her finally turned towards her, an odd expression on his face. "You're killing them," she said louder, loud enough that everyone on the table heard.

"Excuse me?" Cole stood up, his eyebrows creased together.

"She's killing them, absorbing their aura." Poliana started to giggle as if she was a small five-year-old child, and not a full grown woman. "Look at your lions. Can you not see?" Alice gripped the edge of the table, blue sparks coming from her fingertips in irritation. She paused, calming down, willing the fire back inside. "You are their Pride leader, you're allowing them to be hurt."

"They are only giving what they can. We are in the process of enrolling some new blood into the pride."

"Where are all the females?" she quickly asked.

"They don't need any females," Poliana finally spoke up. "Do we boys?" The lions murmured back in agreement.

"You're a witch, how could you possibly understand what it's like to be part of a pride? My wife completes us, fills the void against the members we have lost."

"So you have lost members?"

"Yes." Genuine emotion in his eyes. "My wife feeding on them is a small price to pay for the pride to feel complete again. Whole."

"You're killing them," Alice repeated matter-of-factly.

"No one has gone missing or died since she arrived." He laughed, his eyes fevered, excited. "No one can touch us."

Alice stood up, the back of her chair falling to the floor with a crash.

"Alice I think we should go." Rex moved quickly to stand behind her, growling at the lions next to her in warning. "There's nothing here."

"Why are you even here?" Cole questioned, ignoring Rex. "Poli is stable, together we have learnt to control her cravings."

"Your pride came up in the investigation I'm working on. A lion was found dead with an interesting amount of similarities to another body."

"Which one?"

Which one? Exactly how many were there?

"Francis Carter," she replied, noting the lions recoil.

"Francis." A hollow chuckle. "He didn't listen to any advice. Thought he could control his urges." His eyes glazed over in thought.

"Urges?"

"Drugs, women. To anything and everything he would become addicted. He thought he was invincible."

"What happened?"

"He thought he could beat the system." Cole's eyes stared off into nothing. "How could a stupid boy try to beat *them* when I couldn't do it myself?" He shook his head, eyes flashing yellow. "He was a fool, one who nearly destroyed the whole pride. Without Poli everyone could have succumbed to the same fate." He gazed over his lions like a father would his children.

"Who's them?" Alice pushed.

Cole ignored her, instead turning to glare at Rex.

"This has been a pleasant evening. I apologise we have to cut it short." Cole started to leave, pausing at the threshold. "I might not be in the circle anymore, but I know you are."

Rex's eyes flashed in warning.

"Stop delaying the inevitable. They are growing impatient." He tugged at his lapels. "Is it worth the risk?" With that he left, Poliana and the lions following him out in perfect synchronisation.

Alice stared after them, confused. "What the actual fuck?" Rex was emitting an intense heat against her back, as if she could feel his anger.

"We need to leave." Without checking to see if she followed, he made his way out the house. Alice stomped after him, her temper still blaring.

Her boots started to slide on the loose stones of the driveway as she followed him towards a large black Range Rover.

"Get in," he said without turning. Opening a side door he shrugged off his jacket, throwing it into the back. With a small thwack something fell out of his pocket, landing on the floor by his tyre.

"I have my own car." She bent down to pick up the brown square, realising it was a wallet as she stroked the worn leather.

"You need to come back to the motel," he said, his tone leaving no room for argument.

But Alice liked to argue. "I said I have my own car. I can drive myself home tonight." Besides, it wasn't late.

She clutched the wallet to her, staring down at it intently before she opened the flap. A photograph was pinned with a paperclip to the left fold, a photograph of herself from a side angle, as if someone took the photo without her knowing. Her blonde hair was in a high pony-tail, loose strands dancing around her flushed face as if she had just finished running. Her green eyes were looking off into the distance, a small private smile on her lips.

The photograph made her look delicate.

It made her feel uneasy.

Pulling the picture out she tried to take a closer look.

"Rex, why do you have a photo of..." she paused as she noticed another photo underneath, beneath the transparent plastic. Three men stood huddled together in the picture, Rex was on the left, the biggest grin as he smiled at the camera, his arm stretched behind two other men.

"Those are my brothers," Rex whispered, his voice full of an emotion Alice had never heard from him before. "That's Theo," he said pointing to the man furthest right. "He's my twin."

"Twin," she repeated back at him, only just realising the two men were identical. "And who's this?" She pointed to the younger man in the middle, their features similar, clearly brothers.

"And that," he pointed to the younger man in the middle. "Is Roman..." He took the wallet from her, staring at the picture for a few seconds before throwing it into the back of his car with his jacket.

"Roman? As in the wolf that's missing?" It all started to make sense. He slowly turned to face her, his eyes bright as the wolf prowled behind his irises, his emotions strong. "Why have you only just hired me?"

"What?"

"You've lost three wolves," Rex tried to hide his flinch. "And you've only just asked for outside help. Why?"

He stared at her for what felt like hours. "It's because I'm running out of time." With that he got in his car, closing the door behind him.

CHAPTER 18

They remained silent as Rex used the little key-card to open the motel door. According to Rex, who felt the need to apologise before even entering the building, it was the only place available in such a short time. Which didn't give her much confidence.

The room didn't look too awful in the dark, almost normal as Alice could just make out the bed in the back, the curtains drawn behind it. She flicked on the yellowing plastic light switch, waiting for something to happen. Nothing did. She flicked it a few more times, but it still didn't turn on, keeping the room gloomy. Instead, she pulled the curtain, allowing the harsh light of the street lamp outside to illuminate through the window.

"Wow," she said, appraising the room. "This is... nice." It wasn't.

Rex stayed by the door, his expression intense. The room was a typical motel room with a queen size bed and off-white linen. Taking a closer look Alice noticed the slight yellow rings, the stains being the result of years of sweat and other bodily fluids. She was definitely sleeping in all her clothes. Maybe even wrapped in a towel.

Lifting up the duvet sheet she pulled it off, relieved to notice the sheet underneath was clean. A sofa covered in a pink and blue paisley pattern sat in the corner of the room, opposite the old television that looked like it had seen better days, dust a fine layer across the screen.

The bathroom, which was right next to the front door, actually had a working light, even if it did flick on and off on its own accord. The porcelain tub with attached shower was an avocado green with a matching sink. There was even a large rectangular mirror positioned above, a spider web of cracks along its surface, interestingly growing from a hole the size of a fist.

Rex still hadn't moved from the door, his eyes watching as she wandered around the room.

"You fancy room service? We didn't get to eat at dinner," she asked absently.

"This place doesn't do room service."

She could have probably guessed that.

"Why did you come?" she asked.

"Why did you not call me?" he countered.

She clenched her teeth, not wanting to overreact. "I had it under control."

"Clearly not. If I wasn't there..."

"What? What could have happened?" She strode up to him, her anger vibrant. "You need to let me do my job."

"That *I* hired you for." His eyes flashed arctic. "I'm going to speak to Cole tomorrow morning."

"And ask him what? Why he's with a woman who's eating his people? Or how he could allow Francis Carter to become so entangled with darkness his body was ripped to shreds by his own hands?"

"It's his wife." A snarl.

"Who's killing his people." She crinkled her nose in disgust.

"How could you possibly understand their situation?"

"Understand?" She couldn't believe what she was hearing.

"She might give them protection," Rex laughed emotionlessly.

"Bullshit, protection from what?"

"Pack is everything. I can understand if keeping her around stabilised the pride."

"I'm not listening to this," she replied as she stormed past him, her hand touching the door handle before his palm smacked against the wood.

"You don't have a pack, you don't understand what you would do for them." His arm tensed as she tried to open the door, his strength unmoving. "My pack is everything. There is nothing I wouldn't do for them." He looked straight into her eyes. "My family, however, is my *life*."

Alice froze in place, the emotion coming off of him raw, powerful. "Rex..."

"I would kill for my brothers. I would die for them." His voice quivered, thick with hopelessness, pain.

Alice felt her own heartache, the emptiness her family left behind radiating. She understood, better than anyone else she understood the pain, something that never went away, but it wasn't enough. Her anger stronger, hotter.

"You didn't tell me that it was your brother we were searching for."

"It didn't matter."

"How can you say that?" She heard her voice rise even as she fought to control it. "I'm doing everything I can to help you and you didn't even give me all the information?"

"I said it didn't matter." He stepped forward, his height dwarfing hers as he crowded her against the door. "It's irrelevant information, knowing wouldn't have helped."

"It would give me somewhere else to search, more people to question. Your other brother..."

"Isn't available." He raised his own voice, his tone so close to Alpha she had to grit her teeth. "I have given you everything you need, kept nothing from you that I didn't feel relevant. Yet you still go off on your own, not giving me what I've paid for."

"Do not question my ability." She felt the intense heat in her stomach, rising with each breath as she fought for control. Relaxing into the power overload she calmed herself, keeping the power within limits.

"Is that a threat?" A whisper against her cheek, a hand twisted in her hair. "Do you think you're stronger than me?"

Alice let out a flame, a flash in front of his face in warning. "Don't push me."

Without warning his lips came down on her own, his tongue assaulting hers with teasing strokes. He released a growl as he grabbed her wrist, pulling her hand from the door and removing the concealer charm from where she had tucked it. The illusion immediately broke, revealing the bite mark. Rex licked across it, his chest grumbling as he nipped her skin.

It felt invigorating. It felt perfect. It felt...

"Stop this." She pulled her face away, stopping herself from taking it further, from pulling his lips back to her own.

He ignored her, assaulting her mouth once again.

"I said, no." She pushed against him, the intense lust dissipating the further apart they got. "I don't sleep with people who don't trust me." She pushed at him again, her thoughts clearer as her blue Tinkerbell floated around her wrist.

He looked angry before his face closed off. "It's just a fuck, Miss Skye."

Ice cold water. "It's Agent Skye." She blasted a space between them, making him jump back or risk being burned. "I don't really understand what this is," she pointed between them.

"Well if you need me to draw you a picture..."

"You think I don't see you? You think you hide behind this emotionless intensity, this mask, but you don't. It's a cold rage that your wolf is forcing you to confront." Her tone was husky, emotions running high. "What is so bad that you have to hide from me? Hide it from yourself?"

"You know nothing." A hiss. "You're just a stupid fucking female." He stood with his arms crossed, tension coiled up his spine.

"What do you want from me?"

"I want you to fix it." A shout.

"Fix what?"

"Everything," he snarled, turning to punch his fist through the wall. "I thought you would be the one. You seem alpha enough."

She gaped at the hole, unable to speak.

"But I don't know anymore." He stared at his hand, watching the blood ooze gently down his knuckles. "I don't know." With that he yanked open the front door, almost bringing it off his hinges before slamming it shut behind him.

Alice stood there, cold, unable to move until she heard his footsteps fade into the night.

Alice flipped the visor down as the early morning sun streamed through the windscreen. She had been sitting in the car park of the local market for a while, deciding whether to get out or not. She had been up all night, unsure what to say to Rex. Hours later she had gone down to her car, intending to drive home when she noticed him fast asleep in his 4X4. She felt anger at seeing him, anger at what he was trying to do, but mostly anger at his situation. She knew what a man looked like when he was out of options. So she decided to stay in the motel, her annoyance at the situation dissolving, at least until she read the text in the morning.

Agent Skye,
I'm sorry I wasn't there when you woke up, but I can't let you distract me from what needs to be done. Talking to Cole went well, he has given me a lead about a woman Francis was dating when he went AWOL. She owns a shop in the market a few miles up the road, I'm going to head there now. Will talk when we get back.
Rexley Wild.

"Distract?" Alice closed off her phone, throwing it into the glove compartment. How was she distracting him? *Bullshit.*

Voices filtered in through the gap in the window, couples arguing about who was driving, an old woman gushing over a recent purchase and even a small child wailing at being denied sweets. A few rows down Rex's huge car gleamed, standing out against the other less expensive cars and bikes. She opened her door, the sun instantly warming her skin.

The market was bustling with colour, rows and rows of

wooden and concrete stalls selling everything from hand-made jewellery and clothes to basic concealer charms and amulets. The air vibrated with energy, the exhilaration infectious. A woman bellowed how fresh her fruit and vegetables were, thrusting her treasures at anybody walking too close to her stall. Apples, kiwis, lychees, pineapples, all layered one on top of each other, all glistening in their ripeness. Alice fought not to get sidetracked, her eyes scanning everyone as she searched for Rex.

She had no idea where to start.

At a loss in the busy crowd she searched for someone to ask directions, deciding on one of the stall owners.

Manoeuvring through the crowd Alice found a beautiful collection of stones and crystals sitting elegantly atop velvet cloth and oak slices. Touching one she felt it sing, begging to be bought. Crystals were greedy things, natural formations created by the earth used by magic users for spells, the smooth stones able to store a small amount of chi. Alice reached out and touched another crystal, a beautiful pendant, the rock almost glowing with the attention, the small gold flecks shining against the dark blue of the raw stone.

"That crystal was made for you by the song it's projecting," the stall owner mused, smiling over at Alice, her multi-coloured head turban complementing the colours of all her stones and crystals. Taking the pendant from Alice she held it up to the sun, the gold specks sparkling. "Lapis Lazuli. Nice choice, a protection stone that protects against physical and psychic attacks. Great for protection circles, would you like to buy it?"

"Yes please," Alice smiled, stroking the cold surface. Handing over the money she allowed the woman to tie a leather knot at the back of her neck, letting the crystal sit in the hollow of her throat. "Thank you."

"You're welcome, my dear. I love it when my crystals find their rightful owners."

Alice nodded, bringing up her hand to hold the crystal gently, the smooth texture incredibly comforting.

"Oh, my." The woman grabbed her wrist, twisting it so she could see her bracelet better. "What is that?" Her brows furrowed as she stared at the moon pendant, a frown on her face.

"Alice?" a voice shouted. Alice turned just as Rex stormed towards her, his face annoyed. "What are you doing here?" He pulled her away.

"What, I'm Alice again?" He ignored her. "I was looking for you," she said through clenched teeth. Turning back to the stall owner she started to apologise.

"Do you know what that is?" the woman asked frantically, trying to grab her wrist again. "Do you understand?"

"Thank you but we should be going." Rex pulled her through the crowd, towards the car park. "You shouldn't be here," he snarled.

"What?" Alice dug her heel in, pulling her arm free with a tug. Her eyes narrowed as she noticed his slight smirk, knowing she could only get him to let go because he allowed it. She preferred him when he was emotionless. "I'm supposed to be helping."

"I said we would talk back home."

"Well, I'm already here." She stared at him, watching his pissed off expression smooth out into one of complete detachment. *Ah*, there was the emotionless she was used to.

"Have you found this lady yet?" she questioned.

"Yes," he replied, reserved. "She's in a cabin at the back."

"Have you spoken to her?"

"Not yet."

Nodding her head Alice turned back to the crowd, the number of people thinning as the sun hid behind the clouds, the temperature dropping.

"It's this way." Rex walked beside her, his movements frigid as he controlled his anger the only way he knew how. Deciding not to antagonise him further she quietly walked towards the corner of the market square, following to the half concrete half wood cabins.

Beautiful tapestries hung from the top of the concrete shop to the furthest left, flowing down to separate into sections. Each tapestry was handmade to create different scenes, everything from a field of tulips to a feast in a great hall. Inside, the handcrafted scenes became darker, the once beautiful tulips burning, their beautiful colours twisted and warped from the heat. Further inside one showed a scene with people bowing to a horned beast, blood oozing from bite marks across their flesh. Another showed people burning at the stake, their faces distorted in pain in such detail you could almost hear them scream.

"Can I help you?" asked a woman who had walked into the room and begun draping a semi-finished tapestry over an old wooden chair. Rex remained quiet, his muscles bunched as she went to stand beside him.

"Yes, we wanted to ask some questions."

"Questions?" she frowned, her eyes drifting between them. "I'm sorry, who are you?"

The woman was around the same height as Alice, her hair jet black and tied in twin plaits draped over her shoulders. It was her eyes that held Alice's attention, she had never seen eyes so dark, even darker than Dread's, like charcoal orbs surrounded by lashes. Alice swore she could even see flicks of red as the woman appraised Rex.

"I know you," the woman almost purred as she walked over and dragged one of her long nails across his chest. "You have some 'splaining to do." A sharp cackle.

"We need to ask questions." Rex finally said, his voice cold, no recognition on his face, yet he didn't step back.

"Fine." With a twist of her wrist the front of the shop closed, a lock clicking into place. Once she was happy the door was secure she lifted a tapestry, revealing a hidden archway. "No one will disturb us. Please follow me into my office." Without a backwards glance the woman sauntered through, her black braids swinging behind her.

The hidden room was faintly lit with red candles, the flames creating shadows dancing across the black and white portraits adorning the walls. Not one face was smiling.

"Take a seat." The woman threw her hand out in the rough direction of the table, her attention on the shelf by the back wall. With a little click, the lights above turned on.

Alice carefully studied the room, warily eyeing the shelves along the walls.

She felt something stare.

Turning around she eyed the portraits hanging on the walls, their eyes dead. Yet, when she moved, they seemed to follow. A clatter as the woman removed something from a shelf, dropping it onto the table. Deciding against the vulnerability of being seated, Alice chose to stand behind Rex as he folded himself into one of the chairs, arms braced on the table.

"So why are you here?" the woman asked Rex, completely ignoring Alice.

"I need to talk about Francis Carter."

"Francis?" The woman's smirk that was etched on her

face started to fade, a black look replacing it. "Francis is dead."

"We know. We want to know how."

"How?" Barely a whisper this time. "You want to know how?" A dry laugh. "He was chosen, gifted. He wanted the power, craved it."

"What power?" Alice moved from behind Rex.

"But he was unable to control it. So it consumed him." The woman continued as if she hadn't heard Alice.

"Annie." Rex tapped his knuckles against the table. "I remember. Your name is Annie."

"Ah, so you do know me," she laughed.

"More heard of you. You're the gatekeeper."

"Precisely." Turning away from the shelf she sat at the other end of the table, opposite to Rex.

Sensing movement in the corner of her eye, Alice looked past Annie and regarded the shelves behind, an array of creatures forever frozen in position. A taxidermy rat was bent at an impossible angle along its backbone, beside it an owl with its head turned one-eighty and a boar's head with a rabbit's carcass impaled on one of its tusks.

This place was next level creepy. "What's a gatekeeper?"

Annie glared over at Alice as if she had forgotten she was even there. "I find people worthy enough for the cause."

"The cause?" Alice frowned, where had she heard that phrase before? "Wait." Alice thought back, remembering her conversation with the bouncer. "The cause? Are you talking about The Becoming?"

Rex tensed, refusing to look at her.

"Rexley Wild, who have you brought with you?" Annie stepped closer, her chi electric as she flared, testing Alice's magic against her own. "A witch? Why have you brought me a witch?" She looked at Rex for an answer. "They're not going to be pleased."

"Who? Who isn't going to be pleased?" Alice asked.

"Alice we need to go." Rex stood to leave, his movements edgy.

"Wait, your name's Alice?" Annie's eyes narrowed. "They're not going to be pleased at all."

"Alice, please," Rex begged, his voice urgent.

"Yes, Alice, white magic is so boring isn't it? Never thought about going to the dark side."

"Dark side?" Alice frowned, flicking her attention to Rex, then back again. "No, never."

"No?" Annie stalked closer, her movements slow. "Not even a little bit?" Lifting up her sleeve she showed her scarification tattoo, a ram's head entangled in a pentagram. Twisting her wrist she held out her hand, beckoning Alice to touch.

Alice almost did. Almost. "Rex let's go." As soon as the words left her mouth, he had pulled her back into the market, the crowd having completely dispersed.

"We need to get out of here." His eyes darted around the crowd.

The cold air hit her, clearing her thoughts. "What the fuck was that? This is more than a normal lost person case..."

"Calm down," Rex leant down to hiss in her face.

"Calm down?" She moved towards the car park, deciding only a few steps in that she wasn't finished. "You know what? I can't help you. You hired me to help and yet keep vital information from me."

"I'm not..."

"Don't." She cut him off with a hand gesture. "You knew that witch. You knew what The Becoming was." She barely paused to take a breath. "What even is The Becoming? Some sort of cult?"

"Alice, you have to understand..." He slowly backed her away from the cabin.

"Understand? UNDERSTAND WHAT?" Her voice rose again, anger a vibration beneath her skin. "I'm good at my job but you're giving me nothing. How am I supposed to help you?" She felt lost as she faced him, her energy zapped.

"I don't know what to say..." His eyes widened, flicking behind her.

Annie stood in the doorframe, her head tilted as she watched them argue.

"You can't leave." She stepped out, a smirk tilting her lips. "We were just getting acquainted."

"Alice, please." His eyes darted back to Annie. "We'll discuss it back home."

"I said," Annie twirled her hand, a black ball of aura coating her skin. "You can't leave." The air became static.

Alice felt for her own power, bringing it to the surface as blue flames flashed from her fingertips. She could taste Annie's magic, the strength of it like an acid on her tongue.

A cackle. "Stupid bitch." Annie flung her aura.

Alice rolled, her own spell leaving her lips. "*ADOLEBITQUE!*"

A high-pitched screech as the incantation hit.

"Come on Alice." Rex pulled at her wrist, pulling her attention.

Something burned across her back, sending her careening into Rex, sprawling them onto the floor. Gritting her teeth, she spun, throwing everything she had from her hand.

"*ARDENTI TURRIS!*" Her aura pulsed, pain across her back.

"Alice, she's gone." White noise, flames cracking from her fingertips. "Alice..."

She turned, his face trying desperately to remain blank, but his eyes were anything but. They flashed ice, his wolf at the forefront, appraising her with heat. Heat and worry. He was cautious of her.

"We need to leave."

Alice blinked, trying to control the excess.

"It isn't safe."

She was unable to speak, the pain radiating across her shoulder blades.

Her nightgown ripped, allowing her to stumble into the dirt, her knees hitting the ground hard.

A loud bang as something crashed into the door.

The wood around the lock began to splinter.

She looked around the darkness, the earth feeling familiar against her bare feet as she climbed up. Following the pathway down she ran behind the giant oak tree, using the bushes to hide.

Another bang as the door finally gave, a low cuss as the shadow staggered out the door. "Come here little girl," he snarled. "Come here... your parents are inside, they need you."

She cowered against the tree, holding her hand against her mouth to stop the sobs.

A high pitch scream.

Fear twisted her, leaving her immobile as more tortured shrieks filled the air.

"You hear that little girl?" the monster laughed. "Your mamma needs you, come out, come out where ever you are."

CHAPTER 19

lice jerked awake, her dream dissipating sluggishly, the nightmare leaving a cold essence deep in her stomach. It was as if her memories were blocked, a DVD that had been scratched or software corrupted. Flickers of the same thing over and over again, every year without fail. It was almost like her brain was trying to tell her something, but panicked at the last moment and decided she wasn't ready to see, wasn't ready to understand.

Her grief counsellor had once explained she had never gotten past step two of the five stages of grief, never getting past anger. Alice hated to admit it, but always thought the woman was right, she had never felt the other stages, bargaining, denial and then acceptance. Especially the acceptance.

How could they expect a six-year-old child to accept that?

How could they ask a twenty-three-year-old woman to accept it either?

Rolling over on her mattress she stared at the sun's rays breaking through the blinds, a welcoming sight compared to the last couple of days, the continuing deep ache an annoying reminder. Stretching out her arm her breath escaped in a rush, pain resonating down her back enough to allow a little squeal of discomfort to escape.

"Alice?" A soft knock on her door before it pushed open, revealing Sam who stood there with a mug in his hand, steam billowing from the top. Closing the door, he set the mug on her side table, pulling his legs up onto the bed to sit beside her.

Her eyes narrowed on him instantly, one: he never knocked before entering anywhere, just waltzed in like he owned the place. Two: he closed the door behind him.

"You're staring," Sam fidgeted.

"Sam..." she started before she heard a distinctive click of the front door locking. "Sam?" she asked. "Who was that?"

"No one." He shrugged, a secret smile on his face. Alice was about to question him further when she heard a faint knocking. Sam's eyes went wide as Alice scrambled off the bed, pretty much throwing him to the side as she raced him to the front door. "Alice wait..."

"Oh hello," Alice greeted the blushing man standing on the threshold, his fist held up as if he was going to knock again. "How can I help you?" She smiled at the man, taking in his messy red hair, shorter at the sides than the top, crudely buttoned shirt and black skinny jeans.

"Oh...erm." The man blushed impossibly further, almost the same shade as his amazing hair. "I seem to have left my..."

"Here you go." Sam thrust a wallet at him.

"Oh, thanks." Freckles, the guy had freckles. "So, errr, call me?" An invitation had never sounded so meek.

"Sure," Sam nodded, slowly closing the door so Alice could no longer see the redhead. "I will definitely call you." With that the door closed, turning to her. "Don't comment."

"Comment about what? He's cute." She leant against the wall. "Where did you meet?"

"At the club." Amber eyes met hers. "You do realise you answered the door in nothing but your underwear and a smile?"

Alice fought not to look down, only just realising she could feel a pleasant breeze across her skin. She must have yanked her clothes off before collapsing into bed the night before. The redhead was lucky she had been too tired to figure out the clasp of her bra, or he would have seen a lot more than he bargained for.

"Don't change the subject."

He smiled at the door as if he could see through it. "He's proper cute though."

"Very." Alice couldn't stop her cheek-cracking grin.

"How is this funny?" Sam chuckled as he pulled her into his arms, scraping his stubbled cheek against her wild unkempt hair. She groaned, sucking in a pained breath as her back ignited in a series of aches when his aura touched hers. "Alice?" Concern in his voice. "You okay?" He leaned down into her hair. "You smell different."

"Do I?" She leant back, the ache lessening the further away she was. "I seem to have burned some of my aura."

"Burned it?" Sam's eyes went wide as he looked her up and down, unable to see auras. "What does that even mean?"

"I think I'm missing some." She huffed as pain shot

down her back once again. "I need to replace it before it gets worse."

"Worse?" Panic obvious in his voice. "What do you mean worse? Who do we call for that? Can the hospital deal with that?" He went to pick up the telephone sitting on a side table by the sofa, putting the handset back in its cradle when he remembered they hadn't paid the bill for the landline in months. They never really used it anyway.

"No, we can't go to the hospital. Dread will figure out I haven't dropped the Daemons. He can't find out."

"Wait, wait, wait. Back up. You damaged your aura while searching for Daemons?"

"I wasn't technically searching for Daemons..."

"Alice what the fuck!" Sam shouted, his voice getting higher in pitch. "If Overlord finds out, he will kill you!"

"I know!" Obviously, he wouldn't kill her, but he could make her life a living hell. "We need to find a specialist."

"A specialist? Where do we find that? On www.I-fuckedupmyaura.com?"

"So funny. I was thinking I could even do it."

"You? How? You don't know anything about auras? You even fucked up that shaving spell."

"Did not." Alice scowled, she didn't 'fuck it up' exactly. The spell had worked, it just had a surprising area of effect. Besides, Rose had forgiven her when her hair finally grew back.

"Whatever," Sam snorted. "Where do you think you can find the spell?"

"I was thinking, maybe my mum would have had something?"

"Your mum?" He raised an eyebrow. "Wasn't your mum a gardener?"

"Well yes." She bit her lip, thinking. "Dread used to tell

me when I was young how my mum could stir anything. Give her a recipe and she would be able to do it." He used to tell her stories of her parents when she was still young and scared. Every night he would sit on her new bed and tell her about how amazing they were.

The stories were like crack to a junkie, something a small broken child would cling to for hope.

'Alice, get into bed.'

'But the monsters?' Alice felt her bottom lip quiver, a cold hand squeezing her heart.

'Shhh,' Dread stroked across her cheek. 'Don't worry child, Uncle Dread is here.' He tugged up her new duvet set they had chosen together that day, pink with unicorns.

Alice had giggled when she saw his face, he wanted her to have the superheroes one.

'Do you know what your mum said to me when you were first born?'

'No.' Alice sat up slightly, resting forward on her elbows.

The last few weeks had been a blur, doctors, psychiatrists and specialists all wanted to poke and prod. She wouldn't speak, wouldn't even cry.

She had just sat comatose, barely responding. It was only when a young boy at one of the many grief meetings, a boy with the longest hair she had ever seen, had asked her how she had done her plait did she finally speak. Replying with a story about her mum. That's when Dread started telling her stories about her parents, ones that made her heart hurt and yet fill with joy at the same time.

'She said to me...' Dread tucked a piece of her hair behind her ear. 'That this little girl will be the most amazing person anyone has ever seen.'

. . .

"Alice?"

She shook her head. "Huh?"

"Where did you go?" Sam smiled gently, worry still blatant in his amber eyes.

"Back to when I was a kid." She smiled at the memory. Dread had taught her how to cope, how to be strong. He was always there for her, even though he still treated her like the little girl he took under his wing all those years ago. "I remember my mum sitting with lots of books, reading spells. Maybe the books are still there?"

"Where?" Sam thought for a second. "At the house? You haven't been there in years."

"Exactly. No one has."

"Let me get dressed, I'll come with you."

"No." She pushed her palm against his chest. "I need to do this myself."

"You sure?" He grabbed her in a hug again, his chest vibrating in a soft purr, the gentle noise and vibration instantly comforting. "I don't want you to hurt."

"I know." She snuggled into his warmth. "But I need to do this."

The house had aged in the last few years, the white paint peeling off in chunks to reveal the dark brick underneath. The windows weren't boarded up as she had initially thought, but had white smears across the glass that shops had when refurbishing. The windows themselves seemed in pretty good shape, the decent area having kept the kids from breaking in or vandalising the glass. The bushes around the house, while overgrown, were also surprisingly decent considering no one had lived there for close to seventeen years. The neighbour's obviously didn't want the house to be a total eyesore in the well-kept neighbourhood.

Sam had been asking her for a while if they could talk about moving in, *'anything is better than here'* he had said, complaining about their flat once again. Not that she didn't complain just as much, but the thought of her moving back to her childhood home...

A shiver started to rattle her bones. Shaking the feeling she continued to stare at the old house, irrational fear threatening to choke her, the nightmare the night before not helping the sense of foreboding. Blinking past the black spot invading her vision she walked carefully up to the front, the porch light off. She checked the bulb, noticing a huge crack along the side, a bird's nest neatly hidden inside.

Her hand shook as she inserted the key into the lock, the click echoing through the empty lounge as the door squeaked open. Dust glittered in the air as streams of light shone into the dark house, a musty smell thick and suffocating. Alice could feel her heart beat against her ribs, hard enough it began to hurt. Swallowing her sense of panic she stepped inside, noticing how her footsteps left marks in the dust.

Alice knew exactly where to look, knew she didn't have to go anywhere near the kitchen, nowhere near the window where she could see the garden.

The stairs creaked as she slowly made her way up, the light better upstairs, the windows not having had the same white smear treatment. Her parents' bedroom was the last door on the left, the door ajar.

The vanity had been pushed at an angle against the wall, adjacent to the bed that was a simple metal frame and mattress. Walking over she tugged it back into place from her memory, beside the window that faced the front drive.

Bottles lined up like soldiers against the grime covered mirror. Picking one up she examined it closer, trying to read the worn label before giving up and putting it back in its place. The two drawers turned out to be empty of anything helpful, just old out of date makeup and lotions.

Strange.

Starting to lose hope Alice continued to search frantically through her parent's things, checking under the bed frame, inside the wardrobe and even in the en-suite. Other than the necessities, nothing signalled her parents were magic users. No candles, runes or crystals. Nothing. It's as if the room was purposely staged to look normal, human.

She sat at the edge of the bed, careful to not put her full weight on the frame as it creaked. In fact, she hadn't seen anything witch-wise in the house at all. Admittedly, she had only checked one room and the lounge, but all witches had runes and protection spells carved into the walls. It was part of their nature.

Maybe she made a mistake? Maybe she didn't remember her mother as much as she thought. Her childhood memories were rusty at best, shadowed with trauma.

No.

Alice knew something wasn't right. Going back into the wardrobe she pushed against the hung fabrics, most of them half eaten by moths. When they didn't move she pulled them off the rack, letting them crumble into a pile on the floor.

"There's got to be something..." Fingers blindly searched. "Aha." She finally found the small indent she was looking for. Pushing with the tip of her finger she heard a small click.

'Ready or not, here I come.'

"Ready or not, here I come," Alice repeated her memory, remembering playing hide-and-seek with her brother years ago. Eight years her senior, Kyle was the usual moody teen in the family, his mood worsening when their parents made him play with her.

The cupboard had been Alice's favourite hiding place, somewhere she had found by accident one day and a place Kyle had never located. Alice suppressed a grin as the hidden door squeaked open, the space so dark it absorbed light. Reaching inside she felt a cold hard surface, something wooden.

With a grunt she pulled the heavy box out into the open and picked it up, placing it onto the vanity table so it was in the natural light. The box itself was nondescript. Not wood like she first thought but made of a thick cardboard. There were no markings, no dents, no stains. Nothing to indicate what was inside.

The lid came off easily enough, the movement letting the dust fly up into the air and into Alice's face. Coughing and waving to disperse the grime she finally peeked inside, a smile cracking her face at what she found. A large leather bound book. A grimoire.

This is exactly what she was searching for, it was...

A light flashed at the corner of her eye.

Looking out through the window she noticed a man standing on the street, his face covered over with a hood. She blinked, the phantom disappearing.

Confused, she searched down the street, wondering if she really did see someone standing there or if it was her imagination.

CHAPTER 20

"So, let me get this right..." Sam began as his legs trembled against the kitchen counter. "You're going to read a random book and hope something in there will repair your aura?" He sipped from what must be his fifth coffee, his hands juddering from the overload of caffeine.

"It's not random," she muttered. "It's also a grimoire." Alice stroked across the leather-bound cover.

"What if there isn't a spell?" Sam continued to swing his legs back and forth, his denim covered hips barely perched on the kitchen counter. He must have been on another late shift from the amount of coffee he was guzzling, his chest bare as he scratched across his pecs hard enough to leave marks. "What will you do then?"

"I don't know." She frowned, not wanting to accept it wouldn't work. "But I'll think of something." She watched him from the corner of her eye, his edgy movements concerning her. "Are you okay?"

He ignored her, instead turning to the kettle to refill his

cup. Sam took everything to the extreme, including drinking, smoking, caffeine and even sex. It was lucky that he had never been into drugs, his personality that of an addict.

"I think you've had enough coffee."

Sam slid his eyes to her, the amber narrowed as he flicked his plaited hair over a shoulder. "Let's have a look at this book then," he commented instead.

Alice tried to hide her own shaking hand as she opened to the first page, pictures of stars and moons drawn across the stained paper. Flipping through she started to find spells written messily throughout, some written in a strong, curvy handwriting in the middle of a page and others she found written rough and squished together, as if it was rushed. There were random phrases painted in some corners and dramatic drawings scribbled on others.

"This is a mess," Alice remarked as she tried to decipher all the nonsense.

"You find anything?" A thump as he jumped from the counter, his bare feet making little noise as he padded across the lino.

"What about this one..." Alice squinted as she tried to read the small print.

"This is gonna be interesting," he said mockingly from behind her shoulder, close enough that she could feel his breath against her bare nape. She fought not to glare at him.

"'*How to transmute into a badger*'."

"What. The. Actual. Fuck. Why would someone want that?" Sam started to laugh.

"I don't actually know." Alice couldn't really believe it herself. "Here's another one, '*For the love of your life*'."

"A love spell?"

Alice read through the notes. "Seems to be. Also illegal as hell." What was her mother doing with an illegal spell?

"'*How to remove a soul from a body.*'" Both Alice and Sam just stared at each other, deciding not to comment. "'*Eternal happiness.' 'The black mark.' 'Age definer.*'"

"Wait... fold that page over!" Sam leant across to bend the corner of the page himself. "We could use that spell in a few years' time."

She batted him away. "'*Illusionarium.' 'Aura feeder...*'"

"Wait, go back."

"Okay, it says here...'*When the integrity of the aura is compromised, the person will experience draining of energy and magic. This can manifest in many ways, for example, a depleted and sudden energy loss, a sharp change of mood, headache as well as acute pain over the area affected. Other, more unusual symptoms could be nausea or loss of consciousness. Unhealed holes in the aura can often lead to serious and permanent consequences. Moreover, the presence of holes in the aura greatly increases the risk of attachment or invasion of negative entities.*'"

"I have no idea what you just said."

"It means I have left my aura open to nasties." The idea made her feel both ill and dirty at the same time. "The spell seems simple enough. A circle, candles, I can't muck that up."

"Suuuureeee." Sam dodged the tea towel she threw at his head. "It will be alright baby girl, if not Overlord can save the day like he usually does."

"We haven't had to call for Dread's help since we were kids."

Sam sighed in delight. "And I still remember his face when he saw how many cocktails you had drunk. You threw up everywhere."

"It was graduation and I seem to remember you threw up first."

"Well, you have a defective memory," Sam grinned.

Alice couldn't help but chuckle back. They had been awful kids, even worse teenagers. "No threats. Like I said the spell is simple enough." She quickly re-read the instructions. "Okay, I need my candles back."

"Candles?"

"Yes." She narrowed her eyes at him. "You used them last didn't you?"

"Well," he said, looking away, "the funny thing is..."

———————————

A bus skidded as it pulled into the bus stop outside Mystic Medlock's Magic Emporium, splashing them as they walked along the pavement, the torrential rain pretty much killing the open aired high street. Jumping away from the cold water Alice ran into the magic shop, trying and failing to dodge the rain.

"I don't know why I had to come," Sam said as he shook the loose rain from his hair, the water droplets showering over the gargoyle guarding the door.

"Because you're paying for my new candles," she huffed, still annoyed. She couldn't believe he ruined her candles. That was the last time she'd lend him anything.

"It was an accident! I didn't realise they would melt so fast!" He sulked behind her.

"What were you even doing with them?" No reply, just a chuckle. "Okay, I don't want to know."

She shook her head, leaving him by the door as she stalked towards the wall of candles. Browsing, Alice found the soy versions she preferred.

"SAM!" she shouted in his vague direction, "GET YOUR WALLET OUT!" She heard him snigger, and followed the sound until she found him standing in the corner of the shop. "What are you looking at?" she asked as she stepped beside him.

"That thing is moving." Sam pointed to beside the large paradise palm.

"Moving? What?" Sam had finally lost it.

Walking over Alice lifted a leaf, revealing a very happy gnome. At thirty centimetres tall, the gnome didn't make much of an impact in size, but the hollow eyes and creepy smile caused the hairs on the back of her neck to stand on edge. His blue coat contrasted against his luminous green belt and red-capped hat. A fisherman's pole was clutched in his chubby palms, hidden slightly by his pure white beard.

"Wow, creepy."

"I swear Alice, he moved."

She watched the gnome carefully, feeling stupid until she noticed a pair of big, yellow, unblinking eyes staring at them from behind the fern. "Look, it's just the cat."

"I know the cat was there." His nostrils flared to prove his point. "I swear he moved."

"Leave the nice fisherman alone and help me find the chalk."

"Hello, can I help you? Oh, Alice isn't it?" a friendly voice called.

Alice turned, algae green eyes smiling down at her. "Oh, Alistair."

"Please, call me Al." He touched his fringe, pushing the strands away from his eyes. "You want chalk? It's by the register." He smiled towards Sam. "Hi mate, haven't met you before."

Sam smirked.

"This is my roommate, Sam." Alice purposely coughed,

bringing Sam's attention to her. *Stop it,* she warned with her eyes.

He's cute, Sam replied back, his amber ovals glinting mischievously.

Don't you even think about it.

"Nice to meet you Al," Sam greeted. "You got a girlfriend?" He batted his eyelashes, testing the situation. "Or a boyfriend."

"Sam," Alice hissed.

"Ah, no. I don't have a girlfriend," Al answered to Alice, her face flushing at the attention. "I'm definitely available."

"That's interesting, did you know my friend Alice..." Sam squealed mid-sentence as she pinched the fleshy part of his arm. Turning to rub the small mark he scowled before changing subject. "What's up with the weird gnome?"

"Oh, you mean Jordan?" Al smiled friendly.

"You named your gnome Jordan?" Alice asked, bewildered.

"Well, I didn't name him. He came with that name."

"I think he moved," Sam said, his attention towards the palm at the corner of the room.

"Yeah, he does that." He finished wrapping the last candle, placing all the merchandise into a paper bag along with a single chalk.

"And that's normal?" Alice pulled a face.

Al just shrugged, smiling at her. "Cash or card?"

"Pay up Sam."

With a small growl he handed over his card. "I'm just saying, but being your friend is expensive."

"That will teach you not to ruin my stuff." She grinned as she accepted the bag. "Thanks Al, see you around." She turned to leave, not wanting Sam to make it any more uncomfortable.

"Wait." Al held out his arm to stop them. "You okay?" He jumped over the counter and walked towards her.

"Excuse me?"

"You have holes in your aura."

"Do I?" She played ignorance. "I haven't noticed." Her back spasmed at that moment, making her squeak in pain while dropping the bag.

"Shit." Sam grabbed the candles as they rolled away. "You okay?"

"Fine," she replied through clenched teeth.

"Seriously, you have holes all over your aura," Al said again, looking concerned.

"I'm fixing it," she replied as the spasm subsided.

"You should have used your crystal. It would have stopped your aura from getting this bad." Al eyed the raw Lapis around her throat. "Have you not activated it?"

"Activated?" Her brows came together in confusion.

"It's a Lapis Lazuli, isn't it? A protection crystal, you can use it as a source for a protection circle. You just need to do the ritual to train the crystal to react to an incantation or trigger word."

"Oh, really?" She gently gripped it between two fingers, the crystal warm. "Is it easy to do?"

"Well, it isn't particularly hard, I took a few side classes in protection when I was studying engineering. I think we could do it."

Alice thought for a second, weighing up the options. "Can we do it now?"

"I haven't got the space here, you need to draw a protection circle. Besides, your friend has already left." He nodded to the front where she could see Sam lighting up a cigarette.

"What time do you close here?" she asked as she spun back to Al.

"Five."

"Did you want to come over to my place when you finish? I have space in my kitchen."

"You asking me on a date?" he flirted, eyes smiling.

"A date?" Alice flustered. "Oh, no. I just..."

"I can be over around six. But only if you promise me our second date will be something proper." He patted his apron, finding a piece of paper and writing down his details. "Here's my number, text me your address." With a wink he let go, his smile never breaking as she rushed out of the shop.

CHAPTER 21

A
lice smiled at her neatly drawn pentagram, happy with the lines and symmetry.

"Why do you always use salt chalk?" Sam questioned, his legs fidgeting as he sat on his favourite counter by the sink. After an uncomfortable car ride home in which she stared daggers at him at every traffic light possible, he had happily declared he was going to watch and help. Not that he could actually do anything.

"The salt acts as a catalyst, it controls the chemical reaction without itself being affected, almost like a barrier. If you actually mix salt, on the other hand, it does the opposite, it completely breaks the spell and dissipates the magic. So if you ever get spelled or want to break an amulet just dunk it in a vat of strong salty water."

"Is that why you are using the salt-chalk and not actual salt?"

"Pretty much, if I was to cook with my copper pots I would use proper salt to draw my pentagrams as it has no risk of mixing. I use the chalk when I'm going to be in the centre of the spell as it's harder to rub the chalk off and interrupt the flow than accidentally kicking over granules."

"Is that what went wrong with your other spells?"

"What other spells?" she frowned.

Sam lifted his hand. "Protection ward," he pointed to his pinkie. "Waxing spell," he pointed to his ring finger. "The one where you..."

"Okay, I get it," she scowled. He was always bringing up every time she buggered something up. Sticking her tongue out she reached for the bag of candles, unwrapping them carefully before grabbing a knife. Sam gently tugged her hair, brushing strands through his fingertips over and over again as she carefully carved the first candle.

The symbol for earth was an equilateral triangle with a line vertically through the middle. Once the carving was finished she blew off the excess wax, placing the candle at the bottom left of the small pentagram's star drawn in the centre of their kitchen. Earth, as well as fire, were fixed points within a pentagram, with air and water situated towards the top.

The second sign was fire, an upside down equilateral triangle with two waves on each of the sides. She placed the candle on the bottom right of the star. The third was water, simply three horizontal wavy lines that went on the furthest right point with air being three vertical wavy lines, placed on the furthest left point.

The last symbol was spirit, a simple circle symbolizing infinity and eternity. Sitting in the centre pentagram she lit a match, lighting earth first, then fire, water, air and lastly spirit.

"Does it matter which candle you light first?" Sam asked, genuinely interested. This wasn't the first spell he had witnessed, but probably the most interesting. Watching someone create vanity charms and amulets in an old copper pot was pretty boring compared to a physical circle. She looked down at her pentagram again, hoping it hadn't damaged the already worn lino flooring so they didn't lose their security deposit.

"You're supposed to anchor the protection circle by lighting the two fixed points which are fire and earth, you then light air and water to flow into the centre and lastly spirit, which closes it."

"Why do you even need a circle?"

"It's safer. It's a barrier that protects your aura when you mix it with the spell to consummate." She shrugged, not actually knowing the exact details why you couldn't do it without a circle. She wasn't curious enough to try.

"Being a shifter is so much easier." A smile. "It's also why I enjoy watching you try not to screw up."

Alice replied with her middle finger before she let out a breath, concentrating. Once her mind was empty she opened her third eye, checking to make sure the circle was whole. A thin gold and green shimmery film covered the pentagram in a dome, the circle perfect, bigger than she predicted. Pretty impressive for her first try, not that she was gloating.

"The circle is done," she exclaimed as her face broke into a smile, her cheeks straining from the excitement.

"So what's the next stage?"

"Shit." Alice looked at her neat circle, the gold and green morphing into a blue before changing back. "I might have left the instructions by the sink." Which was outside her circle.

"Can't you just go get it?"

"If I touch the circle it will fall, I'll have to start all over again." Once she touched the outside, her aura would rebound back to her.

"Oh, okay." Sam jumped down from the counter and grabbed the leather grimoire. "Want me to read the instructions?"

"Yeah, I'm not sure I should push anything through the circle," she told him, squinting at the dome.

"Okay, give me a second... it says to create a salt circle, light the candles, yadda yadda yadda, okay here it is. *'To realign your aura to its original state, excluding any permanent damage gained, you must quicken the flames with a blood donation.'*"

"A blood donation?"

"That's what it says." He flipped through the pages.

"Oh, okay." Alice grabbed the burnt match and broke it in half. Carefully, she poked the pad of her thumb with the sharp edge, a pearl of blood appearing at the tip.

"Alice?"

"I need to quicken the flames." She squeezed her thumb, letting a single drop of blood drop into each candle, ending with spirit. "Right, what's next?"

"It says you say the incantation and your aura will just replenish."

"Just like that?" That seemed too easy.

"Just like that." Sam squinted as he read through the book once more. "Ready to repeat after me?"

"Ready."

"Anima ad animam."

"Anima ad animam," she began, nervous.

"Ut aura erat aura."

"Ut aura erat aura."

"Putabas sanare capitii textile."

"Putabas sanare capitii textile." Alice sucked in a breath, her lungs burning as she gasped for air.

"Alice?" Sam asked as pain ripped through every cell in her body. "ALICE!?"

"What happened?" A deep snarl followed by an inaudible reply.

Frowning, Alice opened her eyes, blinking blindly at the light above.

How can eyelashes hurt?

"Is she going to be okay?"

"How am I supposed to know? I felt something was wrong and..."

Noise assaulted her ears, different pitches, voices that were muffled, almost as if she was underwater. Blinking a couple more times her eyes started to adjust, the kitchen ceiling coming into focus.

What the hell was that stain?

She watched as the green hue of her circle changed, mixing with blue like a sea mist, disorientating the suspicious ceiling mark.

"What do you mean you felt something was wrong? That's impossible, you're not even mated."

"That is none of your concern."

"Who the fuck..."

Alice rolled her neck, squinting at the two men arguing in her kitchen doorway. It took a few seconds to recognise them through the circle, the moving colours making it look like she was viewing them through a smeared window.

Sam, she realised, was only an inch or so shorter than Rex, his finger angrily pointing at the Alpha's chest. His mouth was slightly open, his breaths coming in short pants as he tasted the surrounding aggression, his leopard close to the surface. Rex, on the other hand, looked like he was made from granite, his muscles bunched, tense as he snarled at her best friend. They both turn to look at her when she finally crawled to her knees.

"Wow. That hurt." She took in a shaky breath, flexing her muscles.

"Baby girl?" Sam knelt beside her as close as he could get without touching the circle. "Open the circle."

"What?" Her head rolled on her shoulders as her neck clicked. She felt... good. Really good.

"Open the bloody circle," Rex barked, tension still obvious along his shoulders.

Sam snarled, his already prominent canines extending. "Don't speak to her like that." She could visibly see his skin tremble, fur threatening to break through the surface.

"Stop it," she tried to say, but it came out more like a croak. Flicking her hand out she touched the dome, voltage as her aura raced up her arm, breaking the circle.

"What were you thinking?" Rex crouched beside her, the opposite side of Sam. "You could have killed yourself."

"What are you even doing here?" she shot back accusingly.

"Yeah, what are you even doing here? I didn't call you," Sam said, eyes narrowed.

Rex ignored them. "You could have killed yourself."

"Don't be stupid," Alice replied as Rex's eyes flashed arctic. "I know exactly what I'm doing. It's you who hasn't got any trust."

"Careful." Rex's voice was a warning, his wolf close to the edge.

"I think you should leave." She stood up, her back

feeling great, energised even. Inside she felt whole, her core aura electric. As she clicked her fingers her chi rippled, coating her hand with blue flames. It was effortless, the little power she used barely touching her chi reserve.

"Remember who hired you." Rex stared at the flame, eyes still ice.

"You don't let me forget." She made the flame grow before extinguishing it. "I'm just going to be researching, so if I get any information that could help I'll contact you."

His face softened for a second, barely a glimpse as he thought it over. "Fine." A shallow nod. "I didn't realise how bad the necromancer hurt you, for that I apologise."

"It's fine, no harm done."

Alice fought not to touch him, her hand almost reaching up to Rex's skin on its own accord before she clenched it into a fist. It was a weird reaction she couldn't explain. She stepped back into Sam, the distance between them helping the weird magnetic pull.

"Ah, I'll keep you updated."

Sam purred low in his chest, his hand stroking through the strands in her hair as he centred himself with touch.

"You do that." Rex went to stretch towards her before he caught himself, his eyes following Sam's lazy movements as he continued to stroke her hair.

Shifters were tactile creatures, needing the physical response to calm their animals. Rex was itching to touch her, reassure his beast that she wasn't hurt. But she couldn't bring herself to close the gap, allow him some comfort.

She couldn't explain her weird attraction, and until she could, she wouldn't allow herself to indulge in what her body was begging her for. She clenched her fists harder.

"Why are you here Rex?" He seemed to be everywhere.

"I came to inform you that time is running out. Another one of my wolves has gone missing."

"What?" she gasped. "When? How?"

"Not important. What is important is that we need to find a new lead."

"How is the time frame not important...?"

"It isn't relevant," Rex interrupted.

"There you go again, keeping information from me..."

"Look, I need to go. They need me at the den." Ice eyes met her own. "You *will* call me." He growled as he slammed the front door, not giving her time to reply.

"Fuck." She smacked her hand against the wood.

"He's such an arsehole." Sam stood to the side with his arms crossed.

"You have no idea." She stared at her hand, tracing the little crescent moon indents her nails left. "Fuck, fuck, fuck." He had done it again, left her in the dark and expected her to find her way out.

"I don't trust him, he acts like he has something to hide."

"I know he has." She knew as soon as he recognised the necromancer, she just wasn't sure what he was hiding. Yet she couldn't drop the case, not until she found out the answers she didn't even know she was searching for.

"Then what's the plan?"

Oh, I don't know, figure out what the hell is going on before my resistance gives up and I jump back into bed with him.

She knew she sounded crazy even in her own head, so instead she said, "I need to research this cult."

And pray to the many gods that it was going to lead somewhere.

233

CHAPTER 22

"You didn't have to come." Alice crossed the road, dodging past impatient back cabs that couldn't care less that it was a pedestrian's right of way.

"My spidey senses are tingling." Sam walked beside her. "I just feel like..." he paused, unable to explain.

"You know in every situation it would be me, protecting you right?" She glanced to her left, smirking.

"Yeah, but I look scarier." He showed her his canines.

She couldn't argue with that. "Seriously, what can go wrong in a library?"

"A book could fall on you." He shrugged as he peered at her from the corner of his eye. "Or Rex could turn up." He stretched his hand out to stop her. "You need to stay away from him."

"You don't need to worry." A car screeched against the wet asphalt as it dodged a cyclist. Beeps and horns a daily occurrence in a city.

"He's taking way too much interest in you," Sam said, anxious.

"I'm figuring it out." She turned them towards the mammoth Victorian style building located just off the west district. The intricate, architectural structure was a stunning contrast to the neighbouring skyscrapers, and the hundreds of original glass windows reflecting different patterns in a kaleidoscope of colour.

The rain had calmed down to a trickle rather than the downpour that pummelled earlier, the sun breaking through the coal grey clouds to shine bleakly.

"What are we here for?" Sam asked as they walked through the two storey wooden door that led into the main atrium of the library.

"Research."

Sam laughed. "It's called the internet."

"What I want to research can't be tracked."

"Ah, you don't want Dread to find out." Sam's face turned solemn. "Don't get yourself in over your head. I don't know what Rex has hired you for, but you seem to be at a crossroads."

Alice didn't know what to say, the seriousness of the statement unsettling. "I know what I'm doing." She hoped.

The library was the oldest across the British Isles, with the most amount of literature under one roof since before the Great War. Floor-to-ceiling bookcases lined each wall, curving in great arrangements to create a chaotic labyrinth of books, tapestries and paintings. The place smelt dusty with a hint of wood polish, which wasn't completely unpleasant.

Wooden benches and tables were placed neatly in the centre, underneath the glass ceiling Alice knew to be several floors above. Various busts were randomly placed around the different floors, everything from the monarchy to authors such as Shakespeare and Jane Austen to Winston

Churchill and Charlie Chaplin. Most were in reasonable condition depending on their age, others were cracked and vandalised.

"Where do we start?" Sam asked nonchalantly, his hand brushing against the top of an armchair, the old brown leather cracked across the seat, the cushion long gone.

"Oh, erm..." she hesitated. She hadn't thought that far ahead. Biting her lip she looked around, hoping an idea would spring to mind. "What about simply starting at 'C'?"

"And look for what?"

"Cults?" She shrugged. "I'm interested in the ideologies behind The Becoming."

"The Becoming?"

"Yes, have you heard of it before?"

"No." A frown. "This isn't the normal thing you do Alice," he moaned as she began leading them towards the bookshelf headed 'C'. "Daemons, cults. It's pretty hard core compared to your usual stuff."

"My usual stuff hasn't helped me with my dreams, have they?"

"You mean your nightmares? The ones that have been worse since you started this?" He picked up a book, slamming it back in its slot after he read the title. "You're hurting yourself and you don't even see it."

"Has it not occurred to you that maybe I need to break before I can grow?" *Before I can understand.* "You would do anything you could to find your dad. To get back at him."

"That isn't the same." A low growl, his amber eyes glowing.

"The hell it is," she hissed back. "I need to find out what happened that night, and this research is helping. Working with Rex is helping." She felt her voice quiver. "Instead of questioning me, can't you support me?" She met his eyes. "I support you."

He held her gaze. "I do support you." He grabbed her into a hug, his chin resting on her head. "I can't lose you."

"You won't." She hugged him tightly before stepping back.

A nod towards the shelf, his usual mischievous smile in place. "So, where would you like to start?"

"All I have to go with is that cult, The Becoming." She started to scan the hundreds if not thousands of books along the shelves.

"How are you sure it's even a cult?" He leant against the opposite shelf, arms crossed.

"Just a guess, what else could it be?" She selected a book titled, '*Age old Cults affecting modern society*' and began scanning through the pages.

"What else have you got to go on?"

She slammed the book shut.

"Not a lot. I have the autopsy reports showing possible signs of Daemon transitions, but it isn't based on solid evidence. I can't even compare them to the wolves because Rex didn't get any autopsies performed." She blew out in frustration, looking for any other books that could give an insight into a mysterious cult that could, or couldn't help.

"This is why I'm not a Paladin, it seems boring when you spend your time in mind-numbing libraries." His attention wandered as Alice continued looking through the books. "You found anything yet? How long is this going to take?"

"I said you didn't have to come," she huffed, her own patience becoming thin.

"We've already discussed this."

"And I have already told you, I'm fine." Annoyed, she

grabbed several books from the shelf, stacking them into Sam's arms before grabbing some more. "Let's take these to a table it'll be easier to study them."

Back stiff she walked to an empty wooden table towards the centre of the atrium, directly underneath the glass roof. The table was marked beyond redemption, a green and gold plastic lamp was drilled into the centre giving some artificial light that didn't seem to have an off option.

"Here." Sam thumped the books down, sitting himself at the edge. "I think I have something for you," he smirked as he flicked through one of the books.

"You do?"

Sam dramatically cleared his throat. "*His bulging cock penetrated as she moaned his name,*" he read loudly. "*Leaning down he kissed along her throat as he increased his thrusts, her tunnel squeezing his thick shaft...*"

"BLOODY HELL!" Alice knocked the book out of his hand, her face burning as she looked to see if anyone had overheard. Sam just chuckled, his dimples dancing across his cheeks. "If you're not going to help, leave me alone." When he didn't answer she glanced up at him, his attention on one of the aisles as a woman wearing a dangerously short skirt bent over to pick something from the floor. "Sam," she called. "Sam," Still no answer. "Earth to Samion."

"Huh?" He reluctantly turned to her.

"I'm going to be sitting here a while, why don't you go prowl somewhere else."

"You sure?" His brows came together.

Alice smirked. "Sure."

"Okay, see you in a while." He unsurprisingly walked towards the bent woman, one who was happily fluffing her dark hair and pouting her lips at the sudden attention.

Rolling her eyes Alice picked up the next book, the title stating '*Ancient Art of Magic the Personification of Cults.*'

Flipping through the first few pages she frowned, the paper in poor condition with some sheets completely ripped out. A mixture of English, Latin, Gaelic as well as other languages she didn't recognise filled the pages, seemingly nonsense. Squinting, she tried to read the headings in English, stopping when she noticed '*B.e.c.o*' before disappointingly seeing the rest of the word was smudged by ink.

Licking her dry lips she read the small print underneath,

'*For one to 'Become,' an age old one must sacrifice a vessel of clean magic. Doing so will give the bearer the ability to transcend into the next stage, giving unbelievable power over the darker arts, their body reflecting the great power bestowed on them by the mother of everything.*'

Alice blinked, re-reading the passage over several times, trying to make sense of the words. The passage stated it was written in '*The Ancient Kingdom Third Century, now Europe.*'

"Third century?" she mused to herself. "What was around in Europe in the third century?"

"Celts," a light voice answered from behind her.

Startled, Alice accidentally pushed the book onto the floor, her mouth agape as the mystery man bent to gently pick it up.

"Interesting read," he mused, his voice musical. Taking a seat beside her he flicked back to the same page before reading the small paragraph. "Yes, it's definitely the Celts, I believe specifically the druids." He handed her back the book.

"Excuse me?" She cleared her throat as she stared at his eyes, purple iridescent orbs that matched the pastel of his shoulder length hair. She assumed he was a man, but she wasn't actually sure, his features that of complete androgyny. Either way, it was definitely Fae.

"Look here," he said as his long fingers traced across the passage, "It says *'bestowed on them by the mother of everything.'* Druids worshipped nature, specifically mother Gaia who they, at least, used to believe was their source of magic. The time frame is around the same but your best bet would be to ask a druid."

"Maybe." The Fae was actually making a lot of sense. "If it was druids, wouldn't it state Great Britain rather than Europe?"

"Oh, so you know something about druids?" His iridescent eyes sparkled.

"Some. It also says in the same paragraph about *'sacrificing a vessel of clean magic'*. Druids are notoriously famous for their passivity, peaceful people who gained their magic from the earth and atmosphere."

"Passiveness?" The Fae laughed, the sound like little bells tinkling through the air. "When was the last time you met a passive druid? You can't associate an entire race into an expectation. That's the same as saying all witches own black cats, or all faeries eat small children." He smiled, amused at his own joke.

"Okay, point made."

"You're also assuming the *'vessel of clean magic'* is something sinister when it could easily be something as simple as a plant. There is nothing else in here to state otherwise."

"You obviously know more than me on this subject."

"I wouldn't take it to heart, I'm a professor at the local

University specialising in atmospheric magic. I have to know the basics of all magic based Breeds to really understand how to take certain aspects of magic further," the professor stated, his eyelashes the same pastel shade as his hair. "You a student? They have a study on the original history of magic based Breeds in the next semester. You could really benefit from it."

"Oh, no I'm not. I'm just really interested in the history."

"Alice, you find anything?" Sam walked over to the table, interrupting the Fae. "I tried to look for books about Daemon's but couldn't find anything." His amber eyes narrowed to slits as he appraised the professor, his nostrils flaring as he tried to scent his Breed.

"Oh Sam, this is..." She didn't know his name.

"Professor Luanou, but I'm afraid I must be going." The Fae stood up, his black shirt and trousers reminding her more of something a sensei would wear rather than a university professor. "I must have made a mistake in suggesting you should attend the history of magic based Breed's next semester. We do not tolerate any practitioners of the dark arts." His eyes flashed to her numerous books about cults as well as the inappropriate erotica before he walked away.

"What is the faerie on about?" Sam frowned as he took the now vacant seat.

"Wait..." she called after him. "I DON'T PRACTICE BLACK MAGIC!" The professor didn't acknowledge her statement. "I really don't." She sighed, noticing the audience of people watching her outburst.

"So what was that about?" Sam rolled a cigarette between his fingertips, the end creased as if he had stubbed it against something.

"He now thinks I'm studying black magic since you came over and mentioned the Daemon books."

"Really?" Sam chuckled. "You at least find anything interesting?"

"A little. I think I found the description of The Becoming." She turned the page so he could read. "And after speaking to the professor it does sound like something that's druid in origin."

"Druid? Like your Da?"

"Maybe. The professor made some solid comments but I would really need to ask another druid, other than my dad's appreciation for nature I don't know much about his history."

"What about Overlord?"

"He might know something." Dread had been best friends with her father, and while he never admitted his true age, she knew he was old.

Alice closed the books, stacking them up and putting them on a tray for the librarian to put back into place.

"Did you find anything?" she asked.

"Found nothing. The word Daemon is completely missing if the books were in alphabetical order."

"I thought you were checking out the skirt girl?" She crossed her arms, smirking up at Sam.

"Aye, but it's a complete turn off when my nose itches from the amount of glamour that Fae was wearing." He reached up to scratch his nose as if it still was irritated. "So what now?"

Alice looked up at the clock on the wall. "We have time to pop to The Tower, might as well ask Dread the questions before Al gets to our place."

"What about the Daemon books?"

"We can ask the receptionist, maybe we're missing something."

The clerk was right by the front entrance, the small queue having completely dissipated by the time they got there. The desk an oversized mahogany monstrosity, seeming even bigger than possible compared the frail old woman sitting behind.

"How may I help you, young lady?" she asked, her small eyes magnified through her thick circular glasses.

"I'm looking for anything to do with Daemons. We can't seem to find anything."

"Daemons?" Her eyes widened slightly. "Oh, let me check." She tapped her keyboard. "I'm sorry but we do not keep those types of books here."

"Really? We are in the biggest library I have ever seen and there isn't one book about Daemons?" Sam asked dryly. "Bit weird don't you think?"

"Have you checked under 'D,' my dear?"

Alice tried to smile sweetly, ignoring the question. "We are looking more specifically into daemonic transitions."

"I just told you we do not hold those sort of books here."

"Well, where would we find those sort of books then?"

"Not here."

"What about some history on them, maybe?" Alice asked, changing tactics.

"We have nothing like that here." The woman's voice was getting sterner.

"You didn't check your computer," Alice said sardonically, starting to lose her temper.

The old woman tapped one button. "Nothing."

"I don't understand why this is so difficult, we're only interested," Sam interjected.

"We don't practice black magic." Alice had never had to

defend herself so much. "It's just for a project we're working on."

"I have already said we do not have those types of books here." She sniffed unpleasantly.

"Then where are they?"

"Not here. You shouldn't even be looking at that sort of stuff. It's dangerous."

"What's so dangerous about books?" Sam growled. "This is ridiculous."

The woman's eyes slowly bled into panic, the pulse in her throat beating visibly against her skin.

"What do you know about Daemons?" Alice asked as a heavy hand landed on her shoulder. Turning slightly she eyed the security guard. "Is there a problem here?"

"I'm going to have to ask you to leave," the guard grumbled, his fingers digging in.

Sam swore in the background, snarling at his own personal security guard.

"Why? We haven't done anything wrong."

"If you don't vacate the premises immediately, we will remove you."

Alice removed the hand from her shoulder. "Fine. Sam, we're leaving." She pulled at an angry Sam before they were escorted through the door.

"What a load of bullshit," Sam shouted at the guards, flashing them some interesting hand gestures.

Alice looked behind her shoulder, three security guards standing ominously near the entrance. The clerk spoke in hushed tones into the phone at her desk, trying desperately not to make eye contact.

"What was that about?" Sam asked, turning his attention back to Alice as they stood under the alcove.

"She knows something." Alice knew it, the look in the

clerk's eyes was pure panic as well as guilt. But what could make an old woman react in fear like that?

The Tower was busy as they made their way up to the forty-second floor, the noise and chaotic rumblings of her colleagues a pleasant comfort.

"It's getting late." Sam looked around the large room into all the different cubicles, eyes lighting up when he noticed the cat-themed novelty gifts he had gotten her over the years. "You have a date, remember."

"It's not a date." Alice just sighed. "I'm not going to be long, you could have waited outside."

Sam had dated a few of her colleagues over the years, and not one ended well.

"Oh, Alice," a shrill voice called from beside her. "I see you haven't been fired yet." Michael swanned over wearing a green velvet jacket over an off-white shirt, his ginger hair had been recently cut just above his ears. "Shame," he sniggered.

She didn't have the patience. "Bye Mickey."

His arm snaked out, pulling her against his chest, close enough she could smell the coffee on his tongue. She immediately turned and broke his hold, stepping back just as Sam snarled past, his arm extended as he forced Mickey against the wall.

"SAM, NO!"

"Now we're gonna have a little chat," Sam hissed directly into Michael's face, claws erupting from his fingertips as he kneaded them across the sensitive skin of his throat.

"Alice," Mickey choked, sweat dripping into his eyes.

"Control your pussy."

"Aye, pussy." Sam purred low in his chest as he rubbed the side of his face against his. "You want to see what this pussycat can do?"

"Sam, please." Alice caught his eye, the amber glowing to the point she could almost see the leopard looking back. He always reacted badly, ever since they were kids he took it upon himself to be her protector, as if she couldn't protect herself.

Don't do this. He isn't worth it, she begged with her eyes, not wanting Mickey to understand.

He hurt you, Sam replied in the same way.

There was only a handful of people she could have a wordless conversation with, have a strong enough bond to be able read their expression. Sam more than a brother to her, regardless of blood.

No one should be able to touch you like that. Years of abuse flashed across his eyes, uncontrollable pain before he calmed himself. She had never asked for details about his past, knowing only a small amount based on the history of scars decorating his body. A long time ago she decided she never would.

I'm not breakable.

No you're fucking not. His eyes lost their electricity, the leopard still present but not running the show.

With his face still pressed to Mickey's he gently nipped his ear, purring at the flinch. "If you wanted my number precious, you should have just asked." Pushing away he turned back towards the lifts, a cigarette already placed between his lips as he disappeared through the metal doors.

Mickey made an unrecognizable sound, sweat still pouring down his face. "I'm going to report him for that, assaulting a Paladin is a criminal offence."

"I'm sure you will. Make sure to note how you grabbed me first." Watching his face turn various shades of red she turned towards Dread's office, happily noticing the absence of his secretary, Barbie. Lifting her hand she knocked against his closed door. "Dread?" she called.

"Alice? What are you doing here? I haven't released you from medical leave."

"Oh, yes, well I have had some time to think and wanted to ask some questions."

"What questions?" He gestured to a chair before his own. The room bright from the window behind him, the blackout blind he normally preferred rolled to the top to show the amazing view of the city. "Why is Sam here?"

"Sam?" *How does he even know that?*

"He didn't make a scene did he?" Dread raised a dark eyebrow, his bottomless eyes almost laughing as if he knew exactly what had happened. He probably did, knowing him.

"He's waiting outside."

"Hmm." He tapped his ring against the table. "What can I help you with?"

"I wanted to know more about druids."

Dread paused. "Why?"

"I realised I didn't know much about dad's heritage. I was hoping you could tell me."

"Why the sudden interest?"

"The anniversary is coming up again." She didn't have to fake the emotion clogging her throat. "I want to remember them better than blurry memories or old photographs." Which wasn't a complete lie.

He nodded, accepting her explanation. "Well, what do you want to know?"

"I want to know how often druids practiced dark

magic?" She watched his face tick, his expression remaining unchanged as he took a few seconds to answer. "I was just at the library and I read about some druids choosing dark magic compared to earth."

"What have you been reading?"

"Just a book."

He glared at her for a few seconds. "Anybody can choose dark magic, regardless of their Breed, background or religion."

Pretty much what the Professor had said. "So they weren't more prone to dark magic?" She bit her lip, waiting on the answer.

"Not any more than anyone else. Your father was strictly clean, high in The Order, as you already know. A respected man." She knew little about The Order, Dread having explained to her it was an organisation strictly of druids for which her father worked. He never told her what they did exactly, always saying it was *'top secret stuff'* when she asked as a child.

"Would anybody from The Order be willing to talk to me?"

"Stay away from them Alice, they're dangerous people."

"Then why did dad work with them?" Alice pointed out.

Dread just continued to glare, the vein in his forehead pulsing. "You need to drop this, I don't know what you have been reading, but it is clearly inaccurate."

"Fine." She leant back in her chair, staring out the window. "I saw something interesting at the library today."

"Interesting?" His fingers tapped against the top of his desk.

"While I was there someone asked about Daemons, but they were escorted out by security." Only a small lie.

Dread narrowed his eyes to slits, akin to a python watching its prey. "Whom have you been talking to?"

"No one." She tried not to react to his gaze. "I just thought it was weird."

"Daemons are dark magic, so the media has represented them as mythological tales since The Change. All literature based on black, dark or death magic was removed around the same time to stop mundane people becoming infatuated." He shook his head as if remembering something.

"So they lied to the public and said Daemons weren't real?"

"Nobody has ever said they weren't real, it was always up to the general public to make their own decision. Admittedly those decisions were persuaded along the way. Daemons are rare enough that in all my years I have only had to deal with a handful. It is believed that the process to become a Daemon has a high failure rate. The Council doesn't want people going around trying to summon Daemons to gain access to ancient dark knowledge."

"What even is a Daemon, exactly?"

Dread tapped his knuckles against his desk. "Those who choose dark magic. Alice I'm very busy, you should be at home resting."

"Okay, but what about the literature, was it all destroyed?"

Dread shook his head. "To my knowledge they were just moved from the public floors. Only a select few have access to the restricted section of the library."

"Restricted section? How comes I didn't know there even was a restricted section?"

"Because you don't have access."

Touché. "Thanks Dread."

CHAPTER 23

S am mumbled to himself as he paced across the kitchen, his movements agitated as he took his usual seat on the kitchen counter, his legs swinging. He had been uncharacteristically quiet on their way home, a scowl carved onto his beautiful face.

Alice eyed him warily as she prepared the circle she had used earlier, the marking still perfect. She checked each candle separately, making sure the carvings were all still clear.

Sam's voice broke through her concentration. "Did Overlord give you anything to go on?"

"Maybe." She placed the candle marked with fire back down, setting it delicately into its place. "I have a plan." When he just frowned she continued. "There's apparently a private wing in the library."

"How do you expect to get into this private wing? We just got kicked out."

She folded her arms. "Go in after hours. It's a library, all

I have to do is dodge some security guards, open a locked door, look around and leave. Easy."

Sam opened his mouth to reply.

Knock. Knock. Knock.

"That's not exactly a detailed plan. We'll sort this out later," he murmured as he opened the front door.

"Evening Alice. Sam."

Sam nodded a greeting to Alistair before sitting in his usual spot on the counter, out of the way.

"Hey, I've already set up the circle. I wasn't sure what you would need." Alice awkwardly scratched her head, desperately trying not to embarrass herself with her lack of knowledge.

"It looks perfect." Al smiled wide as he placed his backpack on the floor. "Impressive circle."

"I used it earlier."

Sam huffed something underneath his breath. She glared at him until he looked away, his poor mood starting to grate against her. He was always dramatic, sulking for hours when he was annoyed at something, or someone.

"It's really well done, I thought you weren't used to this sort of thing?" He walked over and checked out the placements.

"I'm not."

"Impressive," he said again. "Right, do you have the crystal?" He took off his coat, revealing a dark blue shirt neatly buttoned to the top. His sleeves were rolled to his elbows, grease smeared along his arms.

"I do." She lifted it from under her t-shirt. The instant it was in the open air it started to hum.

"It will stop making that noise once we activate the aegis."

"So, what are we actually going to do?"

"We are going to put a little of your aura within the crystal, once you say the invocation it will create an aegis, a molecule thin shield created from your aura."

"Should I be taking notes?" Alice joked.

Al continued as if he hadn't heard her, instead getting his own chalk out of his bag and scribbling symbols around her own. "Are you ready?" His eyes lit up in excitement.

"Sure..." Alice took a step into her pentagram, her bare feet cold against the hard floor.

Al began to whisper, the runes and symbols beginning to glow as he rummaged through his bag. "Light the candles," he said as he handed her a small mirror.

Earth, fire, water, air then spirit. The circle cracked into place around her. A gasp, her smile dropping as she noticed Al's shocked face.

"What? What?" Alice panicked. "Did I do something wrong?"

How could I fuck this up?

"No, I've never seen a circle like yours." His eyes glazed, a sign he was looking through his third eye. *"Flaminco."* A larger circle erupted around them both, eclipsing her own.

Sam looked at her at that moment, his eyes easily readable. *Someone wants to show off.*

Shut up. She looked through her own third eye, noticing how Al's circle was an unappealing orange. "Okay. What do I do now?"

"Put the crystal onto the mirror, then push your aura from your hand onto the crystal. The mirror will act as a catalyst, a block. It stops your aura from leaking into other objects and helps the concentration on the pendant."

"How do I do that? You can't see your own aura."

"Just concentrate, I will tell you how it is going."

"Okay. Okay. Okay," she whispered underneath her breath.

Sitting down onto the floor she crossed her legs, using her knees as a table with the mirror balanced between them. She carefully placed her crystal on the mirror's glass, hovering her hand over it before she began to chant loudly in her head.

Move. Move. Now. Do something. Anything.

She let out a frustrated growl. "It's not working."

"Alice stop overthinking it. Close your eyes."

She obeyed.

"Now envision a cloud around your hand, imagine the cloud flowing over your fingers and towards the mirror."

Pins and needles over her elbow, flowing down her right arm into her palm. Uncomfortable.

"That's it, keep going."

Alice wiggled her fingers, the tips aching without the warmth of her aura.

"Okay, now hold your aura over the crystal, and say this phrase, followed by the word you will use as your incantation. *In hac sphaera absorbet meam commisisse.*"

"Okay..." She concentrated on holding her place, her eyes still closed. "*In hac sphaera.*" Numbness swept across her fingertips. "*Absorbet meam.*" Sudden pain through her hand. "*Commisisse.*"

Her hand spasmed closed over the pendant.

"*ARMA!*"

Her aura rebounded back like an elastic band. With a yelp Alice jumped up, knocking the mirror from her lap with a crash. Her step back brought her in contact with her circle, breaking the dome with a pop.

"Shit, are you okay?" Al walked over, careful to not break his own circle until she was ready.

"I'm fine, it was just a shock." She looked over at the shards on the floor. "Your mirror," she cried.

He laughed "It's okay." He picked up the necklace through the broken glass, handing it to Alice.

"Did it work?" she asked, eyeing the crystal suspiciously. It didn't look any different.

"I'm going to drop my circle, once it's dropped put the necklace on and say your incantation." He pushed against the invisible wall surrounding them, another soft pop signalling his circle had opened.

Alice held the necklace carefully in her palm, the raw stone warm in her hand, familiar. Slipping it over her head she placed it neatly in the hollow of her throat.

"*Arma.*" An instant circle formed around her, the whole three-hundred and sixty degrees. A thin shield made of a mixture of green, blue with specks of gold.

"Wow Alice, that's really cool," Sam said with awe, his mood suddenly changing. "Is that what your aura looks like?" He jumped off the counter to press his hand gently against the opaque surface. With a hiss, he pulled his hand back. "Ow."

"Erm," Al mumbled. "It shouldn't be that big."

"What do you mean?" Warmth drained from her face.

"An aegis is only supposed to be a shield in front of you. You have made a complete circle, and without a drawn pentagram." His eyebrows creased as he walked around it, touching the barrier in different areas. "I've never seen anything like this." He poked the circle again. "Have you studied arcane magic?"

"No." She eyed the dome. "Is this not normal?" She touched the barrier to drop the circle.

"There's nothing wrong with it, I'm just surprised is all." He clapped his hands together. "You should really practise with arcane energy, I think you're a natural. Can you manipulate a ball of energy?"

"Yeah." *Sort of anyway.*

"Great." He grabbed his coat and rucksack. "By the way, I get to choose our next date." With a wink he let himself out.

"See, I told you it was a date." Sam padded across to her, his fingers playing with the crystal at her throat.

"Hardly a date." She rolled her eyes. "Now let's get back to planning."

———

From the radio came an eerily detached voice. *"Check. One. Two. Three. Check. Alice, can you hear me?"*

"Hear you loud and clear, over," Alice replied, holding down the little button on the side. Placing the walkie-talkie radio back on her belt she looked around the empty street, checking to see if anyone was looking.

"There's a staff door on the side of the building, you will then need to go across the atrium towards the back of the building. There will be a large double door to the left. Go through that towards the private corridors."

"Where the bloody hell are you getting this information?"

"There's an interactive map of the whole library on their website," Sam replied dryly.

Alice burst out laughing, softening the noise with her black leather glove. "Even the private wings?"

"Nah. I've checked the whole map and there are a couple of doors you can't look into which are through that corridor."

Static before she turned the radio down slightly. It was hard to sneak around in a city that doesn't really sleep, the

255

lights illuminated the street enough to make it difficult to look inconspicuous. Acting as casual as possible she walked towards the alley at the side of the building, her black leather catsuit helping her to hide amongst the little shadows available.

"Okay, I've found the staff entrance, no names from now on. Over." Re-attaching the radio to her belt she picked up her small knife hidden in a loop within her boot. Grabbing a pin from her hair she placed both in the keyhole, turning one slowly until she heard a series of clicks, each pin clicking into its correct height. With a little more pressure the final pin clicked into place, allowing her to turn the lock mechanism.

Suppressing a smirk she put her knife back into her boot, her fingers tingling as she pressed down on the handle gently, peering through the small gap. Satisfied that no one was there she crawled through, closing the door gently behind her before checking the room for cameras.

Must be the staff cloakroom. Squinting in the poor light she noticed hangers lining one side of the room while a selection of ugly armchairs and a small table sat against the opposite wall. A coloured photograph of a smiling woman was the only decoration on the otherwise bland walls, '*Employee of the Month*' written in gold across the top.

She searched every corner of the room and saw no telltale cameras. Happy, she stood to her full height, adjusting the leather straps under her breasts and stomach that held her sword flush against her back. She usually wore the straps beneath her clothing, but they were uncomfortable against the catsuit, forcing her to wear them over the top. She probably should have left it at home. What could go wrong in a library?

Walking to the only door available she passed a mirror, her face a stark contrast to the darkness. Blonde strands had escaped her black beany hat, creating a halo around her face, accentuating the thick black eyeshadow and eyeliner she decided to put on to help her blend in. Sam had laughed his arse off when he saw her. *'You look like a gothic panda gimp.'* he had said.

She pretended to be annoyed, explaining she had to wear the outfit otherwise her blonde hair and pale skin, courtesy of her mother's Nordic heritage, would have stuck out like a sore thumb. He just laughed harder. She didn't want to admit he was right.

Moving past the mirror she opened the door, the lock on the inside easily turning as she made her way quietly into the atrium. All the artificial lights had been turned off, leaving only the streetlights to leak through the stained glass windows, creating a dissonant pattern across the already ugly carpet. She kept to the walls, blending into the darkness as much as possible as she walked through.

A noise came from the left.

Dropping to her knees, she quickly crawled towards the clerk's desk.

"So how was your wife's birthday party last week?" one of the security guards asked, sweeping his torch across the patterned floor.

"Terrible, apparently I got the wrong bracelet for her. Ungrateful bitch," the other guy replied.

Alice stayed hidden, controlling her breathing until their voices were distant murmurs across the room. When confident they were far enough away she peeked over the desk, noticing a small green glow across the other side of the large atrium. Careful to not make any noise she sneaked towards the first bookshelf.

"Have you got to the door yet?"

She hushed the speaker.

"Steve, did you hear that?"

"Hear what?"

"A noise, over there..." He swept the torch in her direction, the light creeping under the bookshelf towards her feet.

OH SHIT. She hid amongst the other bookcases, her thick-soled boots making no noise on the plush carpet.

"George it's nothing, your imagination's going wild again."

"Maybe..." Alice picked up a small book, throwing it across the room, creating a soft bang in the opposite direction. "Over there." A jingle of keys as the men ran towards the distraction.

She rushed towards the private corridor, the light turning out to be a *'restricted area'* sign. Alice pushed at the door, but it didn't budge.

Fuck.

Noise close behind.

Running past she entered the only other door available, the door swinging shut just as light swept from beneath the frame. Alice stared, heart in her throat. The light eventually moved away, the footsteps disappearing with it.

"You almost got me caught," she whispered into the radio.

"Sorry."

"I'm in the men's room." She kept her voice low. "It had to be the bloody men's bathroom, didn't it?"

"Babe, if you needed to go you should have just said."

"Funny. Is there any way out of here other than the bathroom door?"

"Give me a second, there's no other exit, but it does back up to another bathroom. Is there a grate or something?"

Alice moved her hand gently across the walls, careful not to touch the urinals. "There's a vent." Getting her knife back out of her boot she used it to unscrew the corners, catching the vent as it sagged off the wall. Leaning it gently against the tiles she peered in, unable to see anything. "I'm going to try it."

She climbed into the small metal hole and pulled the vent back across the opening. No one would notice it was loose until the morning.

Ouch. Her head smacked into the opposite grate. Mouth twisted in a snarl she peeked through the small gap.

Nothing.

Just another bathroom.

Turning slightly she planted both her palms across the metal, pushing. A squeak, the metal resisting. Pushing even harder the metal started to groan, bending at the top and bottom. The corners screeched as the screws were forced out, warping before crashing to the floor.

Fuck. Fuck. Fuck.

She held her breath, and counted.

60. 59. 58. 57.

No tell-tale noise, just a low hum.

25. 24. 23.

No footsteps. No noisy keys.

10. 9. 8.

Crawling out from the hole she stood up, stretching her muscles. The low hum was slightly louder towards the door, more of an annoyance than anything. Pushing the door soft light flooded in, the lighting strips on the ceiling the reason for the hum. Stepping through she planted herself to the wall, blinking her eyes to help readjust to the sudden light.

The corridor seemed to hold a couple of doors, light shining through the small windows. A buzz from above. In the corner she noticed a blinking red light, hidden. Keeping herself low and against the wall she watched it as it slowly turned, sweeping the corridor.

"Adolebitque." The camera sizzled, melting before the little red light flickered off. "Okay." Happy that there were no other cameras she checked through the first door, the window allowing her to see into the surprisingly small room. Metal and glass cabinets lined the back, diamonds and jewels placed underneath the glass.

The second room held paintings, some on the walls while others were just gently stacked against each other on the floor. The third room held some vandalised busts, floating heads that had some bad artwork painted across them, but no books. Alice reached for the fourth door.

"I think I've found the basement," she whispered into the black radio. "Is there any information on the website?" The door opened onto small spiral stairs, leading into darkness. "Hello?" she asked again, making sure the frequency was correct.

Static.

Crap, something must be interfering.

Grabbing a small torch from one of her pockets she clicked the button, the tiny light bright enough to see the ends of the step's reflective strips. Following the curved stairs down to the bottom, she stepped onto the concrete floor.

The light from the torch struggled, flickering on and off before dying completely. With a sigh she dropped the useless device into her bag and reached for a couple of glow sticks. With a satisfying crack she snapped them in half, shaking the liquid before throwing them across the room, lighting up the large square concrete space with an eerie green glow. Holding one stick in her hand she held it before her, scanning the room.

It was bare, nothing against the dark walls. The only thing was a cage sitting dead in the centre.

Weird.

With nothing in the room, she turned back to the stairs.

Alice gasped. "Where are the fucking stairs?" She exhaled as she frantically reached her hand out, her brain refusing to believe the stairs could just disappear. Her palm connected to the brick, the surface intensely cold, even through the gloves.

"Sam?" she asked the radio, panic in her tone. "Sam? Are you there?" No response, not even static. "Fuck." With nowhere else to go she moved towards the cage.

A high-pitched noise filled the room, a shattering sound that made her jump back with a cry. The noise stopped just as suddenly as it started, almost as if she had imagined it. She waited, concentrating.

Nothing. She heard no bugs scattering across the floor, no water droplets. There wasn't even a smell. If it wasn't for the glow sticks, the room would be pitch dark, giving out no sensory output. Hesitantly she stepped forward, the piercing noise screeching again as lights danced beneath her feet. Another step forward and the noise stopped.

She looked down at the floor, not recognising the small patterns lighting up in the concrete.

What the fuck?

Cautiously, she reached down, touching a rune to the left of the light. A pierce shrill filled the air before lighting up, a spectrum of colours breaking through the concrete with a rainbow glow. *Shit. Shit. Shit.* Sweeping her gaze across the carvings she checked the different runes and symbols, each one slightly different from the last, surrounding the cage in a perfect circle. An educated guess would say a circle had been engraved into the concrete, but not a circle she had ever seen. Taking a closer look she tried to make out more of the runes, starting to understand one slightly.

A hiss.

Scrambling back she froze, blood rushing in her ears as she strained once again to hear anything. Her sudden panic excited her Tinkerbell, the little blue ball bouncing happily around her head. Fluffing it away from her face she peered into the dark, seeing nothing but black.

I'm losing my mind.

The cage was around ten square feet, all sides covered in thick metal bars, an intricate mesh patterned in between. The lattice climbed around the whole structure, including the top. No chance of just climbing over. Peering through the small holes in the mesh Alice saw nothing, almost like a void, absorbing any light. Lifting the lock she studied it, her blue ball of flame allowing her to read more runes that were scribed all over the heavy metal. With her pin and knife she started to pick the lock, and with a click it turned.

Yes.

The knife snapped.

Alice stared at the knife dumbfounded as something clattered to the ground.

What the fuck? A metal shard by her boot. *Did that lock just spit it out?* The pin launched itself out in a similar fashion, clanking to the ground next to the remnants of the small blade.

A hiss again, but closer.

She threw the handle, it disappearing into the shadows. She squinted further into the darkness, trying desperately to listen for any movement as she stepped back over the runes.

Drip. Drip. Drip.

Drops of liquid against the concrete floor, sizzling on contact, like acid.

Slowly she reached back and unsheathed her sword, her senses on high alert as she felt the air move to her left. Instinctually she moved out of the way, rolling backwards and across the runes. They lit up un a burst of rainbow.

Another hiss, something being spat in her direction.

With a scratchy sound a long black leg stepped over the light line, long hairs swaying at the movement. Another leg, movements jarred as bones clicked into place.

Click. Click. Click.

A third leg came into sight, accidentally touching an unactivated rune, causing further light to illuminate the dark space. The sudden shrill noise made the legs flinch.

What. The. Actual. Fuck?

Alice felt her mouth snap open, her sword wavering as she watched the three legs click as they moved.

Click. Click. Click.

The thing leant forward, balancing on what she assumed were its front legs, slowly, almost wary of the symbols embedded into the concrete floor. Alice stood frozen, seeing her wide-eyed reflection, mouth agape in the hundreds of dark eyes staring back at her.

Sluggishly, the giant creature opened its own mouth, huge white fangs protruding from black gums. Drool ran like a river between its smaller, razor-like teeth, dropping onto the floor with a sizzle. Another step forward and a fourth leg appeared, slowly scraping its claw against the floor like nails on a chalkboard, leaving a scar across the concrete.

Fast as a whip one leg shot towards her, making her jump out of the way, slashing out blindly with her sword. Something wet landed beside her, big enough that it made an uncomfortable noise when she kicked it away with her boot. Pulse beating impossibly loud in her head she tensed, waiting for it to strike again before a hiss screeched from the darkness only a few meters from where she stood, spittle landing on her leg.

Reacting, she ran towards the cage, activating several runes as she went. The high-pitched noise vibrated against the walls, loud enough to make even Alice flinch, wanting to hold her hands over her ears. The beast roared, spittle landing in front of it before it writhed in pain, its long legs trying to claw at the lights.

"Shit." Holes appeared in the leather, one just above her breast, one on her stomach and a couple along her left leg, exactly where the creature's spit had landed. Flesh peeking through, she faced the creature, the extra light providing a better look even as it continued to fight against the rainbow.

A spider.

Of course it would be a giant fucking spider.

The monster spider was twice the size Alice originally thought. Its head dwarfed by its giant hairy body, three legs against the floor, one held up in the air dripping black liquid into a puddle. Four more legs spaced evenly against the wall, making its body face Alice at an angle. Slowly the spider pushed one of its uninjured legs against the light, pushing past the runes, testing.

Concentrating, she felt the deep heat in her chest expand into her hands. It felt electric as she allowed the overload to manifest, her focus on the spider.

"*Ignis*," she screamed, satisfied when the intense ball of flame formed around her fingertips. "Die fucker." She launched her ball, gasping when it just popped, crashing to the floor as if it had hit an invisible wall.

The spider seemed to chuff through its fangs, amusement in its gaze.

"Oh bugger."

Hand tight on her blade she ran to the unactivated runes, watching as she pressed her foot against the grooves, the light and noise an instant reaction. In a panic the spider tried to claw into the wall, failing to escape the onslaught of raucous sound. Without warning the spider launched itself across the room, a claw at the end of a long leg scraping against her stomach. Doubling over she clutched her midsection, blood pooling beneath her fingers. Another leg hit her from behind, causing her to fly into the cage head first, her blade dropping from her hands.

Alice climbed shakily to her feet, crying out as her shoulder protested.

Another hiss, a patter as liquid was sprayed across her back. Instant burning, bubbles eating away at the leather before starting on her exposed skin. Gritting her teeth, she turned, feeling her burnt skin peeling. At a run Alice shot towards the runes, dragging her foot in an arc around the cage, illuminating every single one.

A chorus of sound, a cacophony of deafening shrills. The noise trembled the floors, causing her to fall against the cage, exhausted. She grabbed the metal lock for stability as it taunted her, laughing. Or it could have been the blood loss.

A glint of light, her blade lying useless against the cold concrete floor. In a burst of energy she rolled towards it, swinging it in the air at the same instant a leg came crashing down. With an inhuman screech the creature reared back, black blood spraying past her face, barely missing her. Before she could react another leg came from the darkness, pinning her against the cage with a sharp claw to her shoulder. With a scream she ripped the claw from her flesh, moving towards the cage door, waiting.

"Come here you fucker," she taunted, no real energy behind the words.

Alice swapped her sword to her left hand, her right badly damaged. The ridiculous blue flame innocently floated by her shoulder, just a spark at the corner of her eye, neither helping the situation nor hindering.

"I'M GOING TO SQUISH YOU INTO A SMALL INSIGNIFICANT BLOB YOU BUG!" It would have sounded so much more threatening if she hadn't slurred most of the speech, her brain slowing down as her blood decorated the floor.

The spider reared around, threatening Alice with his fangs.

"YOU. YOU. FUCKER. YOU." It was best to keep the threats simple and effective, especially if nothing coherent was going to come out.

Alice held the blade up, pointing it unsteadily at the spiders face. With a shriek, the spider spat. She danced out of the way at the last minute, the spittle hitting the heavy lock, searing and smoking at the contact. With a scream Alice brought her blade down, the acidic spit having weakened the metal enough for the lock to disintegrate on impact. She launched herself into the cage door, swinging it closed behind her.

Alice closed her eyes, waiting for the spider to crash through the unlocked gate.

Nothing.

She quickly peered through the gaps behind her, into nothing. Darkness. No lights from the runes. No burn marks on the concrete. No giant murderous spider. It was as if it had been when she was outside the cage, looking in. A void. Absorbing all the light.

Her legs gave out, collapsing beneath her into an unsteady pile. Blood poured from her stomach and shoulder, an impossible amount leaking across the floor. Her sword clattered to the ground, her hand limp at her side. She blinked several times, each time the room brightened before darkening around the corners. Head heavy, she looked up at the chandelier that lit up the white ceiling, wooden beams shooting in a pattern from the centre.

Blink.

A cage, an intricate latticework of metal mesh revealing only darkness above her.

Blink.

White ceiling, pale walls with colourful paintings. A statue stood in the corner, its modesty covered by a leaf beside a bookshelf full of old leather-bound books. Black invaded her vision, creeping from the corners once again.

Her head slumped against something cold.

CHAPTER 24

Oh god, my head.

Alice moved to brush her hair from her face, her wrist stopping short with a rattle. She pulled her arm again, pain shooting through her shoulder sharp enough she hissed.

What the fuck?

She opened her eyes, the harsh light causing her to squint. "What?" She looked down. "Where the hell are my clothes?"

Her catsuit had been removed along with her bag, radio and sword. Her black lace bra, underwear and harness the only things covering her.

How the fuck did they remove my catsuit without removing the harness?

Wiggling her toes she looked further down, her legs cuffed carefully to a wooden chair. She pulled at her wrists again, her arms having been tied behind her back.

"If you pull anymore you might hurt your wrists," a

268

deep voice chuckled. She stopped tugging, her muscles going rigid.

Who the fuck is that? Blowing her hair from her face she peered through the blonde strands. A huge male stood against the wall, one foot on the floor and one against the wall, bent at the knee.

"Excuse me?" she questioned while pulling at her bonds again.

The male just crossed his heavily tattooed arms across his chest. Waiting.

Fighting a snarl Alice calmed herself, thinking. She couldn't burn through metal, and she didn't have access to her bag or sword. "Fuck."

He sniggered, the sound echoing across the room.

"Who are you?" she asked, staring at the stranger. Nothing. No answer. "Why am I tied up?" A thump as his other foot landed on the floor. "Are you going to talk or not?" A small chuckle, but he remained hidden.

Great, she thought. *He has a sense of humour.*

Alice tested her leg restraints. No budge.

"Why were you in the basement?" he asked with a penetrating glance.

"Where's the spider?"

"So you're scared of spiders?" Another dark, irritating chuckle. "That was the Somnlin. Our deterrent against thieves and curious librarians."

"A Somnlin?"

"An illusion taken from your deepest fear."

"That was not an illusion, it almost sliced me in half."

Or did it? Alice peered down, noticing only smooth skin, no sign of the bloody gaping hole, no cuts or bruises.

"It was a physical manifestation taken from your imagination, it's as real as you believe it to be." He walked round to face her, his heavy biker boots making no noise on the wood. "The spell causes you to be delusional, makes you see things that aren't there."

So that's why my spell failed. It's not really there.

"So are you saying that if I just closed my eyes and believed it wasn't there, it couldn't have hurt me?"

"It never actually touched you." He was laughing at her.

"Yeah, well you're a shitty librarian." She blew at her hair again, the blonde strands tickling her cheek.

"Why were you in the basement?" His face morphed to blank, expressionless as he asked his questions.

"Why am I naked?" she countered.

His dark hair, longer on the top than the sides was pulled back from his angular face, the colour matching the long stubble along his strong jaw and neck. His too full lips were straight, all humour gone as his narrowed steel-grey eyes watched her carefully. A faint scar marked his otherwise blemish free skin, a pale pink line that curved gently from his high cheekbone to break into his top lip, accentuating his masculinity.

"You were passed out on the floor." His gaze slowly roamed across her skin, eyes lingering far longer than necessary. "I was checking you were okay."

"You didn't have to strip me."

"Probably, but it was fun." A cheeky grin. "Interesting knife you have."

"It's not a knife!" she sneered, the harness biting into her skin. "That's my..."

"Interesting runes along the blade." His eyes darted to hers. "You do them yourself?"

"Runes?" Alice strained her neck, trying to see her blade. It was alight with colour, patterns bright flaring down the steel. They seemed to brighten as the man stroked down the edge, wanting him to touch.

Her sword had runes?

"Why were you in the basement?" he asked again, his eyebrows pinched.

She ignored the question, instead flaring out her chi. If he wanted to interrogate her, she at least wanted to know what he was. Pushing out her chi she tested, sucking in a breath when her aura hit his, the feeling electric against her senses. His eyes flashed silver, lashes quickly coming down to hide them as his full lips curled in amusement. It was clear from his reaction he was a magic user, something she recognised, yet didn't.

"Are you a faerie?" She pulled her chi back, the connection too strong for her to concentrate. What was he? He wasn't a witch.

"No." Another curl of those lips. "But I know they prefer being called The Fae." He tilted his head slightly, causing some of his hair to cover his expression. "Are you going to answer my question?" He clicked his fingers, the tattoos on his arms illuminating gently against his skin before a ball of arcane encased his hand.

"Neat trick, do you do kids parties too?" Alice pulled once again against the bonds, sweat starting to drip down her skin as the arcane built against his hand.

Shit. Shit. Shit, she chanted, wiggling her bum, the wood uncomfortable against bare skin. *Wood.* Wood burned.

"*Adolebitque.*" She rattled her wrists to mask her voice.

"Are we going to do this the hard way?" He took a threatening step forward.

"Wait, what are you?" She hoped the question caught him off guard.

"A man."

She fought not to roll her eyes. "That's not what I asked." Another groan, the wood weakening.

"So I'm not a man?" He reached down to the zipper of his black jeans. "Shall we check that out, sweetheart?"

"WAIT!" She tried to stall him, feeling the wood continue to weaken beneath her. He hesitated at her outburst, the arcane on his hand hissing.

Alice licked her dry lips, staring at his arms. Black and red intricate patterns wrapped around most of his left arm and all of his right arm, symbols similar to the ones on the floor and locked in the library basement. Symbols she now recognised, her memory sluggish to catch up in her panic.

"I know what you are." The symbols were of Celtic origin, runes that were engraved to give a permanent anchor to a spell the same way she would use the five elements. Runes her father had tattooed around his wrists.

With a final creak the chair gave way. Muscles tensed, she pulled just as the chair collapsed, her feet ripping free from the wooden legs. Within an instant she was pushed against the wall, a strong arm against her throat, no sign of the arcane.

"Careful sweetheart," he breathed against her neck, loosening his hold enough to allow her to turn, pressing her shoulders flat against the wall. She glared up at him with controlled anger.

With a final push against her neck he stepped back, close enough to grab her but not close enough to touch. Her skin continued to burn where his hands once were, a phantom against her flesh.

"How did you move so fast?" She released a shaky breath.

"Why don't you tell me considering you know what I am?" he replied smugly.

She didn't miss a beat. "You're a druid."

"Gold fucking star." He stepped towards her, forcing her back against the wall. "Now, why were you in the fucking basement?"

"I don't know why," she hissed through her teeth, the pain in her wrists fuelling her anger. At least her legs were free, two separate cuffs hanging from each ankle.

The man didn't say anything for a minute, his face immobile. "I know you're a Paladin, you had your license in your bag." Her eyes flashed to his, but she remained silent, deciding to stare at the tattoo crawling up his throat instead. "What's your name?"

"You said yourself you've read my Paladin license. You know it's Alice."

"Progress." He stepped away, his eyes accusing. "Just making sure it's actually your license."

She didn't have to read minds to know he thought she was a burglar. To be fair to him, she was dressed like one.

"Now, I will not ask again. Why were you in the basement?"

"I was looking for literature on a cult."

"A cult?" His eyes narrowed. "What cult?"

Alice bit her lip, deciding what to tell him. "The Becoming." She watched his reaction, noticing his jaw clench.

"So you're chasing Daemons."

"Am I?" That at least confirmed the passage she read from the book. "Who are you?"

"Who I am is not important."

"I didn't ask your star sign, I want your name." She straightened her back, trying to look scarier than she actually was. Especially considering she was half naked with black makeup smeared across her face. She probably looked crazy.

"Fine, I'm Riley."

"Is that your first or last name?"

He just smiled in response. That smile made her frown, his face suddenly becoming more familiar.

"Do I know you?" she asked, trying to place him.

"Why would a Paladin be researching a cult? You on a contract?"

"Maybe." She kept the eye contact. "So do you have any literature I can read regarding this cult?"

Riley clicked his fingers, the cuffs around her wrists and ankles falling to the floor with a clink. Slowly pulling her hand from behind her back she flexed her fingers, but resisted the urge to rub her wrists.

"Your clothes are behind you on the table." He nodded to a table in the other corner. "Get dressed."

"Turn around." She didn't want to get dressed with him watching. He just crossed his arms over his chest, eyes darkening. Biting her tongue she stormed over to the table, noticing her destroyed catsuit. "You didn't have to cut it off." He ignored her, continuing to watch. Quickly stepping into the leather she tied the ripped parts across her breasts, covering her modesty as much as possible. "Give me my sword."

"Oh, this?" He stroked her blade again, watching the lights dance at his touch. "It's nice, never seen anything like it."

"It was a gift." Dread had given it to her when she completed the academy, had explained it was her mother's, passed down through the family. She had never asked how he had it.

"Hmm." He flipped it several times. "What do the runes mean?"

She had no idea. "Don't change the subject, talk." She found her beany, shoving it into her bag before slinging it over her shoulder.

"What do you know of this cult?"

"Nothing, which is why I'm here, researching." She eyed her sword, weighing the options whether she could just grab it back. The way he was expertly flipping it would suggest she probably couldn't.

"When did you first hear of it?"

"A woman attacked us, she said she was recruiting."

"Who's 'us'?" His eyes were piercing, as if he could see the answers through her skin. "Who hired you originally?" She refused to reply. "Maybe we could help each other."

Alice hesitated, not trusting him. Looking around the room she noticed it was decorated the same as all the other private rooms she saw earlier in the library. One wall was encased completely in a huge bookcase, old leather-bound books piled high.

"What do you know of this cult?" It wasn't like he was going to allow her to look at the documents behind.

"It's one of the oldest organisations known in daemonic history." He balanced her sword expertly on his finger.

"Yet fascinatingly enough, it's based on druid arts."

He stopped balancing the sword, instead placing the hilt into one of his fists. "So, you do know something."

"Are you part of The Order?"

"Who have you been talking to?" He threw her the sword, training only allowing her to spin and catch it by the hilt and not the blade. Chest pumping with how fast he could throw she gently sheathed it, feeling instantly better when the weight registered against her spine. She had noticed how, as soon as she touched the hilt, the lights disappeared, and the way his eyes narrowed told her he noticed it too.

Her aching limbs protested, her full bladder deciding to wake up. "Are we done here? You're clearly not going to help."

He jumped forward, crowding her against the back of the room. "You need to drop this subject, let the big boys deal with it." His cheeks creased at her slight flinch. He kept crowding her, enough that she could feel the heat radiate from his chest. Until she had to tilt her head up to keep him in view, his unusual eyes ablaze in challenge.

"You're clearly not doing a good enough job..." Her hand tingled, fingertips alight with blue flame as she pulled her hand up to stop him from coming any further. "Otherwise you wouldn't be just the security guard for a load of books."

That gained her a full-blown laugh. "We will definitely be seeing each other again."

CHAPTER 25

Alice twisted into the kick, knocking the hanging punching bag back. She had been taking her temper out on the bag for a while, allowing the energy to flow out of her fists and feet into the worn leather. The repetitive kicks and punches were relaxing, giving her some control in an otherwise irrepressible situation.

She had gotten home earlier to an empty flat, Sam having gone to work once he had finally heard from her. Apparently, according to the text she had received, he had been permanently banned from the library, having gone back hours later once it was open to try to find her. The idea he had scared people enough to get banned made her laugh.

The gym was quiet as she continued to work her frustration against the sand filled bag, only a few other people working out in the large open space. Another punch, the chain above the bag screeching as it pushed against its restraints.

Fuck my life. Feeling her fists start to ache she decided

to take out her blade, the sword Dread had given her when she had graduated from the academy, somewhere he had persuaded her to go.

Apparently it was an heirloom from her mother's side, something that was supposed to be handed down in the family. She had thought it was a generic sword until he had explained the significance of it, a steel blade with a dark, well-worn hilt. It didn't glow when she touched it, which made it even more curious.

Twisting around the bag she did a series of exercises designed to control the blade as if it was simply part of her arm. Without encouragement the end erupted into flame, leaving a charred smell in the air as it swept across the cracked leather of the punching bag.

Shit.

She needed to get herself together. Her back still ached gently from where she had been tied to a chair, her shoulders clicking as she stretched and started a cool down routine. Swapping the sword to her left hand she practised a sweeping motion, angling her hand to reduce strain. Flipping it a couple times in the air she practised balancing before turning with speed to point it at the jugular of the man standing behind her.

"That's not very nice." Danton's Adam's apple bobbed as he talked, getting precariously close to the edge of her steel. "Your hand is too extended. It would be easier to swipe it off you."

She knew that, and she also knew he couldn't help himself but to comment.

She stood there with the sword still at his throat, a red pearl of blood sliding across the tip.

"D," she greeted, swiftly sheathing her blade in the custom sheath at her back. "Go away." Without a second glance she grabbed her sports bag, walking straight out into the sunlight. The workout had done nothing to calm her, her temper still bubbling as she noticed Danton walk casually beside her, his face slightly scrunched up as the sun shone down. With a grunt he reached into his coat pocket and brought out his sunglasses, letting the shaded glass protect his sensitive eyes. As usual, she was disappointed with the horror movie stereotypes. Vampires didn't turn crispy when they stepped into sunlight, even though Hollywood still liked to dramatise.

"We need to talk." D's accent wasn't as pronounced when he was serious.

"About what?" she asked disinterestedly as she walked to the other side of the road. He casually followed her, looking completely out of place in his matrix style black leather jacket. Alice in comparison was only in a pale blue t-shirt and black yoga pants with 'Cheeky' written across her butt. They looked quite the pair. "What do you want? I'm in no mood for company." Especially company who would repeat everything she said back to her boss.

"I'm here because you broke into the library last night."

Alice stopped, deciding whether or not to deny it. "How do you know that?" A few strands of hair had escaped from her hairband, flapping across her face from the wind. "Have you been following me?" She felt lead in her gut, the realisation she was right when he didn't defend himself. "Why?"

"I have been asked..."

"Since when do you listen to every order?"

D stood a few feet back, his pale fingers pulling his long hair away from his face in an uncharacteristic display of agitation.

"Did Dread send you?"

"Alice, you need to listen to me. This is important." He stepped toward her.

"Back off." She dropped her voice a few octaves.

He pulled the sunglasses from his face, showing her his dark eyes. "You threatening me petite sorcière?" An unfriendly smile.

"Whatever works." The wind whipped at her hair.

"You don't understand. You need to come with me." His leg tensed as he leant forward. "It isn't safe."

The moment she realised he was a threat she stumbled back, his long arm reaching before she managed a shout.

"ARMA!" With a hiss D was repelled as the aura shield touched him, burns appearing across any exposed flesh, healed over within the next second. "Were you actually going to jump me?" Alice felt all the anger leave her, replaced with shock. "Take me by force?"

Danton wasn't just her trainer or fellow Paladin, he was her friend. She didn't want to fight him. She wasn't confident who would win.

"Wow. Nice aegis." A whistle.

Stunned, Alice turned towards the voice, only just seeing the tall man poke at her bubble.

"This is impressive. Did you really make it all by yourself?" The man walked around the circle, appreciating its structure. "You can make this but you couldn't escape handcuffs?"

"Riley?" she gasped. Fate must have it really in for her. "What are you doing here?" She risked a glance at D, who was staring at the druid with a look of pure hate.

Riley poked at her shield again, sparks sprouting at the connection. "How are you, sweetheart? Your back okay from all the action last night?" Alice choked out a cough at the blatant innuendo.

She could hear D growl, his fangs releasing from the top of his jaw. "Do not speak to her."

"Oh. Vampire." Riley smiled, showing teeth. "Hop along now. Alice and I have something to discuss."

"Reculez enfant."

Riley laughed. "Attention aux insultes vieil homme," he replied in the same language.

French. Why didn't I bloody learn French?

"Alice, please." Danton slowly moved around the bubble, further away from Riley, almost as if he was worried, or scared. "You need to trust me."

"Trust you? You were about to grab her if I wasn't mistaken." Riley played his fingers along her shield, smirking as D stepped further away. "Vous devez reculer."

"Boys," Alice shouted, annoyed. "If you're gonna talk about me, make it English." She glared at both of them in turn.

"Sorry sweetheart, your Vamp friend was just leaving."

"Vous avez entendu mon ordre, druide."

"Ensuite, vous pouvez parler avec Le Conseil." D's face burned red at Riley's reply, his lip curled as he stalked off.

Alice watched him go. "What did you say?"

"Nothing important," Riley shrugged as he leant against a lamppost, his black t-shirt rising up before he pushed it down. Not before she noticed his tattoos went across the left side of his abs.

"Why are you here?" she asked.

"Would you believe it's a coincidence?" That smile again, one that lit up his face, highlighting his cheekbones. He studied the structure of her aegis, slowly walking around the dome. "So, are you going to pop this or what?" He poked at it again.

"Not until you tell me why you're here?" She crossed

her arms, dropping them as soon as his eyes dropped to her breasts.

"You said something interesting last night..." He tilted his head to the side, some of his dark hair draping over his forehead. "Something I want to investigate."

"Well isn't that nice for you." She pressed her lips together.

Riley's face turned cold, his grey eyes flashing, almost mirrored.

It must be a trick of the light.

"Now what I want to know is why Jackson Skye's daughter is researching Daemons?" A curve of his lip. "Looking to taste the dark side are we?"

Alice felt her mouth snap open. *How the fuck did he know that?*

"It wasn't hard to find out much about you sweetheart." He stopped directly in front of her. "You're supposed to be dead."

"And you didn't poof and disappear. The world is full of disappointments." Stomach churning she looked around, noticing how the street was empty.

"I want to go speak to this woman who was recruiting. Where can I find her?"

"Oh, so there is something you don't know." She widened her stance. "If you want anything from me we need to compromise."

"Compromise?" His brows came low over his face. It was clear he had always gotten his own way.

"I will tell you where to find the necromancer, if..."

"If?"

"If you take me with you." She watched his reaction carefully. She was so close to piecing her nightmares together she could taste it. Without Riley's perspective on things, she was out of options. She just had to deal with him first.

"You will only slow me down." She didn't budge. "I'll only agree on one condition."

"What condition?"

"We do this my way."

"We are not going on that." Alice eyed the shiny Harley motorcycle parked up on the curb, Riley gently leaning against it. "You'll kill us."

"Don't be stupid." He stoked across the shiny metal, his leather jacket draped over one of the handlebars. Alice just tapped her foot, observing the bike wearily.

No way in hell. She had changed into something more comfortable, something that didn't have the word 'cheeky' embroidered onto it. Tossing her ponytail off her shoulder she stalked towards him, swinging her car keys around her finger.

"I'm not doing a five hour drive on something with two wheels."

"We could make it in half that."

"No." She tapped her foot again. "I'll drive." Riley sombrely followed her as she guided him down the side road.

"That," Riley said as he looked over her beetle. "Isn't a car. It's a rust bucket."

Alice tried not to get offended. "Well, it has four wheels and a metal roof. Already safer than your death trap." She glanced over her car, admittedly it had seen better days. She hadn't actually realised the marks around the door were rust, she just thought it was dirt. "It gets the job done." She smacked the roof in reassurance, trying not to cringe as rust flaked off.

"Fine, I guess it will do." He went to open the driver's side. "I'll drive."

"I don't think so." She smiled at his annoyed face. "My car, my rules." He looked like he wanted to argue before allowing her to slide into the driving seat. He climbed into the passenger side, having to push the seat as far back as he could to fit his long legs in. Even then he had to bend his knees, his shoulders taking over half of the area available in the small space.

"Why are we taking your car again?" he grunted, closing the door.

"Because I'm not getting on the back of that bike. Besides, you don't even know where we're going." She inserted her key into the ignition, the car grumbling to life a second later.

"It's called a sat nav." Stretching, he took off his leather jacket, throwing it onto the small backseat.

"What's with your tattoos?" she asked, not looking at him.

"My tattoos?" He glanced over at her, her face burning at the attention. "They're special runes, but you already knew that."

"I'm more interested in what they mean and why you have so many?" Her father had always told them they were special tattoos, but he had never explained further.

Druids, from her very limited childhood knowledge, were similar to witches in that they were magic based Breeds. However, rather than just using their aura and chi they also could use the earths ley lines, natural forming earth energies that seemed to connect ancient sacred sites, undetectable to anybody who wasn't attuned to the earth. The rumours were that the tattoos were embedded with magic, not that any druid had ever confirmed it, not even her father.

"You're asking questions I'm not willing to answer." She peeked at him then, catching eyes that had gotten impossibly dark, the grey almost black. There was a hint of challenge in them, almost a dare. She looked away quickly.

"So, if you want to be friendly, what's with your dagger?"

"It's not a dagger," she quickly corrected.

"Yes, it is."

"No, it isn't." She couldn't help but look from the corner of her eye before concentrating on the road once again. "It's a sword."

"Sword?" He chuckled. "It's a very short sword."

"How observant of you." It actually wasn't that short, it was slightly longer than her forearm, giving her perfect balance in her swing.

"Does it have a name?"

"A name?" *Is he on something?*

"Don't all swords have names?" He clicked his tongue.

"No, it hasn't got a name."

"What about spiky?" Riley casually drew across the window with the tip of his finger. "Or maybe Pen?"

"Pen? What sort of name is that?"

"It's something small and pointy."

"That's not even a little bit funny." She drummed her fingers across the steering wheel in irritation.

Riley flashed her a smile before turning to stare out the

window. "What about 'Phantom Iron Sword'? Or P.I.S. for short."

Alice snorted. "I'm not even going to comment." She opened a window slightly, letting the breeze play through her hair. "Why are you investigating the cult?"

"Why are you investigating it?" he countered.

She clutched the steering wheel hard, ignoring the slight squeal of the leather. If they were going to act like a cat and dog the whole journey, the drive would be unbearable.

"You're very small for a Paladin," he said, turning so his back was to the passenger door.

"What's my height got to do with anything?"

"It hasn't. I was just making an observation." He tilted his head to the side, his dark grey eyes staring at her intently. "I know for a fact Paladins don't get contracts based on Daemons."

"How would they know Daemons were involved?"

"You're ignoring my point."

"And you're ignoring mine." Alice blinked up at the traffic lights, waiting patiently for green. "Now why are you investigating the cult?"

"It's my job, I am the guy they call when they need something exterminated."

Alice hesitated, surprised he answered. "And who called you?"

A dark chuckle. "Are you going to tell me where we're going?"

"To a market in Hollow Creek."

A nod. "I know the place." He continued to stare, his eyes penetrating as she concentrated intently on the road.

This was a bad idea.

Why didn't she listen to the advice of never getting into

a car with a stranger? Especially a stranger who wouldn't stop staring, his gaze leaving heat on the exposed skin of her arms and neck. She tried not to fidget, the harness against her back, hidden beneath her clothes rubbing against her in irritation. Riley just continued to chuckle beside her.

CHAPTER 26

Car parked in an empty space, Alice climbed out, locking the door behind her. The entrance to the market was surprisingly empty of all pedestrians, the energy and colour of her previous visit a complete contrast to the dilapidated, malodorous state of the boarded up stalls.

"You sure this is the place?" Riley asked, his leather jacket back on to cover his black t-shirt.

"Yes." Alice led the way, trying to ignore the almost haunted looks of the closed stalls and shops. Graffiti was painted badly across the wood partitions, all in bland colours, as if life and colour had been sucked away, leaving behind just monotone. Numerous alleyways broke out from the centre atrium, many previously hidden from view by the bustling market. The sun strained against the thick clouds, shadowing the already dark alleyways.

The streetlights flickered on and off, confused by the lack of light, solar powered bulbs that were fuelled by the sun, but reacted to the darkness. Plastic bags danced in the wind, mingling with the other litter that had been carelessly tossed away.

Looking around, Alice hesitated, not recognising anything straight away. *Shit.* Maybe she had taken a wrong turn. "I think it's just over here." She pointed to the corner of the square.

The tapestry shop was boarded up, absent the same as the rest. A sign hung dangerously off its pivots, telling her it was the right place. Riley pushed against the heavy door, the locking mechanism not moving. Peering inside Alice checked the gaps in the boards, the interior too dark to see.

"Give me a second..." Alice began.

Riley kicked with his heavy boot, splintering the wood surrounding the solid lock.

"Ever heard of a locksmith?" she asked dryly.

"I smell blood." He pushed the door open, the hinges squeaking into the darkness.

"Holy shit, what happened?" A Putrid odour leaked from the open door, undertones of copper.

Riley didn't respond, instead walking into the room. He pushed the burnt tapestries across the floor, scorch marks smearing the hard concrete. "Looks like someone tried to destroy everything, but didn't finish."

Alice remained silent, swallowing the bile threatening her throat.

"You okay?" he asked when he noticed her face.

"Fine." She swallowed again. "Her office is over there." She flung her arm in the general direction of the hidden door, the tapestry barely hanging against the wall. The door opened easily, the noxious smell reaching its peak inside the small airless room.

"It's been ransacked," she stated, breathing carefully through her mouth.

"So it has." He wandered in, inspecting the remnants. "Stay there."

"What?" She took an automatic step inside, staring at the remains on the floor. "So that's what the smell is." She quipped, no humour in her voice. "It looks like she exploded."

"It's a 'he'."

Alice stared at him wide-eyed. "How can you even tell?" He didn't answer, instead looking around the room. Pulling her top to cover her nose and mouth she bent down to the floor, staring at the remains.

The skull was larger than she would have thought, humanoid with oversized canines. Patterns like a spider web cracked across the top, breaking into an eye socket.

"He was hit on the head numerous times with a blunt object. I can't tell if it was before or after he exploded," Alice murmured. Another chaotic pile of human tissue and organs sat in the corner of the room, half hidden by the overturned table. A femur stuck out from the pile, a shock of white against the browns and reds of the old congealed blood. "There's more than one body here."

"It's an ancient summoning spell. Normally someone is sacrificed around an inverted pentagram. The more men sacrificed the longer the connection."

"Willingly?" She couldn't see any evidence of restraints.

"I doubt it."

"What does it summon exactly?"

"There are a few possibilities, but probably Daemons, but only if you know their names. The summoner creates a circle from which the Daemon cannot escape, the blood from the victims fuelling the dark magic."

"People still summon Daemons?" That realisation

floored her, Daemon summoning hadn't been reported since the early nineteenth century.

"Very rarely, not many people still have the knowledge. A Daemon also isn't willingly going to give up their freedom even if it is only while they're in the circle."

"What do you mean give up their freedom?"

"Once they have been summoned, they are magic bound to the summoner, at least, until the timer is up."

She knew nothing of this magic, but she could feel the remnants leak through the floor.

"Is there anything here?" she asked, her stomach recoiling as the black essence leaked from the corpses, almost like a tar caressing her skin, obstructing her airways.

"Nothing I can see." He kicked at the rubble, moving the table across the room. Leaning down he touched the floor, dry blood flaking beneath his fingertips.

The inverted pentagram was carved into the concrete, congealed blood from the three men soaking into every crack. "The spell's still leaking, probably because the bodies aren't even a day old."

Alice saw something out of the corner of her eye, reaching down she gently moved the table, frowning at the small object. "I've found something."

"Grab it, we need to burn this place down before someone else finds it. I don't want to risk someone syphoning off the remains."

Nodding, Alice grabbed the small rectangular object, shoving it in her pocket without giving it a second glance.

"Scintillam." She lit up the walls, holding the flame steady as it slowly ate away at everything that wasn't concrete. The flesh of the bodies began to burn, a noxious cloud filling the air to the point she had to escape the room.

Walking out into the cold she left Riley to finish, the wind cool against her skin.

She was glad she didn't deal in death, didn't deal in the dark magic that was the opposite of her own. Magic was yin and yang, right and wrong, darkness and light. Newton's third law, for every action there was an equal and opposite reaction. Every spell required a sacrifice in various options of severity, whether it was a plant, her own blood or death. There were reasons being a black witch was illegal.

There were times when people actually protested against the use of living organisms in spells, bringing up the morality of killing a living being, even if it was just a plant. But it was quickly dismissed as being ludicrous. If people really got upset over killing plants, then a lot of people would be suffering from guilt when trimming houseplants or cutting their grass.

"Hello Miss," a small voice called.

"Hello?" she asked, looking around the abandoned market.

"Over here," the falsetto tone beckoned, coming from the alley opposite.

Alice hesitated, peering into the shadows. "Can I help you?"

"No, but I may be able to help you child." An old woman stepped forward, her multicoloured patchwork dress brushing the ground as she moved. "May I read your fortune?" She gave a toothy grin, her two front teeth missing.

"No, thank you. I don't believe in fortune telling," she answered, dismissing the woman.

"Very controversial for a witch."

Alice froze. "You sound so sure that I'm a witch?" Alice

almost checked to see if she had a pointy hat on, which of course she didn't.

"Aye witch, can smell you a mile off. Come for a fortune." She held out a dark hand, encouraging Alice to come with her.

"Like I said, I don't believe in fortune telling."

"Please, no charge. I see the warnings in the cards."

"Warnings?"

"Yes. Warnings." She shook her head forward in a violent motion, her grey dreadlocks swinging intensely. "They are coming." She held out her hand again, her over-sized rings catching the light. "You have seen him."

"Who is coming? Seen who?"

The old woman started to turn away.

"Wait..." Alice reached out. "You said 'you have seen him.' Seen who?"

"My cards can tell you." An oversized smile again. "Follow me." She moved away, no care for her dress as it mopped up the grime along the floor.

Alice wavered, debating what to do. *Fuck.* It went against her training, but she needed to know what she meant, so she followed after her.

"Please. Please. Sit." The woman pulled out a chair from the small round table, taking a seat on the throne opposite. The room was as you would predict a fortune teller's shop should look like. The walls draped artfully with velvet fabric, a mixture of reds, pinks and purples. A wooden free-standing bookcase leant against the wall, feathers, skulls, books and candles sitting neatly atop it. The flames flickered, making shadows dance against the drapes.

At least there wasn't a glass orb sitting neatly in the middle of the table, Alice joked to herself. *Because that would be total overkill.*

"Please child. Sit." She shuffled the cards in her hand, the noise sharp against the silence. Sitting in her chair she faced the old woman, her eyes matching her withered dark skin.

"Now, normally you would ask a question and the cards would answer, this time however I feel we need to do this slightly differently. Your first card," she said, shuffling the pack. "This is your past." She held the cards out, allowing Alice to pick one.

"Death," the old woman stated, as she placed the card face up on the wooden table. "The death card is wildly misunderstood. Most people worry at the prospect of death, but that is not what I see with you. The card portrays an armoured, skeletal figure astride a stallion, black. Death passes people from all walks of life and each is affected differently, you see on the card a man, a priest full of his faith rewarding the afterlife, rewarding death. A young woman turns away out of fear, yet kneels obediently, unable to control her destiny. Lastly a child, completely innocent lays dead flowers by the stallion's hooves, blissfully ignorant of the horrors that are happening."

Alice stared intently at the card, not understanding the meaning.

"Your second card. The present." She held out the pack again. "Ah, the high priestess." She placed the card next to death, tapping it gently with her finger. "The high priestess is you."

"Me?" Alice asked, confused.

"The high priestess indicates that you are seeking knowledge, but such knowledge requires great discipline." She tapped her finger against the woman's face. "The woman sits between two pillars, one light and one dark.

One positive and one negative, you are drawn from outside influences, torn between two."

The woman shuffled the remaining cards further before grabbing another.

"The high priestess is not alone, the ace of wands helps guide her." She placed the ace of wands cards below the high priestess, overlapping. "The ace of wands is the element of fire within the tarot pack, the power of will, sexuality, full of passion, desire."

She slammed the cards on the table, making Alice jump at the sudden movement.

"What does this all mean?" Alice asked, still distracted by the death card. "This is ridiculous," she said, heading towards the door.

An arm grabbed her, nails digging into skin. Turning, Alice faced the woman, ice shooting through her chest. The woman's once dark eyes had glazed over, the pupil's pure white.

"Please child, take this." The woman thrust a card into her face. "We have the seven of swords. A man, as you can see is carrying five swords, two still at his feet. He's tiptoeing away, looking behind him to check if he's being caught, being followed. Betrayal or even deception on his face."

"What has he got to do with me?"

"Are you being deceived my child? It is up to you to decide who or what that may be. You are not thinking with your head, you should listen to your intuition."

Erm, what?

"Your last card." She held the card between two fingers. "We have the king of swords. An authority figure, a cold warrior who acts on his own judgments."

"Okay, I think this is enough." Alice grabbed the cards, crushing them in her hand before shoving them into her jacket pocket. Pulling away from the old woman she stormed out of the small shop, to turn face first into Riley's chest. "Oh."

Riley grabbed her arms before she stumbled back. "What are you doing down here?" He frowned, his thumbs rubbing soothing circles along her forearms.

"I was just..." She turned back to the shop, one that was completely closed, boarded up with old posters layered across where the door once was. "I was just..." *What the fuck?* The neon light fixture above the door was smashed, looking like it had been broken for a while. "I was doing nothing. Just needed to walk off the smell."

Riley stared intently, not believing her. Not wanting to get into a staring contest she turned her head further into the alley, stiffening as she noticed someone in a long cloak standing twenty feet away, a hood hiding its face.

"Alice?" Riley tugged to get her attention.

"Do you see it?" she asked quietly.

"See what?" He frantically looked around, his eyes narrowing as he searched for threats.

Alice continued to stare at the cloaked figure. "Nothing."

I'm going crazy. Batshit-la-la-land.

"It's nothing. It's been a long day." She tugged out of his grasp, shocked at the intense cold that instantly consumed his warmth. "We should go." She gently barged past him, walking in the vague direction of the car park.

"Alice, wait." Riley's long legs caught her up in no time.

"Did you get what you need?" she asked to the air, her emotions too raw to face him.

"What was that all about? I turned around and you were just gone."

"I said I needed some air." He didn't need to know she was losing it.

She turned the corner, skidding to a stop when she noticed four men standing by her car. Riley faced towards the empty car park, his eyes hardening at the sight of the men.

"Friends of yours?" he growled.

I'm going to have to add this to my list of other bad decisions. She knew better, was trained better. Yet she was desperate, an increasingly bad feeling that seemed to overshadow her judgement.

"Nope." She unsheathed her sword, pulling it free from underneath her shirt. Riley looked over approvingly. The men all stood on edge as they approached, fidgeting and looking around the car park warily, their eyes focusing when they walked closer, one gripping a baseball bat in his shaking hands.

"May we help you gentleman?" Riley asked, words like steel.

"Our Pride Leader wants a word." One of the men stepped forward, a scrap of dark greasy hair covering the majority of his face. His cheeks were hollow, veins visible beneath his pale skin. Several other men, just as malnourished as the first, stood a few feet behind their eyes vacant as they waited for instructions. She didn't recognise any of them.

"What's your name?" she nonchalantly asked.

He seemed confused for a second before replying. "Rupert."

"Well Rupert. You may tell Cole to go fuck himself for me," she taunted.

"You know we can't do that." His eyes flashed with worry before hardening.

"Who are these guys?" Riley whispered, his face like stone when he faced her.

"They're from the local pride."

"They don't look like lions."

"Enough," the dark haired man snarled, his nails elongating with his anger. The comment seemed to wake up the other guys, making them step together as a unit. "Come now, or we will force you."

"If you wanted a date, you should have just asked," she drawled, flipping her sword absently in the air. "But, you're not my type."

"Your mouth must get you into a lot of trouble." Riley murmured beside her, his fist clenching.

"You have no idea." She thought she heard a chuckle, but decided it must have been the wind.

"Fine." A silent signal passed between the men. The leader walked slowly towards Alice, an almost sad smile on his face. "You're leaving us no choice." His words slurred as his face slowly shifted in his anger, his control weakening.

His nose grew, pulling his face into a contorted point, his jaw clicking as it widened, allowing room for the large canines that had begun protruding from his mouth. With a snarl he launched towards her, his malnutrition not hindering his speed.

"*Arma!*" With a shout her aegis jumped into existence around her, the dark haired leader jumping straight into the side at full speed. The impact shook the shield, making Alice step back, straight into the side.

"Riley, don't kill them!" she shouted.

Riley dodged a punch to his head, bending at the waist while kicking out at the person behind.

"Why?" he growled, throwing more punches. The lion's

head snapped back with an audible crack, falling into his friend.

Two down.

"Just please, don't..." Rupert rugby tackled her, pinning her to the floor.

Bringing her blade up she blocked his mouth as it aimed for her neck, the blade caught between his inhumanly long jaws. "For fuck sake, I'm trying..." She reached into her boot. "Not to..." Unsheathed a small dagger. "Hurt you." She slashed the blade down his side, deep enough to hurt but not enough to be fatal. He howled out in pain, dropping her sword from his mouth.

Kicking up she dislodged him just as a hand appeared around his throat, lifting his weight off of her. Riley threw the lion into his friend, a crash as they bumped into each other like bowling pins. Chasing after them Riley kicked one of them to the ground, making sure he wouldn't get up any time soon.

Jumping up Alice looked around at the chaos. Rupert was crushed against a dent in the driving side door, curled in on himself as he groaned. The last lion ran off, disappearing from view within seconds.

"Shit. Riley, you're hurt."

"Oh." He looked down at the twin tears across the front of his t-shirt, blood oozing from the holes. "Fuck sake, this was one of my favourite shirts."

Alice turned back to her car, ignoring the lion groaning and rubbing his head. "I can't believe you hit my car. I can't afford a new one." She kicked the bat lying absently by her wheel. She had no idea how it got there or how it had been snapped clean in half. She decided she didn't care.

Riley stalked over, pushing Rupert out of the way before leaning over and popping out the dent. "All new."

"Funny." She re-sheathed her sword, eyeing him warily. He just took down two full grown shifters with ease, a third if she counted Rupert who he effortlessly threw against her car. Her fingers tingled, her blade heavy on the back as she weighed her options. He was definitely more of a threat than she first thought.

"How many blades do you have in that small outfit of yours?" he asked, a playful smile on his face.

"Enough." She looked at him, feeling warmth grow in her stomach, her adrenaline reacting. He opened his mouth slightly, eyes narrowing. He stepped toward her as if he could feel the sudden connection.

Fuck.

Without a second thought she grabbed a spare knife from her other boot, and threw it at him.

"Oh shit!" She blinked stupidly, gaping at what she had just done. Riley held her knife in front of his face, a fist circled around the blade. Blood dripped gently down his wrist, hitting the asphalt. Riley glared at her as he dropped the knife, squeezing his hand to stop the blood flow.

What the fuck was that? His eyes seemed to say, but she couldn't be sure.

She had no idea what made her do that. He was fast, but not fast enough to catch the handle. She licked her dry lips, tensing when his eyes followed the nervous movement.

"You're driving," she said after a few moments, the energy in the air still obvious. He accepted the keys silently, getting into the car without another word. The car rumbled to life, the warmth of the heaters welcome.

What the fuck is wrong with me?

She slid a side look towards Riley, his mouth open slightly as if he was gently panting, his throat swallowing as he concentrated on the road.

Unable to stare at him any longer she turned to the window, counting the trees calmly between the streetlights. Feeling inside her jacket she pulled out the two tarot cards she had stashed in her pocket and ripped the death card in two, throwing it out the window. She felt the air move as Riley turned to see what she was doing, could even feel the air expel as he opened his mouth to speak before quickly turning to face the road once more.

Closing the window she looked down at her last card. The king of swords sat on a throne, a long sword in his left hand, an owl sitting obediently on his right. *An authority figure'* the old woman had said, *'a cold warrior who acts on his own judgments.'* She peered closer at the card, bringing it right up to her face, the king, with jewels encrusted around his neck wore a cloak of grey.

Alice crushed the card in her hand.

CHAPTER 27

The car slowed before coming to a gradual stop, the clouds, having released their weight on the drive back, beat against the roof in a comforting rhythm. Britain was famous for the rain, although it did seem worse than usual.

Riley had parked as close as he could to her place, the dark sky looming over them as she reached for the handle.

"We need to talk." Riley's deep voice almost shook the small car. The atmosphere was still there, something she couldn't describe, almost electric, like her chi was energised by simply being near him. It wasn't as strong as before, but still there. Unnerved to say the least she watched his reflection carefully in the glass, wondering if he felt it too.

Or was she simply losing her mind?

Probably the latter.

Sighing to herself she finally faced him, the lights from the dashboard creating a halo around his face, softening his masculine features.

"Talk, huh?" she tried a side smile, feeling her face crack at the fakeness of it.

"I need to see what you picked up from the cabin."

"What?" She felt it then, the weight of the rectangular box she picked up earlier. "Oh." She had completely forgotten, thought of her cloaked ghost figure playing around in her mind. Reaching for it Riley's hand snapped out, grabbing her wrist.

"Don't get it out here, we don't know who's watching." She looked at him like he had sprouted a second head. Snatching her wrist away she opened the car door, the cool rain hitting her instantly as she walked briskly to the front of her building.

The front door had been broken years ago when someone had forgotten their keys and decided to just kick the weak wood down. No one had bothered to fix it so she easily pushed the door open and started to climb the stairs.

"Alice, we're not finished."

She continued her way up, feeling the hair on the back of her head rise as he effortlessly followed behind. "I think we are." She felt anger grow, an unreasonable reaction considering it wasn't his fault. Squeezing her fists tight she fought the sparks that threatened to release. She had to calm herself before it started to leak.

"Alice?" Riley's weary voice beside her as she walked towards her door.

Techno music pumped through the hallway, broken up by the barks from Mrs Finch's dogs. She could feel the fire start to burn up her throat, feel it react to Riley.

"Keys, please." She let out a breath, almost tasting the smoke. The door creaked open enough for her to push herself through, but not quick enough for Riley's booted foot to shove the door the rest of the way open.

"What's wrong?" He spun her to face him, panic in her eyes as his hands held her shoulders. Air expelled out his throat, a growl erupting from his chest. Alice's breasts pumped against the restriction of her clothes, her body too hot as she fought for control of the power that had awakened. She could feel the flames want to absorb him, testing his energy against her own. If she didn't release it soon she might combust, or worse.

Like a tap, the built up energy dissipated, cooling to a simmer.

"Riley," her voice cracked as she met his eyes, a deep grey encircled by a thin black. Glints of blue floated through his irises, giving the illusion of a mirror. She stared at those eyes, ones that weren't just an illusion, they were actually mirroring her own image back at her. Her own eyes were heavy with a mixture of panic and arousal. Hair a mess, blonde strands circling her flushed face. "What did you do?"

He released her as abruptly as he had grabbed her, his face contorting as he controlled himself. "You will kill someone unless you learn to control yourself." His voice had dropped a few octaves, almost husky as he panted gently through his mouth. He stepped back, widening the space between them. "What are you?" he asked, no hint of humour in his voice.

"What am I?" Her voice was weak, an intense calm coming over her. "What are you? You just..." She had no idea what he had just done. "Took my magic away?"

His fists clenched as he ground his teeth. "How could you possibly hold that much chi and not know how to control it?" He mumbled something incoherently. "Touching you was like standing in a big fucking ley line." She couldn't feel ley lines so couldn't compare, however, she once heard it was like sticking your finger into a power socket.

Her pulse fluttered as she tried to remain calm, she couldn't speak, couldn't react. She felt drained as if he took something from her. Feeling suddenly too hot she pulled off her jacket, throwing it against the sofa where it missed and thudded to the ground. Riley's eyes automatically appraised her, his once silver mirrored irises returning to normal.

"Your eyes?" Those same eyes closed off, dark lashes coming down to hide.

"We need to look at the object you found. Everything you have done up to this point is meaningless unless we figure something out. You'll need something to tell your wolf..."

"My wolf?" She felt the fevered skin on her face drain, replaced with an intense cold. "So you knew who hired me in the first place?" *Of course he did, he knows fucking everything.* Needing to think and put some space between them she bent to grab her coat, storming into her small kitchen to place the jacket down on a counter, staring at the bulge in the pocket.

"What did you pick up?" he asked, his deep voice breaking the silence.

"I don't know," she replied to the jacket. If he believed she was solely doing this for Rex she had an advantage, something he didn't know.

"Alice, we need to know what you found at the witch's cabin."

"The necromancer," she corrected him.

"Semantics. All witches can become necromancers. It's the magic they study that gives them the name."

He was right but... still. Biting her tongue she answered.

"I'm not sure what it is, I just picked it up and shoved it into a pocket."

"That's the first sign of kleptomania you know."

"Funny." She opened her pocket to reveal the rectangular object, staring at it intently. "It's a book."

The book was reasonably small, only slightly larger than her palm with wraparound brown leather. What she assumed were either privacy or protection runes scratched around the corners, the leather turning to suede at the deepest points. Alice squinted at the symbols, not recognising the harsh lines. Turning it in her hands she eyed the clasp, an off-bronze latch with a small circular indent. Looking it over she couldn't tell how to open it.

Pressing down onto the small indent she felt an intense cold, cold enough it stung her skin. With a small yelp, she dropped the book from her hands.

Riley snatched it before it hit the floor. Sucking her finger into her mouth she narrowed her eyes as he examined the book himself, seeming unaffected by the intense cold.

"It's locked."

No shit, she smirked to herself before taking her still throbbing finger out of her mouth. "Can you open it?"

"It's locked by a Pandora charm."

"A what?" she asked, genuinely confused.

"You know the story about Pandora's box? A box that wasn't supposed to be opened otherwise evil would reign down on earth. A Pandora charm literally stops people from opening things, such as chests, boxes, doors and in this case a book." He slammed said book down onto the counter. "It's attuned to blood."

"Blood?" *Of course, because nothing is ever simple.*

"Well, can you open it?" she asked, watching the book intently on the counter.

"Probably." He crushed the palm of his hand to his face. "Without the specific blood needed it is hard. But I should be able to do it." He caught her attention. "I'll need to take it with me." He reached forward.

"NO." She exploded from her position and knocked the book onto the floor. "It stays with me." She nudged the book with her foot, bringing it closer. She couldn't trust him, she had no idea who he was, what he was capable of or how to find him again.

"This is more important than your bloody contract," he growled.

Oh if he actually knew.

"It. Stays. Here."

"Stubborn." He unclenched his jaw. "Fine, at least let me void the tracking runes." *Tracking runes?* Alice stared at the book on the floor. *Who exactly was tracking it?* Alice bit her lip at the thought.

"Fine," she grudgingly accepted. Bending down she hesitantly picked up the book, careful to not touch the clasp. "I'm sure you can do it in my kitchen." Riley just glared with his unusual eyes.

"All I need is salt and a container." Riley glanced around the small kitchen, picking up her bag of salt from the corner.

"A container?" Reaching up to one of the top shelves she grabbed a Hello Kitty lunch box, smirking as she offered it to Riley.

"It will do." He opened the obscenely pink lunch box, tossing the book inside before closing the latch. Without turning he poured salt onto a counter around the lunchbox. He started teasing the grains into what looked like a Celtic knot, but one that ended in points rather than curves.

Alice stepped closer, watching the rune being drawn

when she heard his voice whisper in a language she didn't recognise. Stepping even closer she strained her ears. She decides it might be an adaption of Latin? Or maybe Gaelic?

"Is it done?" she asked his shoulder.

She went on her tiptoes to have a better look, never having seen anything like it. Her knowledge of tracking runes, admittedly lacking, was nothing like this. She reached her hand across, intending to see if she could feel anything coming from the salt when Riley grabbed her arm.

"Don't touch it." He turned her away from the salt. "I haven't got time or the ingredients to void it so I have had to just block it. If you remove the box, the tracking runes will reignite. I don't think you really want whoever is tracking that book to find you in a... compromising position."

"I wasn't going to touch it." She wasn't, probably.

Riley broke into one of his smiles, the one that turned his face into something dangerous, highlighting his sharp cheekbones. She didn't trust that smile at all.

"Can I trust you not to try and open it without me?" He stepped towards her, crowding. She instinctively stepped back, right into one of the kitchen counters. He came further, caging her with his arms on each side. "Promise me you will not open the book." His gaze was intense.

"You said not to move the box." She bit out the words, the events of the day wearing thin on her temper. "It's just a book."

"If you try to open it the wrong way, you will ignite the Pandora charm." He leant forward even further, making her bend to keep away. "It turns deadly." He whispered the last part against her lips. Alice struggled to concentrate, the heat of him radiating against her as she felt the energy building within once again.

His eyes reacted, slowly swirling, becoming mirrored,

yet not. His own breath became laboured, mixing with hers as she struggled to control herself. The energy spiked, making her want to moan before she caught the noise.

"ALICE?" A door slammed.

Her eyes widened in panic at the interruption. She pushed against Riley, forcing him to step back, the cuts across his chest glowing through the fabric of his t-shirt.

What the hell had just come over her?

"Looks like your wolf is back," Riley whispered a second before Rex appeared, his usual closed off face awash in anger.

"Who the fuck are you?" Rex snarled, releasing his claws.

"How did you get in?" she retorted, her early anger renewing from the embarrassment of Rex walking in on her. But she wasn't doing anything wrong? Was she?

"She's mine," Rex stated, ignoring Alice before trying to grab her. Only falling short when she quickly stepped away.

"Rex. Stop it." He wasn't listening. "This is Riley, he's a friend."

Riley leant against the worktop, his body relaxed but his eyes hard.

"He was helping me with research."

"She's mine," Rex groaned low in his throat, his eyes completely wolf. He shook his head like a dog, his teeth growing bigger inside his mouth, large canines protruding through his lips.

Alice turned back to Riley. "I think you should go."

At the mention of his name, he looked down at her, his eyes holding the unusual silver gleam in them, something ancient and animalistic staring out of those silver irises. Blinking, they returned to his normal grey.

"I don't think you should be left alone with him."

"I can take care of myself."

Riley hesitated before slowly nodding. "I will be back as soon as I can get the equipment." With that he quickly left.

"Oh, hey baby girl," Sam walked through the partially open front door. "Why did I just walk past...?"

A howl echoed through the flat.

They turned to the kitchen where Rex paced in the small space.

"Rex?" she asked again, concern and a question all in that one word. He snarled, spit spraying the room through his sharp teeth. Spinning he slammed his fist into the wall cabinet, a dent appearing around his hand.

Closing her eyes, she breathed through her anger, not wanting the fire to build to uncontrollable proportions again.

"Who the fuck is that?" he roared at her. Alice ignored him, continuing to just calm her temper with her eyes closed. "ALICE!"

"I already told you," she scowled, her tone like ice. "He's just a friend."

"Bullshit." His eyes were still an electric blue, his control fracturing, the wolf fighting for dominance.

"Who the hell are you to talk to me like that?" She met his eyes.

Sam tensed as he pulled them both down to their knees against the floor. "Be lower than his head," Sam whispered against her ear. "If you are not lower, the wolf will presume you are challenging his authority.

"But I'm a witch?" She didn't have to follow the same rules as shifters.

"He isn't acting rational," he said, worry underlying his

tone. He caught her eye. *He's like a pup, how the fuck is he an Alpha?*

Alice shook her head. She didn't know.

"Who is that wolf?" Rex roared again.

"Wolf?" she asked, confused but keeping her voice calm. "He isn't a wolf." The next roar shook the room.

"He smells like one. A fucking predator in my territory." He started to pace.

Alice stayed on the floor, the tiles cold against her bare knees. Enough time later for her calves to cramp, Rex finally stopped pacing, his movements less edgy. Taking that as an indication he was calmer she stood, staring daggers at him. She had finally hit her limit.

"What the fuck was that all about?" she seethed.

"He was challenging me," he replied matter-of-factly. As if that was a good enough reason to redecorate her kitchen.

"He isn't a wolf. He isn't even a shifter."

"Is that what he told you?" He laughed, rage in the lines of his body.

"Yes." She barely got the word out before Rex was on her, his hand gripping as he crushed his mouth to hers, the force bruising.

"You are mine," he snarled, nostrils flaring. "You smell like him." His voice went deeper. Electric blue swam across his irises as he kissed her again, a fang digging into her lip.

"Rex, back off," Sam hissed beside them, his own cat reacting to the situation.

She called for her aegis, not wanting Sam to make the situation worse. Her circle encased them, leaving Sam on the outside.

"Get. Off. Me!" she snarled against his mouth. Challenge in his eyes he grabbed her hand, sucking one of her fingers into his mouth, his tongue rolling around the tip.

She remained calm, watching the wolf tease across his features. She tuned out Sam's snarling, his hand banging against the circle.

"Are you finished?"

"You work for me." He put on his usual mask, and once again she found herself annoyed, yet amazed at his ability to control his emotions so fully.

Copper filled her mouth.

"Why was he here?"

"He isn't a shifter," she carefully replied, not wanting to set him off again.

"I know exactly what he is." Rex leant forward as if he was going to kiss her again.

"I think you should leave." She stared into his eyes, showing him her anger.

Rex stared back for a few seconds before turning away, facing the edge of her circle. "Miss Skye?"

She reached to the side, fingers connecting to her aegis before her chi resonated back. Rex stood for a moment, facing the wall before he quietly walked past a seething Sam and out of their flat.

"What the fuck was that about?" Sam quickly touched her face, checking her lip for any damage. Reaching for a paper towel he blotted the corner of her mouth, soaking up any excess blood.

"I don't know." Why would Rex react like that?

"Are we going to talk about the fact you left me outside the circle?" Sam threw the paper towel away.

No. She shook her head.

If he touches you again, I will kill him. Sam started to stroke her hair, purring gently in his chest.

"Why was Riley here?" Sam asked.

"Riley? You know Riley?" She leant back to look at his face. His eyes were slightly crazed, the leopard pacing.

"Of course I know him, he's the new owner of The Blood Bar." He tilted his head to the side. "Did you not recognise him?" Sam walked out the kitchen, returning within moments with a magazine underneath his arm. "Look."

Alice scanned over the front, her pulse loud in her ears. "You have got to be joking."

'London says hello to one of our top bachelors... Riley Storm.'

"That's Riley Storm."

He's a fucking Storm? Holy shit.

The Storm family was one of the most influential in London, owning a large chunk of the real estate. They casually touched elbows with high-end politicians and celebrities, one of those families that were just famous for having money. Looking down to the photograph Alice stared into Riley's grey eyes, his face in open joy, laughing at something the photographer must have said. His dark hair was dishevelled as if he had just run his fingers through the strands. He was bent slightly at the waist, his white shirt open revealing a tanned chest, his tattoos peeking through the gap.

'The Storms' only son Riley has returned from his travels to learn the family trade.'

Alice's eyes glazed as she read the article, confusion mixing with shock.

Things have just gotten even more interesting.

CHAPTER 28

Alice paced in front of Dread's office, the rain battering against the large windows, aggravating her further.

I'm in over my head.

"You sound like an elephant stomping around like that," Barbie tutted to herself, her attention on the emery board she was pushing across her nails.

Alice decided to stomp even harder, continuing her course around the sitting area.

"You should have made an appointment," Barbie continued. "He's a busy man you know."

"It's an emergency." Likely, probably, she wasn't sure. Alice finally came to a chair, sitting down heavily. "I only need to speak to him quick."

"Yeah, well, he's in an important meeting. You'll have to wait." She sniffed before turning away. "You could have just called."

Alice sighed, sinking further into the chair as she closed her eyes. She concentrated on breathing, in and out, the fire inside aggravated, reacting the more upset she became. She needed to purge, her chi overwhelming.

But she was scared.

How could she possibly hold as much chi as she was without just combusting? Riley had said it was like standing in a ley line, but surely he was being dramatic?

She needed to speak to Dr Dave.

"Thank you sir, you will not regret it," a voice broke through her thoughts.

"It has been a pleasure Michael. Don't let me down." Dread's voice flowed through the sudden gap in his office door.

"I won't, sir." Mickey swaggered out of the office, a grin from ear to ear that stretched even further once he noticed Alice.

"Oh Alice babe, did you hear about my promotion?"

"Promotion?" she echoed, eyebrows drawn together. She hadn't heard about any promotions going?

"I have been specifically chosen by The Council for some liaison work. They only wanted the best."

"Well Michael, everyone knows you're the best," Barbie added, pushing her breasts out as she leant over her desk. "You obviously deserved it."

Oh, ew. Alice tried to hide her disgust. "Congratulations Mickey, will you be away from the office for a while?" *Please say yes.*

"Probably. I'm hoping to get my own office within The Council. Soon I might even be Commissioner." He smirked, pushing a hand through his slicked back, greasy red hair. Alice wanted to laugh, Mickey the weasel would never have the balls to run The Tower, never mind actually being in the room with all the members of The Council at once.

Alice had never met any of The Council, but had heard the rumours.

Michael would probably piss himself, she mused to herself.

"Fascinating stuff." Alice leant forward so she could see Barbie, "Barbie can I go in now?"

"Oh, whatever Alice, can't you see I'm talking to Michael? You're so rude."

"Yes Alice, once I'm the boss you won't speak to Barbara like that at all. That's even if you're still here." They both shared a snigger.

Ignoring them she walked past to push open the heavy door, allowing it to close behind her gently. She stood by the entrance for a few seconds, waiting for Dread to acknowledge her. He knew she had been sitting there, waiting, just like he knew everything that happened in his Tower.

"Mickey is after your job by the way," she said instead of a greeting. He hadn't even looked up, instead writing on a single piece of paper with his gold pen.

"I need to retire eventually," he commented. He signed the bottom of the paper before putting it into a hidden drawer on his desk.

She fought a chill that threatened to run down her spine as he looked up at her, his eyes, though usually dark, were the darkest she had ever seen. Bottomless pits that encased all the whites of his eyes.

"What's pissed you off?" Alice took a seat in front of him, careful to not stare directly into the abyss. The rumours about Vamps hypnotising their prey were widely spread in the eighteenth and nineteenth centuries, more than likely by the Vamps themselves. While not technically true, the older the Vamp the more influence they wield. It also depended on how susceptible their prey was.

"Language," he scolded. "I hope you're here to tell me why one of my best Paladins has gone AWOL. Danton was supposed to report back but has been uncontactable."

"How am I supposed to know?" she frowned.

"His last contact was with you."

"He's probably hiding with his tail between his legs after he failed to grab me." She crossed her arms.

"WHAT?" Dread almost floated out of his chair, the lamp on his desk somehow vibrating as the vein in his forehead burst, giving his pale complexion a flushed appeal. Alice felt the hair on the back of her neck stand on edge, she thought his eyes were uncomfortable before... "WHAT HAPPENED?"

"Wait..." Sudden realisation hit her. "If you didn't tell D to grab me, then who did?"

A feral sound came from Dread, his fangs punching through his gums to rest below his bottom lip. "Start from the beginning." He seemed to compose himself, his face marble as he waited for her to explain. "Did you say Riley Storm?" Something flashed across his eyes, but it was too fast for her to catch.

"Yes." She left out the part where she broke into the library, he didn't need to know that. "He interrupted D and..."

"How do you know Mr Storm?" Dread interrupted, his fingers like claws on his desk.

"I don't." His face said he didn't believe her. "It was just a coincidence, I hadn't met him before. I didn't even know he was a Storm until Sam recognised him."

"Sam?"

"Yeah, apparently Riley is the new owner of the bar Sam works at."

Dread's eyes finally narrowed, allowing some white to

peek back through. "What a coincidence." He grabbed the handset from beside his desk, punching in numbers from memory. "Get me the Archdruid," he barked into the receiver. "This is Commissioner Grayson."

Alice strained to hear the conversation.

"Tell Mason if he doesn't call back within the next hour I will pay him a *friendly* visit tonight." With that he slammed the phone down, cracking the plastic.

"Who was that?" Alice chirpily asked. *And who's the Archdruid?*

"You need to stay away from Riley, Alice. He's a Guardian from The Order." Alice sat a little straighter, listening intently. He had never been exactly clear what The Order do. "He's one of the most dangerous men..."

"Well, I'm pretty dangerous too."

"Don't be a child." His severe face stopped her next comment. "He is the youngest ever to gain that rank. He is the judge, jury and executioner." He leant back in his chair, scraping his fingernails across the desk. "What are you even doing Alice?"

"What?"

"Do you think I don't know what you have been up to? Breaking into the library for what? Books on Daemons?"

Busted.

"I..."

"You're taking it too far. Do you think knowing will bring them back?" Alice sat there silenced, unsure what to say. It's not like she had a plan. "If the people you're hunting find out..."

"Find out what?" She tried to cover the tremor in her voice. "I don't even know who I'm hunting."

"And that is exactly why I'm worried."

Alice shuddered as the freezing cold rain battered down, soaking through her jacket quickly. She felt hollow as she walked out of his office and into the street forty floors below, the sky becoming dim as the clouds hid the disappearing sun.

"I don't know what I'm doing," she told the rain.

And who was the Archdruid? What does he have to do with anything? She had been so angry she even forgot to ask about her sword. *Fuck sake.*

A car squelched past at a blinding speed, making her back off from the pavement. Sighing, she looked down the usually busy street, noticing how empty it was. Feet slipping, she turned towards the bus stop and froze, her skin turning to the same temperature as the rain. A hooded figure stood a few feet away, the face hidden in shadow. She stared at it dumbfounded, wondering if she was hallucinating.

The phantom suddenly turned, quickly walking in the opposite direction.

"HEY!" Alice shouted to its back. "WAIT!" She splashed through puddles as she chased after it, following it down several streets until it finally turned down an alleyway. Ignoring the crazy looks from other pedestrians she stood in the mouth of the alley, staring at the figure.

"Hey." She tried again, wondering if the hallucination had the capability to speak back. "What are you?" Of course it didn't reply, instead it just stood at the brick wall at the back between two black bins. "Are you from my imagination?" She shook her head. *Yes, I did just ask that.* "Why are you following me?" She laughed at herself. "Why am I still asking questions?"

The phantom seemed to shake, its shoulders rising and falling in a fast sequence.

Great, my imaginary ghost is laughing at me.

With a huff she picked up a can, throwing it at the figure, watching as the metal sailed through to hit the brick wall as if no one stood there. Verification that she was crazy.

"Yeah, well. Fuck you." She turned to leave when the figure stepped forward. Halting, she watched it move slowly towards her, her back stiffening and the hairs on her arms stood to attention. The figure stopped when it was within a foot of her, within touching distance. The rain suddenly stopped, the wind no longer biting. The figure raised its cloaked arm, reaching out...

"Alice?" A feminine voice called from behind, making Alice jump back and turn at the same time.

"Why are you standing alone in the rain?" Rose held her gym bag above her head.

Alice spun back to the alley, blinking through the rain that she could feel once again, wanting to confront her cloaked phantom.

"I don't know."

C hest tight, she carefully peered around the trunk of the oak tree, staring at the shadowed man, his large body covered in darkness.

"Come here you little bitch."

Sudden light brightened the garden, the flash blinding her.

Blinking past the glare she peered over the trunk once again, gasping as she saw the monster standing by her house. His face was distorted into a scowl, twin horns protruding from the centre of his forehead, curling through his hair before finishing by his ears. An off-white teddy bear was clutched between his large palms, the fur speckled with pink.

"Come out, come out, where ever you are," the monster sang.

The light turned off once again, leaving only the moonlight. She felt her heart beat in her chest, a rabbit trying to escape. Salt on her tongue as tears streamed from her eyes, mixing with the snot against her upper lip.

"Shit. Where are you?" Shoes crunched as the monster moved closer.

CHAPTER 29

S omething's watching me.

Alice woke to the sudden realisation she wasn't alone in her bedroom. She blinked, her eyes struggling to adjust to the darkness. A shadow stood ominously by her open door, taller than her phantom cloaked figure but a shadow, nonetheless.

Great. She rubbed her face with her hands, *I'm seeing other things now.* Flopping down onto her back she stared towards the ceiling, deciding it was just best to ignore it.

A squeak, the floorboards protesting.

What the fuck?

The air moved above her.

Acting on instinct she rolled quickly over as a hand came down, a rag pushed forcibly down into the pillow where her head should have been. Kicking out into the darkness her bare foot connected with something hard, someone or something grunting at the blow.

"You're real?" Scrambling out of her bed she fell to her knees, clenching her teeth at the shock of pain.

"SAM!?" she shouted, her heart turning to ice when he didn't respond. "SAM?" she shouted again as she rolled out the way of a kick. Launching to her feet she tackled the intruder, knocking them both to the floor in a heap. "FUCK!" She tried to get up but something clamped around her wrists.

She yanked herself free, scrambling across the floor in the dark.

A chuckle close behind. "Come here, bitch."

"LUX PILA!" A ball of light bursting into existence above her, illuminating the small bedroom with an eerie blue glow. She stood by her curtained window, sheets from her bed piled on the floor in her panic. The large shadow loomed by her doorframe once more, a pale cloth clutched in its big hands.

A fist flew towards her face, connecting with her cheek and throwing her head back. Crashing against the wall she clutched her cheek, the pain sharp as copper coated her tongue. Another fist came towards her holding the cloth, a sickly sweet smell emitting from the white fabric. Sliding out of the way she yanked at the curtain covering her window, throwing it in the vague direction of the attacker. The curtain landed on its head, disorientating it enough that she kicked out with her foot, connecting painfully with its groin.

Distracted with the pain he (it was definitely a he) clutched himself, her knee meeting his nose in the next instant.

A deep growl as the man pulled the curtain and threw it on the floor, his face scrunched up in a snarl as light leaked from the uncovered window. With a roar he leapt forward, picking her up by the top of her arms and throwing her straight through the open bedroom door. She landed hard on her tailbone, her head connecting with the edge of the side table. A weight settled on top of her, hands constricting her throat. She clawed at the man, his dark eyes bleeding into a vibrant red.

"*Ignis,*" she whispered from a strangled breath, sparks flying from her fingertips. His hands tightened impossibly further before suddenly loosening. With a yelp blisters appeared along his hands and arms, red welts that expanded to bursting point as the sparks ate away at his skin.

Alice wriggled, trying to get out from underneath him, her efforts useless as he reached over and grabbed another cloth from his back pocket. Holding it above her head he laughed, showing small pointy teeth along both jaws.

Calming herself she flipped onto her stomach, her sleep t-shirt riding up so her skin gripped the laminate floor uncomfortably. She stretched, trying to grab the side table...

A loud crash, the front door slamming open and ricocheting off the wall with such power it automatically shut itself. A black blur grabbed her intruder, throwing him against the wall between the bedrooms with such force the picture nailed to the wall smashed to the floor.

Alice clutched her throat, her body suddenly remembering how to breathe as she coughed violently, oxygen struggling to recirculate her system.

What the actual fuck?

She pulled herself to her knees, her head swimming. Feeling as if her skull was weighted she turned to look behind, her eyes taking too long to take in any details.

"Riley?" she coughed again, her throat protesting at any sort of speech. "How? Why are you here?" she wheezed in another painful gulp, successfully stopping herself from fainting.

Point to me.

Riley slammed the attacker against the wall, his legs flying wildly in panic. "I was watching the place, I didn't trust they hadn't already tracked the book."

"Did you see Sam?" she coughed again, the pain mingling with her growing headache.

"He isn't here."

Oh yeah. She finally remembered. *He was called into work.*

Alice leant against the sofa for support, attention on her attacker, the view better from the living room as the light from the balcony stretched through the kitchen archway. The guy was huge, easily double her size and wore all black. His red eyes were wide, the pupils slit, like a cat, or a snake.

"What is he?" she asked, her throat painful.

"Daemon."

The Daemon cackled deep in his chest, smiling with his teeth.

"A Daemon?" she parroted. She stared at the man, if she could even call it a man, as it struggled against the hand at its throat. The shadow in her nightmares was nothing compared to the real thing. Over six foot with bulging muscles overlaid with dark veins. Heavy features scrunched with pain, dark hair longer than her own styled to cover the small horns that had been sanded down.

"What are you doing here?" Riley snarled. The Daemon continued to laugh, blood bubbling around his lips. "What are you doing here?" Riley repeated, the words resonating with a power Alice had never heard.

The Daemon gurgled in response, his red eyes glazing over. A light from Riley's closed fist, a ball of arcane held against the Daemon's skin, the power licking against his clothing, almost teasing the flesh as it burned and melted.

Alice stared, her throat dry. Arcane magic was unpredictable, raw power manifested into a ball of light. It took incredible strength to control it so casually.

The Daemon hissed in pain, blood now pouring down his chin in a steady stream.

"I will ask you one last time. Why?" Riley leant in. "Are. You. Here?" The last word a breath against the Daemons face, almost intimate in its rage.

"She is the one," the Daemon gargled. "She is the last before The Becoming." A wet cough, its hands holding onto Riley's forearms so it didn't suffocate.

"Stop with the riddles," Alice responded, her voice hoarse, sore from the strangulation.

The Daemon laughed once again, the sound wet. Something dripped out of his ears, a sea of red across his dark skin.

"He is Becoming."

"Who is Becoming?" she asked.

A scream as the arcane ball slowly burrowed into his chest. Red tears leaking from his eyes.

"What do you want from Alice?" Riley asked.

"Dragon born. She's the dragon born." A hollow chuckle as his chest rattled. "With steady breaths, they ride towards the dawn. Mortals cower in the dark, defenceless, prepare to mourn. Shadows move across their souls, as darkness, corruption and power grows. The four elements, magnets against mortal breath. Generations of lies, of wrath. Power in its truest form, made physical with greed. Are they saviours who wish to lead? Famine destroys along the path, against Pestilence in his wrath. Death stares and waits his turn, as War's flames turn to burn. The apocalypse they bring to earth, destroying it for all it's worth."

"What's happening?" Alice asked, her face in open shock. The Daemon convulsed, shaking violently. Riley released his grip and the Daemon fell straight to his knees, blood pooling quickly around his body. His dark skin slowly turned red, as if he was combusting from the inside out.

"Blood's leaking out of his pores," Riley grunted, absorbing the arcane back into his hand.

"Death is coming, War." A wet snigger. "You are the catalyst." A smile showing red stained, pointy teeth. "With your ascent, the new beginning will start."

A deep inhale. His face crumpling, eyes sinking into his face as skin was absorbed into his body, a shock of white as his skull appeared through the flesh, cracking and disintegrating before their eyes. The body melting into itself, leaving nothing left, not even dust.

"Great," Riley snarled, staring down into what was left of the attacker. Red splashed across his shirt and face.

"What happened?" Alice asked for the third time, her face white.

"He was on a timer."

"A timer?"

"Yes, it's a delayed assassination spell. The spell went off because he was taking too long. If he succeeded and got you out of here the spell would have dissipated and he would've lived."

Riley turned to look at Alice, his face expressionless. "Where's the book?"

"Book?" A confused look. "Oh, it's still in the lunchbox."

Without another word he turned towards the kitchen, opening the lunchbox with a quick click.

Frowning at the book he reached to the bottom of his shirt, pulling it over his head revealing intricate black and red tattoos along the left side of his back. Scrunching the shirt in his fist he squeezed some red liquid onto the silver clasp, right above the circle indent. With a pop and sizzle, the book snapped open.

"It's done."

"How did you know that would work?" she asked, having followed him.

"I didn't."

She walked over to where he was standing, feeling the heat from his skin. "You have blood on your hands," she whispered, carefully taking the book out of his palms.

She scanned the book, flipping through pages.

"It's a list," she said a moment later.

"A list?" he asked, wiping the remaining blood off his face and chest with his destroyed shirt, throwing it into the bin in the corner of the room. Alice stared at the book, careful not to look at him.

Maxi Swanson – Dead – Survived only 2 weeks.

Samuel Lewis – Survived.

Sahari Mooner – Dead.

Stewart Leonard – Survived.

Ernest Rhodes – Infection started.

Alesha Morgan – Dead.

Bobby Dust – Dead – Did not take to the infection.

Mischa Palmer – Dead.

Jackie Nunez – Dead.

Alexus Pride – Survived – Rabid, had to be put down.

Francis Carter – Dead.

Louis Owen – M.I.A.

Tomlin Kar – Started infection – Got caught by target. Had to be made an example of.

Roman Wild – Started infection – Taken to infection perfectly, looks promising.

Alice stared at Rex's brother's name, a million questions forming at the forefront of her mind.

Does Rex know?

She flipped further through the book blindly, unsure how to deal with the information.

"Oh," she gasped, unable to speak past the lump in her throat. With shaking hands she traced the indents the pen had made on the page, the name circled many times. Her name. Repeated over and over.

"Anything?" Riley's voice made her jump.

She glanced at him, wide-eyed. "My name's in here." She held out the book, he accepted it before flipping through the pages.

"So it is," he grunted, tossing the book onto the counter.

Alice walked away to stare out the window of her balcony, the light of dawn threatening to break in the distance.

"May I use your shower?"

She nodded, still facing the window, her emotions too raw to reply. She felt him rather than heard him walk away, silent even though she knew he wore heavy leather boots. The shower started in the bathroom only minutes later. Grabbing a mug from beside the sink she poured in hot water, and simply held it in her hands, watching the water as it settled.

Riley re-entered the room a lifetime later, the mug now cool in her palms, his chest bare, jeans low on his hips. He leant against a cabinet opposite, his eyes reflective in the light.

"What happened to your cupboard?" He nodded towards the dent.

"Rex thought he would redecorate."

"Did he touch you?" A low growl.

Alice refused to reply, instead she looked up from her mug she caught his eyes. "What are you?"

"You know what I am." He turned his head at an angle, an animalistic gesture, something she was used to watching Rex do, or even Sam.

"You're more than that," she stated. Her eyes travelled across his chest, following the patterns that flowed across his left peck, further down his taut stomach before disappearing below his jeans. His right arm was completely covered in the beautifully intricate designs, his left only partially covered. A slight pink scratch marked his chest, the only evidence of the wound from the lions. He held her gaze, the silver sheen reflecting heat. "Rex called you a wolf."

"Did he?" No smile. Only eyes.

"Are you?"

"Am I what?"

"A wolf?"

Riley didn't hesitate. "It's complicated."

"It's a yes or no question."

"I'm not a shifter." Controlled words.

She refused to let him bend. "How can you lift a Daemon off the ground like that?"

"I work out."

"You were faster than those lions."

"They were lazy. Alice what do you want me to say? I am who I am."

"Then who are you?"

"I am me," he stated, face tense. "Now who are you?"

"Who am I?" she laughed. She didn't know the answer to that herself.

"He called you a dragon." He stepped closer.

Alice remained silent.

330

"What did he mean?"

She moved further from him, not liking the fact he was towering over her, her height giving her little advantage.

"I have no idea." She really didn't.

She had no idea why her name was in a book.

Why he called her a dragon.

Why her family was slaughtered and she was the only survivor.

Riley narrowed his eyes as he decided whether she was telling the truth. Alice stared back, daring him to comment, the lukewarm tea forgotten in her hand. What did he expect from her?

"You're not telling me something." A statement.

"Oh, like you haven't told me you're a Storm?" She watched something dark pass across his face. "Or was it just something you forgot to mention?"

"We're not talking about me."

"Like hell we are!" She felt her voice rise.

"You know nothing of me and my family," he said, annoyed as he backed towards the shadows, hiding his face, hiding his eyes.

"And I know *nothing* of mine." She moved up to him, trying to see his expression through the darkness.

She could feel his gaze on her face, could tell when he decided she was telling the truth, that she didn't know what the Daemon was talking about. A light suddenly reflected across his eyes, the iris turning silver in a flash before becoming hidden once again. Swallowing her emotions she stepped away, trying to get her thoughts together.

"What was he talking about? The poem?" She didn't recognise it.

"It's just a poem," Riley replied, his voice soft. "It supposedly depicts the four horsemen of the apocalypse."

She turned to the balcony, watching the pink sky.

"War, he called me war." She felt a warmth against her neck, butterflies in her stomach. Turning she looked up at his face. His eyes were inhuman, something ancient staring out. She didn't feel scared, only a sudden anticipation. It was different with Riley, a natural attraction compared to the torrential longing she felt for Rex. She didn't feel like she needed Riley beside her, but wanted him instead.

He stared down at her, his eyebrows pulled together in confusion. Slowly, he leaned down, giving her time to change her mind. He sighed her name as his lips came down on her own, the contact electric. She melted into the kiss, surprised by her sudden voracious hunger. Sliding his hands down her waist he bunched up her T-shirt, going beneath to touch his warm hands to the bottom of her back.

"Alice..." he groaned as if she were the greatest pleasure, or pain.

Lifting her up he moved her to sit on the edge of the sink, she could feel him through the fabric of his jeans, a large bulge against her most sensitive area, her underwear giving little protection.

She moaned into the kiss, nipping at his lip before he started to peck down her neck. She panted heavily, her brain overpowered with arousal as her chi danced from the electric current. With a small bite to her neck, he let her slide to the floor, her legs like jelly. He took step back, staring at her with a blank expression. In one slow movement he bent at the waist, light perspiration glittering along his back.

He walked out without looking back, leaving the cold to swarm into the space he just stood.

CHAPTER 30

"Fucking stain," Alice scolded the blood that seemed to have permanently ingrained itself into the laminate flooring. "He had to bleed all over the place didn't he?" She pushed the cloth through the red liquid, squeezing the excess into the bucket next to her. Sighing, she scrubbed the floor, the supposedly 'magic' bleach doing little.

After what felt like hours Alice finally sat back, staring at the doomed flooring. It wasn't budging.

"Well, I guess this place needed a new rug anyway." She threw the destroyed rag into the bucket when a loud knock rocked her door. "Shit." She looked around the room for something to hide the stain. "JUST A MINUTE!" she shouted through the wood.

KNOCK. KNOCK. KNOCK.

"For fuck sake." She cringed at the blood. She did not want to explain anything to Mr Tucker or her landlord. "I SAID," she shouted even louder through the door. "JUST A MIN...."

The door swung open, two men dressed head to toe in black swarmed in, their faces covered by oversized black sunglasses.

On instinct she kicked the bucket, letting the mixture of water, bleach and bloody mucus shower the men. Their shocked faces were all she needed as she lifted her elbow up to meet the first man's nose, causing his head to flick back into the wall with a crack. The second one snarled as his arms encircled her, lifting her off her feet as he growled something inaudible in her ear. Chest constricting she threw her head back, catching his face and kicking out at the same time. The momentum threw them both back, hitting the wall with a thump his arms loosened around her. Turning with a snarl she called to her power, lighting up her palms...

"ENOUGH!"

Attention shifted to the older gentleman who closed the door gently behind him. His suit was clearly pricey, ironed to perfection with a silver clip holding his blood red tie in place. His face was aged, but in a way rich people age, someone who has never had to worry about where their next meal would come from. Fashionable laugh lines. His eyes were cruelly pinched, annoyed as he looked her up and down, and from the scowl she knew he was disappointed.

"Bruno. Marco. Please wait outside," he instructed the two men who had taken to stand beside him.

Sunglasses number one held his nose, blood pouring down his face, while sunglasses number two frowned at the broken glasses clenched in his big fist, intricate runes were tattooed around his left eye, pulsating in irritation before he followed his friend out the door. The bleach had already started to eat away at their black shirts, leaving white patterns like a badly designed tie-dye.

"I don't think we have been properly introduced," the older man started. "I am..."

"Mason Storm. You're Riley's father." She could clearly see it after she looked past his severe expression. He had the same high cheekbones as Riley, ones that seem to be chiselled from stone with a strong forehead and jaw. His skin was clean-shaven, hair the same dark tone as his son's but peppered with grey.

His eyes the same unusual shade, eyes of a predator.

"I see you have no manners," Riley's father tutted to himself. He folded his arms across his chest, bringing her attention to his expensive watch. "You may call me Councilman Storm."

Councilman?

That was something she didn't know. Dread had taught her to always be wary of The Council, of the people who believed they ruled everything.

"Why are you here?" Alice breathed heavily as her chest ached, her ribs protesting with every inhale. "Why did your bodyguards attack me?"

"Firstly they didn't attack you, they defended themselves." His eyes narrowed as he took in the bloodstains across the floor. "Secondly, I am here because my son seems to be fascinated with you, Miss Skye."

He appraised her once again, his face turning into a grimace as he noticed her black t-shirt. It just happened to be the one that said '*CLASSY AS FUCK!*' written in white across her breasts. She folded her arms to cover it.

"I like to take an interest in anything my son does. I personally don't see his fascination."

Okay, rude.

"Can I help you?" She tried to keep her voice civil.

335

"Your manners are atrocious, your father would be disappointed."

"Excuse me?" She dropped her arms. "You knew my father?" Alice fought for her voice not to break.

"Of course, he was my advisor, a high-ranking Vector. He left it all for your mother, the fool he was. Right until the very end." He tilted his nose up slightly. "He was corrupted by that woman. I will not let it happen to my son."

Alice narrowed her eyes. "So you're the Archdruid?"

"Well, of course, who else would it be?" he smirked, full of himself. It's nothing like the smirk Riley can do, a smile full of tease and laughter. This smile made her want to run for her blade.

"Now tell me, how did you survive when your family did not?"

Alice remained silent.

"You seem surprised I know that?" He chuckled as he tugged the ends of his black suit jacket. "I'm a man who knows secrets. So, are you going to tell me? No? I'm sure it is an amazing tale. But one for another time then?"

A blue flame burst across her fingertips, her irritation manifesting itself as she swallowed down the excess power.

I need to get myself together.

His eyes watched the flame in fascination. "So much like your mother. I wonder if you will learn to control it? Or allow it to consume you."

She frowned. "Consume me?"

He checked his watch. "Now this has been lovely but I really do need to be getting off. Important people and so on..."

He turned to the door, opening it slightly before looking back over his shoulder.

"Stay away from my son Alice, or else people close to you could get hurt."

He tugged something from his inner pocket, unfolding it before flinging it towards her.

"This is for you. I found it pinned to your front door. I'm sure you don't need any more enemies Miss Skye." With that he left, slamming the door shut behind him.

Alice clenched her hand, crinkling the paper he had handed her before she calmed herself, flipping it over. Her temper instantly cooled, acid coating her tongue as she studied the photograph. It was Sam, unconscious with his wrists and ankles painfully bound by silver, bruises pattered across his face and chest.

Below it was an address.

Sam's phone went to voicemail. Again.

Swallowing her dread she parked up the dirt road, a short walk away from the long driveway of a compound. The address was just out of the city, surrounded by land for miles on all sides.

There was an old manor house built at the end of the drive, surrounded by smaller, similarly designed buildings. Alice surveyed the area, noticing the house backed up to a dense forest. Several cars were parked along the drive, a mixture of cheap run-arounds and expensive 4X4s.

Crouching behind a black truck she analysed the house, squinting to see into any of the windows. There was clearly something happening, shadows moving erratically behind the curtains. She heard a howl, followed quickly by a loud growl.

The front door crashed open and a shirtless man

stormed out, heading straight towards where Alice was hiding. Confused, she stood up from her crouch, arms folded across her chest as she made her way around the truck.

"What the fuck are you doing?" Rex snarled. "Why are you here?" He halted a few feet away, close enough for Alice to see a slight sheen of sweat across his skin, glistening next to the blood that had already started to clot from the deep abrasions.

"How did you know I was there?" she asked.

"Alice, I don't have time for this." He turned back to the house, expecting her to follow.

"Where's Sam?" She ran after him, her voice strained as panic began to rise. "Is he here?"

"Sam? What are you on about?"

She followed him down the hallway, her boots tapping on the wooden floor.

"I got a photo and it had this address on it." She pulled out the photograph, showing it to him when he finally stopped walking. "Where is he?"

Rex looked at it carefully, his lashes low when he handed it back. "I have no idea, he isn't here."

"But he has to be..."

"Oh look who it is," a voice mocked from an open doorway. "How is little Alice?"

She turned to the voice, her hand automatically drawing her sword when she noticed Cole. "What are you doing here?" she asked through clenched teeth, hand tightening on the hilt.

"Helping out my friend," he replied with a curl of amusement on his lips. "Has the little witch come to play?"

"Cole, enough." Rex held out his hand. "Alice, give me

your sword. There are no weapons in the Den. This is a safe place, I will not have you walking around armed."

"No."

"Then we won't help you find Sam," Rex growled.

Panic built further as Alice took a moment to decide, calming herself as she surveyed the room. The calmer she made herself, the clearer she saw.

Cole stood behind Rex, leaning casually against the door jamb, his body language seemingly uninterested in the situation. His eyes, however, were burning, emotions intense.

Rex crossed his arms as he waited, his face grimacing as he opened one of the deep cuts across his chest. Blood trickled down his abdomen to drip on the floor, each drop slowing as his blood clotted once again.

Seemingly out of options she licked her dry lips.

"What happened here?"

Cole answered before Rex could. "Pack matters. We don't need assistance from a witch."

"You aren't pack," she bit back.

"Alice I haven't got all day..." A howl interrupted him, tightening his jaw he waited for the noise to finish before continuing. "Give me your sword, so we can help."

She hesitated, not wanting to be without her weapon. Blade hot against her palm she handed it over.

"Thank you." Rex nodded as he handed it to someone behind him.

She remained silent, not sure about the situation.

A shadow leapt through a doorway, smashing itself against the opposite wall.

Howls of pain erupted as the large man-wolf clawed at its own chest, deep enough to see bone. Alice moved out of the way, never seeing a shift so violent. The beast's snout elongated as razor-sharp teeth erupted from newly formed flesh. Black liquid oozed from open wounds across the creatures bare chest, the fluid thick and stringy. Bones cracked, skin stretched, growing, shrinking and rearranging as the body morphed. The fur looked to be absorbed back into the body, pink muscles and ligaments appearing underneath before hardening like leather, a burst of colour compared to the darkness of the fur.

This shifter's transformation was a violent metamorphosis of one form to another. The strange black liquid continued to pour out of the wounds that didn't seem to heal, the thick substance sticking to the floor.

She had seen enough shifts to know that it wasn't normal.

"Cole," Rex grabbed the scruff of the wolf. "Take Alice outside." He wrestled the wolf as it tried frantically to bite him, his claws digging into Rex's chest.

"What's happening?" She really wished she had never given up her sword.

A hand came down to clutch her shoulder, fingers pinching painfully. Alice turned, raising her elbow high enough she hit it straight into Cole's throat. He snarled, clutching his neck as he choked and gasped for breath.

Not caring about his damaged windpipe she stepped back onto the drive, not stopping until she was at the end of the row of cars. Hands shaking she crouched down, her own breath coming in pants as she tried to control her emotions.

Sam wasn't there.

Then where was he? Why would the paper show this address?

"That was mean." Cole coughed as he walked up beside her, his voice slightly strained.

"You shouldn't have touched me." She straightened,

her gaze taking in the grassy areas that surrounded the house before disappearing into forest. "Where's your wife?"

"She's not allowed to leave our house." He coughed again, spitting onto the dirt floor.

"What's happened?" She nodded towards the house when she faced him, noting that his beard was shorter than last time.

"Rex is being punished. He never was good at taking my advice."

"Punished?"

"He's a fool, one that will eventually learn."

Alice watched his eyes. "What is he being punished for?"

"That is for him to tell, for him to decide." Cole looked towards the house as a wolf howled. "He just needed a little push."

Stupid lion, speaking in riddles.

"I need to speak to Rex, we need to get out a search party for Sam."

"Well isn't it your lucky day, he's walking over." With a sarcastic bow, Cole moved towards the house, passing Rex as he stormed towards her.

"You don't understand what's happening." He shot the words like bullets. "You have no idea what's going on."

"Rex I need help with Sam, he's been taken..."

"You just don't get it do you?" he shouted, eyes ablaze and angry. She had never seen him so angry. "You were supposed to help me, supposed to keep them away. My mate, this supposedly powerful witch..."

"Mate? Rex, what are you on about?"

Rex continued, almost in delirium. "They were wrong. You can't help." His voice broke, pain radiating from every word. "I didn't know what to do. They're my pack, my family."

"Rex, I..."

"You smell like them." His voice dropped, his wolf close to the surface.

Slowly he reached across the small space between them, closing his hand delicately on her throat, his thumb stroking gently across her skin.

"I'm sorry for everything." His hand began to tighten as he wrapped his other hand around her hair.

"REX?" She pulled away, her skull screaming as she felt the hair pulled straight from her scalp. She stared at the blonde strands clutched in his closed fist.

"I have no choice. They're giving me no choice."

"Choice? Rex, what are you talking about?" She eyed him carefully, her heart in her throat. He was a shifter, stronger and faster than her, an Alpha even more so. She was trained to track down his kind, yet she felt a slow terror ache her bones. She had never gone against someone with eyes that held the edge of sanity.

She needed to calm him down.

"Rex. REX, look at me." She kept eye contact, the beast within him unable to look away. "We can get through this, I can help if we talk about it." She slowly edged away, stopping when she noticed him tense.

"You can't help." His voice was no longer his own.

"Of course I can, I'm the big bad witch remember? You said so yourself." She swallowed to help her dry throat. "What was Cole talking about?"

"They're coming for them, for everybody."

"Who is?"

"I..."

The wind erupted around her, throwing her hair into

her face and breaking the eye contact. She scrambled back, but not fast enough. All the air in her lungs was knocked out as she was crushed to the ground, Rex straddling her hips.

"Rex," she croaked. Pinned to the earth.

"I'm sorry." With one hand he held her down, with the other he reached into his back pocket.

Shit. Shit. Shit.

Lifting up her knee she kicked up, connecting to his groin with enough impact for him to be thrown back. With all her anger she released an arcane blast, a wall of flame against Rex's unprotected face.

A shout as he covered his skin, protecting his eyes from the sudden heat. With all her strength she pushed against him, hard enough she was able to wiggle out and half crawl away. He snarled, patting out the small flames from his hair as she gained her feet and ran straight into the protection of the wooded area surrounding the pack's land.

A chorus of howls erupted around her, a discord of noise from behind. Not daring to look back she continued running, dodging trees and jumping over roots and debris, trusting her reflexes to stop her falling. Alice reached for her back, searching for her blade that wasn't there, having given it to Rex earlier.

"Fuck." She stopped, her lungs burning. She quickly reached her back pocket and grabbed her phone, careful of the broken glass. "Fuck." She leant against a moss-covered tree, the howls getting closer. "Fuck. Fuck. Fuck."

She scrolled through her phone, the screen flickering before going black.

"Great, just fucking great."

A crunch to her left. A woman stood at the edge of the trees, her nails darkening, elongating and becoming razor sharp as she watched. "There you are," she whispered, her eyes glittering with excitement. "I've been looking for you." Without another word she launched herself across the clearing, her shifter speed carrying her almost effortlessly over the ground.

"*ARMA!*" Alice shouted as the woman closed in, the aegis of aura popping into existence just in time. She bounced off the circle and crashed into a tree, on her feet a second later.

The aegis flickered, disappearing then reforming.

"Shit."

Alice grabbed at her throat, the crystal pendant no longer there. It must have fallen off when she fought with Rex. The dome flickered again, taking all of her concentration to keep it formed without its anchor point.

The woman circled the dome, her skin darkening with her anger, teeth growing in her mouth.

Wiping the sweat from her face she ignored the pain shooting through her skull, taking everything to keep the shield formed. The aegis shimmered, the woman launching herself across the space as it went down.

A scream filled the woods.

Alice gasped, her arms completely covered in blue flames licked with emerald. The woman rolled around the ground, trying to put the fire out from her clothes, patting them with her bare hands, skin blistering as it started to consume her.

Alice blinked, blood rushing in her ears, something warm dripping down her face as copper coated her tongue. Wiping her face with her sleeve she saw red, blood dripping from her nose.

Arms grabbed her from behind, crushing her against a wide chest she recognised.

A short, sharp pain in her side.

Warmth grew from her abdomen, bubbling through her bloodstream.

Cotton at the back of her throat.

"I'm sorry it has to be this way."

She looked up at Rex, her legs giving out.

Her tongue felt heavy in her mouth, unable to form any words. She couldn't feel herself collapse, her knees hitting the earth with a thump. Her head rolled as she turned to stare into his eyes, blue spheres heavy with regret.

CHAPTER 31

Head heavy, Alice groaned as she opened her eyes, shutting them quickly when the lights above burned. Squinting until her eyes adjusted to the bright light she looked up, noticing that her wrists were manacled together, linked with a chain attached to the ceiling. She stared at it for a few seconds, tugging her wrists gently to the sound of the chain rattling.

"Fuck," she exhaled, keeping her voice low. "Fuck, fuck, fuck." The light was coming from a single point in the ceiling, a spotlight aimed at her alone. Beyond the light she saw nothing, darkness being kept at bay from the single bulb.

Panic grew as she tried desperately to tug at the chains, testing their strength until the pain became too much. Lead in her stomach she lurched forward, nausea rising to the point bile choked her throat.

"You'll dislocate your shoulder if you lean anymore," a voice calmly uttered through the darkness.

Alice froze, straining to hear something other than the rattle of the chain and the blood pumping through her skull.

"Hello?" She tugged more desperately. "Rex?" she whispered hesitantly, shrinking back against the brick wall.

"Why would you call for him?" A quiet monotone replied. "He betrayed you."

Alice strained to hear where the voice was coming from, panic peaking when she finally saw something at the corner of her eye. Turning she watched as a figure walked into the circle of light, her veins turning to ice when she recognised the dark cloak.

"You're not real."

"You look like her," her imaginary phantom replied, voice soft, almost detached.

"You're not real," Alice cried once again.

"Real?" The phantom pondered it for a second. "Am I real?"

It slowly glided towards her, almost painfully as the black cloak swished gently. A pale hand emerged from the sleeve, boney with dark veins pulsating underneath paper-thin skin.

"I don't even know if I am real anymore." It pulled off its hood, pale skin stretched across a slim face.

"Have you found her?" another voice joined in, one that was familiar.

"Alice," her brother called *"Alice. It's me. It's Kyle. Come out from where you are hiding."*

The monster continued to check the bushes and flowerbeds, searching for her.

"She's not here," the monster growled. *"I was promised the girl."*

"Shut up," her brother whispered back. *"Alice."* He raised his voice. *"You know how mum doesn't like you playing out here in the dark."*

A click as he turned on a torch, the light landing on his shoes for a moment, dark red stains marking the pristine white trainers.

"Alice," he called once again, his voice scared.

Blinking suddenly through wet eyes Alice stared at what was once her brother, his features the same as the gangly fourteen-year-old too skinny for his frame, except he had grown into his shoulders. His cheeks were hollow, dark messy stubble speckled across his jaw as emerald eyes, the same as hers, as their mother's, stared at her blankly.

"Kyle?" Alice choked out, tears pouring down her face.

"Why are you crying?" he asked, confusion swirling in his eyes. His hand raised to touch her face, the skin ice cold.

"Why are you doing this?" She tried to shrink back, her head hitting brick. "I don't understand."

"I thought you were dead." His other hand came up to hold her face, his breath just as cold as he moved forward. "Then I saw you, igniting the dragon, saving that woman." His gaze searched for something, she wasn't sure what.

"Fuck this," the monster stormed into the kitchen, returning moments later with her mum screaming, dragged her by her hair as she flailed wildly.

"Mummy," Alice squealed, covering the noise at the last minute, as if she could stop the sound carrying. Light landed just a foot from where she was crouched, huddled by the bark.

"What are you doing?" Kyle shouted as the monster grabbed their mother's hair, wrapping it around his fist as she fought the bonds holding her.

"Please. Please," she begged. "Why?"

"NO, STOP!" Kyle grabbed the monster's arm.

"*I knew this was a mistake.*" The monster pushed Kyle back effortlessly, turning to lift him by the throat with one arm. "*Fucking kid.*" He flung Kyle away as if he were nothing.

Alice closed her eyes, hands shaking as she hid behind the tree. Screams echoed until they suddenly stopped.

She tried to control her tears, her sight watery as she struggled to see in the dark.

"*Alice...*"

She felt her heart beat in her chest, the sobs coming stronger as she struggled to control them.

"*Alice...*"

The monster slowly approached the tree, whispering over and over.

"*Alice... Alice, come here little girl.*" Heavy legs beside the fern. "*There you are,*" a growl as an arm reached down to grab her.

With a cry Alice absently grabbed a rock, throwing it with as much force as she could. The sharp edge hit the monster with a squishy noise, hard enough that he shrieked, grabbing his face as a pale liquid dripped down his skin.

"*Mummy?*" she sobbed, running across the garden to the curses of the monster. "*Mum? Kyle?*"

Her nightdress danced in the cold wind, trying to trip her up as she knelt beside her mother, Kyle nowhere in sight.

"*Mum?*" she whispered, her knees warm in the dirt. She patted her mother's hair, her face hidden beneath it. "*Mummy, it's okay, I got him. Look... Mummy?*"

She lifted up her mother's long blonde hair, confused by the sea of red decorating the front of her mother's nightgown.

A sharp pain along her scalp. "Alice," Kyle wrapped more hair around his fingers. "Don't go away again."

Go away?

Alice felt the nausea growing.

"KYLE!" a smoky voice growled, hidden behind the light. "Control yourself."

Kyle's eyes swam with black, pupils dilating as his mouth turned into a grimace.

"If you ignore him," he spoke against her cheek. "He will go away."

"KYLE!"

Kyle ripped away, nails clawing at his own face.

"WHAT?" he shouted towards the voice.

"Walk her down, the preparation has been finished."

Kyle turned back, eyes completely encased in black. "This way."

"What? Kyle STOP!" Her chains went taut as he started to drag her from the room. "PLEASE." He didn't respond, pulling her chain with agitation. "You don't have to do this."

A heinous putrid smell polluted the air, leaving her gagging as she struggled against the chains. Steel cells lined the hallway beyond the light, groans and whimpers leaking through the bars. One cell held a group of people, their clothes ripped, soaked in blood and their own urine. Scars decorated their skin in a disorganised pattern, white lines along their arms, legs and backs. They all scattered as Kyle dragged Alice through the hallway, their black eyes all rimmed with red, all open, terrified as their tongue-less mouths were agape in fear.

"Where's Sam?" she cried, her neck stretching as she searched into every cell.

"Who?"

The next cell held a naked man, his head sunk into his chest as his arms were locked into the wall, almost embedded into the brick. Black veins pulsated under his pale skin, matching the beat of his sluggish heart.

"That isn't Sam," she whispered to herself in relief.

Then where was he?

Tiles ran along the floor and partially up the wall, what once could have been white was a dirty brown, flaking like rust from the blood moulded into the surface.

"Why him?" Kyle growled, the softness of his voice edged with anger.

"What?" Alice snarled back, feeling her chi fill with her fire as she continued to fight the chains dragging her across the tile.

"The Alpha." He watched her from the corner of his eye. "He's wrong. Too weak," he said with disapproving tone. "He betrayed you."

"Yeah well, people betraying me seems to be a habit." She kicked out at his legs in frustration.

He stopped walking, impatient.

"You need to stop that." He angrily yanked the chains. The wolf in the corner snarled, making Kyle's head whip around with a sneer. "SHUT UP!" He stormed to the cell, smacking the metal with his palm.

Alice froze, realising he dropped the chain in his distraction.

Quietly, she started to pull it toward her, hesitating when a voice behind whispered in a weak voice.

"Ple... ase..." a woman's voice quivered. "Please, help me."

Alice turned to face a naked woman with dirty brown hair, her skin a sickly grey patterned with yellow bruises. One eye was swollen shut, blood stained down her face like tears. A pile of cloth lay to her right, a makeshift bed made from the scraps. A tray rested by the bars with a grey lumpy substance in a wooden bowl, green mould fluffy on top, flies buzzing around it greedily. Red smears decorated the walls, a series of parallel lines covering most of the wall space.

"Get the keys." She licked her lips nervously, the skin cracking open painfully.

Alice quickly checked Kyle, who was still distracted by the aggressive wolf. "Where?" Alice gently whispered back.

"Over there." The woman stretched her arm through the bars of her cell, the skin stretched tight to the bone. "He has it." She waved a hand toward Kyle frantically. "HE HAS IT!" she wailed.

"Shhhhh." Alice grabbed the woman's outstretched hand. "Shhh." She tried to calm her.

"He has it. He has it." Delirium took hold as the woman continued to chant. "He has it. He has it." She started to giggle hysterically. "HE HAS IT!"

"Alice come here, she's dangerous." Kyle grabbed Alice's shoulders, pulling her away from the woman who was now rocking, clawed hands trying to strike out.

Alice screamed as she was pulled, rocking her elbow back and hitting him in the stomach before twisting out of his grasp.

"Oomfff." He bent at the waist.

Breathing heavily, she gathered her chi, holding her flame in both hands. About to throw the fire she stopped, watching his eyes fight to become green.

"Kyle?" her voice tremored. "What happened to you?"

"Run." He dry heaved before screaming in pain, nails clawing at his own eyes. He bolted forward, grabbing the chain in his hand and yanking her off her feet. "Bad Alice." He pulled the chain with force, his eyes once again black.

"CORUSCARE!" she shouted, throwing her hand out towards his face, igniting the cloak.

A growl, the smoke clearing quickly as Kyle calmly shook off the robe as it turned to ash in his hands, his skin showing a history of abuse, pale scars crisscrossing almost every part of exposed skin.

Silver cuffs encircled his wrists, patterns engraved into the metal that seemed to pulsate along with the matching choker surrounding his neck.

Clicking his fingers she flinched, gasping when he held a ball of flame in his hand, green tinged with black.

"Don't do that," his voice was soft once again, black eyes fighting against the green as the flame danced between his fingertips.

"What are those cuffs?" she asked, stomach churning. "I can help."

He tilted his head, pain radiating across his face as he retched.

"NO!" He started to shake, throwing his head around as the cuffs glowed brightly.

Alice gathered the chain around her wrist, waiting for his next move when he turned to face her, eyes unfocused.

"They're coming," he whispered, leaning forward. "Run." He started to convulse, his eyes rolling in the back of his head before he fought back control. Groaning, he dragged himself to the exit, leaving the same way he had forced her in.

Alice stared after him, unable to move from the floor as exhaustion beat heavy on her. She dropped the chain with a rattle, concentring on calming her pulse, ignoring the manic crying from the woman and howling from the wolf. Looking down at her raw wrists she tried to squeeze her hands through, desperation taking hold when she felt someone watching her.

"He's coming," the delirious woman cackled. "60. 59. 58..."

"Shut up," Alice hissed, cursing as her fingers failed to fit. The manacles were heavy, locked tight.

"45. 44. 43..."

"Please, let me think."

Water dripped from the ceiling in the corner, hitting a shallow puddle on the cracked tile. The partial stonewalls were shiny, damp with a light green tinge and metal industrial supports that looked warped. A dirty orange cabinet was broken in the corner, the door hanging on one hinge with dust gathered on the empty shelves. Nothing that could help.

"Maybe something's in the cells," she whispered to herself as she crawled across the floor towards the third cell. The wolf paced, huffing and growling as she got closer.

"30. 29. 28..."

The inside of the cell was identical to the woman's, stonewalls with deep gouges and bloody marks. A tray that had been destroyed littered the floor, mixed in with sawdust, tufts of fur and bone. The wolf leapt at the bars with a snarl, part of his snout reaching out from a gap as he tried to bite his way through the metal.

"The bone." She cautiously watched the wolf. "I can pick the lock with a bone."

But how will I get it?

Unexpectedly, the bone skidded across the floor. Startled she glanced at the wolf, the beast calmly staring back as it pushed another bone underneath the small gap between the bars.

"23. 22. 21..."

"You can understand me?"

She wasn't confident how much of the person the wolf had retained. When shifters stayed in their animal form too long, it became hard to come back.

"Are you from White Dawn?" The wolf gave a sharp yip, pawing at the ground. Alice sucked in a breath, "Roman?" The wolf turned, growling at something as pain struck the back of her head.

CHAPTER 32

"Brothers!" a voice boomed as the room erupted into applause. "It's time."

In igne comburetis. Cinis in nos exsurgent.

Alice's headache matched the rhythm of the chant, a tattoo dancing against the inside of her head. She squinted her eyes as she watched the series of cloaked men, surrounding her in a partial circle. Each acolyte held a single candle, the wax dripping onto their grey palms without a flinch. Swallowing bile she flexed her swollen fingers, the surface cold beneath her. She moved slowly, pulling at her wrists, shocked to feel no resistance.

Lashes low so they hid her eyes she tried to study the room, noticing how she was lying on a stone slab in the centre of what looked like an old storage facility. Steel beams held up the high ceiling, surrounded by large cabinets that were mostly closed. Hooks were planted into the walls, some broken, leaving dangerous spikes while others held old high-vis jackets.

Alice tried to keep her breathing steady, even as an intense cold prickled across her skin.

"Brothers," the smoky voice called. "How long we have waited."

Alice recognised the voice.

Where was Kyle?

He wasn't there, wasn't one of the acolytes. She was sure of it.

"Are we all prepared?"

In igne comburetis. Cinis in nos exsurgent.

Alice tried not to groan, the combined voices of the men rattling against her skull. The intense cold increased as she felt something glide slowly towards the pedestal, followed by a scraping sound across the concrete and tile.

Shit. Shit. Shit.

She couldn't see clearly enough in the candlelit room, she had no weapons, no known exits and the intense feeling of panic was getting greater with every passing second.

She was running out of time.

"You promised me Roman."

Alice's eyes opened wide at the voice.

"A deal is a deal."

She strained to turn her head, barely catching a glimpse of Rex as he intercepted her captor. How could she not have seen his deception? Was she that stupid?

"Did you hear that brothers?" the smokey voice called. "This Alpha is asking for his pup." A laugh as the cloaked men twitched in agitation.

"You said..."

"I *told* you to retrieve the dragon..."

"You implied that if I did this, you would release Roman." Rex's voice dropped, anger coming from his wolf.

"ENOUGH." Alice flinched at the shout. "Do not over-step." Rex was pushed against the wall, his eyes arctic.

"No, this..." Rex snarled as a hand grabbed his throat, stopping his words.

"Go back to your pack. Before they replace the weak Alpha that you are," the larger man threatened, releasing his clenched hand as Rex gasped for breath.

"Yes, master." Rex looked up, his eyes almost sorry before he turned away, leaving the room, leaving her.

Fuck! Alice squeezed her eyes shut.

"Ah, there she is." A hand brushed against her arm. It took everything in her to stay relaxed, not to tense up and give herself away. "I know you're awake." An intimate whisper.

Leaping up she flipped off the stone, landing heavy on the balls of her feet.

"IGNIS!" She flung out her arm, flame erupting from her palm like a whip. A high-pitched screech, pain radiating behind her eyes as the pierce shrill forced her to her knees, head in her hands.

Arms encased her, forcing her to stand.

"HOLD HER DOWN."

"NO!" Alice fought against the arms, pulling at the hoods covering their faces. She gasped as the cloth ripped away, showing empty eye sockets, lips sewn together, white thread a stark contrast against their dark skin.

In igne comburetis. Cinis in nos exsurgent.

The chorus of voices continued to chant, invading her head, needles across her brain. Alice felt her heartbeat in her throat, a cold terror filling her gut. A larger hand closed around her arm, throwing her back onto the stone slab with a thud. Arms and legs pinned she struggled, energy evaporating.

Eyes wide open, she quickly took in her surroundings.

She was wrong before, it wasn't a storage facility.

The stone pedestal was in the centre of an abandoned underground station.

Large gold candelabras stood in the corner, holding hundreds of candles, wax melting delicately onto the concrete floor. The white wax slowly turned a sickly pink, mixing with blood that was running along grooves etched into the floor. Old movie posters and train maps still decorated the walls, the once bright pictures muted over the years, covered in layers of dust. There was even a ticket station in the corner, runes written in blood smeared across the glass. The cavernous room trembled as a train passed overhead, dust and debris raining down. The acolytes stood patiently, holding her down.

"LOOK AT ME!"

Alice whipped her head towards the voice, freezing when she noticed the Daemon standing before her. Eyes that were pure red watched with slit pupils, a slow and satisfied smile creeping across his scarred face. Horns were filed down to the skull, barely visible beneath long black hair. Wide shoulders flexed as he gripped her chin, forcing her to meet his gaze.

Something moved in her peripheral view, a black sheet that scuffed across the floor.

Oh shit. They were wings, wings that were dragging behind him. *Of course he has fucking wings.* Black veins patterned like a spider web across the thin membrane, the arch protruding from his shoulders high above his head.

"Who are you?" she asked, yanking her jaw from his grasp.

"Is it really important?" A cold laugh.

"Why are you doing this?" He ignored her, his attention on the others. "What have you done to Kyle?"

In igne comburetis. Cinis in nos exsurgent.

"Today we meet here my brothers, to start The Becoming." He turned his back.

"Where's Kyle?"

"The blood of the dragon is the final catalyst before we take our power we rightfully deserve. Before we start the end of days."

In igne comburetis. Cinis in nos exsurgent.

"Dragon? What fucking dragon?" She pulled against her restraints.

The Daemon just smirked. "You're more ignorant than your parents, little dragon."

"My parents?"

He grabbed Alice's left wrist, holding it immobile in his large hand.

"The blood of your mother was corrupted by that druid, useless."

A long nail cut across the delicate flesh at the crease of her wrist, blood pooling along the wound.

"But with your life force, we will Become. The blood of the dragon, the blood of war." His head hovered over her wound, an intimate bloody kiss.

Alice screamed, pain searing through her arm. Her flesh tore as she pulled her arm free from his teeth.

A slow smile, his canines covered in red.

"Per ignem enim moriemur. Sanguinis sacrificii nos cogunt. Im igne comburetis. Cinis in nos exsurgent." He raised his arms, chanting towards the sky.

Fire erupted from her blood, a scalding pain that bubbled through her veins. Her life force pumped slowly from her wrist, a red trail across the stone. Head rolling to the side she watched as consciousness flickered, the blood dripping to the floor with her blue fire crackling as it followed the flow.

"Hoc sacrificium, absorbet. Et factus est."

"Fuck!" Alice shouted as pain throbbed through every nerve, flames scorching towards the runes, lighting up in intricate patterns along the concrete.

"In fire, we burn..."

"Why are you doing this?" Alice asked, her vision darkening at the corners, her lungs struggling.

"In ash, we rise," he finished, his arms still raised to the sky, before snake eyes moved to her, glittering with excitement. "Because I can."

A loud crash, the ceiling trembling as concrete and dust showered the room.

"ALICE!" a voice shouted.

The pain pulsated with the beat of her heart, darkness shrouding her.

"ALICE!" That voice, shouting from a distance again. "WAKE UP!"

Someone grabbed her, pulling her into a sitting position against something hard, a hand against her throat.

"ALICE!"

Her eyes slipped open, blurring as she struggled to make out the scene in front of her. Riley danced around the room, balls of arcane flashing into the acolytes as they scattered like skittles. A flash of steel, a head rolling off its shoulders as another man who was dressed identically to Riley fought the others. The stranger seemed just as impossibly fast, his sword blurring as he took down one acolyte after another. He wore wraparound sunglasses, his hair pure white compared to Riley's dark.

Her eyes became heavy, the pain dulling.

"They're too late." Smoke against her face, a mouth against her ear.

Gasping for a breath she struggled, lifting her hands to claw at his skin.

Flames continued to pour from her left wrist, strangely silent compared to the clang of metal and shouts surrounding her. She heard whispers in her ear, a desolate sound she couldn't make out as she watched the fire, oddly mesmerising as it flowed into the patterns along the floor.

She felt the hand tighten.

"Pay attention," he growled.

"Fuck you," she snarled through clenched teeth, blood fragrant at the back of her throat.

A crash, an acolyte thrown against the wall, head impaling into one of the hooks.

"ALICE, SHIELD!" Riley shouted from across the room.

"Fucking Guardians," the Daemon seethed, hand loosening as he watched the action.

"ALICE!" Riley moved towards them, jumping over the flames. "SHIELD!"

Shield?

"*Arma,*" she whispered, her aura solidifying into existence around her, a molecule thin film lasting only a second. The hand loosened against her, a shout of pain. With her last remaining energy, she pushed back.

A silver ball of arcane flew past the corner of her eye, landing straight into the Daemon as he stumbled. With a shriek, he scrabbled at his chest, scraping the energy from his skin with a snarl just as it started to eat into skin and bone.

Flames continued to pour from her wrist, her life burning up as she watched. She turned her head, seeing

Riley and the Daemon circle each other. Riley raised a gun, pointing it steadily as the tattoos across his arms glowed.

"Is that all you got?" the Daemon mocked, his wings pulsating and curling around his shoulders in irritation.

Stepping forward he knocked the gun from Riley's hands, sending it skidding across the floor to land against a fallen acolyte. Alice eyed it, watching her hand reach for it in a painfully slow motion. She slipped off the stone, dragging herself through the flames to reach the weapon, leaving a trail of fire and blood behind her.

Riley stood motionless, his chest barely moving as he remained calm.

"You're too late," the Daemon taunted, blood still staining his teeth. "Only a matter of moments before she is gone, and we Become." His thigh tensed.

Riley moved with him, slashing out with his blade as it sliced across the Daemons chest with a hiss. The Daemon reared back, looking down in astonishment as Riley rushed forward, punching him straight in the face with a crunch. A hand came from out of nowhere, nails slicing across Riley's bare arm. Black foam bubbled from the gouges, acid burning through skin.

"Riley," Alice tried to warn, her voice making no noise against the cacophony of battle.

Her fingertips finally touched the metal.

The Daemon laughed again as he smirked into Riley's reflective eyes.

"I see your beast, it screams for release. You're just like me." A glint in his eyes before black flames rained down from the ceiling. "You just keep it better hidden."

Another ball of red tinged with black was thrown across the room, Riley intercepted it with a blast, returning the arcane with interest.

The spell went wild, crashing into the wall, shattering the tiles.

"Fuck," Riley growled as he turned his claymore blade carefully in his hand. Waiting.

The Daemon hissed, circling him slowly. "It's your own people that did that to you. Broke you as a child, forced you to share a spirit."

Alice tried to scream as a cloaked figure grabbed her ankle, his fist tightening before he became dust, Riley's arcane evaporating him into nothing. She heard Riley shout, his face annoyed as he kicked a minion with his boot, the cloaked figure collapsing into the carnage.

Swinging his blade in a wide arc he cut off its head.

"Enough of this," Riley called as he lifted his sword. "You can never win."

"Is that so? Then how come I already am?"

The Daemon stepped from the shadows, his fist powering through the air before Riley even noticed. The second punch doubled him over, causing him to suck in a breath. His sword clattered to the ground, the Daemon kicking it away as he approached.

Alice lifted the gun, her hand shaking from the weight.

"This is getting tiring. Join the cause or die."

"Fuck you," Riley snarled. Drawing back his arm he released his fist. The Daemon yowled, clutching his nose as Riley hit out again, the impact causing him to stumble back, almost tripping over the bodies.

She pulled the trigger.

A bead of blood appeared on the Daemons dark forehead, the bead growing from the centre between his eyes. Another shot. A hole appearing in his throat, a choked noise as blood gurgled. With a roar Riley jumped forward, pushing as much raw power as he could muster through the small hole in his head, searing him from the inside out.

"You could never win." Riley pushed, putting all his rage into that one concentrated point.

"I am many," a gargled laugh, black blood bubbling from the Daemons lips. "We will Become." A flash of light, a silver glow that radiated from behind his eyes.

"Riley," Alice whispered, a quiet noise, a last breath.

Pushing away from the Daemon as his body eroded into dust Riley turned towards her weak voice. She could barely make out him running towards her, his arms crushing as he pushed the gun away from her slack grip.

"Alice?" He shook her in his panic.

All she heard was white noise, Riley's mouth moving but no sound coming out.

"You can't get attached," the stranger said as he came to stand beside Riley, his hand resting on his shoulder. "She's too far gone."

Alice tried to speak, only a croak coming out.

Riley juddered his shoulder to dislodge the hand. "Xander, go stand guard."

"She's dying."

"I said back the fuck off," he snarled.

"Riley, listen to me." Xander got down on his knee. "You can't. You know what would happen. If The Order..."

Alice tried to speak again, her ears starting to ring as sound slowly came back. "Riley?" she uttered in barely a whisper, her throat dry.

"Hey." He stroked her hair from her eyes, ignoring Xander. "Did you really have to burn the place down? Over dramatic or what." Riley tried to smile, the light not reaching his eyes.

"How did you find me?" she asked.

"Unimportant," he replied, cradling her as if she could break.

He checked her wrist, hand covering her wound even as the fire began to eat away at his flesh. She tried to pull away.

"Stay still."

"Don't boss me around," she moaned as her eyelids became heavy.

The flames licked his skin, her blood continuing to burn her up from the inside out.

"Alice?" He rocked her gently. "ALICE, WAKEUP!"

A groan, her face scrunching up in annoyance.

"Alice listen to me, I need you to expel all the fire. Everything, you need to ostracise your power reserve."

"What are you doing?" Xander asked, his tone deep with worry.

"Alice. Nod if you understand."

A small movement against his chest.

"Ready? On the count of three. One, two, three."

He held her as she screamed, fire pouring from her fingertips, an unpredictable recalcitrant element. The walls creaked, straining against the intense heat.

"We need to move!" Xander shouted over the roar of the flames.

"Give it a second."

A metal beam crashed through the ceiling.

"WE NEED TO MOVE!"

"WAIT!" Another crash as the metal beam landed on the ticket office, smashing the glass into tiny shards. She felt Riley cover her with his body, shrapnel bouncing off his back. Blood no longer poured from her wrist, the fire having died out when she expelled her magic, her energy along with it. She could no longer feel anything.

Riley checked her pulse, feeling nothing.

"FUCK!"

He laid her on the ground, her aura damaged beyond repair as she pushed out everything she had.

"FUCK. FUCK. FUCK," he chanted, hovering his hands over her body.

"What can I do?" Xander asked, remaining calm.

"Pump her heart." Riley started breathing for her, tipping her head back to force air into her lungs. "Come on Alice." He started breathing for her again.

"This isn't working." Xander stopped pumping to check her pulse. "It's not beating on its own."

"MOVE!" Riley pushed him out the way, hovering his hand gently over her heart.

"What are you doing?" Slight panic.

Riley concentrated as he shot a small amount of arcane into her heart, shocking it to restart.

Still no pulse.

"Shit." He repeated the shock, his hand burning as he concentrated it into a small area.

A small beat, faint against her skin.

EPILOGUE

Alice hobbled ungracefully with her one crutch, taking a seat on the dust sheet-covered sofa. She groaned, allowing herself to sink into the cushion, her aches and pains protesting at any sort of movement. Even sitting down seemed to hurt.

She rested her head against the wall with a huff, her eyes tracing the intricate designs plastered onto the ceiling. A few cracks marked the otherwise beautiful work, nothing some DIY couldn't fix.

She could hear muttering from the kitchen, Sam and Dread bickering over something completely ridiculous. They pretended to hate each other, but she knew, deep down, way deep down, that they did at least like each other.

Or it could be more like tolerate.

She couldn't help but laugh to herself as she started to climb painstakingly back off the sofa, intending to go save two of her favourite people from possibly killing one another.

"You don't need this many mugs," Dread grumbled as

he put away yet another novelty mug into one of the kitchen cupboards. "I know for a fact you guys don't have enough friends to use all these."

"Aye, but what happens when one of our mugs decides to grow penicillin? Who are we to stop something from potentially saving the world?" Sam commented back, a smirk on his lightly stubbled face.

Alice just leant against the newly bought table, the chairs yet to be made. Sam smiled when he noticed her, rolling his eyes once Dread commented about the bad taste in mugs yet again.

Returning the smile automatically she stared at the deep bruises across his wrists and face, her smile slipping quickly. Shifters usually healed bruises within a couple of hours at most. It just showed how badly he was beaten, torn ligaments, broken bones, all priority compared to a few bruises.

"Alice you need to sit down. You shouldn't be up." Dread put the mug away with the others, trying to hide his concern.

Alice just sighed. She wasn't stupid, she knew she was hurt. The aches she felt a testimony to that, as was her new crescent moon scar that was a constant reminder of one of the worst nights of her life.

Or, at least in the top three worst nights of her life.

The top of the crescent started in the middle of her left palm, curling down to just below her wrist, the thickened skin several degrees colder than the rest of her body.

"I thought I could help." She had been bed bound, poked and prodded for weeks. She was about to lose it. She either needed to stab something or put away some damn mugs. As she stupidly gave up her sword, she was left with the mugs.

Clenching her fist she looked at Dread, wanting to ask the question she had been asking every day. Luckily Dread knew exactly what she was going to say.

"No," he sighed, shaking his head gently. "I haven't had any reports."

Fighting disappointment she just nodded, deciding to look at the badly drawn pictures that Sam drew on her cast one night after too many wines. She knew it was a long shot. When she heard that Kyle was nowhere to be found at the train station she had hope. Hope that she would get answers, that he could help her understand.

Yet, he was nowhere to be found.

She had decided to move back into her family home, use her happy childhood memories to overcome the bad ones. She needed to learn to accept her past, accept the things she couldn't change. Honour their memory. Renovating the house, making it her own was a start. Second was finding her brother.

"Hey baby girl, have you seen Riley recently?" Sam asked almost absently, his attention mostly on unpacking and not on the conversation. "I haven't seen him in a few weeks. He hasn't been to work either."

"No, I haven't," she replied. It had become apparent pretty quickly that she had no idea how to contact him, which frustrated her even more than the cast. She had so many questions about what happened that night, her memory fuzzy to say the least. He wasn't just a druid, he was more, just as she was more.

Dragon. War.

He had disappeared once he had completed his duty, no longer interested.

"Good riddance," muttered Dread. "All he will bring is trouble. Damn druids."

DING.

"I'm coming," she called down the hallway, the cast on her leg hindering her speed dramatically. Her aching wrist wasn't helping either.

DING.

"I'm coming," she called again, dodging around cardboard boxes stashed high around the living room and hallway.

DING.

"Bloody hell, I'm coming!" She continued her painful journey, her whole body aching as she pushed it.

"Are you answering it or not Alice?" Sam shouted at her.

"I'm bloody answering it," she let out a frustrated snarl.

DING.

"Oh, for... I SAID I WAS...!" She opened the front door, her voice shutting off instantly.

"Hello," the man greeted, a black wolf sitting calmly by his legs.

"Hello," Alice stumbled. "Why are you...?"

"I'm Theo. You must be Alice."

"I know who you are," her voice husky, anger growing. She glared at the man standing on the doorstep. "Why are you here?"

She never wanted to see Rex again, his betrayal scorched into her brain forever. Looking at his identical twin was almost as bad. Theo's hair was cut shorter, the strands barely touching his ears compared to Rex's full head of hair. An old scar split his face, starting from his forehead, travelling across his nose and distorting his upper lip. The darkened skin should have made him ugly, yet it gave his face more character. That lip turned up at the corner.

"I thought you would be taller." Eyes laughed at her

aggressive reaction, or he could be laughing at her nest of a hair, barely brushed ponytail at least two days old.

"I disappoint myself sometimes too."

"You have a nice house."

"Please get to the point." She wasn't petty. Not petty at all.

He gave her a shy smile. "I wanted to say thank you, for what you did."

"Oh." Her arm shook as she balanced her weight on the crutch. "That's okay."

What else was she supposed to say to that?

"And Roman wanted to say thank you." The wolf by his feet stood up, his tongue rolling out of his mouth in a wolfish grin.

"Where's Rex?" Alice asked, hoping he was nowhere nearby.

"Not here." The smile fell from his face.

"What are they doing here?" Sam came up from behind her with a snarl.

"You must be Sam," started Theo.

"Why the fuck are you here?" Sam's hackles rose, his teeth flashing as a threat. Well, as threatening as a man with a tea towel decorated with kittens draped over his shoulder could be.

"We're here to apologise. To you both it seems."

"It's not you who should be apologising," he snapped. Alice put a shaky hand on his shoulder, calming him.

"No it shouldn't be, but let's not speak of my brother, or about the pride."

Theo seemed to hesitate, trying to find the right words.

"They are no longer an issue." His eyes flashed wolf, the same ice blue as Rex before he turned back to Alice. "Like I said, I just wanted to let you know how grateful I am, as well as my pack. I can't even begin to explain the reasons why Rex did what he did." He flicked a look towards Roman. "He broke so many pack laws in his desperation, once we figured out how he tracked you..."

"Wait, he tracked me?" She looked down at her naked wrist, the leather wrap having been cut off at the hospital. "It was the bracelet, wasn't it?" It all made sense.

"Ironically enough it was with the bracelet they could find you at the train station." He shook his head at the thought.

"Baby girl, you okay?" Sam's concern breaking through.

She ignored the question, instead asking her own. "Was that all it could do?"

She waited for the answer, her eyes appraising Theo as he thought about it. Theo was attractive in the general sense, in the same way she had found Rex attractive, yet she felt nothing.

It made her chest ache, a sour taste at the back of her throat.

"There's no way to know, I'm not familiar with the magic behind it."

She gave a shallow nod, not wanting to speak as she digested the information.

"I have put in the request to take over White Dawn. Unfortunately, it means you might see more of me in the city." He attempted to smile charmingly, but it came off more awkward.

"I hope you do a better job." Maybe just a little petty.

A deep chuckle. "I hope so too." He tilted his head, clearly hearing something she couldn't. "That's my signal to leave."

Theo patted Roman on the head.

"Before I go, I just want you to know if you ever need

anything, from myself or the pack please do not hesitate to ask, it's the least I can do."

He turned to leave when Roman nipped at his heels.

"Oh yes, I almost forgot." Reaching back he passed across her sword, her crystal necklace wrapped tightly around its hilt. "I believe these belong to you."

Alice touched the coolness of her sword, happiness at feeling the familiar weight against her palm. With a flash of light runes appeared down the shaft, brightening as she brushed her fingertip down the metal.

"Alice..." She heard the concern in Sam's voice, he knew the sword had never done that before. Unable to comfort him she watched the lights dance, a pain in her gut.

Something had changed. She didn't know if that was for the better or not.

She needed to figure out who she was.

"Thank you," she said as she put down the sword, not wanting to look at it. Not wanting to acknowledge that she wasn't what she thought. What her parents were.

"You're welcome." With a small smile Theo turned away, Roman tight behind. "This really is a nice house."

"Thanks," she replied to his back. "It was my parents."

It's home.

The End of Book One

This series continues with Druid's Storm: Buy here!

A personal note from Taylor

I hope you enjoyed Witch's Sorrow! If you want to show your support, I would really appreciate you leaving a review from the store you purchased. Reviews are super important and help other readers discover this series!

Check me out on Facebook, Instagram and TikTok!

Continue reading for an excerpt of Druid's Storm, Alice Skye book two.

DRUID'S STORM

Walking slowly down the carpet on Dread's arm she stopped and smiled at the reporters asking him questions, her gaze sweeping across the crowd.

Faerie lights had been draped between the street-lamps, creating a fallen star's effect that was eerily beautiful against the darkness of the sky. The red carpet was a darker red than she anticipated, the fine fabric a flutter of activity from the flashes of the photographers.

Gently escaping from Dread's grasp she made her way towards the entrance of the hotel, not wanting to take attention away from anyone else.

The interior was just as beautifully decorated as the outside, a selection of large round tables having been placed around the edges of the grand room, all draped in white linen with silver candelabras. Located at the centre was a large wooden floor placed in front of a pop-up stage. AA podium was set up between two display stands, displaying the Children of The Moon's logo as well as a selection of photographs.

Accepting a glass of champagne from a member of the wait staff Alice placed herself with her back against the wall, able to see the entrance as well as all the guests already walking around.

People chatted amongst themselves, ball gowns and tuxedos mingling as each person tried to compare their wealth of diamonds and expensive watches. Alice recognised a few familiar faces from television, a well-known architect as well as a famous movie actress. The Mayor of London was chatting happily to someone beside the stage, his big gut bursting at the seams of his tuxedo.

"You must be the infamous Alice Skye."

Alice spun towards the woman who spoke, her dark hair blending into the black ball gown she wore on her tiny frame.

Standing at barely five feet, Valentina looked nothing like Alice thought she would, her black boatneck dress emphasising her flawless pale skin with a fitted bodice flowing into a floor-length silk skirt. She looked almost like a child playing dress up.

"Councilman," Alice greeted, nodding her head gently.

"Dread has told me so much about you." Valentina smiled, her ruby red lips tipped at the corner. Alice fought her instincts not to step back from the predator's smile.

This woman is powerful.

"All good things I hope." Alice met her eyes, her own smile wavering as she saw the sombre depths. She thought Dread was old, but this was...

"Alice, it is time to take a seat," Dread interrupted, grasping her arm and pulling her toward a table.

"Mistress Valentina, I hope you make time for me later, we have much to discuss about your trip to London."

"Bonsoir Commissioner Grayson, I was just speaking to your Alice." Her smile was full this time, fangs peaking as white tips against her lips. "It is rude to interrupt us women, non?" A gentle laugh. "How is my youngling doing? He only has praise for you and the organisation."

"Your watchdog is doing well."

"As expected," Valentina nodded. "My Danton has been with me for centuries, I do miss him back in Paris."

Watchdog? Alice thought, sipping her champagne. *Danton's her watchdog?*

"If you trust me to do my job, then you should be able to remove your mole from my Tower." Dread forced a smile.

Valentina let out a laugh.

"Mon ami, we wouldn't have put you in such a prestigious position if we didn't trust you," she said, dark eyes narrowed.

"Alice, be careful of the Mistress," Danton spoke quietly in her ear, careful for the other vampires not to overhear. *"Do not underestimate her."*

She fought not to reply in anger, only remembering at the last minute he wasn't actually in the conversation. How long has he answered to Valentina? Where were his loyalties?

Saving the thoughts for later she did a quick sweep of the room, trying to find him amongst the staff.

"Please, take your seats," a mechanical voice asked.

"Ah." Valentina reached out to touch Alice's hand, her palm cold as she gave it a little squeeze. "It looks like we are almost ready mademoiselle, please find me later. I would love to chat more." She let go slowly, her fingertips lingering on the pulse on Alice's wrist before she wandered off towards her seat.

"Alice, we're over here." Dread guided her with a hand to her back, pulling her seat out for her when they got to their designated table.

Questions bubbled up her throat, her mouth opening to ask before she quickly closed it. It was the wrong time and place, there were too many ears. She needed to get her head back in the game, she could interrogate Dread and Danton later.

"*Something smells off,*" her earpiece rattled.

Alice tipped the champagne flute to her mouth, pretending to drink so she could reply. "What do you mean?"

"*I smell something acidic, but can't tell where it's coming from,*" Rose replied. "*I'm in the kitchen.*"

Alice thought about that for a second. Rose's nose was closer to her panther than human, could smell scents everybody else didn't even know existed.

"D?" Alice whispered quietly, making sure her head was down. "Go see if you notice anything unusual." Vampires had sensitive noses too, albeit not as good as a shifter.

The reply came swiftly.

"*Oui.*"

A waiter dressed in black slacks and a neat white shirt came up to the table, a blood red napkin draped over his right arm.

"Could I get anybody some drinks?"

"Order me a glass of the Chateau du Sang," Dread replied before anyone else could get a say in. "My companion will just have a glass of water." He quickly added before Alice could order herself. Scowling, she clutched her champagne closer.

You're working, remember. His eyes glared.

Yeah, well technically, so are you. Her own eyes replied before he turned into a conversation with the man beside him. *Fuck sake.* She savoured a small sip of her champagne, enjoying the bubbles as they burst on her taste buds.

There were only two people she could have a wordless conversation with, have a strong enough bond to be able to read their expression. Dread had brought her up, had been her parental guardian since the death of her parents.

"Are you sure you would not like some fresh blood, sir?" The waiter asked Dread.

"Anybody holding a red napkin is available," he said as he tipped his throat, holes marking the lightly stubbled flesh.

"I would like fresh," a man opposite interrupted, his grey hair slicked back in a modern style, a complete contrast to the Victorian style suit he was wearing. His fangs were long and pearl white, a shade similar to his pale, yet withered skin.

The thing with vampires is that you couldn't really tell their age at a glance, he could be ten years undead or one hundred, his aged skin unusual amongst most Vamps. The majority of humans applied to be changed before they became thirty, the wrinkles that the vampira virus couldn't remove were fixed before his turn. From the number of wrinkles, Alice guessed he had been turned before The Change, where vampires, as well as all Breeds, hid among the humans. From the state of his skin, his life before wasn't a prosperous one.

His lady friend, on the other hand, was clearly new, her

pupils dilating every time somebody came close, her tongue licking the inside of her lips. She would have been around twenty-five when she turned, as per the law stating all candidates must be in prime health and between the ages of eighteen and thirty-nine.

Before the laws, the death rate of the newly turned was around eighty per cent, the virus temperamental, which was one of the reasons why The Council created the candidate process. The second reason was an agreement with the humans back when they were negotiating Breed citizenship that vampires – who were the only Breeds that were originally human – could only be turned under a strict process. This gave the Norms a false sense of control so they didn't have to worry that they would be overrun with the living dead.

"So do you let your date order for you every time?" a male voice beside her asked.

"Excuse me?" Alice spun toward the dark-haired man. "He isn't my date," she replied before thinking. *Bollocks, yes he was*.

"Well, that's going to make flirting a hell of a lot easier." The stranger's mouth erupted into a full smile, highlighting a single dimple in his left cheek. "The name's Nate Blackwell." He held out his hand, flaring his chi in greeting.

"As in Blackwell Casino?" She felt his chi brush against hers, fuzzy in its sensation.

Blackwell Casino was one of the newer skyscrapers built in the southern district, a beast of a building that stuck out like a sore thumb against the protected Victorian structures that surrounded the expensive area.

"That's the one."

"Alice." She clasped his hand, allowing some of her own

chi to reciprocate, just enough to seem polite, but not enough to encourage.

"Alice." He seemed to taste her name on his tongue. "Pretty name. Haven't seen you in these circles before."

"I don't normally get invited," she replied with a genuine smile.

"Well, I hope you get invited to many more."

"One, two. One, two." A man started to tap the microphone on the stage, testing the sound.

"Looks like it's about to start."

Alice continued to sip her champagne, ignoring the water the waiter had placed beside her.

"Then I guess I will be chatting with you a little bit later," Nate said with a wink.

"Welcome everybody to the tenth consecutive charity gala and the first for 'Children of the Moon.' If you could please put your hands together for the charity patron, Markus Luera."

The speaker on the stage clapped, stepping down as another man took his place.

Markus Luera was dressed in a tailored dark blue suit with black bow tie, his white beard was a shock compared to his jet black hair that was spiked up at every angle possible. Holding a cane against his tanned left arm he held his hand over his breast pocket, smiling to the crowd before turning towards the central table.

"Mistress Valentina, it is a pleasure you could join us."

He gracefully bowed, dipping his head before standing straight.

"It is an honour that you would grace us with your presence for a charity so close to home."

Mistress?

Alice studied Markus Luera carefully, noticed the

nervous gesture of his hand as he tugged at his cane. Mistress was Valentina's title from other vampires, as a member of The Council she stood for all the Vamps, was essentially their leader, their voice. 'Mistress' was supposed to be a label of respect. Or fear. Which meant Markus Luera was a vampire, one with a tan.

Vampires don't tan.

Valentina smiled at the attention, waving elegantly from her seated position.

"Monsieur Luera, I'm interested to hear from the guest speaker, I hear he has been exceedingly generous."

"Then I will keep this short and sweet, Mistress."

He turned to address the crowd.

"Friends, I have gathered you here today to highlight the great work 'Children of the Moon' have been doing for the local children affected by their horrible inflictions. The actions of my fellow board members have helped over one hundred younglings with their life-changing conditions, building moon rooms for the children to live out their final days safely. As it stands, we are closer than ever to a cure, every donation counts towards a future where children who are born with the vampira virus will be able to live to an age where they can survive the transition."

The room was quiet, everybody listening intently as Markus passionately spoke about the condition that had affected around five per cent of children. They still didn't understand the disease, couldn't comprehend how the virus could attack a child while still in the womb of a parent who wasn't a vampire.

"As you have all paid the £10,000 entrance fee you are all greatly thanked by the children who are still going strong, and by the children who are yet to be born."

Holy shit, this cost £10,000 each?

"But my next guest has gone far and beyond to help out the children. He and his family have donated a total of one million pounds over the last year to help build a research facility here in London. Please welcome with open arms, our guest speaker, Mason Storm."

Alice choked on the final bit of champagne, the bubbles bursting in her throat as she tried to control her breathing. Eyes around the table shot to her in annoyance, sniffing and tutting in displeasure at the disruption. Dread silently handed her a napkin, his attention not wavering from the stage. Coughing into the linen, Alice watched as Mason smiled to the audience, their applause loud and over the top.

Her heart skipped a beat once she noticed the other man who joined him on stage. Anger, embarrassment, and, weirdly, excitement all flowed across her brain too fast for her to really decipher. Her emotions were chaotic as she watched Riley stand beside his father, a beautiful redhead clinging to his arm.

You have got to be shitting me.

Buy Now!

ABOUT THE AUTHOR

Taylor Aston White loves to explore mythology and European faerie tales to create her own, modern magic world. She collects crystals, house plants and dark lipstick, and has two young children who like to 'help' with her writing by slamming their hands across the keyboard.

After working several uncreative jobs and one super creative one she decided to become a full-time author and now spends the majority of her time between her children and writing the weird and wonderful stories that pop into her head.

www.taylorastonwhite.com